EPHESUS

A TALE OF TWO KINGDOMS

Mark Abel

ZEPPELIN STUDIOS PUBLISHING

Tempe -Arizona

Zeppelin Studios Publishing
233 East Southern Avenue 27741
Tempe, Arizona 85282

Cover Design by Mark Abel
Cover Photography by Cheryl Abel

Available from your local bookstore and everywhere else books are sold. For more information about this book and the author's other books visit: www.markabelwriter.com

This novel is a work of fiction. Any references to historical events, real people, or real places are used fictitiously. Other names, organizations, characters, places, and events are products of the author's imagination, and any resemblance to actual events or places or persons, living or dead, is entirely coincidental. Any mentioned brand names, places, and trademarks remain the property of their respective owners bear no association with the author or the publisher and are used for fictional purposes only.

All Scripture quotations taken from the New American Standard Bible ®, Copyright © 1960, 1962, 1963, 1968, 1971, 1972, 1973, 1995 by the Lockman Foundation. Used by permission.

Lyric quotations and references:
Crown Him with Many Crowns by Matthew Bridges 1851
Sympathy for the Devil by The Rolling Stones 1968
Feel It Still by Portugal The Man 2017

Printed in the United States of America

First Edition Printed October 2019
10 9 8 7 6 5 4 3 2 1

Library of Congress Control Number: 2019913051
ISBN: 978-1-951265-00-7
ISBN: 978-1-951265-01-4 (ebook)

To my wife, Cheri,
I love you like crazy.

ACKNOWLEDGMENTS

First, to my wife, Cheri, who never tired of listening as I talked endlessly about the story, for her love and encouragement along the way, as well as her help with Scripture knowledge and passage references. Further, for her help with plot ideas and several excellent suggestions. I could not have written this story without her.

Thanks also to Sandra Lee Smith, friend and accomplished author of several novels, who helped with invaluable information and words of encouragement. Additional thanks to Jim Poulin and my writers group, who provided content feedback while pushing me forward when I questioned if the project might ever be completed.

Further thanks to my friend, David Brower, for sharing his near-death experience, when he drowned and saw the gates of heaven opened. And Scott Bitcon, pastor and friend who let me shadow him, as he ministered his gifting of inner healing and deliverance to the wounded and brokenhearted.

I am honored to offer profound thanks to my professional and highly skilled editor, Deirdre Lockhart of Brilliant Cut Editing, who never coddled me, but rather pressed me again and again to do better, shaping and enhancing scenes to bring them alive, all with much humor and laughter to the point of tears, while providing words of praise and encouragement which I so desperately needed to hear.

Lastly, and most importantly, I thank my Lord and Savior. Looking back, I can state with certainty it was He who led and prepared me over my life adventure to write this book.

Mark Abel
Psalm 100

PART I

I, John, your brother and fellow partaker in the tribulation and kingdom and perseverance which are in Jesus, was on the island called Patmos because of the word of God and the testimony of Jesus. I was in the Spirit on the Lord's day, and I heard behind me a loud voice like the sound of a trumpet, saying, "Write in a book what you see, and send it to the seven churches: to Ephesus and to Smyrna and to Pergamum and to Thyatira and to Sardis and to Philadelphia and to Laodicea.

As for the mystery of the seven stars which you saw in My right hand, and the seven golden lampstands: the seven stars are the angels of the seven churches, and the seven lampstands are the seven churches.

Revelation 1:9-11, 20

PROLOGUE

City of Ephesus, 262 AD

THE JUDGMENT boulder missed the mark. Shaking the earth with a thundering boom, the concussion struck the crowd like a flat hand to the chest. Mud and water exploded into a mist that mingled with the fog like a floating shroud above the sprawled body. Except for the rattle of cascading pebbles, it was then quiet.

From below, the old man watched in stunned wonderment.

The push was from the height of a second-story window. Not sufficient to kill, but adequate to crush his rib cage. Two men then rolled him over. It was from that vantage point he watched the boulder tumbling end over end toward him. Seeming to move slowly at first, it accelerated in a flash to strike just an arm's breadth from his torso. The men grabbed him. Each taking an ankle, they dragged his body toward the open area at the quarry's center. His head bobbed as his limp body rose and fell in response to the altar of cut slabs and rubble, a kaleidoscope of rock and sky swirling before him.

The assembly was now making their way down from the outcrop, and the second stone would soon follow. The old man was aware of little, except that his hands were still clutching the writing case. *I do not understand, Lord? My brothers, how can it be they do this...?* It was because of the book, after all, the book within the case.

Through a raspy voice, he asked, "Will you stay with me?"

"Yes, I have your hand." The angel knelt at his side, his piercing green eyes filled with tears of glass.

"But wh–what of the book...? I have failed."

"No, my friend, you accomplished all that was asked."

The old man gazed into the angel's face—Raphael. A magnificent and powerful being with chiseled features and a chestnut mane framing his face. With no facial hair, his skin melded like burnished stone that liquefied as he spoke. He wanted to touch the angel's face. *Would it yield like flesh or be hard like stone?* In this face, he saw a reflection of his own conflicted soul, utter despair and heart-wrenching sadness, yet also, peace eternal and love perfected. The combination of emotions pouring from the spiritual being washed over him.

"Can I go with you—will you take me?"

"My friend, you must travel alone, but I will meet you there."

The next stone would come from the witness, a girl no older than seven or so years. Through his peripheral vision, he watched her stoop at one of the mounds. Picking it up, she held it for a few long moments, her eyes cast down. About the size of her fist, it had sharp edges.

The mob began to circle like a pack of wild dogs. He could feel them, reluctant yet hungry. Gasping through clenched teeth, he drove an elbow into his bed of rubble. Using the extremity as a lever, he managed to roll his head in her direction. Their eyes met. Her lower lip trembled as streams of silent tears washed clean two lines of innocence in her desperate face.

His eyes spoke the words as he struggled to nod. *Be strong for me. It is not your fault.*

The accuser broke the muffled silence. "The judgment boulder missed the mark. Therefore, it is the duty of the witness to throw the second stone." Arms spread, he strode in front of the crowd, wielding a lanky walking staff. "This plague we face is this man's doing. He has a demon. Look at him—do you see the fire in his eyes? He is accursed!" The pacing stopped, and it was quiet again, except for the old man's wheezing.

The girl stared at the stone as if the hand attached to her body belonged to another. She tossed it then, the stone landing harmlessly with a hollow echo.

Again, it fell quiet, like a held breath, the eyes of all on him.

The third stone came from a youth. It moved through the cold gray dawn like a leaf floating downstream, the angel in its path. Gliding through the spiritual being, it entered from the back and exited his chest. Then struck the old man in the jaw and opened a gash that pooled with blood.

Someone shouted, "Kill him!"

The next stone was swift, connecting with a sound like that of a boxer punching a wineskin. The crowd erupted, transforming into a killing mob, stone after stone filling the air in a frenzy of noise, swarming color, and rage.

"He has a demon. Kill him!"

The mob surged in pulsating waves, forward to throw, then aside and back to the stone piles. Shouts and cries clashed with the crack of ricocheting rock echoing through the labyrinth like the sound of battle. The pace quickened as some of the younger men selected boulders which they heaved with a sidestep lunge and a blast of breath.

~~

Raphael remained kneeling at his friend's side, hand in hand until he was covered over. Standing, he walked away, then turned back as the bloodlust waned.

Dressed in black, an old woman placed the final stone at the head of the mound. She stood in silence, head bowed as the crowd dispersed.

Wiping his cheek, Raphael contemplated the savagery of the third-century Ephesians. Not as violent perhaps as some from ages past, and certainly not as cruel as those to follow, and yet capable to love beyond his understanding.

Those present were unable to see him, none that is except for the one lurking within the accuser's body, the dark spirit whose robe of flesh leaned into his walking staff. A gust of wind lapped at his rain-soaked beard.

Raphael returned the glare. In another time, he and Asmodeus had been brothers, united in purpose. But today, and for eons, they'd been archenemies.

Asmodeus made the first move, tilting his head to laugh. It began with a head bob snort and then a chuckle. The chuckle erupted into vulgar hilarity as he bent at the waist roaring to tears, the face of his human body turning red.

"Raphael, you sorry fool—that is what you are, my pathetic friend." His composure transformed to accusing contempt.

"Do you think you won today, by killing an old man?" Despair cracked through the edges of Raphael's voice.

"I did.... But today's victory is not complete." Asmodeus tossed the walking staff aside, stepping forward. "You're a fool, Raphael. You could have joined us, but instead, you cling to that Master of yours—that Ancient One? Do you not understand? It is we who rule this world." Step by prideful step, Asmodeus continued his advance.

"I stand in the presence of the Most High. It is He that I serve and no other." The words reverberated as if spoken by the canyon of stone.

The accuser's eyes widened as the wave of power struck him. It was not the delivery or the volume, but rather the purity of the words themselves. Caught off guard, Asmodeus stumbled. His human body, still falling, tumbled face-first into a slab of rock. Lurching, it curled into a fetal position.

Breaking loose from the carcass, Asmodeus raged. "Damn you, Raphael. I will kill you where you stand!"

Raphael received the instruction then, spoken deep inside his mind: "Your mission is complete, leave this place."

Closing his eyes, he stepped into the rift between time and space. It was over in an instant and would barely have been perceivable to a human if one had been present to witness it. The tear opened with a shimmer of light and a warping ripple. It closed then, and Raphael was gone.

~~

Lunging into nothing, the demon's hands converged on the neck of his opponent at the moment he vanished. Asmodeus whirled around, finding only himself, the quivering robe of flesh, and the old man's grave of stone. Rearing his head, Asmodeus screamed into the stinging rain as a shaft of sunlight broke below the ceiling of darkness.

CHAPTER 1

DANIEL FAIRMONT bit down on the cold slice of pepperoni pizza. He had to pull it laterally toward his ear in order to tear off the bite. He forced the swallow too early. Almost choking, he reached for one of the water bottles clustered in the conference table's center. With a smile, he nodded to the men as he drew a sip. At forty-eight, he was the new guy and also the youngest in the group of seven.

"Let's pray, guys." The chairman glanced at the clock. Three men stood, pushing their leather chairs toward the wall. Taking positions on their knees, they faced the seatbacks with hands folded.

Following their lead, Daniel dropped to the floor to sharp glances from two of the older men. Almost retreating, he drew a breath and bowed his head.

After fifteen minutes, his back was locking up. He shifted position every thirty seconds or so, rolling his shoulders and then sitting on his ankles. The elders took turns praying with profound oratory, sometimes pausing for minutes of absolute silence. *Where did they learn to pray like that?*

Daniel interjected, "Lord, we thank You for this evening and—"

An abrupt bleep interrupted, repeating at five-second intervals. Someone fumbling with a device then cleared his throat.

"And then everyone said... Amen." The words came from the head of the table.

When Daniel opened his eyes, Paul Chambers was leaning forward, a yellow plastic hammer in his hand. He squeezed it like someone doing hand exercises. Short and stocky, Paul had a melon-shaped balding head and manicured goatee he liked to stroke. Daniel didn't know much about Paul except that he owned his own business and loved to golf.

"Okay, guys, we've got a lot on the plate tonight. First, I want to welcome Daniel. I also have the privilege to inform him, he's been selected for the coveted job of treasurer. The truth, Daniel, is you got it because you're better looking than the rest of us, and we're all jealous, in spite of your freckles and red mop top."

A wave of chuckles and aahs rumbled through the room.

Lowering his head, Daniel smiled. "I'm honored to serve, guys."

"Thanks, Daniel." Paul fanned his hammer toward Daniel. "We appreciate you accepting, and don't worry because the pile of weekly checks is usually less than two-inches deep—*usually*." An elation of laughter followed with two of the men exchanging a silent high five across the table. Paul lifted a flat beefy hand, calling for order. "I'd also like to rebuke the rest of you for voting me in as Chair again. I guess you thought either I did an exceptional job last year, or you just figured I was too darn stupid to say no. And you would be right about that if it was the second reason."

One of the men winked at Daniel as the others chuckled.

"For Daniel's sake, I want to say my gifting is leadership, and that's what I do—I lead. That's why I carry this hammer and also why I have this charming device." Paul lifted an electronic timer. "I like discussion but cut it off when it gets out of control. And with that, I'll hand it off to Pastor Jason Stover for the business report."

Jason turned to Daniel. "I just want to say it's great to see someone who grew up in the church has stuck around long enough to end up in here as an elder. Daniel, did you know elder means old man?" In his midsixties, with his slicked-back dark-brown hair emphasizing the crow's feet at his temples, Pastor Jason grinned, his blue eyes twinkling. After sharing a report covering church ministries and upcoming events, he then updated the group on the search to fill the open position for executive pastor.

Pausing, he placed folded hands on the oversized mahogany table, his wristwatch reflecting on the polished surface. He drew a deep breath. "I want to advise the board we will be interviewing a candidate next week. Her name is Amber Lash. For full disclosure, I need to mention Amber was our Realtor when Joyce and I sold our home in Portland before moving here. Joyce and Amber became friends and have stayed in touch. I understand you know Amber as well, Daniel. Is that right?"

All eyes moved to Daniel.

Daniel sat up straight. "Yes, I know Amber. We met in college. We actually dated for a short time, but haven't kept in touch." Unscrewing the cap from his water bottle, Daniel felt his face beginning to flush. "Amber's smart all right. I understand she's had her own business and done quite well."

They continued to stare as he drew a sip.

The business report lasted a full hour concluding with a summary of performance figures including attendance and giving. Daniel offered a few nods and mms. Deciding to keep quiet, he eased into the leather seat, the lumbar support soothing his taut spine. The room still carried the faint scent of fresh paint from last year's volunteer campus renewal project. He had rehung the planning calendar, schoolroom clock, and framed portraits of Faith Bible Church's former pastors. Four of them, one of which now hung crooked. Daniel stared at it.

Paul Chambers scanned his agenda and then stood. "Pastor, we want to thank you. We are truly blessed to have you with us, doing the Lord's work." He spread his arms as the others rose. "Before you leave, we would like to pray for you, if that's okay?"

Jason stood, responding with a pursed smile. "Thank you. I would be honored."

The men then huddled around him, some laying hands on his shoulders and back with Paul leading. Daniel took a position on the perimeter placing a hand on the shoulder of one of the men.

"Lord, we thank You for Pastor Jason and ask You to watch over him as he travels home to his lovely wife. May You use this man, and all of us, to bring glory to Your church. Amen."

Opening his eyes, Daniel glanced at the ceiling. It was a shimmer of sorts, a short pulse in the room. More so, a tingling of his emotions and a wave of vertigo stirring his curiosity. *What was that—maybe the fluorescents?*

Paul Chambers stroked his goatee as Jason departed and the others returned to their seats. "Can we close the door, please?" He rotated his chair to face Daniel with hands on his knees. "As an elder, there are some rules you're going to need to be aware of, Daniel." He spoke slowly, dropping his head with a nod.

Daniel mirrored Paul's head drop. "Okay...?"

"I don't know about your relationship with your wife, but what we need to say to you is this." Paul bobbed his head to the faces around the table. "I'm not exactly sure how to phrase it, but... What I'm saying—or all of us are saying—is what happens in this room stays in this room." Tilting his round head, Paul's eyes widened like a goldfish.

Daniel replied with another nod. "Ah, yeah, I think I understand."

"In here, Daniel, we're like a band of brothers. We need to be on the same page here—even when there's disagreement. And sometimes, the wives can say too much—if you know what I mean." Henry Williams released his suspender straps, which snapped back against his plaid shirt, a blast of air disturbing wisps of his grayish-brown comb-over. "Wives don't exactly understand. I mean, let's face it, when the Holy Spirit is speaking and if you're not in here praying, well, you know—they just don't quite get it. That's what we're saying here."

Paul stood. "He's got it, Henry. I think we're ready to move on." Paul cocked his chin to the far end of the table. "Nick, are you ready? Someone hit the lights. This is important, guys, and I know it's late. But I need us to focus."

Everyone shifted toward the wall bathed in navy. The color washed over Nick Hamilton, who stood before the overhead projector. His finger lifted from his laptop. "Gentlemen, we are about to break new ground, and Lord willing, this church will be blessed."

Nick and his wife had joined the church two years earlier. A year older than Daniel, his friend had the presence of a seasoned statesman. A beaked nose dominated his chiseled face while neatly cropped jet-black hair, dashed with gray in the right places, gave him the look of an eagle. *Brutal good looks—almost ugly.*

"In the corporate world, it's called reorg., and that is what we will call it here as well. Men, this is not for the weak or faint of heart—make no mistake. With a strategic hire to the position of executive pastor, which is forthcoming, we will do this." With head bowed, peering over the rims of frameless square glasses, Nick paused, making eye contact with each. Then, with his pointer finger tapping his lip, as a librarian might ponder silence, he continued, "Reorg. is a process of reinvention—injecting new life. And that is what we are in need of— new life."

A tentative hand bobbed up.

"Hold the questions, guys. Let him finish."

"New life means new blood, and I'm not talking about positions on the lower section of the totem pole. In order to build a new machine, this one will need to be broken. That's right. We're talking key positions, the more senior the better. Let's face it, we can barely keep the lights on. We're a fourth our former size, and we don't even fill the auditorium on Easter. That's failure, gentlemen—failure of leadership—and unacceptable in my book."

Stiffening in his mind, Daniel glanced to blank stares around the table. His throat constricted.

"In the business world, it's easy. Leadership makes the decision, and designated employees are gone by five o'clock. It's surgery. You cut away the cancer and insert the new parts. Being a church, however, will take more finesse and sensitivity. But if this works—and trust me, it will—Faith Bible Church will be written about. Others will take notice and follow our example."

Daniel's stomach churned, heartburn rising in his chest. Leaning back, he covered an exhaling breath with his fist. *Is this what we're doing? This makes no sense.*

Nick spread his arms. "The problem with the megachurch is it eventually fades. It loses track with what it was in the beginning." Drawing hands to his lips once more, this time as if praying, he dropped his voice to a whisper. "For us, it was faith—after all, we were named for it. But let's be honest... Faith left this place a long time ago when a former elder board fired our founding pastor."

Daniel glanced to the crooked portrait where the subject seemed to be bowing his head.

Moving toward his conclusion with the skill of a polished musician, Nick clicked through his presentation by memory. His voice grew in strength, surging to a crescendo. "Gentlemen, we are going to reinvent ourselves. We will have a vision statement to rally around, and we will brand ourselves with a new logo and possibly a new name. We can do this, and if done well, we will prosper." The final slide lit the wall washing over Nick Hamilton. The color was amber.

"We're going to stop it here. I don't want any discussion outside this room, and that includes the parking lot. We're not making any decisions tonight, but I wanted us to hear this and begin to think it over." Paul closed the meeting with a short prayer.

As they departed, the weary faces carried a heavy emptiness Daniel now shared.

~~

Raphael had departed as well, leaving before the final slide.

CHAPTER 2

ASMODEUS swirled dark liquid in the cut-crystal Bordeaux glass. He elevated it at half arm's length, admiring the rich fingering pattern as it faded into the translucent walls. Immersing his nose into the bowl-shaped flask, he breathed it in. The bottle of 1941 Inglenook Cabernet rested slightly off-center atop the round table draped in silk. He pushed it back and to the left, a half-inch or so to balance it with the bowl of floating orchids.

Giving it another swirl, he inhaled the full bouquet and drew a sip. "Incredible."

As dusk approached, the balcony offered a stunning view. The sun had revealed itself below the distant clouds, just above the horizon line which was about to slice into the suspended disk of fire. He soaked it in, mesmerized by the river of red and white lights snaking along Pacific Coast Highway as the waves crashed on the beach beyond. How refined these, the creature comforts of the twenty-first century, truly were. Gazing into the liquid, he sighed. He might dine out tonight, feasting on the finest of food and drink, but only if he chose. For now, the sunset's fading glow, the smell of salt in the air and the cool breeze satisfied.

Tracing his index finger along the rim, he thought about what might await him in the parking structure. After all, he'd been chauffeured in the finest stallion-drawn carriages, not to mention chariots, appointed in black ivory and plated in gold. Then again, nothing compared to a spirited drive on a twisty road, working the gearbox of a four-wheeled chariot powered by a herd of wild horses. Darkness settled in as he breathed another sip.

The battle cry had been loosed, and the prize at stake was great, indeed very great. Struggling to identify his emotions, the dark angel purred. Yes, the moment's quiet beauty pleased, but he hungered for the rage of battle. He was in the eye of the storm, waiting now for delivery of the weapon he needed. He drew another sip, concluding a naked sort of restlessness left him a bit uncomfortable. Perhaps it was the vulnerability of the exterior he felt, yet also, the richness of the internal experience he craved. Soon enough, he'd have his new body of flesh.

<<>>

Amber Lash waved to the barista as she collected her triple macchiato. Twisting her watch, she glanced across the room to her favorite spot at the window—open. Instead, she turned her back to the seat and strode out the door. *No time to sit and savor today.*

Placing her drink in the cup holder, she pushed the start button and strapped in. With a glance at the mirror, she slid the shifter into reverse, backed up, and then maneuvered through the parking lot. After waiting for a gap in traffic, she then merged onto Adler Street, tapped the hands-free button, and said, "Call Richard," checking her mirrors as the phone dialed. "Hi, honey. I wish you were here. I'm missing you already." She bit her lower lip.

"Oh sure, you are. You know you can't wait to get away—poor baby." The smile leaving Richard's voice, he said, "I wish I could join you, Amby. But getting away right now, at the beginning of the semester, it's just not possible. But I'll be praying for you. Promise you'll be careful—especially on the road?"

Amber fumbled with the green and white cup as the traffic light switched to yellow. "Don't forget to send up a prayer during the interview. It starts at eleven. And tell me why I'm doing this? The thought of actually picking up and moving—it's crazy."

A horn blasted as she started to switch lanes. As she swerved back, a silver Mustang roared past on her right. "Sorry..."

"What was that? Are you okay? Are you driving?"

"Yes, honey. Don't worry. I'm fine. People on the road are just insane. He must have been late for work."

"Listen, Amby, we've been talking about making a change for a long time, and—like I've said—when the Lord speaks, it's our job to listen. The interview will be a great experience, regardless. Besides, you're going to have fun getting away—you know you are."

She tipped the cup, drawing a sip through the small hole in the white lid. "Ouch. I think I just burnt my tongue. You're right. I should have pulled over before calling. And you're also right about it being a good experience. I better go. I'll call you when I get to the resort—okay? Love you."

Driving into the sun, she flipped down the visor and squinted. *Nothing but rain for a week and now the sun comes out.* She groaned. With just over ninety minutes to reach the airport, drop off the car, and make her gate an hour before the flight, she certainly didn't need to be fighting the sun. Her Buick Enclave had plenty of power, hitting speed halfway up the ramp. She eased it back at seventy as she merged onto the I-84. Opening the sunroof, she let the freedom of the crisp morning whip through her sandy brown curls.

At forty—six years ago—she'd put on a few pounds, but her figure could still turn the heads of men half her age. Proud of her spunky natural beauty, she hardly needed makeup. She considered her petite five-foot-two frame and beauty to be assets, just right when dealing with men. Not overly intimidating, but helpful when pushing for what she wanted.

Amber tilted her head, twisting a curl. Could Richard actually leave his buddies and what about the church? It did have its strong points. After all, they had made some friends there, and it had been a great place to raise their son. But Richard took it all so seriously, prodding her to join the Women's Bible Study and even asking her to pray with him. Eventually, he'd let it go.

The call had come from Joyce, asking if she might consider joining their staff. She'd initially discarded it. Then later the idea had begun to make sense. After all, she'd built and managed a successful company. What would be so different in running a church? True, the products were different, but the skill sets were essentially the same. Besides, Richard would be so pleased.

The application was extensive, asking questions about her morality and spiritual beliefs. How she'd laughed at some of her answers. *All those years, sitting in church for Richard, are finally paying off.*

After finalizing the application, she attached the various files. Her finger then hovered above the Send button. Shoving the keyboard away, she picked up her coffee mug and warmed her palms. *I should probably wait. This whole idea—this is crazy.*

She squinted as she changed lanes, taking the airport exit. Checking her speed, she was there again, at the keyboard. She'd heard a voice, a soft whispering in her ear or maybe in her mind.

"You can always say no."

Her finger seemed to move then by itself. The command was

executed, and the message flew away into space. She shrugged and then tapped the brakes to release the cruise control. *Oh well, I can always say no.*

<<>>

Arriving at the Newport Coast Villas two hours before check-in, Amber crossed the entry tower's stone medallion. The grand lobby doors opened to a sweeping balcony overlooking a tapestry of undulating pools and gardens.

On familiar turf, she bypassed the check-in counter and headed directly for the concierge, her heels clicking on the polished marble floor. The gentleman behind the white desk, out of place in a stodgy tweed sport-coat with elbow patches, lifted his head to view a monitor over the top of his half glasses. "Mrs. Lash, I have you booked for just tonight, Villa 420. That's right here, facing the ocean on the fourth floor, and this is where we are." He delivered the words in a monotone while sliding a colored map toward her. He drew two circles with a blue marker, connecting them with a sawtooth line.

"Have you stayed with us before?"

"My husband and I have been here several times. We just love the Villas—it's our favorite." Amber drew a deep breath, refreshed by the pristine salted air.

"That's wonderful, and will it be the two of you tonight?"

"No, just myself. I'm traveling on business. I know I'm a little early, but I was wondering if I might leave my bag with you and come back for it later?"

"That would be fine. I can give you the cardkey now. It will get you into the pool area and also access your room when it's ready. If you like, I can have the bellboy deliver your bag to the room."

"That would be perfect. As always, your service is the best."

He nodded to the monitor again. "I also show Executive Motors dropped a rental for you. It's in the garage, space 120." He pointed, drawing again on the map. "We have the keys for you. In fact, they're right here." After fumbling in a drawer, he produced a set of BMW keys and slid them across the white granite.

Amber's mouth fell open. "Are you sure those are mine? I'm sure they said it was a Toyota."

"No, these are right. It says right here—Amber Lash."

"Well, all righty then. I'm not going to argue with that."

"If you're hungry, you might try the poolside Cabana Bar. The food is quite good."

~~

Finding a stool, Amber ordered a fruity tequila drink from the bartender in a bright Hawaiian shirt. She inhaled the paradise, letting it wash away the day's stress. The design of the meandering resort was Tuscany. Overlooking a kelly-green golf course, the buildings were strategically terraced to maximize the ocean view. Freestanding pergola walls, capped with cantilevering trellises, flanked the pool area, serving as backdrops to manicured planting beds accentuated with exotic floral arrangements and pigmy palms. Beyond the pools, a steel drum band played Jamaican music on a grassy mesa with a white gazebo, where a small wedding party was setting up.

The sun's warmth and a soft breeze caressed her face. She closed her eyes, listening to the laughter and music dancing in the background. Stirring her drink with the little umbrella, she purred, "Hmm... this is nice." *A massage, followed by a bubble bath and dinner, or then again, maybe not...*

As she opened her eyes, the bartender placed another drink in front of her. "This is from the gentleman across the bar."

When the bartender moved, she saw him. He smiled, a little older, but very handsome. Amber replied with smiling eyes, sipping from the fresh glass. She touched her wedding band with her thumb, leaving her hand on the counter screened from view.

Looking away, she pretended to watch the wedding preparations, but her eyes soon drifted back. He was doing the same, and more than once, their eyes met with a shared smile. She had cheated on Richard but only once, telling no one. She'd vowed it would never happen again. But the passion of that night was a memory she treasured. A memory she took out from time to time and relived—what was the harm in that? *It was as if it had never happened.* She thought about it now.

As she stirred the ice, another drink appeared, followed by another over-the-shoulder nod from the bartender. Another exchanged smile. And then the woman. Younger and quite beautiful, she wore a wedding band. Amber turned again to the steel band. Lifting her left hand, she stroked her cheek. He stood. Motioning for his wife to walk ahead, he looked back. Their eyes touched again with the smile of a shared secret.

She pushed the half-empty glass toward the drink rail. Standing, she steadied herself with a hand on the barstool. The moment was nice, the cool breeze, the steel band, and the relaxing sensation throughout her frame. She ran her fingers through her hair and nodded to the bartender. Letting go, she did her best to walk without drawing attention.

The suite included two master bedrooms, split with a central kitchen and walkthrough dining area. The living space, large enough to accommodate a small gathering, featured a glass wall opening to a balcony. She took the forward bedroom with the soaking tub and window overlooking the ocean.

Resting in the bath of bubbles with eyes closed, she recalled a rafting trip, the boat gently drifting. A memory about the danger of alcohol and hot tubs floated through her mind compelling her to rise. She gripped the safety bar as her head continued downstream. Bypassing the towel, she snuggled into the cozy white robe while looking to the bed with turned-down sheets.

Soft but firm, perfect in fact. Sitting on its edge, her mind drifted back to the candles, still burning on the tub surround. And the gentleman at the bar. *Being desired is nice, and besides, it was just flirting—an affair with the idea of having one.* Her eyes faded shut, and she was in the stream again. Her last thought—the candles.

"They'll be fine...."

CHAPTER 3

THE ANGEL spoke, "Wake up and pray."

No—I'm so tired. Sleep returned, overpowering consciousness.

"Wake up. It's time to pray." The angel leaned forward with an open hand, speaking gently.

I'm tired. I just want to sleep. Let me sleep. He pulled on the covers, slumber again prevailing.

"Won't you pray with me for just one hour?"

Richard Lash opened his eyes. Turning to the nightstand, he read the numbers—1:26 a.m.

It had happened before. Many times, with Richard dubbing it The Wake-Up Call. Months since the last occurrence, the timing was off. Typically, it woke him at 3:00 a.m. sharp or sometimes at 3:02. Other times, it came as late as 3:10. But it was always close and rarely early.

He'd grown to embrace the interruption but sometimes resisted, especially when it was cold and the bed warm. But knowing the Lord wanted to speak to him was always comforting, and each time he heeded the call, he received a message of significance.

The first time, the Lord told him Shana, his student teacher, was struggling in her marriage. Richard asked, "Are you sure, Lord—Shana seems so happy?" But the message persisted, and after praying, he returned to bed in peace. After classes that day, he asked Shana if everything was okay. As she began to respond, she poured out all that was wrong in her life. An hour later, he was able to share the gospel, leading her in a prayer of surrender. He then watched in wonder as the burden was lifted from the young woman's shoulders and the tears replaced with a quiet peace and joy.

Another time, after praying for an hour and hearing nothing, he asked, "Why, Lord, did You call me to pray?"

The wave of the Spirit broke then, crashing over him as he heard, *"I have a message for you to speak to the church."*

He wrote it on a sheet of paper, which he carried in his Bible. At the time, it had been so clear, but now, more than three years later, it had faded and seemed distant. From time to time, he unfolded the note. Reading it, he would ask, "Is it time, Lord, and did I hear You correctly?"

Richard had sat in the darkness that morning weeping softly. Not because the message was so precious, but rather, it was the experience itself. God Almighty, the Creator of all, had spoken to him, a simple man. The message itself was somewhat harsh, not a rebuke but definitely a warning to change behavior. *Why, Lord, would You speak this to my church? We seem to be so healthy and full of the Spirit?*

The display blinked to 1:27 as he sat up. Reaching into the darkness, he found the arm of his wheelchair and began the process of shifting his body from mattress to chair. He then maneuvered through the door into Amber's closet. The muffled solitude of the dark enclosure felt distantly familiar—a place where he could almost capture a lost memory of being in the womb. Settled in, he listened to his beating heart.

He began as he always did. "Lord God, I praise and bless Your name. You are holy and pure—"

"Be still."

Yes, Lord... Startled by the interruption, Richard stared into the blackness, his eyes open wide.

"Pray for Amber."

Is she in trouble? Richard waited. "Should I call her, Lord? Is Amber in trouble?"

"No. Pray for her."

<<>>

Amber opened her eyes to the room awash in a glow of soft deep blue. The candles on the tub had burned out, and the numbers on the alarm clock read 1:26 a.m. Her head still swimming and her mouth dry, she swallowed. Then swinging her legs over the edge of the bed, she watched the slow wave of the white curtains, the cool breeze caressing her skin. The flowing veil parted and then closed again, a shaft of moonlight washing up and over her legs. Thirst overpowering slumber, her gaze fell on the robe draped over the bed's foot-bench. A glass of water and the beauty of the night called to her.

The full-length curtains billowed in as she pushed the sliding glass doors open. She stepped into the night, the moist balcony deck cold on her feet. The view and cool breeze enveloping her, she touched the stone railing to center herself, the glass of water against her cheek. A silent sky framed the full moon between clouds of cascading blues and purple. The ocean's surface lit in shimmering silver. Its rolling edge breaking white as the rhythmic waves crashed into the shore.

So beautiful... incredibly beautiful. She breathed it in, deeply and slowly. Lifting a foot, she curled her toes as she placed the glass on the railing. Turning then, she saw him. Alone on the next balcony, no more than ten feet away, a stone balustrade between them. Feeling her heart accelerate, she cinched her robe tight to her neck. Covered in shadow, he seemed to be staring into the night. *Surely, he saw me?*

The clouds broke then, caressing the balustrade. It gleamed. Amber took a half-turning step toward him. Tilting her head, she spoke in a shy voice. "Hi, neighbor."

He continued to stare into the distance. She stopped and then touched her water glass with her pointer finger. *Is he meditating or maybe praying?*

A glass of wine in hand, he faced her and then stood, emerging from the shadow. The purple light touched his feet, then rose up and over his body.

As her hand lifted to cover her mouth, a soft gasp escaped her lips. She froze, unable to breathe, her heart suddenly squeezing with pressure. His unveiled presence was astonishing, the essence of beauty and perfection, masculinity and raw power. *How can... Who...?*

His presence, as though a living statue carved by Michelangelo himself, possessed a radiance that glowed like polished metal. Or was the moonlight playing tricks with her? He stood there, draped in flowing white silk with sleeves rolled to the forearms, his unbuttoned shirt revealing a godlike torso of interlocking steel. *How could—is he real?*

Amber tried to breathe and then move. With legs of lead, she felt herself buckling sideways, flailing an arm toward the rail. And then he was there, catching her with an arm of stone, balancing her in a single fluid motion, all the while holding the glass. Her voice and body slack, both refused to obey. Amber then heard her voice exhaling a question, "H–h–how...di–id...?"

"I have you now. Don't be afraid. You nearly fell. I'm sorry I startled you. Would you like a glass of wine? It's very good. I promise."

How could he—the strength? Head swimming, she clutched at him, arms and legs rubber as if she were a rag doll draped over his arm. He waited for her. Finding her bearings then, she began to draw of the strength that seemed to flow from him.

He was breathtaking, his face—like polished white marble—flowed as he spoke and smiled. His obsidian-black hair, slicked back in thick wavy locks, hung at his shoulders. His chiseled features, beautiful yet also brutally rugged, held her like a silver vise. Amber gasped, captivated by mesmerizing eyes of gray steel. Her heart leaped then, racing forward.

How could...? Her hand flat on his chest, she pushed and then yielded.

"I'm so–so sorry. It's hard... for... me to...speak." She managed a full breath. "I–I must have... almost fainted."

"You did. But I caught you—you were falling. Would you like that drink now?"

Amber clutched his forearm, swimming in his eyes.

"The evening is beautiful, is it not?" His eyes caressed her soul.

She heard it then, someone speaking into her mind, a voice she recognized. *"You're so beautiful—you want me."*

"Yes, it's incredibly beautiful, impossibly beautiful." Unable to look away, she managed to compose the words. "Some wine sounds so good right now. Yes, thank you." She took the glass from his hand, lifted it to her lips, and drew a sip. After holding it for a moment, she swallowed. "Wow, this is amazing. I think this is the best wine I have ever tasted."

"Please, you need to sit." He motioned to the table and chairs. "Can I get you anything—a cool cloth or some water?"

"No, no. I'm fine. How did you do that?" She held onto his arm.

"Do what?"

"Jump over the railing. I didn't see you—did you do that?"

"You were fainting. I didn't think. I just wanted to catch you before you hurt yourself." Smooth and enchanting, yet strong and compelling.

"You caught me—thank you. I think I'm feeling better."

"I should leave. Is there someone I can call for you? Do you need anything?"

"No. No, I'm fine, but don't... Can you sit with me for a minute?" She spoke without thinking, still lost in his eyes.

"You're a little unstable. Let me help you." He took her hand, placing his other on the small of her back. The touch startled her, ever so light yet pulsating with tingling energy.

She heard it again. *"You're so beautiful, every contour of your body, every pore of your flesh. You're desirable, the fragrance of your hair, the perfume on your neck, the taste of your lips, and the beat of your heart. I want you...."*

"I think I'm better now, thank you." Turning to him, she brought the glass again to her mouth. "Mm, that's nice." Mesmerized, she lowered it in both hands, parted just slightly. He lifted it from her, leaning in, his finger touching hers. Her mind began to swim again. Feeling a gentle tug, her trembling body arched against his frame. She rose to meet him, their lips touching in a soft kiss.

Melting again, she was aware of being lifted in his arms, her surroundings spinning as she devoured his mouth while clutching at his face. She felt the curtain flowing over her body as he carried her through the opening. Heart pounding in her heaving chest, her entire world had become the singular moment in his arms. *I want you, too.*

Amber felt the bed beneath her, his hands peeling her from his face as he stood above her. "Come here—come to me." She heard her voice, desperate and pleading, but didn't care. Pulling her robe open, she rolled her head back and to the side, lifting up then dropping. "Please— I want you."

She heard the voice again, realizing he had been with her from the very beginning. *"I've always been here, just out of reach. But you can have me now—I want you...."*

~~

He looked down at the naked body. She was quite beautiful, and he needed her flesh. But it was her soul he craved. Asmodeus straddled her as she arched her spine, again his hand under the small of her back. He met her with his mouth, breathing her deeply into his lungs and then exhaling himself into her.

Biting his lip, she clawed at his chest with her nails. "Come into me. I want you...."

He tasted her, inhaling and exhaling the shared breath. She panted now, the oxygen of life waning with each breath as he floated above her rising and falling breasts. Holding her hands above her head, he waited. Savoring her desire. Hearts pounding in unison, the life force within her veins and spirit coursed through him. Eyes to eyes, mouth to mouth, flesh to flesh, he whispered into her mind, *"You will have me now."*

Releasing his lips from her mouth, she gasped for breath. At the moment he entered, every muscle and nerve within her body contracted, pausing like a held breath. Her head rolled back slowly. Then, exploding in release, she cried out, letting go every essence of self to him.

Asmodeus rushed through every cell, coursing through her veins, grasping every nerve ending, then penetrating the pathways of her mind. His spirit saw all of her, every memory and emotion, every passion and desire. Lastly, he engaged her soul, plunging into her spirit. The two of them were one.

<<>>

Asmodeus stepped out of the shower into the sun-filled room, his head pounding. Standing in front of the mirror, smiling at the reflection, he dried his naked body. Dropping the towel, he combed fingers through his curls. His hands swept across his chest and abdomen, then back again. They lingered.

It had been a long time since he dwelled within a woman, and this woman had quite the body. "Beautiful—incredibly beautiful, are we not?"

Testing its facial expressions, he spoke softly. "We have a big day ahead. It's time to get going." He tried it again, listening to the voice. "This is going to be fun, my love, but one thing is going to change. No more cheap tequila. From here out, we drink wine—only the finest." Asmodeus smiled and then receded into the depths of her soul.

CHAPTER 4

BEFORE the kids had moved out, they called it the refuge, their getaway, where they could lock the door and decompress after a hectic day. The huge master suite with its sitting area and fireplace had sold them on the house. Even though the four-bedroom, two-story was no longer realistic for just the two of them, they weren't ready to downsize. They sat on the couch before the fireplace, overhead the ceiling fan spinning in lazy circles.

Daniel looked at his wife. Surrounded by a chaos of books, commentaries, and notepads, she was marking in her Bible with colored pencils. He loved her now even more than when she had said yes to him twenty-two years ago. A few pounds heavier with crow's feet at the corners of her sky-blue eyes, Rhema was still his beautiful and captivating bride.

Swiping at copper curls, she removed her cat-eye glasses, turning to him. "You're awfully quiet tonight. What's going on?"

"I'm thinking about the board meeting. It was disappointing. I thought we would be reading Scripture and trying to hear from the Lord." He sighed. "We spent some time praying before we started, actually a lot. But I didn't get a sense the Spirit was even there. It felt more like our prayers were bouncing off the ceiling. It seemed no different from a group of guys having a business meeting. I was just expecting something different."

Rhema put her dilapidated burgundy Bible on the coffee table. "I understand what you're saying, but you need to remember they're just men. So tell me what you talked about?"

He shook his head. "Apparently, I'm the treasurer. It sounds like it's an initiation for the new guy. They were joking about it, but I don't mind. And then they explained how we're a band of brothers, and we're not supposed to tell our wives anything."

"Seriously, did you agree to that?" She rotated toward him. Pulling her feet up, she sat cross-legged. Didn't he know that look of shock and confrontation he saw in her eyes?

"Well, sort of. I nodded." Daniel dropped his head, looking at her as if over the top of glasses that were not there. He swallowed. "I was thinking I would be telling you what we're doing. Your feedback's important to me."

"Are you sure you can trust me?" She crossed her arms. Then cocking her head, she added a slow nod. "What if I start telling all my friends about what's going on in the elder meetings? Hmm?"

At least, she was smiling. "Some of it's confidential, and I'm not sure I would share everything. Like, if we were talking about someone and it was sensitive or if it was something that might hurt you."

"Scripture says the man is supposed to protect his wife, so it makes sense you shouldn't hurt me. But what would you be talking about that might hurt me?" When he stiffened and started to turn away, she put her hand on his knee. "What happened?"

"I've been thinking about it all day, and I do want your input." He opened and closed his hand. Then making a fist, he drew it to his lips.

Squeezing his knee, she leaned closer. "You don't have to tell me if you don't want to."

"It's extremely confidential, and you have to promise you won't repeat it. If it was to get out, it would be horrible."

"Well then, don't tell me." She pulled her hand back, again crossing her arms.

"But I think I need to. I don't want to carry it without your help." He bit on the corner of his lower lip.

"Okay then." She slid her hand into his and squeezed. "What?"

Daniel let go. Standing, he put his hands in his pockets and stared into the unlit fireplace as he hesitated. "Nick made a presentation about reorging the church. He did a great job presenting, but, well..."

"What's a reorg.?" Twisting toward him, she rose to one knee. "Do you mean switching the staff around and giving them different positions?"

"Partly. But the main thing is reinventing ourselves as an organization. It doesn't feel right. We're supposed to be the church."

"Seriously?" She stood. "You guys talked about reinventing the Body of Christ?"

"It wasn't expressed that way—but well, yeah." He shrugged, turning back to the disbelief twisting her pained face. "They're good guys, Coach, and they love the Lord. But, well, yes, that's what it was.

It makes sense if you think about it from a business point of view."

"What does that mean...exactly?" Her voice was so quiet.

Didn't I just say I wouldn't tell her something that might hurt her? He clenched his jaw. "If a corporation is failing, they make changes to survive. Nick was saying the most effective way to do that is to break the mold and then remake yourself into whatever you want by firing the CEO, and if you really want to make a statement, you replace the entire leadership. Sports teams do it all the time, new coach and staff, new uniforms and stadium." He stared at her hands, so petite and delicate. Exhaling, he met her brimming eyes.

"You're going to fire people—who?"

"According to Nick, it doesn't really matter, except the more senior the positions the more effective the outcome." Again, he focused on her hands. The engagement ring glinted where it had rested since the day he had dropped to one knee sliding it onto her finger. He turned back to the dark fireplace.

"You're going to fire Pastor Stover? That makes absolutely no sense. Everyone loves him, and he loves the people. Remember the woman who came to church when her son was in a coma after being hit on his motorcycle? Pastor Jason dropped everything and rushed to the hospital. All night, sitting with her family, and he didn't even know them. This is crazy. Can you imagine how many people are going to be hurt?"

"So far we're just talking and praying about it. We're not likely to do anything until after we hire the new executive pastor who will execute most of it. The whole thing just doesn't feel right."

"Of course it doesn't! It doesn't line up with Scripture. How could it be right?"

He swallowed. "What do you mean?"

"In John—where Jesus is praying. It's right here." Rhema snatched up her Bible. Almost tearing the pages, she flipped to the passage. Then, holding a finger on it, she read aloud, gesturing with her free hand. "'I do not ask You to take them out of the world, but to keep them from the evil one. They are not of the world, even as I am not of the world. Sanctify them in the truth. Your word is truth.'" She glared at him and waited. When he didn't respond, she slid her finger down the page. "And then here—listen to this: 'I have made Your name known to them, and will make it known, so that the love with which

You loved Me may be in them, and I in them.'"

Rhema tossed her Bible on the couch. Looking like she was about to walk out of the room, she instead stepped in front of him. "Does that sound like instructions for running a business or sports team? And what about where it says the world will know them by their love for one another? And also, where Jesus says no greater love has a man than to lay down his life for his friend? That's what the church is supposed to look like. How does that line up with firing our pastors?"

"You're right, Coach." The pain in her face put a knot in his stomach.

"I don't get it." As she spoke, he took her hands. They were trembling. "Scripture says nothing about kicking someone out of the church because you don't want them or because it's a good way to reinvent the church. It does describe removing someone if sin's involved, but this is not about sin. It sounds more like selfish ambition."

He pursed his lips and pulled her close, smelling the scent of her hair. "That's why we're a good team. You know the Scripture so much better than I do." Pulling back, he cupped her shoulders. The ceiling fan blades stroked her face with a soft pulsing shadow. "There's another thing we talked about. We're going to interview Amber Lash for the executive pastor position."

Rhema's mouth fell open. "Amber? Amber Lash?"

<<>>

Amber stood in front of the mirror, weighing her options. She caressed the high collar of her gray suit, one of her favorites. The tailored jacket drew attention to her curves without being overly sexy. Draping it over the shoe-bench, she wiggled into her purple dress. Just plain seductive, the stretchy material hugged her shape while accentuating her cleavage, perfect for the theater or a wedding. If the interview was with a woman, it would likely work against her. But if it were a man, or better yet, a group of men, she'd go with the purple. She reached for the gray, hanging formal and sexy beside the mirror. The gray was always a safe choice, and considering it was a church...

The voice inside disagreed, *"You look stunning, and besides, who cares if they even hire you?"*

Her face lit up as she swept away a few wrinkles from the skirt.

"That's right. I am stunning and who cares. Purple it is."

Leaving the room, she glanced at the neighbor's door and thought about knocking. But what to say exactly? Call me or how 'bout coffee? And by the way, what's your name? She shook her head. *I'm just glad he was gone when I woke up.*

She thought of Richard. *I should have called. But now, will he know? Will he sense it in my voice?* She'd wait until after the interview. The news, good or bad, would make it easier to conceal her mistake.

She walked briskly away from the memory and toward the lobby. The tweed-suited concierge was there again. "How was your evening, Ms. Lash—I trust everything was satisfactory?"

"Yes, it was. Thank you." She offered a half smile. "I met my neighbor last night, just briefly—the gentleman in 419? I understand you have rules, but I was wondering if you could tell me his name? I slipped and fell on the walk, and he helped me. He was very kind, and I thought I might leave him a note." She fumbled with her suitcase.

"I trust you were not hurt?" He gazed into the monitor.

"Oh no, I'm fine. I just thought..."

"That's quite all right. I believe I understand." Looking over the top of his glasses, he met her eyes. "I'm sorry. Villa 419 is vacant. It was unoccupied yesterday."

"But I–I'm sure he was. Someone surely... Are you *sure*? I guess it must have been another one of your guests." *That's impossible. Does he know?*

<<>>

Amber froze as her suitcase collided into her thigh. Lurking in the darkness of the parking structure, it stared at her from bay 120, the black saloon branded on the hood with the unmistakable blue and white roundel. When she touched a button on the remote, it woke with a throaty growl and wink from the headlamps. After loading her suitcase, she slid into the cockpit. As she reached for the shifter, she realized she had a problem. *A manual six-speed? I've never driven a car with a clutch.*

"Too good to be true. It was a mistake, all right, and the joke's on me." She was about to hit the steering wheel when Asmodeus took over. Depressing the clutch, he slid the shifter into reverse. Then eased the clutch out, and the car glided with the grace of a canoe in quiet water. Reversing and working the gears, they floated through the meandering drive, coasting to stop at the intersection with Newport Coast Boulevard.

"Whoever said driving a stick was hard?" The light turned green, and Asmodeus launched the Bimmer, shooting up the hill passing traffic.

Their eyes met when she shifted to fourth. The officer was perched on the shoulder, straddling his motorcycle with a radar gun in hand. Amber lifted her foot from the gas, glancing to the speedometer as it fell, passing 110 miles per hour. In the rearview mirror, their eyes met again. He smiled, gesturing with a two-finger salute.

Her face lit up. "The gods are with us today, or maybe he just likes the car?"

"It was the purple dress."

CHAPTER 5

BATUSH stretched and then rubbed his neck. Beyond the deep opening in the clay brick wall, Sarah was chasing the spotted goat with a stick. In her multicolored dress and long dark hair, she fluttered like a butterfly dancing in the sun.

"Come to me, Noah, you bad boy." She squealed laughter.

He loved his son's daughter like his own. *Life is hard, but God is good to us.* Checking the cupboards again, he packed a lunch—goat cheese, a few olives, and a wedge of bread torn from a grainy loaf. He then jostled with the wineskin, pouring the liquid into his day flask.

Meraiah slept as he entered the bedchamber, the morning sun edging toward her, the smell of spring and jasmine in the air. He sat on the edge of the wood-frame bed, clad with a woven blanket over a straw mattress. He watched his bride. Her once luxuriant long black hair, now thinned and gray, framed her wrinkled face. She was still young and beautiful to him. Creeping up the pillow, the sun caressed her cheek as she blinked dark-brown eyes. A warm smile curving her lips, she drew the feathered pillow under her chin.

"I dreamed about them last night. It was before the plague, and we were all together. It was First Fruits, and we were in the courtyard." Her eyes opening again, she lifted her petite hand and gave his freshly shaved chin a tug. "You were giving them your blessing."

He cupped her small shoulder in his hand. "They are in the hands of the Lord now. We must praise Him for the years we had," he spoke softly, then kissed her forehead.

"Sarah and I will bake today. Will you be home for supper?"

"I have transcribing and will then go to the library. I will hurry, but the Fathers are expecting the copy completed by Sabbath. I may be late."

"Try to be home before dark. There was another Goth attack only last week. It was less than a half-day's walk from here. I worry about you."

Batush wrapped his lunch in sackcloth and packed it into his writing case. He then ducked under the hewn lintel and stepped into the sunshine, to Sarah running toward him. Bending down, he swept her into his arms. "My sweet butterfly, you are getting too big for me to carry. Did you catch Noah?"

"I did and scolded him too." She locked her arms around his neck.

"I need you to help Grandmother bake the bread today. It will bring a smile to my face. Can you do that for me?"

"I will, Papa. You will see." Sarah twisted as he let her down to run. "Grandmother, get up. We need to make the bread."

He strode down the slope with a spring in his stride, the song of the morning birds filling his ears. *Yes, we are getting older, but remember Father Moses? He was still vigorous when the Good Lord took him home.*

At the base of the slope, the path merged with Curetes Street, which fed directly into the heart of Ephesus. Others were converging on the road, all headed toward the city. Before joining them, he detoured to an overgrown trail leading toward a stand of trees.

Stooping, he swept back the hanging growth to enter the shaded shrine within the gnarled olive canopy, its branches draping to the ground on all sides. John's Prayer Garden, as it was known, had once been a popular stop for pilgrims following the Trail of the Apostle. A listing stone bench rested before a birdbath centered on a slab of variegated pavers.

Legend had it, the basin contained the tears of the Virgin Mary, who had lived in a house on the slopes where the Apostle John cared for her. A great earthquake destroyed the home when the Apostle breathed his last. Only the stone bench and basin survived the quake. It was believed the basin's water had healing powers and never ran dry. While he'd seen a deacon pour water into the basin on more than one occasion, it didn't bother him. After all, it was true the basin did not fill itself, but it was also true that it never ran dry.

Kneeling in front of the bench, he smiled at his reflection in the pool. Although his hair was now receding and mostly gray, his olive skin was hardly wrinkled, and his slender short frame yet strong and true. And to Meraiah, he was still her youthful champion—how blessed he was to have her! Bowing his head, he prayed softly, "Mighty God, Creator of all that grows and breathes, make me a temple fit for You. In Your boundless loving kindness, wash me with the blood of Your Son, that I might bring glory to Your name and a smile to Your face.

Amen." When he opened his eyes, the water rippled as a swallow took flight.

<<>>

Batush loved the City, especially in the morning. He jumped out of the way as children ran past, shouting and laughing. Just ahead, a shepherd herded a cluster of bleating sheep as a woman passed him, a small pig in her arms. Merchants on both sides of the street hoisted the tarps of their shop fronts. The smell of animals and cooking filled the air.

"Batush, my friend, will you be joining us?" Zophar called as Batush entered the open market square.

"How can I escape from you? It is impossible." Batush grinned as they embraced.

"Will it be the usual?" Zophar's white teeth glinted within his burly black beard.

At the counter, his son stood crafting a drink at the stove with a copper vessel. He held it in the flame until it boiled up and then withdrew it to cool. He repeated the process several times as the brew condensed into black syrup. The young man then poured it into a small ceramic cup and placed it on the table.

"Gibeon, you will do well to follow your father in business." Batush nodded, raising the drink, capped with a film of golden froth. He drew a sip. "Now that, dear brother, is what all of Ephesus is talking about."

"Remember, Batush, when you said I was foolish to think a shop with only one drink could ever make it? Look now at the customers— they line up for my brew every day." Zophar leaned back, folding his big arms. "Next year, God willing, Gibeon will open his own shop in Smyrna. But first, he will master the art of serving." Zophar glowed as his son greeted customers. Gibeon, unlike his father, was lean and lanky. Transitioning from boy to man, he wore his medium-length straight black hair oiled and slicked back.

Zophar uncurled his arms and pulled up a three-legged stool. "What brings you to the City this morning?"

"Church business... I will record a discipline hearing and then spend the rest of the day in the library. God willing, I will complete the copy I have been working on. The Fathers want it by Sabbath."

"Is it true, the bishop will render judgment on Brother Shebaniah? I know he is a new convert, but he is zealous for the Holy Scriptures." Speaking in a hushed voice, Zophar gestured loudly with both hands.

Batush placed a hand on his dark friend's shoulder. "The Fathers have been praying and seeking the Lord. The bishop is a holy and righteous man. You know also he sent his wife away to live with her sister, so he can be married only to the Lord. The Fathers are wise and know more than us. We must trust and pray for them."

<<>>

A single shaft of light cast an oval disk of brilliance on the meeting chamber's mosaic floor. The accused sat in a lonely chair beneath the opening in the domed ceiling. Four radial benches formed an elevated perimeter that descended as one entered the sunken room. The circular footprint was symmetrical, except for a linear platform that sliced into the steps. The raised platform supported a sweeping crescent-shaped table, skirted with ornately carved panels, twelve of them, depicting the unique death of each Apostle. Carved in matching wood, five high-backed chairs with red cushions stood like sentinels behind the table. The walls were finished in smooth plaster, punched with three equally spaced openings, one centered behind the table with the other two serving as entrances for the meeting hall.

Church guardians monitored the entry points, two at each corbeled opening. Clad in the traditional brown cloak of the clergy servants, they also wore a sheathed knife hanging from a rope belt.

Batush sat in the middle row, across from and to the left of the platform, tablet and quill-pen ready. A single woman waited in attendance in the front row behind her husband.

A hush fell over the room as a late-arriving vicar shuffled in, his linen robe rustling. Batush had experienced the chair of focus when the Church Fathers interviewed him for his position of scribe. The room's shape focused every sound to that singular location. He remembered hearing the soft whispers of everyone in the room. His heart pounded thinking of it now.

Cupping a hand, Batush whispered, "The Lord says do not fear, for I will never leave nor forsake you."

The heavyset man responded, turning slightly with bowed head.

They entered through the opening behind the table in robes of scarlet, adorned with white tassels on oversized sleeves. Bishop Jonness took the middle chair, a gold chain with jeweled cross swinging from his neck. He squinted into the room and, upon spotting

Batush, nodded.

"Shebaniah, son of Azaniah, you have been summoned before the council of your elders, for the rendering of judgment. The council has reviewed the charges brought against you and prayed over these matters."

Batush wrote quickly, dipping his quill to reload.

Jonness lifted a leather folder from the table. Slowly unwinding its twine tie, he opened its cover flap and withdrew a singular parchment. "Based on the testimony of witnesses, you are accused of teaching the Holy Scripture outside the walls of the church. Do you confess this to be true, Shebaniah?" Lowering the document, he narrowed his gaze on the man in the chair.

"Yes, it is true. I have—"

Jonness raised a hand. "Let it be recorded the accused admitted guilt to Charge One."

The woman whimpered.

"You have also been accused of praying over certain sick persons for healing. Witnesses have seen you do this on three separate occasions." After dropping the parchment to the tabletop, Jonness tugged on his short white beard. "Is this true, Shebaniah?"

"Yes, it is true." His head bowed, Shebaniah seemed to be watching the disk of light inching its way across the floor.

Batush recorded every word.

"But the sick were healed, all of them." The rebuttal came from the sobbing woman, her arms outstretched.

"Silence." Jonness rose to a half-standing position, his pointer finger stabbing the table. "Women shall be silent in the church. Remove her."

Batush lifted his pen, following Shebaniah's gaze to the disk of light now illuminating the depiction of a dove on the mosaic floor. Two guardians met her as she stood, every eye watching them usher her out.

"The record shall state the accused admitted guilt in the matter of Charge Two. Shebaniah, you are guilty of preaching doctrine and practicing works of healing. These ministries are the sacred duties of the Apostolic Fathers only." Jonness fanned his arms toward the other elders. "Shebaniah, you proclaim yourself to be an apostle—and you are not. Do you admit this?"

"I admit to sharing the gospel and praying for the Lord's healing, that His name would be glorified. I admit also the Lord is with me and will never forsake me." Shebaniah looked up, his voice trembling.

"Shebaniah, by your own testimony, you have admitted to practicing the acts of an apostle, and this council finds you guilty. Therefore, you and the members of your family are hereby excommunicated from the Church, and your salvation is taken from you."

The room rested in subdued silence.

~~

Two majestic beings witnessed the proceedings. One of them, stoic, sat next to Batush, the other like a stone of fire stood in the arched opening behind the crescent table. Asmodeus moved slowly, his iridescent robe of silk flowing ghostlike in the light of dancing torches. Eyes of steel fixed on the other angel, he laid a flat hand on the bishop's shoulder. Palm raised, he drew it up the neck and jaw. Dragging it gently behind, over and down, he stroked the bishop's chin. Bending down—eyes locked and drooling lust—Asmodeus opened his mouth and kissed Jonness on the cheek. Holding the man's face in his hands, he loosed the softest of smiles laced with seduction to Raphael.

<<>>

The sky had clouded over, the temperature dropping. Batush pulled his cloak to his neck as he shuffled away from the meeting hall. He had taken the side exit, avoiding the grand portico where a group congregated. Today's late-morning hearing would cover use rights for the public restrooms. The debate would be driven by whatever policy most bolstered the governor's popularity. Batush had little interest in the issue. The Council Chamber served various public and private functions including government hearings, theatrical performances, and large weddings. This morning, it had served as the church, and this afternoon, it would decide the fate of toilets. Batush shook his head. *Strange times we live in... Someday, God willing, we will have a building of our own dedicated for the Lord's work.*

Halfway down the slope, Batush stopped to catch his breath, unaware of the dark spirit cascading down the steps behind him. A sudden chill washed over him as the swirling demon curled itself around his torso. *How is it that teaching God's Word and praying for healing can be wrong? And Shebaniah's wife...she said they were healed, all of them.* Batush rolled his shoulders, feeling a kink in his neck.

The dark spirit laid its flat hand on Batush's chest, wrapping its arm around his neck. The angel's lips almost touched his ear as he whispered, *"We don't know all that the Fathers know. We also do not know what Shebaniah was teaching. And by whose authority did he ask for healing? The Church Fathers know what is best. We must trust them."*

My trust is in You, Lord. Help me in my weakness. Batush glanced behind him. In the same instant, a war club impacted the tormentor, ripping it away from Batush's body. At the bottom of the steps, Batush rubbed his neck. The kink was gone. After merging onto Marble Road, he headed uphill, away from the harbor district and toward the library. Feeling the first drop, he quickened his pace. The sky was growing darker.

CHAPTER 6

DANIEL'S PHONE pulsed in his back pocket. His plumber had just canceled again having trouble with his truck. The electricians were late, and his mechanical guy tied up on another job. *Now what?* Withdrawing the phone from his Levi's, he glanced at the display. Nick Hamilton.

"Daniel. I'm in a jam and need some help. Got a minute?"

"Sure. What's up, Nick?" Daniel shifted his phone to his other ear and walked away from the screaming chop saw slicing through a metal stud with a shower of sparks.

"I'm supposed to meet Pastor Jason and Amber Lash at eleven, but I can't make it. I've got a client in town who's on his way over—he needs to move some assets. Get this: he's doing a 1031 Exchange on a hotel that's closing in ten days, and he asked me to broker the deal. The commission is going to be huge. Anyway, I need someone to cover for me. You know Amber, right? I'll try to make it, but with a transaction like this, the meeting could easily last all day." Nick panted, sounding out of breath.

Removing his hard hat, Daniel walked through the open storefront. "I can make it. But I'm not so sure I'm your best choice. You remember I dated Amber in college, and I don't want anyone thinking I'm bias."

"That's why you're the perfect choice. You, of all people, will be sure not to be biased because of what you just said. And your honesty in sharing it tells me you're a man of integrity."

Daniel glanced at his watch. "I don't know about that, but thanks. I better head out if I'm going to make it. And you better get ready for your client."

"Don't worry. I'm ready for him, and thanks."

<<>>

The black BMW prowled through the main entry of Faith Bible Church. With her touch of a button on the console, the four panels of glass reacted simultaneously. It was hot and Amber was early. With nearly an hour to kill, she'd take a tour.

Centrally located, the campus fronted on two arterial streets, spanning half a block in length and depth. Two buildings had apparently served as worship centers—small and plain, large and grand—the latter clearly the most recent. Probably twenty years old, it was contemporary in appearance, with sweeping curved walls, tall windows, and scalloped metal roof. Rising from the sprawling campus of simple white stucco and red tile, it looked like a ship in the desert.

The campus included several classroom buildings, a youth center, and a small chapel located on the intersection hard corner. Apparently the original structure, the chapel was surrounded by a chain-link fence and knee-high weeds. *With a little work, it would be perfect for small weddings and banquets. And being on the corner, it's a billboard to the community that's being wasted....*

Asmodeus suggested, *"It would also make a nice senior center. Imagine casino nights and the 'old money' that would pour in?"*

Rolling to a stop, she waved to a large man with a shaved head, dressed in a white tee shirt and khaki trousers, on his knees in a flower bed. The Welcome Center sign beside him cast a convoluted shadow over mounds of gold and purple lantana.

"Hi there—wow. You must be the floral artist." She beamed with hands spread out to the canvas of color.

"I've been called lots of names around here, but artist? That's a first, ma'am, but thanks for the encouragement. Most of the time, I'm fixing overflowing toilets and picking up trash. I'm also the painter, door fixer, roofer, and yes, I'll admit, the gardener." He lumbered to his feet and swiped his palms on his pants. "Name's Tom Evans, welcome. Can I help you find someone?" He smiled as he extended a beefy dark-skinned hand.

"I'm Amber Lash. It's a pleasure."

Asmodeus held his breath. *"Don't touch him. Do not touch his hand."*

Amber squinted, looking up with a tilted head, her hands on the wheel. "I have a meeting with Pastor Stover and Elder Hamilton. Do you know where I might find them?" She fumbled with her sunglasses.

Tom continued to smile, his hand still extended.

"Don't do it. Don't touch him."

Reaching up, she adjusted the mirror, glanced away, and then turned back. The hand was still there.

"I saw the pastor a minute ago. Likely, he's in his office upstairs. I would be happy to show you." The smile and hand remained.

"Don't do it.... Don't!" Asmodeus shouted.

Amber extended her hand slowly. Nearly retracting it, she took the tips of his fingers. "Thank you, Tom. I'm a little early. I think I'll look around. You're so kind. I'll let you get back to work." As she let go, the warmth faded from Tom's face as surely as the glass had dropped into the doors of the BMW. *What was that?*

"Good luck with the interview, Ms. Lash."

Asmodeus slid the shifter into first, releasing the clutch a little too fast. The 5 Series lurched forward. Stomping it back in, he avoided a stall.

Amber watched in the mirror. Tom stood in the center of the drive, staring as they drove off. Like a statue, he remained until he disappeared from view as they rounded the corner behind the youth center.

"Be careful. He's dangerous."

The far end of the campus was dedicated to the school where a long two-story classroom building and a cluster of smaller structures fronted two sides of a worn-out ballfield.

She rolled to a stop beneath a shade tree, a backpack dangling in its branches. A whistle blew in the distance where a woman chased a herd of children playing soccer. Amber twisted a curl, thinking of what Tom had said. *Overflowing toilets and picking up trash, not to mention climbing trees to retrieve backpacks.*

Minutes later, she opened the heavy glass door, one of four pairs, located between the foyer and the auditorium. As she entered, a hushed reverence enveloped her as though the room were watching. The low ceiling beneath the balcony and the sloping floor drew her forward. She touched the back of a pew, nearly jumping in response to the cracking echo of her ring striking wood. Emerging from the overhang, she gazed upward, her mouth hanging open. *Wow.*

The plastered ceiling was scalloped with a series of linear planes spanning the room's width, meshing with a series of masonry fin-walls. The dividers formed a series of alcoves that framed side exits, six on each side, with full-height stained-glass transoms. Each grouted glass panel depicted a stylized rendition of an Apostle. Amber lingered at the window featuring an old man with a long white beard, who stood in a large pot above a blazing fire while gazing heavenward.

The entire room focused on the platform, its simple metal podium standing alone at the center of the black stage. Large enough for theatrical performances, it was balanced with a stone baptismal pool, a concert grand piano, an oversized pipe organ, and a handful of potted trees. The back wall, clad with an elegant patchwork of slate and dark woods, served as a backdrop for a large cross in hammered iron. Standing resolute, it guarded over the room, washed with the soft glow of a single spotlight. The only other light source in the cavernous room came from the colored glass and red exit signs.

She imagined herself on the stage.

"You would have them in the palm of your hand. Like Jagger, performing to a stadium of worshipers."

Alone in the big room, she felt a little uncomfortable. Rubbing away chills from her bare arms, she headed for the ladies' room. There, Amber stared at herself in the mirror. *Maybe I should head for the airport right now. I could leave the car and fly home to Richard. Maybe I should call?*

"After the interview would be better," Asmodeus responded in a soothing voice. *"You'll either be excited or disappointed, and that'll make it easier to forget about last night. We've come this far so we might as well talk to them. What do you have to lose? Besides, it'll be a good experience."*

"That's better. I'll call after the interview." She splashed water on her cheeks. Patting them dry, she touched up her lip gloss. *Hi, my name's Amber. Hello, I'm Amber Lash. You have a beautiful campus. You must be so proud. Remember to ask questions and don't push. Let it unfold.*

The soft voice added, *"Don't worry. I'll give you the words."*

She drew a slow deep breath and then another. It was time.

~~

As the woman behind the desk looked up, her face beaming, Amber drew a quick breath, a little shocked. Not by the bulging double chin, but more so the garish makeup. Her short blonde hair cupped her face, emphasizing her overly plump shape. *Who would put her in that chair? Her face looks like a pie, and a pants suit—in canary?*

"Welcome to Faith Bible Church. My name's Karen. Can I help you?"

"I have an interview at eleven with Pastor Stover and Elder Hamilton?"

"I thought it might be you, Ms. Lash. It's so exciting to meet you. Between the two of us, I think it would be so great if we hired a woman to run this place." Karen winked, adding a double pumping fist clench. "They said to wait until they buzz us. Elder Fairmont just called. He should be here in a few minutes. Apparently, Nick has a conflict, but he'll try to make it if he can. You'll love Pastor Jason and Daniel too. They're both really friendly."

The smell of lavender perfume clogged the air as the woman emphasized her chirpy speech with dramatic hand gestures. Amber held her breath, repressing a sneeze. "Actually, I know Pastor Stover professionally. And Daniel and I are old friends. We were in college together."

Karen raised painted-on eyebrows. "You knew Daniel in college— was he your beau?"

Beau? Seriously? That's what my great-aunt used to say. "No. We dated a couple of times, but it wasn't serious."

"So Daniel's an old flame?" Karen teased with a gaping mouth.

"No, no, just friends." Amber shook her head. "I need to tell you I just love your outfit. You look as radiant as those flowers out front." Amber turned to the window where Tom was hosing off a patio.

"Thank you, Amber. Oh, that's Tom, our custodian. He's been here forever, and everyone just loves him. You will too, just wait and see. Tom keeps things sane around here, trust me."

The phone buzzed. Eyes wide, Karen grabbed it up. "Yes. She's standing in front of me. I'll send her up." She gushed, "They're ready for you, and don't worry about anything. They are going to love you. I'm sure of it."

Picking up a folder, Karen stood. "I almost forgot. This is for you."

"Thank you, Karen. You are so kind. It's been a pleasure." Amber bit her lip. *Wow, she's enormous.*

CHAPTER 7

A LIGHT RAIN was falling when Batush arrived at the library. With a muttered reminder to be careful on the slick surface, he hurried up the steps. Crossing the plaza, he could not help but look up, always awestruck by the Library of Celsus, one of the largest structures in Ephesus. Its delicate façade, articulated with a two-story portico, was vertically divided with three protruding alcoves, each capped with ornately carved pediments. The alcoves were constructed with slender stone columns supporting a band of midheight header beams. A second row of columns sprang from the headers, creating a divided frame to surround three pairs of matching entry doors, each with a punched transom.

He grasped the iron key swinging from his leather waist strap. Placing it into the keyway, he used both hands to turn the heavy lock. The door released with a metallic clonk. Motivated with his body weight, the door began to rotate with a grinding squelch. He entered through the deep opening, then pushed the door closed to wall off the weather. After selecting a task lamp in the vestibule, he touched its wick to one of the burning sconce fixtures centered between the doors. *Such a wealth of books and scrolls from every corner of the earth, yet valued by so few. Perhaps a pilgrim will venture in for a look.*

Once he'd made his way through the antechamber, he entered the central atrium reading room. The footprint was octagonal with soaring walls running full height to a vaulted ceiling surrounded by eight round clerestory windows. He placed his lamp on one of the worktables grouped about the mammoth statue of Celsus, former governor of Asia.

The strategically located reading room controlled access to the treasure trove of documents beyond its perimeter. Lighting a second lamp, he opened the stair tower door accessing the floors above. The dry smell of dust and parchment greeted him like a feeble old friend. The stair creaked as he climbed the switchbacks. Except for his lamp, the document storage floors were pitch black.

He stood for a moment before the stacks packed with scrolls and tablets, sorted by origin and topic. A bound papyrus wedged between scrolls in a compartment labeled Babylon / Suza – Chronicles of Daniel caught his eye. Pulling it out, he shook his head. The leather binder cord and hammered-copper cover told him where it belonged. Opening it carefully, he caressed the embossed illustration of an open pomegranate below the title "Beloved". *Who put you here? And yes, I would love to read you, but not today.*

He found what he was looking for on the outer wall, on a rack above a step-up stool. From the top rung, he stretched, placing the book alongside several similar-bound volumes in a compartment labeled Israel / Jerusalem—Solomon's Poetry.

"That is better, my friend. Now you are home where you belong."

He collected his assignment from the church rack in the work area. Then he descended the stair, back to the reading room where he laid out his writing tools. Opening his scrolling tablet, he began as his grandfather taught him.

"Thank You, Lord, for the gift of Your sacred Word. Thank You also for the honor to do the work You have prepared for me. Guide and steady my hand, O Lord, keeping me alert and protecting me from error. May the work I do today bring glory to Your name and a blessing to many. Amen."

Batush dipped his pen and began to copy from the book of prophets. *My people are destroyed for lack of knowledge...* Lifting the pen, he pondered the words. He heard it then, the unmistakable sound of heavy parchment curling under, the edge scraping against the surface of a table. He turned toward the open stair tower. *Someone is here. Did they arrive before me or slip in after? Surely, I would have heard...*

He picked up his lamp and approached the stair. At the top of the first switchback, he lit another sconce and peered into the dark room. Level One contained the tablets, mostly on stone and clay, with some on wood and various metals. They were stored on shelves supported by linear study tables. He glanced up the stair to the upper two floors, which held the scrolls and books.

"Hello? Is someone there?"

Silence responded.

Batush steadied his breathing. *Be still but check to be sure.*

He entered the tablet room and then walked the perimeter of the inside wall separating him from the full-height atrium. Stopping at the center of each octagonal wall face, he lit the protruding wall sconce while scanning the room. Returning full circle, he climbed to the second floor. Again, making the rounds, he lit the lamps.

"Hello...?" After checking the top floor, he stopped. *Foolish old man, the mind is playing tricks.*

He heard it again, parchment scraping against wood. This time from below. He descended the stair back to the tablet room, again peering inside. He then strode the perimeter a second time. Reaching the stairwell, he poked his head inside and cocked his head.

It was parchment. I—I'm sure of it. But where?

Ducking back inside, Batush saw him. At a worktable, he faced the wall with head bowed. Broad in stature, he wore a sage tunic, its weather hood pulled over his head.

"Can I help you, brother?" His heart raced.

The man was silent. As he raised his hand, a large scroll curled under, its edge scraping against the tabletop.

Batush hoisted his lamp. With his arm extended, he took two steps forward.

The man turned, his face hidden in shadow, wavy hair at his shoulders, the trembling lamp between them.

When he took another step, the light advanced, washing up and over the angel's face. Batush staggered backward, banging into a chair. Dropping to his knees, he heard his voice say, "Lord..."

"Do not worship me. I am not the Lord. I am a messenger. Get up, Batush, and listen."

Fumbling with the chair, he managed a half-sitting position, eyes fixed on the angel's face. "Wha—? Who?"

"You are highly esteemed, and the Lord loves you, Batush." The angel smiled, speaking softly, his right hand extended with spread fingers. The words washed over Batush, overwhelming him with wonder. The magnificent creature, humanlike almost, and yet different, possessed a face like weathered stone that yielded as he spoke.

Batush placed his hand over his heart, gulping breath. "Are—are you...?"

"Yes, Batush I am an angel. I bring a message from the Lord, and you have been chosen to deliver it. It is for the church. Will you deliver this message, Batush?"

"Yes, I will—yes. What message?"

"Listen carefully. It is written in a book you will find at the feet of Celsus. Make a copy of the book and then deliver the original to the Church Fathers." A serious clarity replaced the angel's smile.

"What should I tell them to do with the book?"

"That is not your concern. The book contains a message with instructions they will understand. Your task is only to deliver it. But now I must leave you."

"Where are you going, and who—can I know your name?"

"I am the Archangel Raphael. We both serve the Almighty." The smile returned, the angel's emerald eyes glinting. The room pulsed then, like the leap of a lamp's flame as Raphael vanished.

Batush inhaled shocked wonder. "Thank You, Lord. All praise and blessing to Your name." His lips trembling, he realized he was weeping. *Never forget—never.*

"The book—the book at the feet of Celsus..." He ran down the stairs, taking two risers with each stride, feeling twenty again. After bursting through the opening, he rushed to the statue and circled its base.

"At his feet... Where? No panel to open. Nothing." He again circled the stone pedestal. "Lord, where is it? Show me, Lord. I don't understand?" He panted as he searched the room. *Four tables, the chairs, the room is empty. Where, Lord? Show me, Lord. Help...*

He heard a whisper from within, *"The scroll."*

Running again, he ascended the stair, even faster than he had come down. He stopped at the landing. After removing the wall sconce, he approached slowly, eyes fixed on it, afraid to look away. The scroll had curled itself closed. Placing the lamp on the table's light stand, he unrolled a meticulous series of construction drawings. The first plates appeared to be plan views of the library. He scrolled through the document, unrolling it from his left hand while feeding it to his right. It read from the top down, beginning with a foundation plan, followed by floor plans, including the ground level and storage floors, each wrapping around the full-height atrium. He placed his index finger on the spot where he stood.

The ground level showed the pedestal but no indication of the statue or a hidden compartment. "At the feet of Celsus. It must be here?" He spoke softly, drawing a deep breath followed by a blowing exhale. "Surely, Lord, it is here."

He made note of the drawing symbols referencing various construction elements. The symbols were comprised with letters and numbers divided with a slash, the letter corresponding to enlarged views with the number listing the scroll. The entry doors were tagged X/VI. The margin at the top of the scroll in his hands read II/VI in large Latin script. *Scroll II of VI.*

Taking a step back, he spotted an open compartment containing four scrolls labeled Library of Celsus. Selecting scroll VI, he unrolled a series of details labeled with an X. Incredibly extensive, they displayed elevations of the entry door, along with cross sections and an exploded view of the pivot hinges. Setting it aside, he returned to the drawing Raphael had been looking at.

"Why this one, Lord?" In addition to the doors, references marked the exterior columns and various corners of the building. The drawing was tagged with arrow symbols, relating to building section and elevation views, to be found within the other scrolls. *The level of precision is considerable. Notes describing the patterned flooring and there—even the sconce lamps.*

Batush stared at the rectangular pedestal. *Nothing at Celsus's feet... Why?*

He scrolled back to the foundation plan showing the building's stone pier and wall supports. The drawing was hatched with a herringbone pattern between the foundation walls with a note reading: Rubble Infill. His finger rested on the central quadrant depicting the statue's pedestal above with dashed lines. *No hatching below Celsus. No rubble beneath the feet of Celsus? Possibly, it is solid stone to support the weight, or... The piers at the corners of this volume are larger... If it is solid stone, would not the drawing show a single huge pier? But if it is a vault... Where is the access?*

"Lord, give me eyes to see."

He heard it again, parchment scraping against wood. It came from within. He then heard the soft still voice say, *"Turn it over."*

He did, and the parchment curled up and under with a scrape. The back of the sheet was blank. *Where, Lord, show me.*

"Look up, Batush—look to the Light."

He looked into the lamp's flame.

"Help him, Raphael. Show him." It was the gentlest of commands.

He watched as his arms moved, almost feeling the angel's hands. Moving between his face and the lamp, a hidden image revealed itself on the backlit drawing. Emotion flooded over Batush, his eyes filling with tears.

"Thank You, Lord. You are so good—thank You."

The hidden plan depicted a linear tunnel with steps leading to a vault beneath the pedestal. The tunnel originated from a small building appendage drawn on the parchment's visible side. He had seen it a thousand times but never been inside.

The Caretaker's Hut. The tunnel backed up to a closet labeled Tool Storage.

CHAPTER 8

"HELLO, DANIEL, it's been a long time." Amber extended her hand. Leaning in, her breasts pressed against his torso, his physique still firm and strong. As she stepped back, she looked up, met his eyes, and then glanced away when he flushed. *Would his reaction have been the same if it were just the two of us?*

Asmodeus answered, *"See? He's still attracted to you."*

"It has, but you haven't changed. You look great." Daniel's words were a little rushed. "Amber, I'd like to introduce you to John Warner, our worship and arts pastor, and I understand you already know Pastor Jason."

"It's good to see you again, Amber." Jason took her hand as one might ask for a dance. "I understand you drove down from Newport. I'm sorry you had to leave that paradise to join us here in the desert. You know, if I wasn't the senior pastor, I could have just been honest and said, join us here in Hell's Kitchen." He beamed. Then bowing, he ushered them into the conference room.

Amber took the chair with her back to the wall, facing the door. Jason took the head of the table beside her, with Daniel and Pastor John across from her.

"Let's begin with a word of prayer. Daniel, can you lead us?" Pastor Jason's grin yielded to a reverent smile.

"Lord, we thank You for this day. As warm as it is, we are grateful for the opportunity to serve Your church. Give us wisdom as we seek Your will in this decision, surrendering all to You. We thank You for sending Amber to us, and we thank You also for her desire to serve You. We pray in Your Son's name, Jesus... Amen."

Asmodeus barked, *"Let's go."*

"Well, gentlemen, what questions do you have for me on this beautiful day in Hell's Kitchen?"

The men roared as Pastor Jason flipped open a file folder—Opportunity Profile, Amber Lash—wiping an invisible tear from the corner of his eye. Fumbling through a few pages, he closed it. "Amber, can you tell us about yourself and how you became a believer?"

Folding her hands, she sat up straight.

"Like clay in your hands. Go ahead and tell them—everything."

She tilted her head. Her pointer finger grazed her lower lip. She waited a moment and then engaged each of them with her emerald eyes. Daniel first, then John, and Jason last.

"My story is a little hard to share. But it's mine, and it made me who I am. I grew up in Chicago, and we didn't have a lot of money. I have four brothers, and I was last, the baby of the family. We were raised Lutheran, and my mother made sure we went to church on Sunday—every Sunday, without exception."

"My father was a policeman and, well, a drinker, and there was a lot of yelling in the house. My mother did all the housework, and for a family of seven, that was hard. She also worked outside the home, cleaning houses for wealthy people. Eventually, she left us. I guess she got tired of being poor and enduring all the shouting. Anyway, she met a wealthy banker who lived in one of the houses she cleaned. I was thirteen and haven't seen or heard from her since. After that, the yelling and drinking got worse."

"There was a gap of six years between myself and Jake. I think I was a mistake. No one ever said it, but I think I was. Anyway, my brothers left after Mom was gone, and then it was just Dad and me. I was in high school, but all of the housework fell to me." Amber tugged on her chin, and then turning to Jason, she swallowed.

"Tell them about finding your father. Go on, do it."

"One day, two weeks before my graduation, I came home, and I remember it was quiet. The window was open, and a breeze was blowing in. We had lace curtains above the kitchen sink. I can see them now—flowing, like a slow wave. There was a stack of dishes in the sink, and a drip of water was hanging from the tip of the faucet. It was as if time had slowed down. Somehow, I sensed something was different. It was blowing past me and away."

They were mesmerized.

"I remember walking down the hall and my father's door—it was open maybe six inches. I walked up to it and stood there for a minute. I felt the breeze moving through the hallway. I touched the door, and it floated open like the curtains. And I saw him. Slumped over in his green chair, his head resting on his chest, and his arm dangling over the side. He was covered in red like a sheet had been draped over him. And his revolver was hanging from the tip of his finger. He looked so peaceful. He was free—and I was too—and I wasn't afraid or panicked. I walked in and sat on the floor next to him. I remember, taking the gun out of his hand and putting it on the floor. His hand—it was still warm. I didn't look at his face—I didn't want to see. But I knew he was gone. I sat, I think for a couple of hours, just holding his hand. I hadn't done that since I was a little girl. It was so quiet and peaceful."

When she lifted her head, the men had tears in their eyes. Struggling for composure, she drew a deep breath and blew it out.

"What did I tell you? You've got 'em." Asmodeus snorted.

"Anyway, after that, everything changed. My father's pension had a provision that paid for his children's education in the event of death before retirement. After the funeral, we split up the pension money and Dad's savings. It wasn't a lot, but it was enough for college. And the pension covered tuition as long as I kept my grades up. So I was off to the University of Illinois to study business. It was the logical choice. After all, I had been running a household ever since Mom left. Business came to me naturally.

"I met my husband, Richard, in college. Actually, I met Daniel first, and he introduced us. Daniel and I were dating, that is until I met his roommate. It was love at first sight—I mean with Richard. I'm sorry, Daniel. You were so sweet and smart too, but no match for a baseball player."

"Ouch, that's got to hurt." Jason pulled his glasses off as the men laughed.

"I did my best to hide him from Amber, but it was inevitable they were going to meet," Daniel replied with a sheepish grin. "It wasn't meant to be. But if the two of you hadn't met, I would never have found Rhema. But I do admit it hurt a little."

"I hurt you, Daniel? You never told me that."

Daniel flushed again.

"Be careful. Don't embarrass him."

The door flew open then with a handsome gentleman entering. Pastor Jason stood. "You made it. Amber, this is Elder Nick Hamilton. Nick's in charge of stewardship and finances and also helps most of us with our personal investments."

"I'm sorry to be late, but I was closing a huge transaction. I wasn't expecting to make it, but everything went incredibly smooth."

"This is the one. He's the key."

"What sort of work do you do, Nick?" She met his eyes, rotating toward him as he took the chair beside her.

"Touch him."

She let her knee touch his with the slightest pressure, then pulled away. Only the fabric of his pleated slacks separated their flesh.

"I help people with their finances and assets. You could say I'm a financial planner, but I like to think of it as asset protection. It's more comprehensive." Their eyes touched.

"I want to hear about the huge transaction. Are you allowed to tell us?" Amber added a tinge of seduction in her voice.

"Careful, Daniel can see."

"Well, yes, actually, I can. On Friday, an old client called. He was moving some assets—this guy is incredible with money. Get this, he bought a hotel just four years ago, the place was barely making it. Anyway, he fixes it up with some strategic improvements, and then markets it to European tourists, mostly Germans. He then lines up a buyer and calls me to help with the transaction, the six-point-four-million-dollar transaction." Nick bobbed his head, enunciating the number while grinning.

"Wow. That says a lot—he trusts you and knows you're good at what you do." She nodded to the others. "So it closed today, just now?"

"Not only did it close, but I also helped him redirect the investment." Nick's excitement surged.

"Stroke him. Don't stop."

"That's amazing. Did you help him diversify?" She touched him on the arm, her other hand spread over her bosom.

Nick's eyes widened. "I was prepared to do just that. I had a spreadsheet ready with a list of investments and suggested percentages. When I started to talk, he puts up his hand and says one word." Nick waited.

"What, what did he say?" She touched him again.

"Gold." Nick's face remained deadpan for a full five seconds before he grinned. "I didn't argue because he'd clearly made up his mind, so I executed the transaction. The funds were in place, and I confirmed the buy. And I notice the guy looks at his watch. He then engages me with some small talk about family and vacations and stuff like that." Nick changed his voice, mimicking a professor. "Now I want everyone to know I mentioned the church and invited him to join us on Sunday. Trust me, we could use his tithe."

Amber winked. "I was thinking about *your* tithe, Nick Hamilton."

The room erupted, except for Nick who grinned.

"So we're talking for about ten minutes and I'm thinking about this meeting and getting over here. I'm being careful not to let him catch me glancing down to check the time, and I see gold is up twenty-two bucks an ounce. While we're chatting, the guy makes a hundred and fifty thousand dollars!"

"I guess you should have waited to execute that transaction, Nick. Your commission would have been higher." She placed her hand on her chest again with a gaped mouth as the men again roared.

"Actually, my fee was discounted. When you work with clients like this guy, the commission structure is totally different. You need to consider the circles you're dealing in and who he might be introducing you to next week."

"Hmm, that's wise. I can see why the church has you taking care of the purse."

The pastors nodded approval, but Amber's attention was on Daniel's questioning face.

"Don't worry about him. What's he going to say? Don't trust her. She's working us? Mission accomplished."

CHAPTER 9

DARK CLOUDS crawled through the early-afternoon sky above Ephesus, the light sprinkle now a swirling mist. Batush cinched his cloak hood tight to his chin. Descending the steps, he tried to remember the last time late spring had been so cold. He followed the overgrown perimeter path, cradling his lamp under the flap of his garment. He checked behind, and then glanced from side to side. *I am the church scribe of duty today, and it is my task to watch over the library. I am only checking the Caretaker's Hut to ensure all is in order.*

A layer of thin fog mingled with the brush as he reached the hut. The fog hung in the damp air, muffling the sound while he struggled with the stubborn swing-latch. Made of slat-wood, the door dragged when he jostled it open with one hand, protecting the lamp with the other. Again, checking behind, he ducked inside.

Except for a haphazard pile of tools on the floor, the shack didn't appear to have been occupied in years. A broken cot against the wall, apparently used for stacking firewood, had long ago avalanched to the cobbled floor. He shook his hood back and hoisted his lamp. A stone oven stood next to the door with a workbench on the return wall, heaped with piles of clay pots, many of them broken under the weight. A thick layer of dirt coated everything.

Resisting the urge to organize the room, he focused on the open cabinets covering the back wall. They were filled with clay bricks stacked from floor to ceiling. Access to the cabinets was further blocked with a waist-height wall of stacked brick in front.

He exhaled a laugh. "The one thing organized in the entire room is the bricks. Lord, You have been protecting this place for some time, have You not?"

Batush visualized the drawing depicting a single off-center compartment, not the continuous wall of cabinets in front of him. The cabinets were divided into six uneven sections constructed with uniform joinery and materials. Butt joints on each side of one of the center sections interrupted the fascia member. "There you are, my friend. Praise You, Lord, for lighting my path."

Moving a stack of pots, he found a suitable location for his lamp on top of the oven. It would take at least two hours to move the brick and another two to put it back. Who knew how long he might be inside looking for the book. He thought then of Meraiah asking him to be home by dark.

Should we come back early or start now? When he tipped his head up, a drop of water struck him in the forehead. "We will likely be late. But, with the clouds, is it not true it is already dark?" He laughed as he started with the chaos of tools. He then moved to the wall of bricks between him and the cabinet that hid the tunnel.

<<>>

"Anyway, after college, Richard and I married and moved to Oakland. I had landed a job with Eastern Savings, and Richard was playing for the A's. We got pregnant and had our one and only, Ricky. He's married now, and I've recently become a grandmother—I hate the title but love the role." She pulled her phone from her purse. "Here we are. This is Richard. And this is Ricky and his wife, Anne. And in the next few, you'll see me holding our precious granddaughter." She handed her phone to Jason, who passed it along to those around the table.

Pastor Warner said, "I see... Richard's in a wheelchair. Can you tell us about that?"

She drew a slow breath. *Richard.* At fifty-two, he looked younger than his age, despite his thinning, neatly cropped gray hair. He still had his boyish smile and warm peacefulness that defied his physical limitations.

"He was injured, actually paralyzed from the waist down. It was a car accident. He and his buddies had been drinking. That ended his baseball career. It was just five years after we married."

"That had to be hard—it must still be."

"It was, but we've managed. It's made us stronger actually—both of us. Richard says it was a blessing because that was when he gave his life to the Lord."

Nick nodded, his tongue resting on his lower lip. "That's beautiful. And I see you in this one, holding an award?"

"Oh yes, that was after we moved to Portland, it was a banquet with the Chamber of Commerce when I received a plaque for Business Woman of the Year."

"Nice transition. Stay humble."

Pastor Jason scanned her résumé. "I remember you owned your real estate company from when you helped Joyce and me sell our home. Was that when you won the award?"

"Yes, but the award was based on my body of work, which included a leads group I started that was exclusive to movers and shakers in the business community. We broke it into subgroups based on industry and synergy. CEOs loved it because they would make business connections and deals every Friday morning while enjoying a fabulous breakfast. They took the information back to the office and handed it off to marketing. Their companies benefited, and the membership fees paid for everything. I hired a small staff to help run it, but mostly, it ran itself. It was a lot of fun, and I made loads of contacts."

Nick slid forward in his seat and leaned closer. "That's impressive. You started a leads group exclusive to the most influential, not to mention wealthy. The organization obviously grew, paid for everything, and fueled your business. Now that, gentlemen, is what I call a sustainable growth model. We could use some of that around here." He fanned his arms over the table.

"I see you worked for the bank—what, ten years?" Not waiting for an answer, he continued, "You then worked your way up the ladder in retail, before engaging real estate, and then sold your business just before the housing crash. Can you tell us about how you acquired your company?" Leaning back, he removed his wire-frame glasses. Then, lifting them to his mouth, he bit on one of the frame tips.

"I was marketing director for Metropolitan Cosmetics and had pretty much learned all I could. They had structural issues, and the board was never going to let a woman rise above the VP level. So I made the move to real estate. I had always loved design and furnishings." She shrugged. "It just made sense."

"Get to the point before you lose them!" Asmodeus shouted.

"As an agent, I studied the business with the intention of one day having my own agency, so it wasn't long before I bought my first property. It was a cute two-bedroom cottage, on a big lot with a great location. I paid a little under two fifty for it, but the average home in the neighborhood was selling for between three fifty and four twenty-five. I had made some great connections, so I went to see a friend at Eastern Savings. I took my contractor and a rough sketch of what we had in mind, and Sally was eager to help. We split the floor plan by adding a huge master suite and home office. We also did the normal things you do—you know, new finishes, fixtures, and landscaping, stuff like that."

Asmodeus snapped, *"Not so much about you!"*

"In three months, we were back on the market, listed as a three-bedroom luxury bungalow. I had put seventy-five in the remodel, and it sold in one week with multiple offers. I had financed all of it and paid off the loan in less than four months."

Nick asked, "So what did it sell for?"

She waited with a smile.

He nudged her arm with his elbow. "Tell us, Amber. It's just us guys in here."

"See that? One of the guys."

"Keep in mind, this was when real estate was booming—anyway, we got a little over six fifty." She blushed in response to the whoas and gaping mouths.

"I did make some mistakes, but I learned from them. And I never lost money on any of my deals. I also took some night classes and got my broker's license. I then approached the agency owner and asked if he might consider a partner. We talked about it on and off for a few months, and it wasn't going anywhere. So I let it go. Then one morning, he walks into my office and asks if I would be interested in the whole thing. So we struck a deal. His attorney drew up the papers, and it was mine. It was so exciting.... I can't tell you."

Nick placed his glasses on the table. Turning to face Amber, he chewed on his thumb knuckle. "What did you do when you took over? Did you make changes?"

"Now we're getting there."

"I approached it like one of my remodels. I've always believed, when making something yours, you need to change it, and my instincts told me a complete reimage was needed. So I rented a ground-floor suite on Main Street. Our door opened directly to the street. The sidewalk was brick and really wide—like a patio. So we put a couple tables and chairs out and then furnished our reception area like a living room. We had a great storefront, and people would walk up to check the listings in the window. We kept the door open whenever possible and would invite them in for coffee. Amazing how many deals we made in that living room."

Daniel withdrew his fist away from his mouth. "What else did you change?"

"Don't worry about him. The others will make the decision."

"Like I said, just about everything. I let go of the staff and agents. They represented the old business, and I wanted a new look."

"Tell them but show compassion."

"We were as bland as the color beige, and I wanted fuchsia. We were selling single-family homes in the suburbs, and my vision was high-end. The staff was older and several of them were—well, you know—they didn't know how to dress or present themselves. They didn't understand appearance is everything."

"Be delicate—this is the moment. Make or break."

"It wasn't easy, but it had to be done. And I needed to be intentional."

Nick edged closer, his knee grazing hers. "Explain that, what do you mean exactly?"

She spoke directly to him. "I weighed the options. I could have spread it out, letting them go one by one. But I knew that would be a mistake because the staff would be working in fear, wondering if they were next. You don't want that. It's not fair to them. So I called a meeting on a Friday and explained I would be making some changes and some of them would be let go. I wanted to give them a chance to think about it and talk to their spouses in order to prepare." Amber's focus moved from one man to the next.

"How did you prepare?" Pastor John's gaze darted to Jason and then back to her. He swallowed.

"Well, I drew up severance papers with a signature block. The agreements were generous, giving them twice the amount they were entitled to. That was intentional because I didn't want anyone badmouthing the company. I was also ready with my new hires, so I could move quickly. The following Monday, I had each of them come into my office and explained they were being released because I was reorganizing. I told them they were appreciated and how important their contributions had been. I did that to honor them, showing I cared about them personally."

Nick jumped in, "That's amazing. You were able to let them go, without having to deal with any HR fallout. Because you were restructuring, no one could claim they were being fired. And you also took the time to shepherd them through it. That's compassionate, gentlemen, and that's impressive."

"Perfect. Now close it out."

"After signing the release, I gave them their last check, which included severance, plus the cost of benefits and earned vacation time. I told them they could come back later in the week to clean out their desk. That way, I didn't have to worry about the others seeing any potential emotions on display. It was easier with the agents because they were on commission. I gave them a generous bonus and had them sign a similar agreement, promising not to pursue any of our clients for twelve months."

The men stared at her.

"I'm sure all of you understand leadership is not easy. And sometimes, well, leaders need to make difficult decisions. It comes with the territory. I also understand leadership is not for everyone." Amber turned to face Daniel.

He held her gaze as the room rested in silence.

"Wait for them to ask. Just wait, they will."

Pastor Jason folded his hands. "Amber, if you joined us as my executive pastor, what changes would you make?"

"Careful.... Tread softly."

"I think, with a church, you would need to approach it differently. If you were to offer me the position—first of all, I would be honored and humbled. And if I were to accept, I would start by evaluating your ministries and getting to know the staff and congregation. I would be putting my finger on the pulse of the church, if you will."

She shifted to Pastor Warner. "I would approach it like a symphony conductor being handed the director's wand during the middle of a performance. You wouldn't stop the music to rearrange the chairs and instruments. You would be listening, and when you took the wand, the movement of your hand would be in sync. Not changing a thing, you would continue the concert. And if you did it well, no one would even notice. You would be sensitive, and you would be evaluating the strengths and weaknesses, building trust and fellowship. Then, over time and when the musicians were ready, you might begin to introduce some new songs. But you would be doing it together, and if you were leading well, the music would blossom into something amazing." She unfurled her hands like two flowers. Both pastors and Nick were beaming.

"Now ask if they have any questions."

"Can I answer any questions?"

Daniel cleared his throat. "I have a couple."

"And what are they, Daniel?" She leveled her gaze on his statuesque face, ever chiseled in defiance of his unruly red curls and baby blue eyes.

"Don't take the bait. Be gracious."

Daniel swallowed. "Tell us who Jesus Christ is to you."

"The Scripture says He is the way, the truth, and the life."

"The Scriptures teaches He is the way, the truth, and the life."

Daniel cocked his head. "Can you tell us about your calling as a believer?"

"Scripture says let your light shine."

"The Scripture says we should let our light shine in a dark world. I believe we are called to reach out to the needy and those who are hurting." She stared at Daniel. Holding eye contact, she neither offered nor concealed anything.

"One more. What does it mean to you to be filled with the Holy Spirit?"

"Scripture says He is the Spirit of truth, the counselor, and He is in us."

"Scripture says He is the Spirit of truth, our counselor, and He lives inside us."

"I'm not sure you're understanding. Let me ask again: What does it mean to you, Amber, personally, to be filled with the Holy Spirit?"

"Tell them about me—it's okay, trust me."

"This may seem a little strange, and I don't want to scare anyone. In fact, I'm not sure I understand myself. But—he's inside me. He gives me counsel and helps me see things. As we've been talking, I hear his voice. Right now he's saying trust me." She placed her hand over her heart.

Nick stood. "Gentlemen, I don't know about you, but I am quite impressed and would like to make a proposal. We have an important board meeting on Tuesday. Regardless of whether we hire Amber, I believe her input to be critical for us as a church." He moved to the far end of the table using the chair as a podium. "If acceptable to all of you, I would like to ask if Amber might be able to remain or possibly return for that meeting. The church will cover the cost, of course. We have a budget line for travel."

Pastor Jason turned to her. "What do you say, Amber—you could stay downtown in the missionary loft? It's vacant right now and very nice. It's owned by a wealthy parishioner—you'll like it, I promise."

She bit her lower lip. "I reserved a room at the Hyatt for tonight. I was planning to grab some lunch and then head over there next, but I could cancel. Yes, the loft sounds nice. I think I'd like that."

Nick responded, looking directly at her. "Then it's settled. Amber will join us for the meeting. And if it's okay, I'd like to get together with her later today, to go over the agenda? I'll be making the presentation and would love your input, Amber, if that's all right with everyone else?"

When Nick turned to the men, they nodded.

"I'll look forward to it. Will we be meeting here?"

"Actually, let's meet at the loft. It's near my office, and it's a lot more comfortable. I'll have Karen meet us there to take notes."

"You'll need to call your husband."

"I'll need to call Richard, to see about staying on, but I'm sure he'll be fine with it."

"Could he possibly join you? I'm not sure the church would cover that cost, but he would certainly be welcome. Both of you could stay as long as you like. The loft will be vacant until the holidays."

"That is so generous—thank you. It would be great if Richard could be here, but he's quite busy with the semester just starting and planning the year's schedule. I'll certainly ask."

Pastor Jason pushed back his chair. "Both of you could join us Sunday, to see us in action and hear my message. I'm titling it 'After These Things'. It's from the first chapter of Revelation, where John gets his vision about the end times. Scholars have debated that phrase for hundreds of years. We're going to be looking at the different positions and ideas they have on what John was talking about."

"That's an interesting message."

"That sounds really interesting. I'll be looking forward to hearing it, Pastor."

CHAPTER 10

MOAZ WAITED. He'd been there for more than a hundred years. A day had come when he had been tempted to release the wood shim, which he held now tightly. Countless times over the past fifty-three years, two months, and four days, he relived the moment. It was a hot summer day when the girls had ventured into the little house. Inside they found a stove, a cot, and a long pile of bricks. They took turns with a straw broom and swept the floor, and then climbed atop the bricks. And they played with their dolls—the bricks were cool.

Behind them, the cabinets were filled to the top with more bricks. Moaz was there also, waiting on the other side, his hand on the shim holding back the heavy wall. He wanted them desperately, and it would have been so easy to pull the shim and kill them with his wall. Fearing the master's punishment, he restrained himself. Waiting instead for the one who would come one day in search of the book he protected.

That day he longed for so patiently had finally arrived, and he was ready.

Moaz squeezed his shim between slimy clenched fingers, his mind racing with exhilaration. On the other side, he could hear the old man removing the long pile of bricks one by one. He could smell his life scent, taste him, in fact, and now he would have the man's life and finally be free. It was then quiet. Moaz felt him looking at the tall pile inside the cabinet between them. He would start at the top, stretching for the first brick, and that is when Moaz would strike.

Heart pounding, he held his breath.

Moaz felt him wipe his brow, then reach for the first brick. The tormentor's face twisted into a sneer, glee pumping his heart. Moaz pulled, but the shim did not budge. He pulled harder. It held fast.

Jumping up, he gripped it with both hands. Feet against the wall, he heaved and yanked with every fiber of his being. Fear struck him like shards of ice. His eyes darting in all directions, he whimpered. Thinking of the master's fury, he braced for one last try. That was when he heard it—a rumbling deep within the earth. Looking up, he cocked his head as the shim popped out into his hand. Without a sound, the massive wall tilted forward, toward the warm body of flesh and bone.

<<>>

Amber sat in the BMW staring at her phone. Tapping recent calls, she brought up Richard and drew a slow breath. *He's so good at reading me. It's like he can see inside my mind.* Teeth clamped over her lip, she pushed send. After the second ring, she was yearning for voicemail when he answered.

"I was just about to call—is everything okay?" A clash of concern and relief pursed Richard's voice.

The connection, cutting in and out, loosened her shoulders with relief. "I'm fine. I wanted to call sooner, but I was rushing to get here and didn't want to call when I was driving. I'm sorry." She bit deeper on her lip.

"I'm just glad you got there safe, Amby. I prayed for you during the interview. How did it go?"

"It was great. I think they're going to offer me the job. They asked if I could stay for the elder meeting on Tuesday. They want the others to meet me, and I also have a strategy meeting today at three with Nick Hamilton—he's one of the elders. I think both meetings are going to be important. I booked a room at the Hyatt but canceled, because they're letting me stay in their condo that's vacant, and that's where I'll be meeting with Elder Nick. He'll be bringing the church secretary along to take notes."

"Slow down, relax. It never happened. There's no way he could know." Asmodeus reinforced the message she was telling herself.

"Are you okay? You sound like something's wrong."

"You're excited but not sure."

"I'm just excited, but not sure about the whole thing. It's happening so fast, and I guess... I don't know—I wish you were here. They said you could join me if you want."

"What's wrong with you? What if he says yes?" Asmodeus squeezed her heart.

Suddenly faint, she leaned back in her seat.

"It sounds fun, but you know I can't, Amby. I could probably find a sub to cover, but I better not. Besides, without your help, it would be hard, but thanks for asking. For sure I'll come down if you end up accepting."

"That was close. Now relax."

He released his grip, and Amber drew a breath as the faintness rushed away.

"I woke up last night and almost called. But it was late, and I didn't want to wake you. I prayed for you instead. It was strange, I felt like you were in danger. How did it go at the resort?"

"You didn't feel good and went to bed early!"

"It was nice, but I wasn't feeling very good. It was my stomach. I had a drink by the pool and went to bed early. I didn't sleep very well. I think all of this is making me tired. But I'm fine now—just missing you."

"Wait and see what he says."

"I miss you too." The words were right, but a question lingered in his voice.

"My phone is beeping. I think it's ready to die. I'll call back later. Love you." Hanging up, Amber stared at her fully charged phone.

<<>>

Suddenly disoriented, Batush reached forward, dropping the brick. When his hand touched the wall, he realized it was tipping toward him. Pushing against the mass, he tried to repel backward—clawing and kicking. Parallel to the floor and scrambling, his open hand pressed against the avalanche. With the wall an arm's length from his face, his back struck the floor. There was no escape.

"Jesus!" he screamed as a picture of Meraiah and Sarah flashed through his mind. Everything seemed to stop then, nothing moving, not the wall, his body, or even his pounding heart. Yet he was aware of every detail. The variegated color of red and brown clay bricks suspended before him. The broken corners and crack lines, smudges and dirt atop protruding edges, dust and fragments floating weightless before him. All fear vanquished, he felt nothing except the purity of perfect peace. The wall began to move again, not toward him but downward, like a sheet being lowered, row after row of brick passing just inches from his face.

A ripping tension gripped his scalp as something solid crashed into his back. His body lifted as the room exploded in a blur of thundering brick and dust. Rolling off the edge of the oven, he crumpled into a bedlam of debris and blinked back dirt and sand, his ears ringing. He managed to sit, a blanket of stunned numbness overtaking him. Dust settling, he realized he was staring into the blackness of an opening in the wall behind the now-empty cabinet.

Something moved then, just inside the opening. He wanted it to be the settling dust, but the churning orb of smoldering slick goo was not.

Somehow, it is alive.

Springing forward like a cat, the blob pounced just in front of him. Liverish in color, it pulsated ugliness and evil. Morphing into an eellike shape, it reared upright. About to strike, it constricted. Then darted back into the hole and slithered along the top of the opening.

Batush dug his fingers into the dirt floor, his throat constricting.

Is—is it watching?

Something solid fell, bouncing into the bricks. A wedge-shaped piece of wood. Flipping forward, it landed at his feet. The orb descended toward it. Then morphing into a ball, it dodged side to side. Retreating again, it disappeared into the black opening.

Batush rubbed his burning eyes. Pulling his hand back, he found blood on his fingers. Ears ringing and room spinning, the top of his head seared with pain. He patted it gently, feeling a gritty warmth, slimy and stingy. Fearful of what he might discover, he eased his hand back. He gasped. It was covered with dirt and blood and a mat of snarled hair attached to a flap of scalp.

Something or someone pulled me... saved me.

Batush drew his knees beneath him with face to the floor. "Praise be the God of Israel, I am Your servant. I thank You, Lord." Joy filled him then, overpowering the fear. A tingling heat flowed through his frame, washing away the pain, like the elixir of life itself.

With eyes fixed on the dark entrance, he felt a hand on his back. He turned. Face to face with the spiritual being, he gazed into the open room. Lifting a trembling hand, he touched a cheek and then a nose, invisible to his eyes but not his leaping heart. A soft gasp escaped his lips as he pulled his hand back.

"Thank you, my friend, for saving me." He spoke to the open room. A grin on his face, he jumped to his feet. "You are there, Raphael, aren't you? I will not worship you, but I will praise the Lord who sent you." He was crying then. Joy and release beyond anything he'd ever experienced overwhelmed him.

Peering into the face he could not see, he cocked his head toward the tunnel. "Should we have a look? What do you say, my friend?"

Batush turned to the oven and laughed. Somehow the lamp, resting on top of the clay pot, was still lit. After picking it up, he clamored over the rubble. Dark and narrow, the opening with a low arched ceiling was no wider than his shoulders. The tunnel was lined in brick with a small landing just inside. Its steps, honed in stone, descended at a steep angle into the blackness. Extending his lamp, he stooped. Then, tucking his head, he entered.

"Hello, Death. We are coming in, and we are not afraid of you. I am Batush the Scribe, and I think you know my friend, the Archangel Raphael? Oh, you have heard of him—yes, of course, you have. I believe Raphael spoiled your plan for me today, didn't he?"

The whisper at his ear was soft. "His name is Moaz. He's been waiting a very long time for your arrival, but he was not expecting me. He is a tormentor and quite upset. Your weapon is the name of your Savior."

"Moaz, you ugly one, I know you are there. Leave this place in the name above all names. In the name of Jesus—come out."

Batush smelled him first, a foul stench of sewage and rotting meat. He then saw movement. The tunnel wall just ahead began to shimmer with a dark fluidity. It spread in all directions—up, over, and down the walls onto the steps. The fluid bubbled out from the wall, revealing a niche as it emptied.

A chill swept through the space, temperature dropping as it rippled toward him, spreading uniformly over the tunnel surface. It parted, flowing around his sandaled feet as though he was standing in an icy stream.

Rotating at the waist, he watched it part around two, foot sized gaps on the step behind him.

"You are with me, Raphael—thank you."

It constricted again, slinking along the tunnel ceiling. Stopping at the opening, it hesitated and then darted out.

Batush exhaled. Checking inside the wall niche, he found a Roman lantern covered in thick dust. When he touched his lamp to the dry rope wick, it lit with a hovering yellow flame and dancing red particles. The flame receded to a quivering blue vapor as he withdrew his lamp.

Taking hold as it drew fuel from the copper flask, it transformed to orange and grew in strength, washing the tunnel in white light. He exchanged his hand lamp in favor of the lantern.

As he descended, he counted twenty steps before the shaft leveled out. Lifting the lantern, he shielded his eyes with his free hand and peered into the blackness. Cleanly cut stone lined the horizontal section of the tunnel, offering a taller ceiling. Arching his back, he stood erect. Then, rolling his shoulders, he forged ahead, again counting his steps.

He sniffed the dry air. "You are in a good place, my friend. The Lord has been protecting you for a very long time."

The blackness was no longer moving forward with his progress. *The vault...* Reaching the end, he counted, "Fifty-two and three."

The chamber's floor was elevated, a step higher above his feet. Ducking, he extended the lantern as he entered.

The vault, smaller than he envisioned, matched the reading room's octagon shape above. A series of arched piers, springing inward from the eight corners, supported the space. The arches landed in pairs, atop four squat columns arranged in a central square. A pattern of triangular vaults, inset between the arches, divided the ceiling. A second set of arches, spanning from column to column, supported a dome.

Something crunched beneath his foot. Lifting it, he found a broken blue tile, one of several scattered across the floor among patches of white powder. Above, the scalloped ceilings were clad in a sky of variegated blue tile with random patches of white. *How long ago did you fall, and did Moaz hear you?*

Unable to escape the feeling of being buried alive, Batush stared at the object centered beneath the dome. A sarcophagus—formed in slab stone. It bore the insignia of Rome cut into its face.

CHAPTER 11

RHEMA sat on the barstool at the kitchen's peninsula bar, the granite countertop cool to her touch as Daniel piled ingredients on a cutting board. Then balancing his tray, he crossed the kitchen to stand before her and spread the array of goods around the bamboo board as one might assemble tools for a complicated job. When the toaster popped, he met her eyes with a mischievous smile that suggested a secret about to be shared.

"Are you going to tell me why you're home so early?"

The smell of slightly charred sourdough caressed the air as he retrieved the toast and lifted his brows. "Patience, I'll tell you in just a minute. Watch and learn."

"Oh brother." She drew out the reply, adding a slight humph.

He dashed a pile of spicy mustard on two sourdough slices. Next, he selected the rough-skinned avocado, split it with a hooked paring knife, and twisted it open. Using a butter knife, he carved soft meat from the bright green center to cover the other two faces of toast. Selecting a serrated knife, he then sliced and diced his vegetables—cucumber and red onion, yellow tomato, snap peas, and Baby Bella mushrooms. Applying the precision of his German heritage, which seemed to infect everything he tackled, he began the final assembly with a generous foundation of Boar's Head buffalo chicken reinforced with a slice of pepper jack cheese, followed with strategically stacked courses of cut vegetables and leaves of crisp romaine.

One leg swinging beneath her, she couldn't help grinning as his brow furrowed in utmost concentration. "No onion, mushroom, or green beans on mine—just one lettuce leaf and don't forget the mayo."

"Don't worry." Fanning a lettuce leaf, he painted the tip of her nose. "I have a memory like a fox."

She huffed again.

He capped each sandwich with a mound of pepperoncini, dousing his with a drizzle of balsamic vinegar. When he flipped half his sandwich over to land atop the other, several ingredients cascaded to the paper plate, and the laughter she'd been holding back escaped.

"How are you even going to eat that? It's not possible to open your mouth that wide."

"Woman of little faith, it's been done before."

Using both hands, he balanced his sandwich with two fingers on top of the almost four-inch tower as he slid it across the counter toward the other stool. "One more thing."

His back to her, he removed two chilled champagne glasses from the freezer drawer along with a bag of black cherries. He then withdrew a bottle of Pellegrino seltzer water from the refrigerator door shelf. Back at the counter, he graced the long-stemmed glasses with fruit cubes. The frosty concoction sizzled as he poured.

"So, what's the occasion?"

"We made the short list for River Run Crossing."

The memory of their son holding his kindergarten diploma washed over her as Daniel's face lit up. "That's fantastic, Danny. See, you said they'd never consider us. But I told you they would, and you're going to land it too."

"I'm not so sure about that. I'm confident we can beat out three of the guys. But Desert Fox made the list, and Ernie always seems to pull it out of his hat. He's crafty for sure, if not downright unethical, but I've got to admit I admire the guy. His subs are loyal, they're solid, and I hear they give him discounted numbers."

"Our guys are good too, and they respect you, honey. I'm sure they'll be competitive, especially on a job like River Run."

"It'll depend on their workloads, and some of them are going to be too small for the job, so we'll need to find new guys. It's going to be tough, but who knows? Maybe it's our time to break out of the pack with some larger projects. Anyway, I don't want to jinx it by talking too much about it." He lifted his glass. "The real stuff will wait until we win the job."

Matching his gesture, she smiled as their glasses clinked.

She drew a sip as the fizzing droplets tickled her nose. Except for the hum of the refrigerator and their munching, it became quiet. Placing half her sandwich on the plate, she engaged his blue eyes.

With his Dagwood tilted, he navigated a bite, tore away a mouthful, and tried to smile.

"So, how did she look?"

After chewing for a while, he gulped a swallow and then puckered his lips. "How did who look?"

"Amber, of course. Is she still the most beautiful woman you ever met?" Rhema turned to him, but only with her eyes as her index finger floated along the rim of her purple champagne glass.

"Whew." He lowered his sandwich, holding it above the plate as it dripped.

"What do you mean whew? Whew, what...?" Cocking her head, she kicked off her sandals and placed her hands on her hips.

"Well, if I was an honest man..."

"And you know you are not, Mr. Fairmont. I'm waiting..." The smile returned with a wagging finger.

"Do you want some more?" When he placed the sandwich down, it toppled over. Ignoring the demolished structure, he extended the green bottle.

"Don't change the subject, and yes, I would." She met the bottle with her glass, eyes not leaving his.

"I'll have to admit she looked pretty good. She's taken care of herself, but she's nothing compared to you. You're the most beautiful of all. You know it's true."

Effervescent liquid foaming, it rose to the rim of her glass. Hoisting it, she held the cut crystal to the light, as one might inspect a fingering pattern.

"Does she still have her tiny waist and large assets? *Hmm...?*"

"Honey, everyone ages, and honestly, I didn't really notice." He wiped his hands with a napkin.

"So, she does." She saluted his attempt with her glass.

He rolled his eyes. "Okay, if you have to know—yes, she looked great. You should have seen the guys gawking. It was sort of embarrassing. I don't think they even realized they were ogling her—nodding up and down every time she spoke."

She arched a brow while drawing a sip. "Are you sure you weren't ogling her too?"

He reached for her hand. Lowering the glass, she took it with head bowed.

"I'm serious. I could never be attracted to her again. She is beautiful, and I do admire—or, well, appreciate—her looks. But the way she manipulates people? I can see what she's doing, and it's repulsive. It's hard to put my finger on, but there was something else that wasn't right." Daniel released her hand and began to reassemble his sandwich. "It seemed like she was lying."

Having lifted her glass, she placed it back down. "Lying, about what?"

"All of it. Well, some of it was true. But when she was talking about Richard and his accident, it was almost like she was saying she was available. And then she told them about her father killing himself and how she found him. She went into this whole description of walking down the hall and how there was a breeze blowing on the curtains. The whole time I knew her, she never shared that with me. It's terrible to say, but it felt like she was using her father's death to make us feel sorry for her. Maybe I'm wrong, but I've got a bad feeling about her leading our staff." As he drew his hands away from the sandwich, it listed precariously. He rotated on the stool. Facing the kitchen, his eyes remained on her.

"I'm sure there are things she never told you. I think you're being too hard on her—it's possible she was just being honest. Maybe you're seeing something that's not there because she hurt you? People can change, you know. You've changed." She took a sip and lowered the glass, looking at him with the tender smile that had won his heart.

"It was a little awkward with the guys knowing she'd been my girlfriend. The whole thing was weird, but if I had to guess, I'd say we're likely going to hire her. Nick was totally swept away, and Pastor Jason liked her too. Maybe I should take a step back and let it play out. Besides, with all her business experience, maybe she'll be perfect."

He spread his arms. "I do love you—you know that, don't you? The Lord picked you just for me. You balance me out, Coach. You know it's true." Wiping his finger with the napkin again, he leaned in and cupped her shoulders in his strong hands.

"I know. But don't forget you belong to me." She smiled. Extending her toe, she poked his calf.

<<>>

"There you are. Why are you hiding?" Asmodeus hurled the accusation, ignoring the two scribes. A task lamp between them, they sat like frozen statues of stone in the dimly lit cold room. The sound of the steady rain fractured the still air with intermittent booms as droplets struck the tile roof above.

"I was not—I *am not*—hiding, master. I–I was only looking for you." Moaz rocked on his haunches beneath the heavy study table on the library's second floor. The scribes remained motionless. Bent over the desk, one gazed at a scroll, the other a tablet.

"You...were looking for me?" Asmodeus thrust his arm through the table with the swiftness of a striking cobra. Grasping Moaz by the throat, he jerked him up, took two lunging steps, and drove his sniveling subordinate into the wall.

The shorter demon resisted, his legs kicking the air between them.

Leaning in, Asmodeus slowly drew Moaz out of the wall and to his face as the tormentor's desperate ashen face contorted like molded wet clay. With just a finger's length between their lips, Asmodeus paused, reached behind, and drew his weapon from his shoulder scarab.

Precise and swift, he leveled the glinting sword tip on the center of Moaz's forehead. Then motionless, elbow drawn back, he watched beads of sweat bejewel his brother's face.

The beads coalesced into a droplet. Growing in size, it formed a rivulet that trickled down the tormentor's forehead, then split as it met the needle-sharp blade. Applying pressure, Asmodeus watched as the weapon slid into the demon's brain. With it half buried, he stopped.

"What happened?" He eased his grip on the tormentor's throat.

"I... did what you asked. I–I waited—forever, I waited!—and then, I did it."

"Did what?"

"I pulled the shim."

"And then what happened?"

"The wall, I released it and–and killed him." Moaz squirmed again, his oozing stench overpowering the smell of dry parchment.

"I understand you released the wall, but why are you lying to me?" Asmodeus applied pressure again, drawing closer.

"It's not my fault! I did as you commanded. He–he had help from... from the enemy. It was the enemy," Moaz sputtered. Surrendering again, he went limp.

"Who helped him?"

"Raphael—he was there. He plucked the scribe out of the way. And then he was in the tunnel. I fought him there, and he... he fled from me."

"Don't lie to me. Do you seriously expect me to believe that *you* fought Raphael by yourself? And Raphael feared *you*?" Asmodeus squeezed tighter, slowly rotating the blade. "You worthless piece of... I will report this to the prince, and you will be punished."

"No, n–no! It wasn't my fault. I can finish it. That is why—I am here. I am waiting for the scribe's return. He will bring the book. Please, master? Let me complete my mission. I will not fail. Not the prince. Don't tell him—please?" Moaz started to convulse. It began with a pulse and then a shudder. Rippling through the tormentor's body, it blossomed into violent uncontrolled shaking.

"I did not send you here to wait for him. You were to kill him in the hut, and you failed. It was the simplest of assignments. And you wonder why you are not promoted beyond tormentor status?" Asmodeus shook his head in disgust. "I will finish this myself."

Moaz gulped, his throat slithering beneath Asmodeus's hand. "Let me help. We can do it together—*pleeeeease*?"

"I would not ask for your help if you held the fate of all eternity in your hands. I have another operation for you, and I will wait on my decision about reporting this." Withdrawing the blade from the demon's head, Asmodeus gave Moaz a half-hearted shake and then tossed him to the floor like discarded refuse. "Get it right this time. And do not—*do not*—ever lie to me again."

Moaz crumpled into a heap. Then leaping to his feet, the tormentor backed against the wall, the stench of fear pooling at his feet like stale urine.

Asmodeus glared at the pathetic creature. "Giving you another chance defies all pain and even death herself. What I should do with you, and if I could... I would throw you into the Lake of Fire right now. Do you understand?"

"Yes, master. Yes, I do. I will do whatever you ask and will not fail you. Thank you, master—please...?"

"Please what? What are you asking for now?" Asmodeus drew his hand back as the tormentor covered his head.

"Noth–nothing, master—don't strike me," Moaz blubbered.

"Moaz, you smell."

~~

Feeling the pulse, one of the scribes lifted his head. Was it the lamp's flame or possibly a draft? He saw nothing but did notice dust particles suspended before him and a lingering stench. Shifting away from the other scribe, he wrinkled his nose.

<<>>

Asmodeus gauged the scene. He had all eternity and then some, but needed only a moment. The tomb was as he remembered, the sarcophagus still resting in the center, but the rising incense and professional wailers were long departed. A single human stood in the room, head tilted up, frozen with a lantern in one hand, the other reaching out for balance. Asmodeus followed the old man's gaze to a blue tile. Suspended in space below a tuft of white particles midway between ceiling and floor. Turned on end, it formed a perfect diamond as if hanging from a wire.

He approached the scribe. Droplets of sweat beaded his face like pearls of fear. Asmodeus measured his stature. Sniffing at him, he was tempted to kiss the man but knew better.

"So, you are the one causing all the commotion. But you will not succeed. No, my friend, you will not." Asmodeus circled the thin man. "You do not look like a powerful warrior. Just a small and feeble old man, full of fear with matted blood in your hair. True, you had help today, but you will fail. Do you hear me, Scribe?" His lips pressed as close to the man's ear as he dared without touching. Breathing on him, Asmodeus whispered, "Receive my spirit." Snorting, he turned his back. The tile, a bit closer to the floor, now rotated flat.

He approached the sarcophagus, dreading the thought, but knowing it was the only option. "Celsus... Celsus... What grand times we had, you and I. We ravaged Rome together, did we not? And the women. Oh yes—how could I forget?—and the treasures also. Do you know what I miss most? Of course, you do—the power I wielded through you. Now that was quite special. I do wish you were alive, old friend, but sadly, we both know this is the only way, don't we?"

Asmodeus ran his hand across the face of the cold slab. Extending it through, he touched the corpse. "How I loathe incompetence. Moaz, you will owe me for this. You little piece of steaming excrement..." *And you lied to me?* Resting his hand on the body's sunken abdomen, he delayed.

The falling tile had made another half rotation. Exhaling a long breath, he then entered the vessel of dry bones, shrunken organs, and shriveled skin. Withdrawing, he descended into death's soul, hibernating in silence. The sack of death would be difficult to maneuver, but he had done it before. *At least the worms have departed.*

Asmodeus heard it then—the crack as the tile hit the floor.

CHAPTER 12

THE BELL screeched and Richard's head lurched. It was three. "Finish up, guys, two more minutes." He tapped the square basket on the corner of his desk with a Dixon Ticonderoga No. 2. "Make your final points and don't forget to sign it."

Warmth filled his chest. He had some good writers. "Okay, that's it—bring them up. And don't forget the reading. We're going to be discussing Chapters 5 and 6."

The students jostled around his desk as papers fell into the basket.

"Edward." The lanky sophomore with a shock of blond hair was dressed in oversized gym shorts and a Pink Floyd tee shirt. He was chewing gum. "Can you stay for a minute?"

Edward's posture slumped as the room emptied. "Sure. What is it you want to talk about?"

"Last week's paper. Pull up a chair." Richard rotated his wheelchair, applying a simultaneous pull and push to each large wheel.

"I liked the story, but parts of it sounded familiar." He glanced at Edward, whose rotating jaw tightened into a clench. "The part where the old man ties the fish to the boat and his hands are blistered. And also when he fought off the shark with a paddle and made it back to shore with just the skeleton."

His shoulders rounding, Edward shoved his hands into his pockets and scuffled his sneakers.

"I liked the parts *you* wrote, Edward. You don't need to copy someone else's work."

Looking up, Edward's eyes brimmed with tears. "I found it in my mom's room. It was an old book. I knew it was wrong. I couldn't think of anything, and I didn't start until the night before. I had a club track meet and..." Folding his arms, he slouched.

"Look at me." Richard leaned forward, tilting his head. "You're a good writer. You have great potential. There are published authors out there who can't write as well as you. But you need to write your own stories, okay?"

Edward stared at his untied shoelace.

"Here's what we're going to do. I'm not going to fail you on the paper, but I want you to start over. I'll give you another week, but you'll need to do your other work also. And this time, I want twelve pages instead of fifteen. And shorter doesn't mean easier. You're going to discover it's actually harder. Okay?"

"Thanks, Mr. Lash. But what if I can't think of anything?"

Richard pointed to Edward with his eraser. "Write about something you know. You said you run track, right? Has anything interesting happened at practice or in a meet?"

"Well... Last week, I was running the hundred-meter highs, and I was in second place. With one hurdle left, the guy next to me wipes out. He hit the hurdle and flew into my lane, and we both went down. I was so mad—I spun around to cuss him out... and..."

"And what?"

"He was on his face an–and from the knee down... his leg was on backward. All of a sudden, I felt so bad... I didn't even care that I lost, and..."

Richard nodded. "There you go. Sounds like you've got something to write about."

<<>>

Batush studied the scarlet wax stamp, expecting it to be Roman. It looked more like the seal of the church, likely an older version, with an X-shaped cross but missing the surrounding square. Regardless of age, the message was clear. *It cannot be broken without proper authorization from the Church Fathers.*

"You will find the book at the feet of Celsus," Batush whispered the words, his eyes fixed on the sarcophagus. Lifting the lamp, he circled the sarcophagus and found a matching seal on the opposite side.

He'd heard the tale but never given it much thought. Julius Celsus Polemaenue was buried beneath the library bearing his name. His son, Julius Aquila, had commissioned the library, but the official tomb of Celsus was later discovered empty.

That is where the stories began. Some said the body had been resurrected by Zeus and sat as a god in the heavens. Others believed it had been stolen and desecrated by the Goths in one of their periodic raids. The stories of what the Goths did to the body varied but shared a barbaric theme of horrific atrocities.

Mystery solved. Aquila moved his father's bones and buried them here beneath the building and statue honoring his memory. How, Lord, will I explain this to the Church Fathers, and what will they think?

Batush felt it then—a tremor. He stretched out his free hand for balance, gazing upward as a flash of panic swept through his mind. He did not see it fall, but he heard the pop as a tile released. A chill of fear followed like an exhaling breath flowing from the mouth of a cave. Batush froze for a lingering moment, hearing a dark whisper.

"It is true you had some help today, but you will fail. Do you hear me, Scribe?"

A sharp crack echoed through the silent room as the tile hit the floor, fracturing in multiple directions.

"Lord, protect me...." Drawing a breath, Batush touched the floor as he dropped to one knee. A deep-throated rumble rose in the distance and then dissipated like a wave crashing on the beach. Building again, it accelerated toward him. Rising to a pounding shake, it rolled through the chamber. The room erupted with a crackling noise like scalding water poured over ice.

Hands flat on the floor, he looked up. "If You are taking me, Lord, I am ready."

It was quiet then, except for the pounding in his chest. He hoisted his swinging lantern to see a film of white dust hovering over the floor, now patched with a new pattern of broken tile. As he turned to the sarcophagus, his mouth fell open.

"The wax seal." *It is clearly cracked.... Broken by the hand of God.* "A request of the Church Fathers is not required to open a wax seal that is already open."

Grinning now, he recircled the sarcophagus and found the second seal with a matching horizontal crack.

Batush noticed it then—the lampstand. A bit odd standing alone in the open room, it listed to one side. "You have been watching over this room for a long time, waiting to be useful again."

Hanging his lantern on the hook, he touched the sarcophagus's stone lid. The thickness appeared about equal to his hand spread. *I do not have the strength, Lord.* Feeling a pulse, Batush spun around—quite sure he was not alone.

"Raphael? Are you there?"

"I am ready, my friend. Where do you want me?" The words came from the empty space.

Batush pointed. "You take that corner, and I will push on this one."

"I am ready on your command." He followed the voice as it moved to the back corner.

"Ready...?" Taking a sideways heaving position, he leaned into the cold slab with arms extended. "Push..." The lid moved before he could apply pressure, feeling like it was gliding on water, yet hammering through his bones as if being dragged by an ox. "You are very strong, Raphael. I am not sure you needed my help." Almost falling, Batush caught himself with a laugh.

"You are strong also, Batush—remember that. I am sorry, but I must now leave you again."

"But you cannot—I need your help. Where is it you are going?"

The empty space replied, "I do not know, except that I am being called. Stand firm, Batush. Everything you need is within you. I was only sent to bring you the message and help you move the stone."

"Will you be back? Will I hear from you again?"

"I do not know, but I must go now without delay. Listen to the Spirit of God. He is within you and will lead you, if only you have ears to hear."

"Thank you, Raphael, thank you." A bit disoriented, Batush placed his hand on the stone lid to center himself as the space in front of him seemed to warp, like a taut sheet poked with a finger. Batush was then alone again, of that he was certain.

The sarcophagus was now open at two corners where the lid had rotated. Retrieving his lantern, Batush approached. The smell was dry, like an old blanket stored away for a long time. As he lifted the lamp, the beam washed down the side of the stone box, revealing a torso beneath a white robe accented with a leaf pattern stitched in gold. He then lowered the lantern and pulled it back. As the beam shifted, it exposed the withered face of Governor Celsus, a silver coin covering each of his eyes. Suddenly faint, Batush gripped the edge of cold stone for balance.

An ornate medallion, inlayed with red rubies, lay across the governor's chest. Attached to a heavy gold chain, the medallion's jeweled design matched the wax seals. *It must have been placed there after the burial.*

"Were you a believer, Celsus?" Batush placed his hand on the lid.

"Forgive me, Lord, for disturbing this place. Wash and cleanse me, Lord, with Your Spirit."

He approached the other corner. *Please, Lord, I do not want to reach inside.* As he elevated the lamp, light washed over shriveled feet and a cylinder-shaped object. His heart leapt—a wooden scroll sleeve bearing the emblem of the X-shaped cross carved into its face.

"And there you are—at the feet of Celsus. Praise and honor be to You, Lord." Batush released a breath, his eyes welling with tears. He then rushed to the lampstand and moved it into position before rehanging his lamp. Holding his breath, he reached inside with both hands and lifted out the scroll sleeve. He cradled it in his arms like a sleeping child. "You are well preserved, my friend. And what mystery is written on you?"

Should we have a look or take it to the reading room? There could be questions if someone is there. Home, yes—read it there.

Batush laid it on top of the sarcophagus. "We have a lamp and desk right here, do we not? Let's have a quick look." Sliding the lamp closer, he brought folded hands to his lips. Heart pounding, he withdrew the sleeve and tested the parchment which felt quite fresh. He began to unroll it. His left hand above, he fed it with his right.

The crudely drafted text tilted downward and to the right with no embellished lettering or decoration. *How is this? A scribe's days are over when the steady hand is lost. Unless...?*

The text was Greek, one of the most familiar. Reading the first few words, he began to tremble. *It—it is an original. It must be.*

"Lord God, I am not worthy." Holding it at arm's length, he drank in the words, awash in the purity of nourishment to his soul.

The Revelation of Jesus Christ, which God gave Him to show to His bond-servants, the things which must soon take place; and He sent and communicated by His angel to His bond-servant John, who testified to the word of God and to the testimony of Jesus Christ, even to all that he saw. Blessed is he who reads and those who hear the words of the prophecy, and heed the things which are written in it; for the time is near...

His head swimming, he willed himself to focus, afraid he might drop it, speculation and questions racing through his mind. *It must be John the Apostle. Our first bishop, he spent his final days here caring for the holy mother, Mary. But how is it I have never read this, and why is it here, buried with the governor? And who would have put it here? The church seals are a clue there can be no doubt, but why?*

Batush forced himself to stop reading. As he began to roll the scroll, the light started to fade. His gaze darted first to the lampstand and then about the room. He made note of his surroundings—lampstand to his side, tunnel behind him. Quickly rolling the scroll, he fumbled while trying to slide it into the tube. *Too wide, it needs to be spun tighter.*

He faced the corbeled opening as the lantern sputtered. The glow behind him waning, he squared himself with the entrance some ten paces away. The lantern wick dimmed from yellow to orange, then deep red, a pulsing blue vapor circling it. Wavering in the blackness, Batush held the scroll in one hand and the tube in the other.

The excitement of his discovery dissipated with the light, replaced now with a creeping fear rising from the darkness. The face of Celsus seared in his mind, he thought of Moaz. *Has he returned? Did Moaz quench the lamp?*

CHAPTER 13

THE TWELVE-STORY condominium, situated between a greenbelt and Main Street, dominated the heart of downtown. Peering skyward, Amber eased the black sedan into the roundabout and lifted her foot as the asphalt transitioned to cobbles. The building's skin was clad in a patchwork of green glass, raw concrete, and perforated metal. Randomly placed balconies served to break up the vertical planes, adding depth to the clean but elegant façade. Crafted in cut aluminum, the words *Green Oasis Lofts* arched over the entry. *I guess we need to be "sustainable" and "going green". I'm a little weary of it all.*

Asmodeus disagreed, *"It's about packaging a vision. Don't you see...? Get them thinking they can change the world or maybe even a church?"*

"Hmm... The Sustainable Church?" The security arm swung open as she swiped her cardkey across the magnetic kiosk reader. Pulling forward, she followed the double row parking drive that looped the building's footprint.

A man behind the gray desk scooted back as she entered. The sedentary job matched his heavyset frame and slouching posture. His red-cheeked boyish face contrasted with his mantle of longish gray hair. He tipped forward in the swivel recliner, a nametag dangling from his soiled brown uniform read Tank. "You must be Amber Lash."

"Why yes, I am. How did you know my name?"

"Owner called, said you would be coming." Swiping at greasy straggles, he ogled her up and down.

Amber's nose pricked to the odor of flatulence.

"It's on twelve, right?" She started toward the bank of stainless-steel doors.

"Yep, penthouse. Right on top. You'll need the last cab. It's dedicated."

She pushed the green button. When she turned back, his eyes darted to her face. Smiling then, he leaned back while visually groping her as she stared at him. She was relieved to hear the elevator rushing toward her.

"Let me know if you need anything, Ms. Lash. I'll be ready to take care of you." He was nodding, the grin on his face peculiar.

She backed into the cab, swallowing as the doors closed.

Asmodeus selected the word for her, *"Revolting."*

<<>>

Cold sweat coated Batush's sticky neck. Wavering in the blackness, he dropped to his knees, the scroll in one hand and the sleeve in the other. He took a deep breath and placed the tube on the floor, his open hand hovering above it. Then, holding the scroll in both hands, he located the edge. Unrolling it one hand's length, he began the process of reverse rolling it.

"There we go, nice and tight." Scroll in one hand, the other patted the floor, locating the scroll tube. Bringing them together, he inserted the scroll to midpoint. He then worked his hand upward, careful not to let it unfurl. "Relax, old man. Have we not done this a thousand times? Breathe in, breathe out. Easy and slow. Easy and..."

He heard it then—a rustling followed by a scratching.

Batush froze, holding his breath. *A rat... It must be a rat or mouse.*

Lifting the sleeve to his chest, he applied pressure as the book eased home. As he released pressure, he felt it unwind.

He heard it again, muffled and larger than any rat. His temples pulsated in unison with his heartbeat. Again, the rustling, followed this time by a thud and the stuttering of a long exhaling breath. Like that of a dying man's last rail, trailed by a staccato gasp.

The sound was directly behind him.

<<>>

With the turn of a key, the heavy bolt slid, granting entry. Amber drew a soft gasp as her pupils constricted to the flood of light. The view beyond the wall of glass wasn't Manhattan, but the cityscape and mountain ridgeline was quite beautiful.

Asmodeus purred as they spoke simultaneously, *"Nice..."*

She parked her suitcase on a Persian rug, centered between the elevator door and a huge antique mirror in a gold-leaf frame. The penthouse was split with public functions on one end and private on the other. Amber surmised it to be a single bedroom of roughly two thousand square feet, not including the balcony.

The space integrated an artful blend of contemporary and traditional with polished hickory flooring and twelve-foot open ceilings. The end walls and three large square columns, finished in tumbled brick, complemented the balance of refined finishes. Held three feet below the concrete ceiling, the interior partitions— freestanding, finished in ultra-smooth texture and painted stark white—served to frame space and function with no interior doors.

A kidney-shaped soffit, floating above four Vandero chairs, drew her forward. Centered perfectly on a faux zebra rug, the chrome and leather seats rested in front of a curved wall of chiseled stone. With a two-sided firebox, the thickened wall served as a divider to an opulent library. Full-height bookstacks, equipped with a rolling pipe rail ladder, wrapped the perimeter walls. Amber circled the room's centerpiece, touching the rusticated oak finish. The Arts and Crafts style table, with opposing red leather chairs, was a museum piece. Overall the look was powerful and masculine, but the feel intimate.

Again, they spoke in unison, *"Very nice..."*

The kitchen's sweeping black-granite island bar formed the heart of the penthouse. Placing her purse on the cool slab, she admired the sleek European cabinetry and stainless Gaggenau appliances. Her motion woke a backlit glow that emanated from a reveal line between the countertop and millwork, lacquered in sage. A recessed refrigerator and full-height wine cooler bookended a twelve-burner gas range, both lit inside with glass doors.

"Check the labels."

Amber was about to look when she changed her mind. Heading instead for the owner's suite, she walked through the central entertainment space. An overstuffed leather couch faced another divider-wall clad with the largest monitor she'd ever seen. The wall served as a headboard to a king-size bed centered on the other side. Finished in rising-sun red metal, it provided a striking backdrop for the pillows and slippery quilt colored in gold umber, hunter green, and deep purple.

A painting above the bed drew a purring chuckle from within. The image captured a soaring angel with black wings flung behind her naked body. The ebony frame included the engraved title, *Raven Wing.*

Amber leaned toward the face of the angelic beauty. "Do I know you?"

Asmodeus answered, *"Oh yes, we know her all right."*

Two suspended sheets of frosted glass, internally lit from above with a ribbon of white light, defined the bathroom, the plumbing fixtures visible through the glass. A bit obscured but clearly discernable, two black pedestal sinks, a large glass shower, and an open-platform tub. The silhouette of the commode was visible as well in matching black porcelain.

The elevator chimed, followed by a swoosh.

She glanced at her watch. *Three o'clock, he's here.* After straightening her skirt, she headed back to the kitchen where she found Nick standing at the island bar with a shoulder bag and an arm full of notebooks.

Looking up, he smiled. "Karen's on her way. She should be here in a couple minutes. So... what do you think?"

"It's amazing. I've seen a lot of homes in my day, but nothing like this." Amber beamed with open hands. "What's the owner like?"

"It's a bit of a mystery. As far as I know, he's only here on New Year's Eve. That's it, just one night a year. He's a church member, single, midthirties. No one I know has ever met him. I have a few details because I handle the church finances and a portion of his portfolio. His name's Karl Bernhardt, and he's extremely wealthy. Most of his money is parked in low-risk bonds."

"Really—that's intriguing. Have you ever spoken to him?" She stood in front of Nick, her hand on the counter.

"Never. He communicates in writing only—mostly email. He's always prompt, replies within the hour, sometimes longer but always the same day. And he travels a lot, has a Gulf Stream V and a private pilot. I saw his tax return once. A lot of it was redacted, but there was enough there to see he owns properties all over the world."

"Ask him where."

"Wow, do you know where?"

"London, Moscow, Hong Kong, Odessa, and Dubai, mostly residential—I've done a little research. His place in Odessa is a two-hundred-year-old castle overlooking the Black Sea. And his Dubai property is high-rise luxury apartments, sixty-three floors." Nick lifted his brows, looking over the top of his glasses. "He owns it, the whole building. He developed this one too, but sold it off as condos, except for this space that he keeps for himself. But that's just the residential stuff, the commercial side was redacted, but I did see the total he paid in taxes."

Amber covered her open mouth. "What was it?"

"Touch him."

"Total combined—eight figures." Nick showed the suggestion of a smile.

"No. Seriously? Wow." She touched his elbow, her other hand falling from her mouth to cover her chest.

"Let him lead."

"Would you like to join me in the library?" Nick asked in a stodgy voice.

"Yes, darling, but I fear I've forgotten my smoking jacket." She mimicked his tone.

"I believe there's one hanging in the armoire."

"Oh my, you don't say? But alas, we have no cigars."

"Oh, but we do, my dear. Over there in the humidor, that is if you like Cubans?" Laughing, they took chairs at the study desk. Nick slid three notebooks toward her. "There's a lot of information here you'll want to familiarize yourself with. I'll leave this, but I want to give you an overview. And then I'd like to talk strategy for Tuesday's meeting." He adjusted his glasses, opening the first notebook.

"He's suggesting the job is yours. Get clarification."

"It's so nice of you to take the time with me, but do you think the board will actually consider a woman? A lot of churches don't allow women to serve as pastors, and I'm sure they'll be looking at some qualified men." Hands folded, she leaned forward.

"You are very qualified. And the board will, in fact, hire you—trust me. The women-in-ministry thing is easy. You'll be running the church all right, but your title will be minister or director of administration."

"Probe him."

"How can you be so sure? After all, a group of seven will be making the decision—right?"

"Correct. But this is between just you and me." Nick lowered his head and voice. "This board of elders is stupid." He paused, looking directly into her eyes. "When I came on, I couldn't believe what I encountered, a group of guys with no clue of how to run an organization. They had zero process for making decisions, and they were talking in circles. Just the other day, I proposed we open a credit line, as a safety measure because our reserve account is overly stressed. We own everything outright, and we've never borrowed to cover costs. But you never know. We might need to, and a credit line is a no-brainer. We went round and round discussing it for two hours—I kid you not. One of the guys said a church shouldn't borrow money, and another didn't even know what a credit line was. I was ready to tear my hair out."

Again, she covered her mouth. "Oh my... How much were you asking for?"

"Eight million, but the property is worth twenty-three—and we'll likely never need to use it. Anyway, they finally agreed, but the point is, I have to teach these guys how things are done. But you, Amber, you're different. You get it and we need you. The position is yours if you want it. I'm going to clarify the job description and ensure the compensation package is appropriate—don't even worry about that. Ready to get started?"

"Show him how amazing he is."

"The church is blessed to have you. This is so exciting. I can see we have similar perspectives, and it's reassuring to know we would be working together. Well, I mean—if it works out."

"I feel exactly the same way. I sensed it when we first met."

CHAPTER 14

THE SWOOSHING doors matched Karen's state of mind. Reclining with his feet on the desk, Tank lowered a magazine, then lifted his eyebrows as his smile expanded.

"Hi. I'm late for a meeting. The Bernhardt residence? I lost the number. I think it's 1204?"

Tank stared at her, locking his eyes on her breasts. "And you must be Karen. I was expecting you."

She glanced away, tugging on the neckline of her yellow vest.

"You'll need the first cab, that one. Yup, it's 1204, all right. You got a good memory." Leaning back, he tilted his head as if trying to see around the corner of her backside. "I can help you with the code from here. It'll open right into Mr. Bernhardt's loft. Now, let me see..." He fiddled with a button on his monitor. "Here we go. I got you covered, Karen—Penthouse, Level 12."

~~

As the doors closed, Tank pulled his feet off the desk, concentrating on his monitor. After opening a window, he clicked on a tab labeled Fire Alarm.

Mayhem spoke first, *"Hurry up. Don't blow this. Open it and scroll down."*

Madness cut him off, *"Shut up, fool. Let him think. Steady... Wait for Moaz. Wait for the signal..."*

"Do it now. Do it. No, wait... Wait for the signal... Wait for Moaz."

His hands shaking, Tank opened a screen labeled Override Control. The graphic displayed four cabs, each with an *X* on the building's core plan. Green bars, rendered above, indicated each cab's vertical position. Three were stationary with Cab 1 rising through a series of horizontal planes. Tank's index finger hovered over the mouse, the arrow pointing to the Stop button.

"Five, six, seven..." With eyes locked on the monitor, he missed the co-ed walking through the lobby in an overly short white tennis dress.

"Steady now. Wait, not yet... Wait for the signal..."

"Do it. Do it! I can't..."

"Silence, fool! You are going to blow this."

"You're the fool. You shut up. Steady, almost there..."

~~

Moaz looked up into the shaft, his hand gripping the greasy hoist cable, flashes of light glinting between the doors as they rose. He began to dance, jumping into the air as he crooned one of his favorite made-up songs.

"Knocking on the gates of Hell, yeah baby... Banging on the doors of pain... Banging on the doors of pain, yeah, Karen... Knocking on the gates of Hell... Yeah. Oh yeah... Banging on the gates of Hell, yeah baby... Knocking on the doors of pain...

"Eight, nine, ready, ready... Now!" Moaz screamed, gripping the cable with both hands.

"Now—Now—Now!" Mayhem and Madness relayed the message, shouting into Tank's mind as his finger jerked to execute the command.

Moaz spun around the thick cable like a stripper in a nightclub.

~~

Karen's body bobbed forward and then back. Tank viewed her from the cab's security camera on his monitor, standing in front of the control panel. The green bar on his split screen showed Cab 1, stopped just above the letter *M*, between floors nine and ten. His mouth hung open as he watched her pushing buttons on the keypad, gently at first and then harder. After, hitting the display with her fist, she then pawed through her purse.

"Who ya gonna call, Karen?" He smiled when she opened the emergency phone panel. "Hello, this is Tank."

"Concerned... Sound like you want to help."

"This is great. This is so great."

"Shut up!"

"It's me. Karen. The elevator's stuck. I'm on Floor M. I can't believe this. I forgot my phone, and I'm late. I'm stuck in here. Can you help me?"

"Now you just relax, Karen. We can help. Floor M is the Mezzanine. That's the equipment floor. Is the door open?" He chomped down on his tongue.

"Don't laugh."

"This is so great. We got her. She is going to get it."

"Shut up, idiot."

"Of course not. I–I just said I'm stuck in here. Can you please call the Bernhardt residence? I'm supposed to be there for a meeting. Can you let them know what happened?"

"Sure thing. I'll call in just one minute. Right now, I'm trying to move it from here, but it seems to be stuck. It happens sometimes, but don't worry. It looks like we'll need to call the Up and Down Boys." Tank bit down on the side of his pointer finger.

"Who the... Who are the Up and Down Boys?"

"The elevator guys. I'll call them right now."

"How long will that take? This is very uncomfortable, and I need to use the restroom."

"Yep. I'll call them and then call you back. They're usually right quick. Everything is going to be okay. We got you covered, Karen."

"She's going to piss her pants. This is so great."

"Let her wait. We're in control here. She deserves it."

Hanging up, Tank returned to his magazine and kicked his feet up again. Cab 2 opened with a chime as the co-ed emerged with a racket. "Hello, sunshine. Beautiful day for some action. Can I join you for some *strokes*...?" He stretched out the last word, smiling as she cringed.

<<>>

Nick opened the third binder. "This one covers mission, vision, and values. For sure the vision statement needs some work." Tugging on his lower lip, he huffed.

Asmodeus responded quickly, *"Show him you agree."*

"Love God and all people. That sounds a little vague. I mean—shouldn't a vision statement be directed toward the church, calling them to action? I would think it should start with something like we exist in order to do such and so. I'm sure you've thought about it. What do you think?"

"I love this, you get it, and I totally agree—actually, I've been talking to the board about changing it. But I don't think we want to throw it out, but we definitely need to rework how we're conveying the message. It should be cogent but also inspiring." His hand hovered above the binder, the diamond on his wedding band glinting under the halogens. "We Exist to Impact the World."

"We like it but add something."

"That captures everything the church is called to do. But we might want to add something—give it a twist. Something that resonates with where people are coming from." Amber focused on the singular eyebrow whisker protruding beyond the hedge of his impeccably manicured brows.

"What would you add?" He scrunched his lips.

"Make sure it's his idea and don't hurt his feelings."

"Well... It seems everyone these days is talking about sustainability and going green—you see it everywhere. Something that ties in with that might resonate with Millennials. I don't know—maybe that wouldn't work for a church?" She tilted her head, letting her big green eyes smile.

"You're on to something. No, really, Amber, that's good. Maybe something like... We Exist to Impact a Sustainable World. Wait—I got it. We Exist to Sustain the World for Christ. No... It needs to include the word *sustainable*. Here we go. How about this: We Exist to Impact a Sustainable World for Christ. How's that? Maybe it's too long...?"

"Not sure about Christ."

"I like it. But I'm not sure it should include the word *Christ*. That word is so loaded these days. It might offend someone, especially if they're new. But then again—we are the church, so maybe it's good?"

"Mm... I got it. What about this? We Exist to Impact a Sustainable World for Goodness."

Amber's mouth dropped open. "It's perfect—but I would make one small tweak. We Exist to Impact a Sustainable World for Kindness." They lit up with smiles as Amber extended her hand for a high five.

Nick inched back the shirt-cuff of his cobalt blue Giorgio Armani, checking his watch. "It doesn't look like Karen's going to make it. Something must have come up. We could keep working. But it's nearly five o'clock, and I seem to remember Mr. Bernhardt has quite the wine collection. Would you like a glass or a soda or something?"

"Yes. Chalk Hill Chard sounds good."

"That sounds great. But I'm not much of a wine connoisseur. Actually, when I do order wine, I usually ask for white Zinfandel."

"Nice move."

"Trust me." His lips drew together in a knowing smile. "I think I know what you'll like."

<<>>

Karen sat in the corner of the elevator with knees tight against her chest. Tank's mouth hung open as he watched her reach for the phone again. He let it ring three times.

"It's me again. Did you call the Bernhardt number? I really need to use the restroom."

"Yep... I was just about to call you. I tried the penthouse twice, but no one's answering."

"What about the Up and Down Boys—are they on their way?"

"They're coming but stuck in traffic. They said about an hour or so." He covered a grin with his hand.

"An hour or so? I can't wait that long. What am I supposed to do— can you get me out of here? I'm about to pee my pants."

"Well... I could open the door from here if you like."

"She's going to burst. This is so great."

"We got her. She's going to pay. Yes!" Mayhem and Madness laughed hysterically, kicking and throwing wild punches into the air, a war dance of sorts that had become a signature ritual when tormenting humans.

"You can open the door?" She scrambled to her feet. "Why didn't you tell me sooner? Yes, open it. Please."

"You'll need to be careful. I can't tell from here if the cab is level with the floor. And I can only open the outer doors. You'll need to pull the inside doors open yourself." He grinned at his display, which showed the cab elevated four feet above the mezzanine's floor. "Let me try, and we'll see what happens."

"Unbelievable—this is unbelievable. Please hurry." She began to pace.

Moaz peered into the gap between the cab and the elevator shaft. *"Get ready, guys—on my mark. Wait for me..."*

Tank clicked on the button labeled Outer Door Release, gawking as Karen flattened her hands on the elevator doors with legs spread apart. Giving up, she grabbed the dangling phone receiver.

"It's not moving. It doesn't want to move." She was puffing.

He bit his tongue again. "Did you try to open it?"

"Of course, I tried—I just said that."

"Try putting your fingers in the joint between the doors. That might work."

"I tried that. It's not budging. Please..."

He toggled his display to the camera in the mezzanine. *Sure enough, four feet.* "You're a little bit above the floor level, Ms. Karen. But you should be able to climb out and then follow the exit signs to the stair. That will bring you down here, and you can use the restroom."

"Get ready. This is it. Here she comes."

"This is great. This is so great. This—"

"Shut up, idiot. Be quiet."

"Here we go, Tank. You can do this. You know you want to. She's just like Mother and all the others. She thinks you're stupid, and she's gonna pay."

Tank split the screen, watching from both sides of the doors.

Karen pushed her fingers into the gasket again with elbows wide. "This is insane. It's not moving!" she shouted. Her yellow pants darkened then, flowing from the crotch down. "Please... Damn doors. Ah—move!"

"Look, she's pissing herself. Yes!"

"Take that, fat cow. How do you like that?"

Karen sobbed. "Please open—please."

"Ready..." Moaz was kneeling, his head protruding through the cab ceiling. *"On my word..."*

Tank's finger trembled over the Inner Door Release button.

"Now!" Mayhem and Madness screamed the message into his brain as his finger punched the mouse.

The doors flew open with Karen crashing into the cab's sidewall. Approaching the edge, she leaned over.

Tank glanced up, checking the lobby. His heart raced, fueled with fear and excitement.

"You can do it, Tank. Wait, wait for her... Not yet..."

Tank watched from the mezzanine camera as Karen sat, her legs hanging over the edge. With her hands flat on the floor, urine drizzled into the open shaft. "I'm going to jump for it. Can you hear me, Tank?"

"Don't answer."

"Tank, are you there? Can you hear me?"

Two men approached in the garage. Tank hung up and then switched off the monitor's audio, nodding with a plastered grin as they waited at the elevator doors. "Beautiful day out there, isn't it?"

"Sure is."

"Tank? Tank, are you there?"

Hovering above, Moaz primed his comrades, *"Get ready... Wait for my signal. Almost there..."*

Unable to contain himself, Mayhem shouted, *"Do it. Do it now!"*

"Shut up! Wait for the signal... Wait." Madness grabbed Mayhem's throat. *"Can you for once shut up?"*

Looking back to his screen, Tank saw Karen on her stomach, legs extending from the cab, kicking in the air. His hand opened the video control, toggling camera resolution to high speed. Karen slipped, lunging forward with her cheek pressed against the floor. Her hand slapped at the pool of urine.

"Are you here for business or pleasure?" Tank asked as the chime sounded.

"Family. Here to visit our mother."

"That's nice. Enjoy your visit." Bobbing his head with an open mouth, he turned back to see Karen's backside extruded from the opening. His eyes widened.

"She looks like a sausage. A big fat sausage."

<<>>

Amber eased back in the high-back red leather chair. Across from her at the desk, she watched him. Clearly, he was trying to impress, so polished and well mannered, a little overly so, but quite handsome. She nodded, and then she smiled, stroked her hair and laughed, and then did it again. *Men are so easy.*

Nick extended the half-empty bottle of Talbot Sleepy Hollow Chardonnay.

"More?"

"Just a bit. This is really good. It's so light and crisp. I better be careful. I could probably drink the whole bottle."

"The Chalk Hill is better. How 'bout changing?"

Amber was floating. "Would you mind if I changed?" The question escaped before she realized it. "I've been wearing this all day, and these shoes are killing me."

"Not at all—I'm the same way, especially when traveling."

"I'll be right back." She wavered toward the bedroom, feeling a little tipsy. Remembering her purse, she abruptly turned around. Nick was standing in the library, his wine glass at his lips. Their eyes met, and he glanced away to the skyline.

"He wants you."

She selected an oversized tee shirt and a pair of jeans. *Is he watching?*

"Of course, he's watching."

Amber stepped behind the sheet of frosted glass and switched off the overhead can lights. A single spot remained lit above the tub behind her.

"Leave it on."

She kicked off her heels and then wriggled the purple dress over her head, draping it over the top of the shower door. Hesitating for a moment, she unclasped her bra, instinctively wringing the tension from her breasts with both hands. Threading her arms through the tee shirt, she checked herself with a glance at the mirror, fluffed her hair, and switched off the backlighting before jostling into her stretchy Wranglers. As she emerged, he was opening the sliding glass door at the balcony.

"That's so much better. Thanks for your patience." Wine glass in hand, she joined him at the railing. The sky was on fire with the sun about to drop below the mountain ridge.

"It's getting late. Do you need to go?"

Nick leaned against the railing with both hands. Facing her, he cocked his head. "I still want to prep you for the meeting." He then sighed, his gaze returning to the sunset. "Sometimes when I look at a view like this, I can't help but wonder about life and what I'm doing. If I had made different choices, who would I be and what would my life be like? Do you ever think about things like that?"

"Not really. I just decide to change my life instead, and I do." She shook her curls over her shoulders and took another sip.

Nick nodded slowly, his chin protruding. "And that is why you are going to make a great executive pastor." He pointed at her. "Amber Lash, you are going to reinvent us—that is what you are going to do." He gestured toward the door. "I have about an hour. Brooke is out with the ladies tonight and won't be home until eight."

Back at the desk, Nick slid a pamphlet from his satchel and laid it on the table. The title read Elders of Faith Bible Church.

CHAPTER 15

COAGULATED GOO in the bottom of the flask was slowly absorbing into the lantern's rope wick. The glowing ember at the tip ignited, rising with a dancing blue flame. Now facing the sound, Batush perceived the sarcophagus's shape in the pulsing glow. Fixed on it, he clutched the scroll while jostling with his writing case. Heart pounding, he held his breath as he struggled to unclasp the leather flap with one hand.

Again, the thump followed by the exhaling breath. It spoke then out of the cold darkness. "Come to me."

The voice sounded like Raphael.

"Who are you?" Nearly dropping it, Batush slid the scroll tube under his arm.

"I am Raphael. You know me. Come here, Batush."

The lamp pulsed, revealing a dark shape emerging from the open corner of the sarcophagus. Shifting to the side, it morphed larger with a struggling scrape followed by a metallic clang. The image of the necklace resting on the corpse's chest flashed through his mind.

"What do you want?" The clasp popped open as Batush drew the writing case to his lap.

"Bring me the book, Batush. I need the book." The glow pulsed again, illuminating a torso with lowered head. Shifting, the form faded to blackness.

The words trembled from his lips. "You are a liar. You cannot have it." Remembering Raphael's departing words, he hurled a command into the blackness. "In the name of Christ, I rebuke you."

Another pulse revealed Death's hooded face, staring through him. The glow began to strobe as the lamp flame danced around the wick, the hideous shape shifting position with each pulse.

Heart racing, Batush stuffed the tube into the case. *Now close it. Close it.*

Death replied in chuckling disgust. "It will take a bit more than harsh words to stop me, Scribe. It seems you do not know who you are contending with."

<<>>

The coffee table between them, Amber leaned forward, trying to focus. She pulled a sofa pillow into her lap and then covered her mouth repressing a yawn. Beyond the glass curtainwall, the horizon was glowing red as the city's streetlights winked awake.

Nick opened a folder and removed a smiling portrait. "Paul Chambers, chairman. We've talked, and he's impressed with you—he'll vote yes. Paul has his own business and does quite well, sells appliances—lots and lots of refrigerators. I handle his investments. Paul's not that smart but likes people to think he is, and he throws his weight around. He's a little insecure, hides behind his gruff persona—you know what I mean?"

Amber picked up her glass, giving it a swirl. "He looks friendly."

"Oh, he's friendly all right once you let him know his place. In my first elder meeting, he was pushing the guys around, so I stood up to him."

"You did? What happened?" She covered her mouth.

"I don't remember what we were talking about, but he was lecturing—oh yeah, he was saying how we should all be out in the foyer on Sunday mornings, greeting people. So he stands up and starts yelling at one of the guys. Don't get me wrong, I agree we should be out there with the folks, but I wanted to establish territory in the room, so I took him on. I stood up and got in his grill. I was poking him in the chest. We were face to face, and I didn't back down."

"No, you didn't? I can't believe it." Amber uncovered her gaping mouth, eyes wide. "Seriously?"

"Absolutely. I stood my ground until he sat down. I then apologized—to him and the group—but the line was drawn. He may be chairman, but I control the board."

Her expression of shock unmoved, Asmodeus blurted, *"Enough with the damsel in distress bit. Yes, he's full of himself but not stupid."*

He moved to the next face. "This is Henry Williams. He always votes with the majority—never has an original thought. He's worthless—except that you can get him to do anything you want." Nick pointed. "This is Lewis Kolsby—all he does is pray. He's a nice enough guy, just a little wacked out. He thinks he can 'feel' what the Holy Spirit is doing. Just let him know you care about prayer, and he'll be impressed."

Amber picked up her wine glass. Floating her index finger around the lip, she nodded thoughtfully and tilted her head to the ceiling, allowing him a break from trying not to look at her breasts. "I can work with that, thanks."

For a moment, it was quiet. As she faced him again, his eyes swept back to the photos.

"Now Earl Dempsey's a bit of a wild card, so it's hard to pin him down. He's retired and serves as a hospital chaplain. He's charismatic and believes in healing. You'll need to be careful because Faith Bible doesn't embrace the sign gifts. Now this guy, Vince Fogel... He's running for city council, and it could be good for the church if he gets elected. He's impressive and extremely conservative on issues like abortion and gay marriage." Nick met her eyes over the top of his glasses. "Anyway, just let him know you understand where he's coming from."

<<>>

Karen was slipping. Unable to stop, she'd have only one chance—push off and away from the open shaft. "No. Don't panic. Ready... Please, God—please."

On all fours, Moaz watched from the gap between the cab and the elevator shaft. *"Get ready."*

She drew her body weight tight to the cab, her forearms screaming with pain, the threshold cutting into her skin. Her hand slapped at the floor as she shoved herself backward with an exhaling grunt.

Moaz reached for the cable. *"Now!"*

The command was screamed into Tank's mind as his finger dropped on the Hoist Override button. A warning flashed in bold yellow letters—Cab Doors Open.

The cab lurched upward. A high-pitched scream filled the shaft.

<<>>

"And then we have Daniel, the new guy. I handle his investments too but don't know a lot about him. But I understand you do, and I expect he'll support you?"

"Well, I'm not so sure. I mean, we knew each other, but that was a long time ago. And you know people change. Tell me how the voting works." Amber smiled. Then twisting a curl, she rubbed the back of her neck.

"The constitution only requires a majority. But on something like this, we'd want to be unified. Sometimes, when it's close, we'll take some time to think and pray. But I'm hoping we'll be able to get this done on Tuesday. I'm pushing for you." He looked up from Daniel's dossier, meeting her eyes. He then reached across the table and touched the back of her hand with two fingers.

"I may have let him down a little too hard when I broke it off." Withdrawing her hand, Amber picked up the glass again. Drawing a sip, she held it in her mouth and then swallowed. Their eyes touching again, she watched as he mirrored her swallow. "I hope he wouldn't hold it against me if I broke his heart."

"And I'm sure you did—just kidding. But seriously, Daniel has integrity and wouldn't let a past relationship cloud his judgment. He'll be a yes. I'm sure of it."

"Enough with Daniel. Ask about the pastor."

"What about Pastor Stover?"

"Pastor Jason's an elder, but he doesn't vote. It would be a conflict of interest because he's also paid staff. He'll weigh in on the decision, but he likes you. I could see it in his face when you described the symphony analogy—brilliant, by the way. I asked him what he thought about you after the meeting." Nick leaned back, laying his arm across the top of the couch. His eyes twinkled.

"Tell me... What did he say?"

"Like I said, he likes you. He said, 'Get her in here as soon as you can.'" Nick mimicked Pastor Jason's voice.

Hearing it, they froze—the shrill scream of a woman.

<<>>

Startled by the crash, he felt the case slip from his hands. It sounded like a sack of dry wood hitting the floor, followed by the rattling and hollow echo of his tools splaying across the stone tile. The flame pulsed, again fading. The corpse piled in a heap at the sarcophagus base, the scroll tube between them, rolling away. The next pulse lit the face of death. With mouth hanging open, it stared at him from open eye sockets. Falling forward, it shifted shape with each pulse. On, and then fading again.

A voice inside nudged him, *"Get the scroll."*

The flame continued to strobe. On—the body closer, propped on an elbow. Then fading. On again—the body falling forward onto its chest.

Fading. On—the scroll within reach, seesawing to rest.

The voice shouted, *"Grab it!"*

The flame pulsed again. Batush reached as Celsus surged forward. Grabbing it, Batush felt the brush of death against his hand.

"Give it to me," the voice rasped.

Spinning backward, Batush wailed as Death gripped his ankle like a slamming door crushing through flesh. The staccato drumbeat of his heart filled the chamber.

Clutching the scroll, Batush pulled, twisted, cried out. Focused on the searing pain, he kicked into the blackness. The light flared again as his heel connected with the gaping mouth, the sensation like crushing dry brush. The jaw broke away as the light faded.

Laughing, it squeezed like a closing vise.

Batush screamed, hearing his voice morph into a wail.

"You cannot escape, Scribe. You are mine."

Thrusting again, his foot connected as the flame pulse illuminated a torso raised on one limb with head dangling.

The exhaling laugh continued as blackness returned. "Where do you think you are going, Batush? I am going to put you into that box. Both of us and the book, back where we belong."

Batush shoved the scroll into the case, slung around his neck.

The grip tightened. "We will be together."

"Help me, Lord." Thrashing, with elbows driving into the cobbles, his flailing body dragged against his will. "Help...!"

The shimmer came from behind, flaring like the sun.

Slinging an arm behind, he arched toward the light.

Motion swept past him as the shout rang out: "Run."

Heaving with all essence of being, Batush beheld the angel wielding a shattering weapon. Lunging forward with the swiftness of a pouncing leopard, Raphael stomped on the body's neck.

Still clutching the case, Batush repelled backward as his ankle released. As Batush's eyes adjusted, the powerful archangel stood over the thrashing corpse.

Lifting his weapon, Raphael twisted to Batush. "Run. *Now.* Go!"

Batush scrambled backward on all fours, unable to look away, eyes locked with Raphael. Bumping into the wall, his groping arm located the opening.

Raphael's arm rose. He hesitated as the warping tear sizzled to brilliant green. He started to move toward it, then back, the enemy still pinned.

Asmodeus gurgled, "You're too late, Raphael."

Over in the blink of an eye, it seemed to unfold in slow motion. Raphael hoisted his arm to a punching position, the spiked ball following. It hovered for a second. Then lunging with a driving blow, the ball vanished. The motion, fluid and swift, ended with a bowing follow-through, the iron crushing through Death's skull into the floor. The deafening impact shook the chamber with fragments of rock and bone ricocheting from the walls.

Batush blinked back a stinging pinch below his eye. He had seen men fighting before, even to death, but never like this. *The deliberate power and veracity, to kill with such vengeance...* They stared at each other for a silent moment. Raphael's face contorting to sadness, he stepped into the rift.

Batush ducked into the tunnel's blackness as the strobe pulsed behind him. One hand steadying the writing case, the other brushing the tunnel wall, he ran.

<<>>

Smiling, Tank watched on the monitor. As the woman pushed off, he executed the command, lurching the cab upward and flipping her back. Hitting the edge of the shaft squarely on her back, she reverse-flipped forward and disappeared into the shaft.

In that same moment, the angel arrived from a tear in space, reaching into the open shaft. Looking over the edge into the scream, he pulled back. Unable to watch.

"*Yeah baby, we got her. Nice try, Raphael. You're too slow. Ha!*"

Mayhem and Madness celebrated with delighted shouts as Karen's high-pitched scream rushed toward them. Tank jolted upright as it passed just beyond the closed doors. Moving down and away, a muffled crunch and silence followed.

He hadn't considered a scream and was surprised by the volume. *So loud... so loud... Someone will be looking. What do we do? It was an accident. I was in the lobby and heard it.... What scream? I was at the trash compactor. I didn't hear anything....*

Madness answered first, "*They will know you did it.*"

"*Yeah, they're not stupid like you, Tank.*"

"They'll see it on your computer, idiot. Even if you erase it, they'll still find it."

"You are going to be arrested, and you'll be on the news, stupid."

"Yeah, Mom is going to be really pissed off."

Tank's heart was pounding. *Stay cool. Stay cool. It was an accident, a bad, bad, accident—that's all.*

A siren droned in the distance, closing fast.

Erase? Erase? How do we erase...? Should we run? No, they'll know for sure. Stay cool. Figure it out.

"The roof, Tank. I think you better go to the roof."

"It's the best option, Tank. The roof..."

"Better hurry. They're coming right now." Mayhem and Madness bit on their tongues and fingers trying not to laugh. *"The roof, Tank—look, they're here now."*

Tank ducked into the stair tower as a police car entered the garage. Panting, he lumbered up the stairs. One hand braced on the wall, he paused, gulping for air. He then stumbled up several more steps, tripping on one and slamming his knee on a hard corner before pushing himself upright. *Hurry. One more flight. Get to the top. Just get to the top...*

Bursting through the door, he heard more sirens. At the edge, he looked over. A group of teenagers stood smoking beneath the glowing streetlight.

"It's for the best. You better jump, Tank. If you hide, they'll find you."

"It's the only option. It'll be fast, just like her...."

Fast, yes, and finally free. The wind felt good in his face as he flew. Glass and red sky rushing past in a blur, he soared. A little over eighty miles per hour, he hit the pavement still smiling.

<<>>

Batush staggered out of the tunnel, tumbling into the bricks with one hand on the writing case, the other breaking his fall. A glowing luminescence emanated from the gaps between the shed's roof planks. He considered heading to the library for a lantern and then changed his mind. A numb weariness overtook him as he stared at the chaos of scattered brick. He then thought of Meraiah, wondering what time it might be. *The bricks can wait.*

Lifting and pushing the dilapidated door, he peered into the night.

A full moon hung in a gap between crawling clouds, a knee-deep layer of fog hugging the earth. He walked into the lonely beauty, following the path to the road below and home.

His legs as heavy as stone, he nearly tripped, his head and limbs clogged in stunned numbness. He struggled to recall the day's events, giving up as they jumbled. *Lord, help me remember. I want to remember all of it.*

The moon's position suggested it was nearly first watch. Again, he thought of Meraiah. *Be careful on the road, only last week there was another Goth attack.*

He drew his hood up as cold mist stung his face, the iridescent night ebbing to darkness. The thick fog was waist depth at the bottom of the hill where the path merged with the familiar cobbles of Curetes Street. He didn't see or hear it coming. From behind, it struck just above the neck. He crumpled, enveloped in blackness.

<<>>

They were in the corridor when they heard the second scream, this one coming from outside. Nick ran through the penthouse to the open balcony, Amber right behind him.

Arriving first, he braced an arm to stop her. "Don't look. Don't."

Amber recoiled, turning her face from the crushed body below the streetlight surrounded by teenagers and a symmetrical red splash. Gasping, she buried her face into his chest.

He held her sobbing body. It felt good and right to hold her in his arms.

~~

Asmodeus whispered but only to his brothers, *"We did well today. And, Moaz, you redeemed yourself. You will be rewarded."*

PART II

To the angel of the church in Ephesus write: The One who holds the seven stars in His right hand, the One who walks among the seven golden lampstands, says this: I know your deeds and your toil and perseverance, and that you cannot tolerate evil men, and you put to the test those who call themselves apostles, and they are not, and you found them to be false, and you have perseverance and have endured for My name's sake, and have not grown weary.

Revelation 2:1-3

CHAPTER 16

THE ANGELS faced one another on the windswept plain. They waited. Each had responded to the call, arriving moments apart at the location where they always met when receiving directives.

In every direction, it was perfectly flat to the distant horizon, the surface like a sea of silica, reflecting the colors of the overhead expanse. Today, it ebbed and flowed deep hues of sapphire and emerald split apart with flowing currents of lapis and ruby. If the kaleidoscope were to emit sound, Raphael imagined it would be like that of rolling thunder. A rushing layer of mist hugged the plain, parting at the ankle line. It was windy, as it was always, sweeping toward them from all directions.

They stood at the rift, a fissure in the glass, seven of them on each side. The rift varied in width between three and four strides, having knife-sharp edges. It was the destination of the wind and fog, flowing over the edge in a continuous Niagara. He had approached it once, long ago in fearful wonder, beholding a sight he would never forget. The jagged cut was precisely vertical and very deep. Peering into the abyss that day, he saw what appeared to be stars, churning in liquid obsidian.

The fire was centered between them, hovering over the rift at knee height. Its fuel source being itself, centered within. Without a base, it flared outward, uniform in circumference. Like the pilot coals of a furnace, it rested now, waiting to ignite. Waves of heat pulsated as the fireball's shape morphed in unison with the shifting tide above.

The angels had met here countless times throughout the eons. For Raphael, it had always been a humbling experience. His emotions ebbed and surged in synchronicity with the throbbing fire. Although he stood in the presence of his beloved comrades and his fiercest enemies, his attention was riveted to the fire.

Gabriel was the first to speak, his powerful voice booming across the divide. "We are gathered to receive a message of challenge." Swept away by the wind, the spiritual beings heard the message reverberating in their core. Gabriel stood in the center of his row, Raphael on his right, Michael to his left.

Glaring with unyielding stance, the Prince of the Air responded from his mirrored position on the other side. "We are ready for any challenge. Any place—any time." Delivered with no emotion, a soft whisper of seething hatred emanated from the beautiful being.

Asmodeus stood next to him across from Raphael, his posture less revealing than his master's. His whisper interrupted, spoken deep within Raphael's mind, *"You are—"*

Closing his eyes, Raphael lifted his hand, repelling the words. *"I will not listen to your lies and taunts. Not here—not now."*

The Holy Fire flared with pounding flashes of golden orange and yellow, intensifying in rapid succession. Raphael drew a soft gasp, his spirit trembling.

Having experienced it many times, he was never prepared for that which was about to unfold. Conflicting emotions of fear and exhilaration surged within as a memory darted through his mind—the day they held back mountains of churning waters, he and the others. Myriads and myriads, standing in defiance of the torrents, protecting God's chosen, and then crushing Pharaoh's army.

There was no turning away—the sequence had commenced. The fireball exploded then in a nova, like burning metal. The wave of power struck at the knees a millisecond before the shockwave, blasting them backward.

Raphael met the silica with his forearms and chest, digging in with his fingers to break the backward slide. The sand in front of his face reflected the erupting sky, blinding white through eyes squeezed shut. Unable to breathe, he surrendered to the crushing weight, his heart pounding.

The thundering voice like no other followed, shaking the ground, flowing through his frame like rushing water.

"RISE AND LISTEN."

The weight lifted as the One with Many Names spoke. Struggling to his knees, Raphael squinted, his head tilted in wonder. Rising out of the fire, waves of pounding heat flowing from His form clad in white linen, a golden sash across His chest. His face glowed like liquid metal, burning with the brilliance of the sun. Flowing white hair framed eyes of fire that understood all and knew all.

He engaged Raphael's soul, mind, and spirit. Without moving, He saw them all. Across the chasm, the inner ugliness of the dark angels was exposed in flashes of truth.

Repulsed by the demons struggling to their knees, transforming from creatures of beauty to gargoyle-like monsters, Raphael's skin crawled. Their robes flashed from white linen to black silk, and then back again. He focused on Asmodeus, reminded of his adversary's true evil. Clad in the copper scales of a snake, with drooling fangs to match, he bore hands and feet like that of a bear with the talons of an eagle. An oozing tumor, twice the size of his head protruded from his left shoulder. The smile being his only recognizable feature snarled from a doglike face with the glaring yellow eyes of a cat.

Again, the voice thundered like a ripping torrent.

"THE SEALS ARE BROKEN, AND MY CHURCH SHALL BE TESTED."

It was still then, the wind silenced like a hushed breath. The fog began to dissipate, lifting as it vaporized.

He spoke again.

"TWO OF YOU WILL CONTEND FOR MY BRIDE, MY EPHESUS, WHO HAS LOST HER FIRST LOVE."

Raphael and Asmodeus rose to their feet. Just the two of them as the winds returned, the eternal rushing winds of time.

CHAPTER 17

THE MEN entered quietly, taking their favored positions. Any eye contact was unintentional. After sitting, they gradually lifted their gazes. Reluctant yet resolved, they acknowledged one another with pursed nods. The somber silence was measured by the ticking schoolroom wall clock. Daniel stared at its reflection on the mahogany slab.

"Apparently, it was a murder." All eyes turned to Nick Hamilton. "I spoke with the detective this morning. There's not a lot to speculate on. The building's surveillance system captured it on video, which backs up to the cloud. They can also look at the keystrokes and see where they match up with the video." He spread his hands. "It won't be official for another few days, but that's about it. Looks like he picked her out of the blue... Who can say?"

Face blanched, he shrugged. "Amber and I actually heard her scream.... It was horrible. We were in the hallway and heard it coming up the elevator shaft. I've never heard anything like... We didn't know it was Karen until later. But we saw him on the pavement."

Silence held the room for about thirty seconds as one by one they turned away.

Paul Chambers cleared his throat. "Pastor Jason, can you update us on the family and funeral plans?"

Daniel swallowed, the lump in his throat unmoved.

Jason took his glasses off and laid them on the table. "This is one of those times when it's just impossible to understand why something like this happens. The Apostle Peter, writing to the scattered believers, would have said it this way... I know you're hurting and suffering, but stand firm in the grace of your salvation. This struggle we face is short, but remember, we press on, living in righteousness and waiting for our Lord's return. And this is our hope—He is coming again, and we will see Him and be with Him."

As Jason engaged them, his gentle gaze moved from one to the next, some with glassy eyes, others with heads bowed. "I shared this with Bruce and his two sons, and that will be my message at the funeral. They're going to be okay. Their faith is strong. Gentlemen, this is the time when we need to shepherd our flock. This is what eldering is all about."

Daniel drew a stuttering breath. "When I think of Karen... I'll remember her smile and mischievous personality. The other day—we were right here—and she said... Well, she was teasing me and laughing... Karen had the gift of joy, and she was the face of the church. When people walked in the door, it was Karen they saw, shining the love of Christ to them and all of us. If you think about it..."

Paul broke the hushed moment, "I think we should spend a few minutes in prayer." The men nodded as he began, "Father God, You know each of us and how we're hurting. But, Lord... Lord, we thank you for Karen's life and her service to the church and all of us. We ask You to be with Bruce and the boys. Wrap Your big arms around them and comfort them, Lord, with Your peace. Give us the right words and help us to be sensitive. Thank You also for being in control of all things, even when we don't understand."

It was quiet again except for the ticking clock and buzzing fluorescents.

Placing flat hands on the table, Paul stood and then rubbed his face. "Guys, this is hard—and even though we don't feel like it, I'm going to need your attention. I thought about putting this off. But we asked Amber to stay in town to meet with us, and she has. She'll be joining us in a couple minutes." Paul held his timer, slowly shaking it up and down. "I know you guys are going to have some questions, but... I need us to remember Amber's just been through a trauma. She's strong, and I'm not saying we should treat her any differently because she's a woman. But try to be sensitive. I've got my timer, and if it starts to get out of control, I'll be using it, understand?"

Nick swiped his phone. "She's on her way up right now. I'll bring her in, but I'd like to add a couple thoughts." He stood. Fanning his hand slowly, he lifted his pointer finger to his lips. "Our chairman has given us good advice. Be sensitive but also know you can ask anything you want. I believe you will all find Ms. Lash to be quite impressive.

"I had the opportunity to spend some time with her. I walked her through our history and shared our vision in where we want to lead the church." He opened his hands and then stopped. "I'm wanting to share more but hesitant—I believe it should wait until after the interview."

Daniel was about to shake his head when he caught himself. *Forgive me, Lord. Give us wisdom and peace. We need You.*

Nick arched his brows to Paul. "I think we're ready. Was this going to be an open session?"

"Oh yeah, uh... The interview will be an executive session. Pastor, you've already met Amber, and we or... I was thinking because the executive pastor will be functioning side by side with you but under us... Or we'll be in the position of providing oversight that is... And if we hire Amber, she wouldn't be your boss, but you would be working together. Both of you would be under the power—or headship actually of us—your elders. Is this making any sense, or am I just confusing myself?"

Paul gave his goatee a tug. Then performing a double-take freeze stare, he finalized it with eyes bulging. Daniel joined the others with a laugh to break the tension.

Jason offered a forced smile, biting on the corner of his lower lip. "I believe I will look forward to whatever decision you make. For me, it's about submission. When I'm here, I submit to your headship as my elders. But it's mutual, of course, because when I'm ministering to you like I just did... All of you are submitting to me as your pastor. You see, that's the beauty of the church. It's very different from a business, isn't it?" Jason stared at Paul as they stood.

Paul clapped a hand on Jason's shoulder. "Thanks, Pastor, for joining us tonight and ministering to us. You're right. The church is a beautiful thing, and we want to thank you for pointing that out... um, as beautifully as you did."

<<>>

Batush opened his eyes to a swirling blur, his head pounding. "Whe– where am...? Where is...?"

The blur faded to gray.

A muffled reply hovered over him, the words garbled, "Batush. You are... with... here... safe."

Feeling like he was tumbling backward, he gripped the bedsheets as gray yielded to darkness.

CHAPTER 18

"HELLO GENTLEMEN. I'm honored and pleased to join you. I just want to say how much I appreciate your time because I know how important your work is." Amber's heart quickened as she offered her perfected smile, the one radiating a seductive charm and innocence blended with a quiet self-assuredness. She wore the tight gray dress-suit. Spreading her hands, she continued, "This is a little intimidating. I don't think I've ever been interviewed by seven gentlemen as handsome as all of you, but I believe, I'm going to enjoy this." Her tension lifted as the men laughed.

"The pleasure is truly ours, Amber. We want you to know how much we appreciate you staying in town in order to join us, especially considering the tragic events. It must have been awful. Please know we've all been praying for you." Paul leaned forward, hands clasped on the tabletop, buzzer at his elbow. "How are you doing? Are you okay, or...? Is there anything we can do for you?"

"Remember her and tell them to pray."

"Thanks, you have done so much already. The condo is beautiful and... But yes, it was difficult—being there when it happened. I'm just grateful Mr. Hamilton was there for support. I can't imagine what it would have been like to go through that alone." She nodded to Nick, then turned to the others, her eyes welling up.

Henry Williams reached for a box that was passed to Paul, who extended it as a gift.

Pulling a tissue, Amber dabbed the corners of her eyes. "I must have pushed it out of my mind, but it's all rushing back. But... It must be so much harder for all of you. You knew Karen, and I just met her the one time. What I saw in her was kindness and hospitality. She was such a beautiful woman, I wish... I will remember her as my friend. I would just ask you to pray for her family—for peace and comfort."

"That's plenty—move on."

"Is there anything I can do for any of you or for the family?"

Lewis cleared his throat. "It's inspiring to be here with you. Clearly, you've been blessed with the gift of mercy and helps."

"What a clown. Stroke them with a little respect."

"I'm not sure what you mean by helps, but I certainly see the sensitivity and discernment evident in all of you."

"Perfect. Now wait."

Paul Chambers eased back, folding his hands across his protruding belly, his thumbs tapping each other in a satisfied rhythm. "Men, this is a sweet moment, sitting here watching all of you—ministering to Amber and to each other. I just wanted to share that." His voice cracked at the edges. "Leading a church can be challenging at times, but we still have to do the work. You've had some time to look over Amber's résumé. So, I'd like to open it up for questions. If there is anything, anything at all you want to ask—keeping it in bounds, of course. I mean, don't ask about her underwear or something dumb."

A couple of the men chuckled uncomfortably as Paul shifted his weight.

"Seriously, guys... If you have anything on your mind, now's the time. That's why I called an executive session without staff because, if we do hire Amber, she'll be the CEO of the church. Even though we're all family, the executive pastor will be the boss."

Lewis Kolsby lifted a slender finger from his chin. His gaunt face, slightly ashen and wrinkled, needed a shave. The slicked-back white hair and tired pinstriped long-sleeve accentuated his feeble frame. "After reading your testimony, I'd like you to please share what faith means to you?"

"Abraham was called. And don't forget prayer."

"When I think about faith, I'm reminded of Abraham. He was called by God, and not knowing where he was going, he stepped out in obedience and went. And that's why prayer is so important. Because without it, we're not able to hear God's voice when He's speaking to us. I'm not sure I'm making sense—does that help?"

"It does, yes. Thank you." Lewis nodded, the long finger returning to his chin.

Henry followed, "Amber, I read these documents and was very impressed. I just wanted to say that." He released his red suspender straps with a snap.

"Henry, do you have a question for Amber?" Paul smiled at Amber, raising his eyebrows.

"No, no, that was it. What I'm saying here, I mean, when you look over these reference letters and accomplishments and everything else here... This is high-caliber stuff. I mean, let's face it—it doesn't get much better than this." Henry waved a hand over the documents.

Nick waited with elbows on the table, the tips of his mirrored fingers touching like a spider on glass. "Gentlemen, it is no coincidence this candidate sits here tonight. This is the Lord's work. We've been talking about reorganization for a full year, and now, we have the potential to make a strategic hire. Amber Lash has the finesse, the boldness, and also the sensitivity to execute a reorg. Doing it is one thing, but doing it well—without upsetting the flock—will be a challenge."

He stood and began to pace. Stopping, he engaged eyes with each man and then leveled on her. "If we were to hire you with the intention being the execution of a reorg...? One: Would you be interested in the job? And two: How would you plan to accomplish it? And lastly—and this may be the most important question of all."

She sat up straighter, arched her back, and lifted her chin.

"As you know, we're struggling, and if that doesn't change, our days as an organization are numbered. Now that's a lot of pressure. As a woman—are you prepared for that? The responsibility of the church would be in your hands."

"Give it to them straight."

"Well, that's quite a question or series of questions, but I appreciate your boldness in asking. So I'll be equally direct in answering." Amber let her eyes of emerald float from one to the next. "First of all, yes. I'm interested in the job. I see it as a challenge, and challenge has always motivated me. Secondly, I agree reorganization is needed, especially given your challenges with the struggling attendance and finances."

"Pour it out—they need the cold truth."

"When I met with the smaller group, I talked about taking the pulse of the organization and not making changes right away. But then, Nick and I went over the financials on Thursday. The day when..."

"Stay on topic!"

"You know, when *it* happened... But, considering the numbers, and Nick agrees, something needs to be done right away. If we wait, the holidays will be on top of us, and we'd then need to wait for the dust to clear. What I am saying is... The church is hanging by a thread, and that thread is ready to snap."

"Between the eyes."

"If I were leading, I would approach it like I did when I bought my business. If you're wanting a clean break from the past, well—regardless of, who you hire—I believe it will be important for that individual to establish themselves early on."

Paul let go of his goatee and leaned forward. "Go on, Amber. Trust me, you're making a lot of sense. Understand, most of us have been in leadership. We get it."

"It's time to be bold. Not only to reorganize but also to reimage. The purging can be done with compassion, but the rebuilding will be exciting. Breathing life into something that's dead—there's nothing better than that. It's like remodeling an old house. You decide to do it and move forward, but what you get is transformation. A new and beautiful creation, and it's yours." She spread her hands, bobbing her head.

"Nehemiah, the wall..."

"I believe the Spirit has a word for us. I didn't plan this, but right now, I'm hearing: Nehemiah. Do you remember when he rebuilt the walls of Jerusalem? He did it because the people were hurting and vulnerable, and he had compassion and acted, remember? Now think about that—what did he do first?"

"The rubble..."

Nick jumped in, "He started with a bold decision and went to the king for approval like we're doing here. And then, he financed the entire operation, getting the money for the timbers to build the gates." He stabbed the table with his pointer finger.

"Financed the gates? Like he was there—what a fool..."

"Correct you are, Nick." She took control again. "Nehemiah rolled out his plan and rallied the people around his vision. But they started with the foundation, clearing the rubble before rebuilding. And then, the people were protected, at peace, and comforted—ready to move forward and to grow and prosper.

"If you hire me, I would rebuild the walls of Faith Bible Church. Doing nothing about the condition of this church would not only be sad, but it would also be wrong. We—all of us, I believe—would be squandering our responsibility."

<<>>

When Batush opened his eyes, Zophar stood over him holding a wet cloth. Batush blinked, straining to focus, his head still pounding. "Where—where is...? The book—do you have it?"

"The book is safe, Batush." Zophar leaned down, dabbing at his forehead. "A bit wet and smeared, but legible. It is drying by the fire. We have hot soup and bread when you are ready."

Beyond a blur of mud walls and timbered ceiling came the steady patter of rain. Then, again, the silhouetted shape. *Zophar...*

The tumbling sensation again sweeping him away, Batush murmured, "Meraiah, Sarah—where?"

"I sent Gibeon to tell them what happened. He is bringing them as we speak. They will be here soon, my friend. Soon."

Batush exhaled, surrendering again to the fog and darkness.

CHAPTER 19

VINCE FOGEL lifted his fingers from the keyboard. "Do you have any thoughts, Amber, about who you would be looking for as new hires?"

His face—well tanned and cleanly shaven—along with his spiked yellow hair worn in a taut crew cut conveyed a look younger than his years. Sharply dressed, with olive khakis and crisp tucked-in short-sleeves, the aspiring politician clearly valued image and made regular visits to the gym a priority.

"That's a good question. I haven't studied the demographics in detail, but what I'm mostly seeing is an older population. But, when I was downtown, I also noticed a lot of young people and children. I'm not saying old is bad, and old money can certainly have advantages." She leaned back in her chair as the men chuckled. *Men—all the same, so easy to manipulate.* "I'm thinking our goal would be a more diverse and younger look. And that's not exclusive to congregation and staff. I'm talking about vision and image. Programs and music that will attract the youth.

"As an example, when I toured the worship center, I noticed the pipe organ and choir platform. The organ is impressive, and I'm sure the choir sings beautifully—but honestly... Millennials are not going to show up for that. Most growing churches have a band and video presence. And—"

"We've got the only pipe organ in Palm Desert," Henry interrupted. "A parishioner donated it, and our choir sings some wonderful music, let me tell you. Some of our choir members have been singing with us for twenty years plus. You should come visit one of our organ concerts. The care homes bus in the folks and fill the place."

Paul rapped the table with his plastic hammer. "Will you listen to yourself, Henry? It's no wonder we're struggling—most of the choir are retirees, and we're busing in the dying folks. Some are giving, but most of them are stingy old goats."

"Smooth it over."

Amber leaned across the tabletop toward Henry, gently unfurling her fingers to lay flat with palm raised. "I'm not proposing we get rid of the organ or the choir. That's part of our heritage, and we want to honor that. I'm just suggesting we consider shifting the focus toward more contemporary music. Perhaps a band could be blended with the organ? And the choir might be highlighted for special services, like Christmas and Easter."

When Henry responded with a reluctant nod, she spread her hands to the others. "I see so much potential. Did you know more than fifty thousand people live within five miles of this campus? A lot of minority families are moving in, and not far from here, there's an art district and a farmer's market. I'm seeing a harvest waiting to be gathered. And if we don't bring it in, who will—and why shouldn't it be us?"

Nick gripped the back of his chair, bending forward over the table. "Gentlemen, some of this is difficult to hear, but Amber's saying all the things we've been talking about. I, for one, am humbled and honored to be part of this. This candidate has vision, and the Holy Spirit is clearly speaking through her. These are exciting times—the Lord is working in our midst."

"Daniel—here it comes."

Daniel unfolded his arms. "I want to summarize what I believe I'm hearing you say. If we hire you, you'd establish yourself by firing the staff. You would then hire some new, younger, and fresher-looking faces. You'd also change the music and ministry, in order to attract a younger congregation. Is that what you're saying?"

Paul leaned forward, nearly standing. "Daniel, I think you're being a little harsh with our guest. I understand you know her from your past, but honestly, you're being rude."

"Cut him loose—let him dangle."

Amber waved a hand toward Daniel. "No, that's fine. Really—I understand this is hard, but I'd like to respond. My answer is yes, Daniel. That's exactly what I'm proposing. I don't agree with how you phrased it, but yes, that's what needs to be done. And what I would say to you, Daniel, and all of you..." Amber dropped her fist on the table. "Each of you has a decision to make. This church is dying. I'm available to do the heavy lifting if you're willing to hire me. And if you are going to disre..." Her voice cracked.

"Easy."

"That's okay, Amber."

"Let her finish."

"Leading is hard, Daniel—but I'm good at it, and maybe you're not. And that's okay. Each of us has different strengths and weaknesses." She glared at him and then turned away.

Paul shifted in his chair. "Earl, we haven't heard from you? You're always so quiet. What are you thinking, brother?"

Earl was leaning back. His arms, folded across his abdomen, crinkled an overly tight and soiled polo. His poorly dyed purple-brown hair gave him the appearance of an elderly Elvis impersonator. *Surely, he must be single. No wife would have let him leave the house like that. And if she had, I don't want to meet her.* Noticing his ringless finger, Amber stifled a smirk.

"We need to do something—this place is dead. What we need around here is the Holy Spirit. That's my opinion. I'll leave it at that."

Paul leaned forward. With elbows on the table, wrists together, he slowly clapped his fingertips. "Any more questions for our guest? Speak up, guys—now's the time." The room was quiet. "Amber, do you have any questions for us?"

"Get authority."

"I'm not expecting an answer right now, but I would want it addressed if I were to take the job. I would need clarity on my authority in terms of hiring and firing and making ministry decisions and if there would be spending caps. It sounds a little corporate—but the position, if I was to accept, would be, I heard someone say, CEO of the church. So, I would want you to discuss that and let me know." Amber smiled at Paul.

"Perfect, that was beautiful."

Paul stood and then fanned his hands as the others rose. "I just want to say, from all of us, how much we appreciate your honesty and the wisdom you shared tonight. I think we're about ready to make a decision, but before you go, we'd like to gather 'round and pray over you, if that would be okay?"

"I would be honored, thank you."

~~

Asmodeus waited until the prayers began. It was the touch that allowed him to move between the bodies, all of them being safe except two. It was a victory dance of sorts. Whispering insults, lies, and temptations, he darted from one to the next as they took turns praying.

"Look at those beautiful breasts. No—don't look, that's bad. Wait, it's okay. Take another peek. Grace, remember? You're already forgiven...? Don't you wish you could touch them? It's just a harmless fantasy—old men will dream dreams, right?"

He encountered two old friends. "Mammon, you beautiful sack of vomit! It's been a long time. How's the project coming?"

"Very well, master. We're halfway there. He thinks the enemy is blessing him with great wealth—such a fool. We are building his confidence slowly like you said. He will soon be stealing from his friends—I promise you. Humans never change. It is so easy."

"And you there, Longshanks. We need to stop meeting like this. Tell me, how are you faring, good sir?" Asmodeus slapped him on the back.

"I am excellent, as usual, and quite hungry. His liver weakens by the day—look, I have been clawing and gnashing. Be sure to tell him, he deserves a drink to celebrate the meeting. Oh yes, remind him again, his hard work is paying off, and his plan will help so many churches." Longshanks roared to tears. "I have been encouraging him also, but your words are so convincing, master."

Asmodeus continued the rounds, here and there and then back again. Stopping short of the bodies he could not enter, he hurled some encouragements.

"Daniel is a problem. Allowing him in was a mistake. You tried to warn them, but they're so stupid. But tonight, we celebrate. This is going to work.

"Go ahead—no one's watching—take another look. So sweet, I wonder what it would be like...? She wants you, you know, and she's so beautiful. Look at her... Don't worry about the husband—he can't even please her. But you could. It would be a blessing for her and even for him. It would be a secret—our secret. Like it never happened..."

CHAPTER 20

BATUSH SLURPED another spoonful. The hot broth warmed his soul. Spiced with yellow curry and red pepper, it was a favorite, but nothing compared to the sight of Meraiah. He met her hand with his to help steady the spoon. She smiled with warm eyes, blinking back tears of relief and a richness of love cultivated over a lifelong relationship and nearly six decades of marriage. He reflected the smile, the dizziness gone now but not the lingering ache at the back of his head. *Thank You, Lord. I am so blessed to have her.*

"You did a lot of talking in your sleep. It must have been quite a dream." Withdrawing the spoon, Meraiah leaned over him, her hand cupping his cheek.

"What did I say?"

"You talked endlessly about a book, and you were also speaking to an angel. An angel named Raphael, who was helping you?" Lifting her brows, she tilted her head.

"Where—is it here?" A sharp pain shot up his neck as he tried to lift his head.

Zophar intervened, "The book is here, Batush. It is safe. But you, my friend, have been through much and need to rest."

"My tools—where... Do I have my writing case?"

"The case is here, but your tools are gone, all but your blotter and stamp."

"I must go to the library—to make a copy of the book. Raphael was quite clear—I must transcribe a copy and take the original to the elders. But how can I, and... How long was I sleeping?" The shed and the exposed tunnel flashed through his mind.

Zophar placed a hand on his shoulder. "You can work here, Batush. It might be better for you to make the copy here."

"But I will need pen and ink—and parchment."

"Indeed. I sent Gibeon to your home. He is getting them as we speak. Rest and let your bride feed you. You should see yourself—you are quite the sight. Apparently, you were attacked by robbers. You are lucky to be alive."

Batush patted the top of his head.

"That's right, my friend, and you do not smell so good either. Rest some more, and then Meraiah will bathe you. The book can rest—and you can rest."

<<>>

Two bowls were passed around the conference table. One, which seemed to never empty was filled with assorted wrapped candies. The second overflowed with overly salted stale popcorn. Daniel passed both to Henry, opting for bottled water. As the men chatted and munched, some of them milling about, strangely he felt alone. *I'm never going to be one of this group....*

"Okay, guys, I know it's late, but I'm thinking of taking a straw poll. Let's have some discussion and then see where everyone's at." Paul Chambers tossed a glance toward the hanging schoolroom clock—10:22.

Henry snapped his suspenders and then rubbed his hands together. "I think Amber's tremendous. She has the experience and has done this kind of thing before. Making changes like she did with her company—and really getting it going. I think we should hire her and you know—that's the way it goes."

Nick stretched. "Does anyone have a problem with her in the pastoral role being a woman?"

Daniel straightened his back, a little surprised, expecting another long call to action speech. *Now, that's a first. What's his angle?* "I have a problem with it."

Everyone rotated.

"And what's your problem, Daniel?" Paul emphasized his irritation.

"Well, *problem* might not be the best word choice. But I do have a concern. Scripture says women are to be silent in the church. I understand that was written a long time ago when the culture was very different. But the principle is that God established a leadership structure for the family and the church. I'm not saying men are more qualified than women—I'm just saying God placed the leadership responsibility on men. As executive pastor, Amber would be running the church. She wouldn't be over us, because we're elder-led, but she would be in the meetings and have a lot of influence."

Daniel fanned his hands out. "Faith Bible is a community church with a fairly diverse congregation. Some will be okay with it, but others are going to have a problem. We need to be sensitive about that, and that's my concern."

"Okay—what do you think about Daniel's point?" Yawning, Paul rubbed his face.

Nick lifted his pointer finger. "What if we give her the title *minister* instead of pastor? That would frame her in the role of serving rather than leading. She wouldn't be preaching, but we would want her up front making announcements and putting a face on ministry. A man would be preaching, and he would have the title of *pastor*."

Heads nodded.

The room jumped to another snap from Henry's suspenders. "I like that. I move we hire Amber as executive minister of Faith Bible Church."

Paul glared at Henry, arching his brows. "Henry, I didn't call for a motion yet. I think we need more discussion. What do you think, guys? If we give Amber the title executive minister or director, would we consider her for the position?"

Lewis Kolsby hoisted a slender finger from its resting positing at his temple. His head remained tilted as if propped. "I'm okay with any of the titles, and I don't have a problem with a woman having authority over men. Look around, it's everywhere. And I don't have a problem with her preaching either. Not every week—but I think a woman in the pulpit might attract a younger crowd."

Paul scanned the group. "Any more thoughts on the woman thing?" He waited. "Okay, so what do you think about hiring Amber? Do we need to talk some more or are we ready to vote?"

Suddenly dizzy, Daniel closed his eyes. *Shouldn't we check her references or pray about it? This is crazy.*

Henry blurted, "I think we need a motion."

"Whoa, Henry. I want an answer to my question first. Vince and Earl, the two of you have been quiet?"

Vince looked up from his keyboard. "I've been listening to the group dynamic. I think we agree—Amber has a lot of talent and would be an excellent choice. I also agree with Lewis. It would be good to have a woman up front presenting a softer face. But I'm not so sure about having her preach—we don't even know if she can, but I wouldn't be surprised. Amber Lash is quite impressive, and we saw how she handled herself in front of us. And that's not easy for the average woman. I know my wife couldn't do it—she'd be scared to death. I also sense some tension in the room. Maybe it's the woman in leadership issue—I'm not so sure, but we need to flush it out. But I like her and think we should make her an offer."

"What about you, Earl, what do you think?"

"We need to be led by the Holy Spirit—that's what we need around here. And as I sat here and listened to this woman, I'm not so sure my spirit was resonating with her. I also agree with Daniel, putting a woman in charge of a church isn't wise. It might be fine in the business world, but this here is a church. This is the Body of Christ, and we need to be looking to the Scriptures and not making compromises." Earl folded his arms, nodding to Daniel.

"Anything else—Daniel?" Paul waved his yellow hammer.

"I guess I have an observation. In both meetings, I noticed Amber spoke about herself a lot. For me, it came across as being self-focused. She mentioned her husband and grandchild, but it felt like a show to me. I also know her from the past, and she, well... Maybe I shouldn't say."

"Go on. You can't say you're going to say and then not say." Paul shook his head back and forth.

Daniel shifted, torn between wanting to speak and wanting to let it go. He swallowed. "When I knew her—it's been a long time, and people can change. But Amber has a way of getting what she wants, and typically, she wants a lot. I guess I'm saying I'm not so sure she's changed."

They stared.

"Anything else?"

"Maybe it's a little picky. But when we asked her spiritual questions, she quoted Scripture. And that's good—I mean, we should all be reading the Word. I try to, and Rhema does—she's really good at it, in fact, but I'm drifting." He spread his hands. "It felt like she was evading. Sort of like, well, like she wasn't being truthful. As if she was saying this is what the Scripture says, but I'm not telling you what I say. Maybe that's a little harsh, but that's the vibe I got." His neck tingled as his face began to flush under their unrelenting stares.

Paul glanced at the ceiling and then back to Daniel. "So, what you're saying is you have a problem with Amber because she's a woman and she quotes too much Scripture. But you also think we all should be doing more of what she is doing—quoting the Scriptures. Is that what you're telling us?" He rubbed his face and then shook his head. "Are you sure it doesn't have something to do with your past? I mean, she dumped you for your roommate. Are you sure you're not just wanting to get even, or you don't want her at your church?" He leaned toward Daniel, pointing with his hammer.

The memory of an old boss flashed through Daniel's mind. Big and brash, cruel and obnoxious, that man was key in his decision that one day he'd have his own company. Daniel stared at Paul and saw that man. Drawing a slow breath, he calmly spoke matter of fact.

"I'm just telling you what I see. And I can see why you might think those thoughts, and that is why it's hard to be honest. I'll recues myself from the vote if you think I have a conflict or can't be objective—that's fine, I will."

Paul eased back. "No, we want to hear your thoughts, Daniel, but we need—or I need—to be sure you're on the level. And that's why I asked. I wanted to be sure, and I want you to vote. Does everyone agree?"

Nick stood up. "I am seriously concerned with what just took place. We've seen this before. It's not right and needs to be rebuked." Nick began to pace. Stopping in front of Daniel on the other side of the table, he pointed. "This man, an elder mind you, has just slandered a good woman and sister in Christ. This is wrong, and I, for one, do not and will not stand by and accept this." He waved his arms. "Am I alone on this? Does anyone else see what just happened here?"

The others turned to one another, exchanging slow nods with protruding chins and raised brows.

Nick began to pace again, gesturing as he spoke. "Amber Lash has traveled to meet with us. She is willing to serve in our time of need. And this young man slanders her good name and bases it on his *feelings*? He doesn't *feel* right about her, and he has a *feeling* she's not being truthful and she's self-focused. I believe it is this man who is self-focused and also judgmental. It's not all about you, Daniel, and we don't care about your *feelings*. No, this is wrong." Again, he pointed at Daniel. "This behavior has no place at this table and needs to be stopped right now."

"Maybe you're right." Daniel squared his shoulders and then continued, speaking softly. "But here's the thing. As an elder, it's my job to tell you what I see and think. Each of us is called to sit in judgment on many things. So, I will share my thoughts and feelings, especially when I believe the Spirit is prompting me to speak. And I hope I will also hold my tongue when I believe the Spirit is telling me to be quiet."

"Guys, it's late, and this is getting out of hand." Paul laid his hammer down. "Discussion is good, and both of you are right. We need to be careful in what we're saying, but we also need to share what the Lord is showing us. And that's why this is hard and gets, well, sort of exciting. But let's bring it back to Amber—is there anything else?"

The room was silent.

"Okay, do you guys want to take a straw poll now and vote later? Or we can do the real vote now if we're ready?"

The silence continued.

"Do I have a motion?"

Nick stood at the far end of the table, his hand on the back of the chair. "I move we draft the acquisition documents as necessary to execute the hire of Amber Lash to the position of executive minister of Faith Bible Church."

Daniel stared as Nick spoke cryptically as if reading from notes. *I thought I knew this man, who is he?*

"Said documents shall grant full hiring and firing authority to the executive minister, with the exception of the senior pastor, which shall require Elder Board approval. Additionally, the executive minister shall have the authority to spend church funds to further ministry, with a ceiling limit not to exceed twenty thousand dollars, for any single expenditure, without Elder Board approval."

Too fast... Daniel's head was swimming. *We haven't talked about spending authority or hiring and firing, not to mention salary. Do they understand?*

"Discussion...?" Paul looked to the men as the room remained quiet.

Daniel's mind raced forward in a panic.

"Do I have a second?"

Henry flexed his suspenders, running the insides of his thumbs up and down the straps. "I second the motion."

Daniel gripped his water bottle as Henry spoke, his lips seemingly moving in slow motion.

"All in favor say yea."

Four of the men replied.

"All opposed—same sign?"

Daniel and Earl lifted a hand.

"We have four yeas and two opposed. But I didn't vote, and my vote is yes, which makes it five to two in favor. Looks like we have a decision, but I wish we could be together on this."

Earl Dempsey unfolded his arms. "For the sake of unity, I'll change my vote."

"Thanks, Earl. I really appreciate that. Daniel—how 'bout you?"

Daniel pursed a smile. "Sorry... My vote stands."

Paul dropped his head, covering his mouth with a fist. "Now that we have a decision, we need to stand together. And we all need to support and pray for our new pastor—or minister, I mean. Can I count on that from all of you—including you, Daniel?" He shuffled his papers as Daniel offered a nod.

"I'm going to close us in prayer, and I want to thank each of you. These are exciting times for our future, and it's a blessing to be serving with you. I love you, guys, and I mean that—all of you." Paul surveyed the table, his roaming gaze falling on Daniel—the new elder who had voted no.

CHAPTER 21

QUILL IN HAND, he leaned back. It was not a lengthy transcription, and beginning early with a single break for lunch, he had completed the copy before dusk. Then he read and back-checked it twice, comparing the copy to the original. Batush finished as he started. "Lord, I thank Thee for granting me the strength to complete this task and for Thy peace which now resides in my frame. I know not what lies ahead, yielding that burden to You. Use me, Lord, as Your messenger, I pray in Thy Son's name. Amen."

A man named John had authored the scroll, which included several clues identifying him as the Apostle. The book also described a being, who appeared to John dressed in a robe with a golden sash. His face and hair were white like snow, and His feet glowed like heated metal. The description went on to say He was dead and now alive.

Clearly, Lord, it is Your Son, the resurrected Christ.

The message itself was one of evaluation, which Jesus had received from the Father and then given to an angel who then spoke it to John. A report of sorts, it included commendations and reproofs, along with calls to return and repent and the promise of a blessing to all who might heed the instruction. The heavenly being told John to write the message in a book and send it to seven churches, one of which was Batush's church, the Church of Ephesus.

He had read the Apostle John's confusing revelation, but this he had never seen. *Could it be this is part of the revelation that begins with the phrase "After these things"? Does this lost letter come first, and the balance of the message then follows? A letter from You, Lord, written to my church—now resting on the table before me. A bit damaged but protected by You. Soon I will deliver it to the Fathers, and after that, it will be in Your hands. The elders are godly men chosen by You. They will decide what to do with it. Give them ears to hear what Your Spirit is speaking to them.*

He rubbed his eyes as fear crept into his mind. *The tool shed and the scattered brick. And the exposed tunnel—what if...?* He flexed his aching fingers. *The bricks can wait. We will return in two days when I am scheduled for transcription. Before sunrise, the streets will be quiet. Afterward, I will wash at the bathhouse. That will give me time to think and pray. How, Lord, will I explain this?*

"You are a hard worker, my friend. I did not see you look up even once all day. It is good to see the burden now lifting from your shoulders." Zophar pulled up a chair, his white teeth gleaming within the curls of his burly black beard. The big man spread large hands, his dark eyes sparkling. "Now that you have finished, I am hopeful you can smell dinner cooking? Your bride has prepared a stew of lamb and turnips. We have bread also, and Gibeon is brewing coffee—Ethiopian, the very best. You are blessed to have a godly woman like Meraiah. I envy you, stubborn old friend." Zophar chuckled, nudging Batush's thin frame as he cuffed his shoulder.

Sarah burst into the room. "Papa. Did you finish—can I see?"

Batush groaned as he hoisted her to his lap. He then scrolled the copy mounted in the tablet frame for Sarah. The frame held two pins, resting in triangular cradles. Turning one of the pins would advance or retract the parchment over the writing surface. He was working with two tablets, one for his working copy, the other displaying the original.

"Yours is beautiful, but that one is messy and old."

Batush intercepted Sarah's finger just before it touched the book. "You are right. It is very old. It was written by Jesus's best friend. It is sacred and holy."

"Can I touch it?"

"Gently. It is a very special book."

"Where did you get it, Papa?"

Batush lifted his eyes to Zophar. "It was hidden, but an angel named Raphael told me where to find it."

"An angel!" She wiggled on his lap, tilting her head from the scroll to his face. "What did he look like?"

"He was big and strong, the most beautiful sight my eyes have ever seen." Batush touched his finger to her nose. "Well, almost the most beautiful."

"Will he be coming back so I can see him?" Her brown eyes opened wide.

"I hope so."

"Me too." After sliding from his lap, she ran to the kitchen.

"What more can I say? It was..." Batush floated his hand above the original.

Zophar rocked on his heels as he stroked his beard. "You don't need to explain it—I believe you. There are angels all around us, if only men had eyes to see. This book is a calling for you from the Lord—it is quite clear."

"Raphael said I was to make a copy and take the original to the Fathers."

"Then that is what you must do, and I will go with you."

"Zophar, you are my friend and blessing, ministering to me in my time of need, cleaning my wounds, and sitting at my side through the night. You should be working at your shop. You do not need to be there, but I will let you—we will do it together."

Batush patted the copy. "Raphael told me to hide this, but I do not know where. Will you do this for me? Put it where no one will look—a safe but dry place."

"Where could I—wait, I could put it—"

Batush lifted his flat hand. "Don't tell me. It is better if I do not know." Leaning back, they both folded their arms saying nothing. Batush then smiled. "I have another question for you, Zophar, and I believe you know what it is."

"And what is that, dear brother?"

"Why is it you have never taken a wife? It would be good for you and Gibeon as well. Find yourself a young bride who can help you grow old. A strong woman would be a good helper. Someone to keep you warm at night, and you could have more children. More arrows in the quiver are a blessing." Batush poked at Zophar with his fist, cocking his head toward the cot, covered with animal furs. "Why do you not listen?"

"How many times must I tell you? I am content without a wife, and I have my son. I am blessed to live a simple life—a brewer of fine coffee, enjoying the company of so many from all around the world."

"You have never spoken of how it was you lost your wife. It is good for the soul to speak of these things."

"I will share something I have told no one." Zophar frowned at his hands, rubbing them together. "I have never been married. My Gibeon I found when he was just a child. The Goths killed his family, and that is when I saw him in the market. He was no more than three years old.

I had never seen such a young child being sold as a slave. 'What is this world coming to?' I thought. And so, I purchased him and raised him as my own. I taught him the pleasure of working with his hands and that our joy comes from the Almighty. And when he was fully grown, I adopted him as my own."

Batush relented with a nod as Meraiah appeared in the doorway. "Dinner's ready and coffee too."

<<>>

"There it is. Did you see it?"

"I didn't see anything. You're losing it."

"Okay, watch again. I'm slowing it down some more. The guy turned up the camera speed to ensure he didn't miss anything."

"I'm just glad the bastard jumped—saved us all some grief. Are you saying he was planning to watch this later in slow motion?"

"I'm sure he was. Okay, here we go... It's right—here." Detective Ryan Green froze the video, his pulse spiking as he waited. Using the mouse, he advanced it one frame at a time. "See? There it is. It shows up on just three frames. That's a person—look. But he's moving superfast."

"How fast?" His partner stood in the doorway, sipping coffee.

"Fast. The cameras are state of the art. The default setting is one frame every three seconds, but you can adjust it, which he did. He turned it up to full speed—one-hundred-twenty frames a second. The file size is huge. Watch... She goes down... See? And then here—he's at the door. It's blurry, but that's a man. Next frame, his head and arm are in the shaft, and his other hand is on the doorjamb—there. Then next—he's on one knee, looking directly at us. It's fuzzy. But you can see his face, and he's wearing a robe or something. It's white. Next frame—poof, he's gone. But here's the thing—you asked me how fast. That's beyond human fast. I don't know exactly, but I can figure it out. Less than blink-of-an-eye fast."

Scooting back his chair, Ryan looked up, his trigger finger twitching on the mouse. "So, what do you think?"

"Are you saying the guy in the robe pushed her?"

"No. If you count the frames, he's not even there for almost a half second after she's on her way down the shaft, and I can prove it using the equipment. It looks more like he's reaching in to catch her, but he's too late. You want to see it again?"

"No. I think I got it. So, you're saying someone was there and tried to save her? A super-speedy guy. Is that it?" Grimacing, Howard McCain withdrew the green mug from his lips.

"Yeah. We both saw it, and the equipment doesn't lie. You want to see something else?"

"Can't wait."

"Watch... The image is blurry, so I was playing with the settings. The camera has infrared to see in the dark. It's automatic in case the power goes out. But the cameras shoot in both spectrums simultaneously, and we can turn the visual light off—watch."

Ryan clicked on a window and then slid a toggle switch. The background faded to black as the image facing the camera transformed from red to orange, then yellow to bright white. "That's his heat signature. It's hard to see any detail when it's all the way up because he's so hot. He's on fire. A normal person doesn't get this hot. I tried it on myself, and I was only glowing red. When I dial it down, between yellow and orange, it's the clearest. Check this out..."

Scrolling with the mouse, he zoomed in. "Look. See his face...? His nose and mouth? But look at the eyes, they're pure white—that's heat. Now we're zooming in and dialing down the temperature." The eyes expanded, filling the monitor. "Here, at the bottom, and there, in the corners."

The eyes displayed in hues of orange and red with a thick yellow-white line at the base, pooling in the corners.

"Tears? That's what I'm seeing."

"So, the superhero is crying, is that it?" Howard gave his mug a swirl. "Can you add some color and give me a face?"

"I can't, but I bet the lab guys can. I'm going to send it to Los Angeles and see what they think." Ryan scratched his neatly cropped brown hair. "I don't think it's human. It's a ghost or spirit or something, but it's real." He stared at his partner.

The older detective straightened up from the doorjamb and walked away. "It's got to be a mistake. No one moves that fast, and I don't believe in ghosts. And I don't believe in Superman or the Easter Bunny either."

Stopping, he returned to the doorway. "Ryan. Let's keep this between the two of us until we hear from Los Angeles. I don't want to be the laughingstock of the department. If this gets out, they'll be calling us the Ghostbusters."

CHAPTER 22

JASON STOVER checked the dashboard clock and winced. *If I still had Karen, she would have called to be sure I was up—what a disaster.* It began when his alarm didn't go off. *But I'm sure I set it—or did I?* Then, in his rush as he made breakfast, the coffee pot had slipped from his hand, smashing to the floor in a splash of glass and eight cups of scalding mess. He growled. And topping it off, his computer froze when he was trying to print his outline for the funeral—forty minutes. *We're still good. I'll use my handwritten notes. Thank goodness, Joyce is out of town.*

Headed down the two-lane highway, the gated neighborhood behind him, he would soon merge onto the I-10 freeway and be at the church in fifteen minutes. Exhaling, he applied pressure to the gas pedal of his red Mini Cooper. *In spite of the distractions, I know You're in control, Lord. Lift this stress from me now and use me to speak to those who don't know You. Prepare their hearts for Your gospel that they might receive salvation today.*

Rounding the corner, he saw the approaching white delivery truck. Ahead and to his right, a boy on the sidewalk peddled a bicycle.

~~

On the truck's hood, Moaz spread his arms like a surfer riding a wave. As the red Mini Cooper rounded the curve, he spun around to face the windshield. Extending his face through the glass, he shouted at Madness and Mayhem, "Here he comes! Get ready." He leaped to truck's roof. The wind in his face, he grinned. "Now!"

Standing on the driver's lap, Madness punched his fist into the man's left eye as Mayhem kicked at the man's wrist, centered on the wheel.

They screamed in unison, "Look out!"

<<>>

Why is there so much evil? His hands resting on the balcony railing, Daniel stared at the ebony coffin flanked with flower arrangements and family portraits. A single spot fixture washed the platform in a somber white glow.

He lit his phone, checking the time—*forty minutes.* The worship center was empty except for himself and the man below, sitting some ten feet or so from his wife's body. Bruce Peterson was not a regular attendee but appeared with Karen faithfully twice a year at Christmas and Easter. *Maybe I should try to talk to him, but what would I say...?*

Turning then, Daniel saw him, the dark figure in the top far row, a big man. Daniel approached. "Tom, how are you doing?"

"I'm good—I'm okay." They spoke in hushed tones, extending hands to clasp. Tom gestured for Daniel to sit. "She was a beautiful soul, wasn't she?"

"She was." A picture of a Baptist preacher flashed through Daniel's mind as he eyed Tom's black suit. Daniel took a seat in the oak pew just in front of Tom. Rotated with his arm on the seatback, he again checked the time. "I'm sorry. I'm helping with the service and will need to head down in just a minute." He exhaled slowly. "I was just asking the Lord why? I know God is in control of everything, but this?"

<<>>

The truck swerved into Jason's lane. Tires locking in a puff of blue smoke, it tilted as the back end swung toward him. As if moving in slow motion, his windshield filled with the face of the truck, the gap closing, the curb, the boy—falling now with his bike. *Not enough space!* The car stuttered as his ABS engaged. Hands pressed against the wheel, he heard the horn blasting, tires scraping curb, the boy stumbling toward him.

~~

In the middle of the road, a searing green flash sizzled as the tear opened. Shield drawn, Asmodeus lunged forward, driving his shoulder into the side of the careening truck.

~~

Lurching, the truck's back end rocked left as the gap opened, and Jason shot through. Bouncing and grinding against the curb, the boy flew past his window in a blur. His clenched hands gripped the wheel as the car ground to a halt. In his mirror, the truck rested in the middle of the road ahead of arcing skid marks. The boy rose on both arms, his bike down, front wheel spinning.

<<>>

Tom leaned forward. Elbows on his knees, he clasped his Bible between large hands. "Life here is short. But for the believing man, it's forever. Let me show you something." He flipped through his worn leather Bible. "Psalm 116—listen." He extended his index finger as he read. "'Precious in the sight of the Lord is the death of His godly ones.' Think about that—Karen's death is precious to God because she is now in His arms. He is wiping away her tears and showing her around heaven. It was her time, and now she's truly free."

Again, Tom turned the delicate pages. "You were saying you don't understand—right? I want you to hear this, Daniel, with your heart. This is a word for you. Isaiah 45, here verse 5—you read."

Daniel unfolded his reading glasses, the metal arms cool against his temples. "'I am the LORD, and there is no other; Besides Me there is no God. I will gird you, though you have not known Me; That men may know from the rising to the setting of the sun, there is no one besides Me. I am the LORD, and there is no other; The One forming light and creating darkness, causing well-being and creating calamity; I am the LORD who does all these.'"

"Did you catch that? People want to say God is only in control of the good things and not the darkness. But this says He created both. Think about it... God is in control of all things, good and bad." Tom's finger extended toward Daniel's chest.

Daniel pursed his lips. "You're not saying God killed her, are you?"

"I'm not saying that at all, but I am saying He allowed it and had a purpose in it we can't understand. Remember Job and how Satan had to ask permission to torment him? God told Satan he was not allowed to kill Job, but in Karen's case, it was different. No, God didn't kill her, but He allows the evil that did. Why? That's not for either of us to know—someday maybe, but not likely."

Daniel's phone vibrated with a chime. "It's Jason." He brought the slice of glass and plastic to his ear.

Jason panted between broken words as he explained what happened. "Everyone's okay, but the three of us are pretty shaken. I just talked to the boy's mother, and she's on her way. But I'm going to need to stay here until she arrives."

"Wow, that's unbelievable. It sounds like you had angels protecting you."

"No doubt about that, but I'm not sure I'm going to be able to make it. If I don't, I'm going to need you to cover for me." Jason's breathing filled his pause. "My notes are on my desk. The message is the same I shared the other night at the board meeting." More panting. "John's out of town, and Victor has the flu. But Jenny will be there to do the music and can help with any questions. Can you do it?"

Daniel's throat tightened as he squeezed the phone. He glanced at Tom. "Me? I'm not so good in front of a crowd.... But sure—yes, I'll do it."

Tom's face glowed in the dim light of the overhead cans. "The Lord is seeking servants with open hearts like you. Someone who is willing to surrender all of it, no matter the cost. The Lord has plans for you—I can see it—but you have got to be willing."

Daniel swallowed. "Did you just hear that? Pastor Jason was almost in an accident and might not make it. In twenty minutes, it could be me down there delivering the message." He pointed over his shoulder with his thumb to the platform.

"Evil is for real, Daniel. Do you think that was random? Don't kid yourself. The enemy knows funerals are ripe with souls ready to receive. And look at this—a godly woman like Karen...murdered? People talk all the time about evil and spiritual warfare, and they even talk about demons. But do they believe it? If they did, you think they'd get some armor on and fight." Tom's eyes narrowed. "Truth is, most people don't believe demons are for real."

The exit stair door opened with Earl Dempsey emerging from the opening. Washed in white light, he threw open hands into the air, tossing a head-fade to Daniel. "I've really got to go, Tom."

Tom reached forward, poking Daniel in the chest. "The church is supposed to be the light, but most of the time, we're no different from the rest of the world. Amen?"

"Tom, I've—"

"Don't worry, Daniel, the Lord has this covered. He has everything covered. If Pastor Jason does the speaking or if you do. Trust me. The Lord's got this."

"Okay, I hear what you're saying, and I agree. But why does it seem like evil is always winning? Listen to the news any day of the week— murders and death, disease and immorality, you name it. I guess I'm asking: if we're the church and we have God's power, where is it?" As Daniel started to stand, Tom capped his shoulder.

"Let me ask you, Daniel. If you were in your house and the place was surrounded by a bunch of bad guys with guns coming for your family—what would you do?" Tom arched his brows. "Let me tell you what the average Christian would do. Right in his closet, he has a .50-caliber machine gun, a flamethrower, and a box of grenades. But he doesn't go to the closet. He goes to the pencil drawer and gets a peashooter or grabs some flowers from the garden."

Feeling pressure on his shoulder, Daniel eased back in the pew.

Tom lifted his hand, again pointing. "The guy doesn't believe the enemy is for real. And if he does, he shoots some peas at him or tries to make friends. But it's too late because he's either wounded or dead before he even knows what happened." He dropped his voice. "Daniel, do you believe the battle is for real?"

"I do, but..." Daniel studied his hands and then Tom's eyes. "I guess I don't understand how we get the weapons on. How do we open the door to get the power?"

"You just answered it, Daniel. The closet is full, and the power is in there. But you got to open the door—you got to ask."

Daniel sighed with a nod, his eyes drifting back to the exit.

Tom cocked his head. "Have you ever prayed with the Intercessors, Daniel?"

"The old—I mean—the ladies who pray, on Monday mornings?" Daniel stood, again glancing to the door.

"Old is right." A rich chuckle interrupted his words. "Those ladies got some firepower. You should check it out. They would love having one of the elders show up to pray with them and ask how they're doing." Tom bobbed his head. "Those ladies are strong, let me tell you, mister."

"I need to go—but thanks, I mean it. I'll be thinking about our discussion, and I'll visit the Intercessors—I promise." Daniel's phone chimed again. Swiping the screen, he read the message and then exhaled as the pressure lifted. "You were right. The Lord has it covered. Jason's on his way. He'll be here in ten minutes."

<<>>

Asmodeus gripped Moaz by the throat. About to rip the cowering rodent's head off, he changed his mind and threw him to the pavement. "What, in Lucifer's name, do you think you're doing?"

Moaz stammered, "W—w we were only m—murdering him. We

thought... y—you would be so pleased. He is their leader master, their pastor—we..."

"I know who he is." Asmodeus bared his fangs, his eyes narrowing into slits. "You're a fool, Moaz—don't you see we need him? Sympathy for his death will not divide them; it will make them stronger." Towering above the useless tormentor, Asmodeus bent at the waist and drew his open hand back. Then shaking his head, he stood upright and kicked Moaz in the chest.

Jumping to his feet, Moaz quivered. His eyes darting about, he then pointed to the boy. "We could, or... Look, we can kill him. That is, at your command, of course."

"No! That would be a distraction. I have a better idea, how 'bout you kill yourself instead? Why oh, why do I put up with you...?"

<<>>

Slapping at the alarm, Nick nearly knocked it off the nightstand. *Twenty minutes...* Forcing himself to rise, he wavered in the darkness as he reached out to touch the wall. Finger on the switch, he braced for the flood of light. *Cheap wine. We've got to ease off.*

He rubbed the dull ache at the back of his head and squinted in the mirror. He didn't mind the worry lines or the graying at his temples— after all, they conveyed wisdom. It was the dark circles under his eyes he didn't like. *I'll be stronger, Lord. I promise.*

After groping in the dresser, he pulled a tee shirt over his head, Brooke's reflection filling the mirror's background. She was lying on her side, snoring, a corner of the sheet partially covering her plump body. It was a picture of their relationship—him busy with his career while Brooke spent her time at home. At least she got out once a week with the girls. They called it Thirsty Thursdays based on the idea of thirsting for conversation.

Amber flashed through his mind, startling him that he would think of Amber while looking at Brooke. It had been nearly a year since they tried to make love. It seemed she was going through the motions for his sake while inwardly enduring it. Wincing, he thought of how it ended.

A soft voice whispered from within, *"It would be different if she wanted you. But Amber, she's beautiful and exciting. Can you imagine what it would be like...?"*

He glanced again at the clock and then dashed downstairs to his home office. Lighting his Lenovo, he then ducked into the kitchen to start the coffee. Having done his research the night before, he was set with three potential plays. Rehearsing the action about to unfold, he filled the cone filter with five scoops. Then pouring water into the tank, he checked the microwave clock. *Four minutes—no time for market news. This is crazy.*

The coffeemaker dripped as he turned on his wide-screens. Two in front for trading with the other on his desk return for confirmations and monitoring accounts. As he clicked his browser, the screen flashed to his home page. He glanced at the lower right corner.

Three minutes... His fingers flew as he logged on to his trading platform, the front monitors split with a graph on each side preset with his picks, commodity plays—an oil driller, a natural gas producer, and a mining company—each displaying real-time features of the trading action including fast-stochastic interval shift, as well as macro dynamics and volume. The fourth graph displayed the value of the US dollar in relation to the basket of world currencies.

Two minutes... He scratched his stubbled chin, thinking of the journey that had brought him to this moment. He'd always described himself as a buy-and-hold guy. But after the crash, the markets had become a game of shifting momentum with the traditional approach of accumulating slow-and-steady growth no longer working. He struggled to protect his clients from losses, and they were not accustomed to not making money. They were frustrated, and he was frustrated, which led him to Day Trading. But there were risks.

Nick had started with a seminar, taught by a highly successful Wall Street trader. As recommended, he began slowly, trading only on paper. There were rules, and he forced himself to follow them. The first being, one always entered and exited the market on the same day because no one could control what happens in the world overnight—a storm or natural disaster, a political scandal or terrorist attack. Additionally, an unexpected news release could impact any stock.

There were various strategies for the day trader, but he liked the Open Wave. The idea was to trade on the first-wave cycle, buying at the bottom and then selling at the top of the rebound. It was a lot like fishing. Sometimes he'd be in the stream for just a few seconds, other times for several minutes or even an hour or more—but always out before the close.

After two months of paper trading, he moved to real money in limited amounts, keeping track of gains and losses. There had been days when he lost a couple hundred dollars or broke even, but typically, he was making three to five hundred dollars a day.

Today, he'd be using client money for the first time, clients who had given him full discretionary authority to trade on their behalf. Although legal, pooling monies from more than one client crossed the ethical lines of most brokerage firms. As sole owner of his small company, he justified the practice that simplified transactions and saved on trading expenses. He'd moved the monies into a separate holding account, which included ten thousand dollars of his own money, as well as ten thousand each from four clients.

A glance at his currency graph showed the dollar up. *Beautiful. Commodities are going to dive. One minute...* He dashed into the kitchen, poured coffee into his favorite mug, and returned to his station before drawing a sip.

Mammon whispered, *"Now we enter the stream. Let the fish come to you. No fear. Wisdom and discernment, art and science—you are the Zen Master.... Master of the markets..."*

Nick quietly prayed, "Give me favor, Father God. Expand my territory that I may provide for my family and give to others. Protect me now from fear, granting me boldness, Lord, for Your glory."

The graphs lurched forward in unison. He focused on the price indicators, all three falling like stones. *Beautiful. In and out and call it a day.* Nick was learning to feel the market-flow, but knowing the difference between a real shift and a head fake was tricky. The indicators could also be deceptive. Early on, he'd often fallen for the bait, buying or selling too quickly or slowly. The goal was to execute in the fade zone, between the up-and-down waves. The skill was in knowing when, and he was getting good. *One with the stream...*

The trajectory of the falling stones eased slightly and then spiked upward while moving forward, then turned again falling. His picks were leveling and would soon rise. The cycle would then repeat throughout the day. His finger on the mouse, he selected the oil driller which had the most dramatic drop of nearly three points. *Keep it simple—cool as a cucumber...*

The blue volume bar pulsed upward with a second bar following, price spiking nearly a dollar in seconds. *The buyers are coming on... Is it a head fake?*

Mammon coached him, *"Not yet—patience..."*

Nick jerked, his rigid finger lifting as the price reversed falling again. *The sellers aren't done yet.* Much of the trading was automated with computers doing the buying and selling, triggered by any number of shifting parameters. *Hard to beat the machines, but we have the advantage.*

Again, he heard the whisper, *"Wait, one with the stream... Not yet... Now!"*

He dropped his finger, exhaling as price and volume surged. *Climb, baby, climb. Yes... The stochastics are off the charts. Looking good. Steady...* He had learned the price of a stock would often climb or fall throughout the day, but the up-and-down wave cycle would typically follow a momentum trajectory. *Ride the wave. Don't be greedy.*

His jaw went slack as his pick turned sharply down, again with volume rising. The macro indicator, climbing, had crested and was now declining. His eyes widened as it broke through the baseline. *No! Don't do this. Not today.*

Mammon whispered, *"Your instincts are good, feel the market. She won't lie to you. Trust yourself, trust me."*

Finger cocked, Nick watched his gains rapidly draining toward breakeven. Having experienced it before, he'd placed just half his money. *Okay. Reselect and double up...*

Calculating his position, he was suddenly dizzy. *Down nearly two thousand—no, Lord, please... We're out at five, no more.*

Nick rubbed his face. He was sweating. Down another thousand, the indicators began to level. *Stay cool. This is no different from trading paper.*

Mammon spoke calmly, *"Almost there, almost there...Now."*

Nick executed his second buy of twelve hundred shares. *Here we go. We're out at breakeven.*

"Nick...? Can you help me with something?" Brooke stood at the top of the stair.

The price again reversed, pumping down. His hands shaking, he queued up a sell order for twenty-four hundred shares. "Wh–what is it?"

"The toilet—it's running and won't stop."

"I'll be there in a minute. I'm busy."

"It's wasting water. Can you come now?"

"No. I need to finish this first." His hand gripped the mouse, his finger aching. *This is insanity.* It turned then, like a kayak exiting the rapids. The move was sharp and decisive, the ascent smooth and steady. Glancing at his dollar chart, he saw it had spiked but was now fading. His heart rate slowed as the graphing crossed his breakeven point with leg strength.

"Master of the Markets—yes!"

He sighed as his profit pushed beyond two thousand. *Thank You, Lord, for protecting me and granting me favor.*

Mammon interrupted, *"Don't be greedy. Take your fish."*

Clicking sell, Nick exhaled and then checked the clock as he did the calculations. *Forty-eight hundred in twelve minutes—not bad.* He then confirmed the sale and began to move the monies back to the client accounts.

"You took the risk, and you earned it. Besides, you were ready to absorb the losses." The voice was convincing.

Stopping short of splitting the profits, he instead gave each client half a share. *That was intense, and I took the risk. It's a bonus fee. That's fair. And besides, I was prepared to absorb the losses.*

"Honey, can you come now? It's going to overflow."

"I'm on my way, babe." He smiled. *What a rush!*

CHAPTER 23

RICHARD SAT alone in the dark room, an empty chair pulled away from the table, exactly as she left it. Overhead, the pendant fixture emitted a high-pitched ring. It was the first time he'd noticed it. His fingers rose and fell, gently tapping his wheelchair arms. Two objects rested in front of him—his Bible and cell phone. He'd been praying for nearly an hour. "Lord, I understand You're saying no."

With a slight nudge, he woke his phone, displaying 9:38 in large white numbers. Scrolling to contacts, he tapped Amber. He then stared at the number as it faded to black. "Okay, Lord, I'll wait. I know she belongs to You and not me. But I ask You to protect and watch over her. I pray in Jesus's name... Amen."

<<>>

The rain had yielded to a fine mist now swirling about him in the early-morning darkness. Batush tugged on his cloak, cinching it tight to his chin, his steaming breath mingling with the fog. *Winter, it seems you have not yet relented.*

He followed the edge of the slab paving, moving slowly to keep his bearings. He prayed in the muffled stillness, "Prepare the hearts of the elders and bishop, Lord. May they receive Your words with grace. Protect them also from the spirits of fear and doubt and grant me peace to complete this task. I praise and worship Thee."

Dribbling water pricked his ears before he saw the landmark. The fountain served as a washing station for the public brothel. Oval shaped with a flush perimeter lip, it sloped toward the center. The shallow basin allowed patrons to walk directly into the mosaic-clad pool. Shrouded in mist, the fountain's focal point—Priapus the Aphrodite, dancing with head flung back, her arms wrapped around a phallus from which the water gurgled—cast a dark silhouette. Glancing away, he crossed to the other side of the road.

The cobbles underfoot signaled he'd merged onto Curetes Street, the swirling fog so dense he could barely see his sandals. Inching forward, he searched for the trail leading uphill to the library and toolshed. He counted his steps, doubling the number to allow for his slow progress while estimating the distance. Thinking he had passed it, he was about to turn back when he stumbled onto the trailhead.

He skirted muddy puddles as he slogged on. Stopping every few paces, he glanced ahead in search of the building wall. *Surely, it is close.*

As he reached forward, his hand disappeared into the thick blanket. He was pawing at the fog when he heard it—the unmistakable sound of a heavy belch. He held his breath, a wave of fear sweeping over him. Voices followed as a dim light appeared, swinging back and forth.

"Wake up, sloth. You let the fire burn out—get up." The clatter of scattering pebbles was followed by a thud and grunt.

"I was watching."

The voices spoke Latin.

<<>>

A handful of shop owners huddled under the coffee shop's canopy. In hushed tones, they spoke of the fog and cold, the raspy crying of an unseen child not far away.

"It is in the Lord's hands, my brothers. If it rains or even if it snows, there is one thing we know—the Lord is good and He will provide." Zophar smiled with Gibeon at his side. They stood in front of the linear stove serving as a counter. "Gibeon. Fetch some wood. The fire is about to fail us."

Zophar had two flasks in play. One contained coffee, which he was boiling down for strength and richness. The other, goat's milk bubbling on a stone warming plate. He withdrew the coffee from the burner as it again began to boil up. After letting it cool, he then returned it to the flame.

"Your patience will be rewarded, my sister. Trust me." Zophar lifted his brows. Mischief bunching his cheeks, he gave the flask a swirl. "And because you are the first to try this concoction, there is no charge for today."

A warm smile crinkled Rehab's weathered face.

"And now we are ready." Zophar poured the hot fluid into a clay mug, capping it with frothing milk.

As the brew's color changed from tar to a medium mud, the spice trader extended a small hand toward the drink.

"Patience, my sister, there are two ingredients yet to add. I think you will like this." Zophar lifted two small jars from a wood box.

Laughter slipped from her thin lips, a gnarled hand rising to cover her mouth. "From my shop?"

Zophar winked. "First, the cane for sweetness. And then, two dashes of cinnamon for aroma." He presented it with both hands. "What do you think?"

She lifted it to her nose, inhaling deeply with closed eyes before drawing a sip. "This is the finest coffee I have ever tasted. You are a blessing and bring warmth to the soul of an old woman—even on a dreary day like this. You must have been sent from God Himself."

Zohpar's smile faded as two Roman soldiers walked toward them.

Rehab was making way for the next customer when he heard the message whispered into his mind. *"Batush needs you. Go to the church."*

He stepped toward Gibeon, who was wrestling with an armful of firewood. "I must go to help a friend. You will manage the shop." He tilted his head toward the approaching men. "Be sure to take good care of our Roman friends."

<<>>

Batush's heart was pounding when he entered the library. *They have found the crypt....* He instinctively glanced at the wall sconces, relieved to see them burning. After lighting a hand lamp, he headed for the stair tower, his head reeling. *The sarcophagus and broken seals—surely, the elders have been informed.... What will I say, Lord?*

At the top floor, he entered the workroom awash in a blue glow emanating from the clerestories. As he slid into a seat at the center table, his mind filled with images of Meraiah and Sarah. *Keep them safe, Lord. I do not understand. Please, Lord, I beg You.*

He began to weep, his body shaking. "It is too much, Lord. Raphael and the book—and then Death come alive? And now, Rome and the Church Fathers, what will I say?"

A wave of warmth poured over him then. With his eyes closed, the blackness shifted to bright red as if he were looking into the sun. He continued to weep as the fear and panic began to wash away. Looking into the light, he leaned back and spread his arms. "Give me strength to complete this. You are my Lord and God. There is none besides Thee."

A soft still voice spoke from within, *"The Lord is pleased with you, Batush. He is your strength. Hold fast to Him."*

The waves of tears transformed from despair to surrender and joy.

"I worship Thee and thank Thee—praising Your holy name. You are the God of Abraham and Moses and Father of the Christ. I am just a scribe, Lord, a simple man. And You have chosen me? I give all to You and ask only for the strength to honor and serve You. You have authority over all things, and Your will shall be done for Your glory. I will hold fast, Lord. That is what I shall do."

A rustling shuffled from downstairs.

Raphael...? After rushing down the three flights of stairs, Batush burst into the reading room. A short young man spun around, cradling the oil jar in his arms.

"Naaman? I—I did not know..."

"Batush, where have you been? The Church Fathers are looking for you. Two nights past, they sent me to your home, but I found no one. And Rome also, the guards are looking for grave robbers. The body of Celsus has been desecrated. Do you know of this?"

"Four nights ago, I was here... working into the night. I was attacked on the road, a—and injured and..."

Naaman's expression stopped him. "I was here four nights past also. But I did not see you, Batush. You must go to the bishop and the elders. They said you should come immediately."

CHAPTER 24

THE FLUORESCENTS buzzed overhead as Daniel watched Nick. *He's doing it again, wearing them down. Can't they see it?* Daniel squeezed his temples between thumb and index finger, his head pounding. It was a mistake to sign checks before the meeting. In the future, he would make a second trip. Perhaps it might also be a mistake to continue with Nick handling his finances. *How would I bow out...? It's a conflict with us both on the board. It doesn't look good....*

With a red laser, Nick pointed to the slide. "This represents a summary of where I believe our offer should be. I pulled this from churchjobs.com—which was quite helpful. The model allowed me to enter parameters based on position, title, and congregation size. It included an option for gender designation, which I removed. I also changed the title to executive minister. In any case, this is showing we fall between eighty-six and ninety-four, plus benefits with two weeks' paid vacation. I would like to encourage us to consider a performance bonus as well."

Nick glanced at Paul, who nodded. "I recommend we offer ninety for the base. If we come in lower, it'll look like we're taking advantage because she's a woman. Keep in mind, there'll be a lot of responsibility on this woman's shoulders."

The smell of stale popcorn, thick in the air, tormented Daniel's churning stomach. He felt the room begin to spin as the men responded with nodding heads.

"Why would we offer a performance bonus? Is that appropriate, and how would we measure something like that?" Lewis Kolsby removed his glasses and placed them on his copy of the proposal.

"It's completely appropriate, and it's also measurable. We take attendance every week and track the giving numbers. If they move up under her watch and hit predetermined targets, she earns the bonus, and the church benefits."

"I don't like it." Lewis jabbed at the mahogany slab with his index finger. "This is a church, not a business. We're doing kingdom work here, and I'm not sure attendance and giving figures are appropriate for measuring results. You can't measure the number of saved souls or hearts being touched. I hear what you're saying, but that's my opinion." He lifted his finger and put his glasses back on.

"You're right. There's no way to measure ministry or see what's happening inside people's hearts, but that's where the data helps. If attendance and giving are up, then I think it's fair to say the Lord's work is being accomplished."

Another glance passed between Nick and Paul.

Paul leaned back. Lifting a hand, he cradled his chin. "What do you think, guys? Does anyone disagree with ninety plus benefits? It's a little less than what we're paying Pastor Stover, but considering the responsibility and work involved, I believe it makes sense. After all, Pastor Jason just blows in on Sundays to preach, but Amber will be running the place. She'll be doing everything from leading staff meetings to ordering toilet paper. I can see where we would pay her more, but that can wait till later. I also agree we could give her a bonus if she grows the church, but we would consider that when we do her performance review. We also want to leave some room to give her raises moving forward."

Daniel's heart was racing. Lifting his hand, he drew it to his lips. *We're not ready. This is crazy.*

Paul turned to him. "You got something?"

"I've already said it. You guys know where I stand."

"It's awfully quiet, gentlemen. Do I have a motion?" Paul leaned forward, tapping the table with his yellow hammer.

"I move we offer the position of executive minister to Amber Lash, with a yearly base salary of ninety thousand dollars plus benefits as per standard policy. Additionally, the offer shall include a performance bonus, the parameters of which shall be decided at a future date." Nick read his motion from a yellow notepad.

"Do I have a second?"

Henry Williams quickly responded, "I second the motion."

"All in favor say aye."

The men responded in kind.

"All opposed, same sign?"

The room was silent.

"Any abstentions...? Then I guess we can call it a night."

Paul was beginning to stand when Daniel said, "I abstain."

Paul blew a long exhaling sigh as he stuffed his bag with three notebooks and a handful of file folders. Shaking his head, he huffed a burst of breath. "Why does that not surprise me? Guys, let's be sure to get that in the minutes—Daniel abstained."

<<>>

Seven powerful warriors of light escorted the human. Raphael held the point position, tight at the man's side. "On the ready—stay alert."

The angels surrounded them, three above and three below, equally spaced. The formation was known as the sphere, designed to maximize protection. With six, the formation was quite strong. However, twelve was preferred. "Weapons…"

The angels closed tighter. Their backs to the scribe, they were separated by the distance of a tall man with outstretched arms. Raphael drew his spiked war club. The others unsheathed glinting weapons, four with wide-bladed gladius swords, the other two wielding twin-headed lancing staffs.

"On my command…"

<<>>

The elders lifted their heads as he entered. The dancing light of wall torches overpowered the dim glow emanating from the overhead circular opening. A chill gripped the musty air, more like a cavern than the familiar council chamber.

Batush descended the steps to his favored position, across from and level with the platform, meeting their eyes as he sat. The elders glanced away. Bishop Jonness was leading with his elders on each side. A middle-aged man sat with bowed head in the chair beneath the domed ceiling.

"Do you believe in Jesus Christ the Son of God?"

"Yes, Your Holiness, I do."

"Do you surrender your life in obedience to follow Him?"

"Yes, Your Holiness, I do."

"Do you renounce your life of sin and worldly lust?"

"Yes, Your Holiness."

Jonness waited for the convert to look up. "Do you renounce your lust for the flesh and your sins of sensuality and fornication?"

"Yes, Your Holiness."

The volume increased. "Do you repent of your adulteries and

idolatries?" His voice then softened to a whisper. "And do you confess your sins before your God and the Holy Church of Christ?"

"Yes, Your Holiness—I do."

"And do you renounce the spirits of darkness that dwell within you?"

"Yes, Your Holiness."

Lifting his gaze, Jonness locked eyes with Batush. "In the name of Christ, I rebuke the demons within you." Leaning forward, he spoke slowly. He gripped his jeweled cross in his right hand.

Eyes shifting to the convert, he lowered and raised the cross as if sprinkling water from it. "Demon of lust, come out of him. Demon of adultery and fornication come out. Demon of hatred and anger, demons of pride, murder, and lies—come out. Demon of drunkenness, come out in the name of Christ."

The shaking began with the last command. "Demon of drunkenness, you cannot hide from me. I command you—in the name of Christ—leave him!"

The man fell to his knees crying out, his hanging head swinging from side to side. "No... No—I will not."

"You will come out and be gone from him. I rebuke you."

The man lurched violently, falling to his face, then flopping over as if kicked.

"What is your name demon? Tell me."

"I will not. No!" The man's rigid body, overtaken by convulsions, began to kick, knocking over the chair. The shaking so violent, his body seemed to vibrate, almost lifting from the floor.

Seeing veins protruding from man's neck, his face bright red, Batush felt the hair on his neck standing on end.

"N–no. I will not—I..." His body then went slack as he began to weep.

Jonness lifted his right hand, again staring at Batush. "By the power of God, you are forgiven and accepted for baptism into the church. Go now and sin no more." Returning to the convert, he asked, "Do you, Simon, son of Josiah—surrender all to follow Christ? And do you Simon, son of Josiah—surrender also to follow me?"

The sobbing man responded, "Yes, Your Holiness, I–I do."

Two church guardians entered swiftly to help the man rise as an elderly blind woman was ushered in. Wiping his brow with a white handkerchief, Jonness waved them off. "Batush, we would like to speak with you. Come—come sit with us."

<<>>

Longshanks came out with an exaggerated wail, followed by a snort. Hovering below the domed ceiling, he surveyed the scene. The body of his host was lying on its back like a wax figure with mouth agape in contorted horror.

The dark angel taunted the angels clustered around the scribe, "Woe is me... Ha! You think that's going to hold? I'll be back before sunrise with a wine flask and some friends. Or maybe, I'll just take the scribe instead. Yeah, that's better."

He glided slowly, arcing around the dome's perimeter. Coasting on his back with arms extended, he accelerated, his robed form transforming into a blur of whirling scarlet. The stoic angels watched as he then decelerated, the blur of color again revealing the demon prancing about the perimeter wall. With a hand on the wall, Longshanks rotated his body and stepped to the floor, walking.

He dusted his hands as he approached. "The book and the scribe belong to us, and we will have them both. You cannot stop us. We are too many. Too maaaaaaannnny." He spit a laugh into the air while patting his weapon. "I admire your dedication, although it is difficult to understand. Gotta love you guys—this is crazy, what am I thinking?" He shook his head. "I'll be honest. I do love you, but mostly, I hate you. And that is why I believe—I shall kill you all right now."

He drew his battle-ax from its low-slung satchel. The frozen torchlight glinted from the polished blade. Crescent-shaped and razor-thin, it was quite wide, about equal a man's head. Still smiling, he extended his upper jaw allowing his fangs to flop over his lower lip. Freezing, he locked eyes with Raphael. "Do you think you can defend that which is already ours?"

Longshanks applied pressure to the weapon's slide release. A metallic zing sliced through the chamber as it sprang forward and locked into place with a click, the blade nearly touching the floor.

"We stand in obedience to the Almighty." Raphael stood motionless at Batush's side. "Test us if you must, but we will not yield."

"Yes, Raphael, I got it. 'We obey the Almighty'—'we obey the Almighty.' I've heard it a thousand times, but where's the humor,

brother? Don't you ever laugh? Do you even know how? Here watch."
Longshanks began to chuckle. Then forcing a deeper tone, he gave up.

The angel cluster rotated around Batush. Oscillating in overlapping directions, it transformed into a sphere of white light.

Longshanks lifted his weapon level to his chin. With both hands, he wielded the blade in a wide circle, dipping in front and behind, then up and over, loosed in a blur. Making a single rotation, it stuck the sphere's center, shattering into fragments that ricocheted from the walls and ceiling. After following through with the low bow of an entertainer, Longshanks rose and folded his arms, his flabby lips stretching into a smile. He then patted his weapon's handle to confirm it had reassembled in his satchel.

His eyes widening, he pivoted toward the warping shimmer as Asmodeus emerged behind the row of elders.

"Longshanks, enough. This is not the appointed time or the place."

"I was only testing the blade, master." Shrugging, he sauntered to the platform. Not bothering with the steps, he hopped onto the table and squatted in front of the elder on the far end. The man's fixed gaze stared past him, puzzlement scrunching his face.

"What the hell are you staring at, fool?" Leaning in, Longshanks bared his teeth, then hacked up a mouthful of phlegm and spewed it into the man's face. He then shouted, "That's right. I'm the demon of demons. That's me, Longshanks. Do you hear me?"

~~

The Church Father at the far end of the table blinked and then rubbed his face.

CHAPTER 25

HIS TILE SUB was behind, and the millwork installer wasn't returning calls. Daniel walked the space checking on his plumber and electrician, both busy installing fixtures and trim. Without the millwork, his plumber would need to pull off the job, unable to complete. For now, it was quiet, but tomorrow morning would be quite different when the owner arrived with his kitchen equipment. Mr. Yee was expecting his second Tea Lite Café to be open by the end of the month, and he was not fond of excuses. *It's going to be tight.*

Daniel scrolled through his emails again. *Come on, man. Where are you?* He was about to close the screen when the phone chimed. The message was from Amber with the subject line Hi There. *Okay, what's your angle?*

Hi Daniel,

I understand you didn't vote with the other elders to hire me as your executive pastor. Now that the decision is set, I trust you'll put the past behind you and support my staff and elders as we begin to move the church forward. I also hope you will not cause problems, as unity in leadership is something I value. Thanks for the hard work you are doing, Amber

Amber, Amber, Amber. Still speaking in not-so-coded messages—I think I got it. I'm the boss of the church now, and you're working for me. I know you're the only one who didn't vote for me. Now get in line or else...

Daniel exhaled, noticing the time. "Hey, John—I've got to run. I'll be back in an hour, hopefully with a good word on the millwork."

"No worries, Danny boy." John was on his knees, an open-end wrench in one hand, a yellow flex-line in the other. "But don't forget—I'm gonna be down the road."

"I know. It's not your fault."

"Where are you off to?" John spoke from behind the water heater.

"A prayer meeting."

<<>>

His hand on the writing case, Batush drew a breath while telling his heart to be calm. Twisting in the chair, he scanned the room behind him. The council chamber was empty except for Naaman, the young scribe, and three church guardians framed like statues within the arched exit openings. The smell of oil and smoke lingered heavy in the air while torch flames lapped at the walls. Movement caught his eye when one of the guards stepped back, allowing a man's entry. Assurance flooded his frame as Zophar descended the steps.

"Coffee Trader, I did not request your presence. Why are you here?"

"I have come to stand with my friend."

"Will you stand only, or do you intend to speak?" Jonness gently rapped his open palm with his jeweled cross.

"I am here to stand only but can answer any questions you have for me."

Jonness leaned toward his elders, three on each side clad in white robes. Cupping his hand, he spoke softly. When he eased back, his gaze returned to Zophar. "I will allow this. However, you will be removed if you speak without permission. Do you understand?" He leveled the cross on Zophar.

"Yes, Your Holiness, I do."

"Batush... We have been in search of you for three days. We were concerned and sent a messenger to your home, but you were not found and nor was your family. We are comforted to see you now safe again with us. Where were you?"

"I was at the home of my friend, Zophar."

"Were you hiding there?"

"No, Your Holiness, I was attacked on the road and beaten. Zophar helped me."

"Zophar, is this true?"

"Yes, Your Holiness." Burly arms at his sides, Zophar stood motionless, his long shadow darting before them in the torchlight.

Jonness stroked his short white beard. "Then you are a Good Samaritan, Zophar. And we are blessed you helped our scribe in his time of need." Jonness fanned his arms over the table, the draped sleeves of his scarlet robe embroidered in gold shimmered like the wings of a dark angel. "Batush, you have served the church faithfully from the days of your youth as a page. We are all aware of this."

Reaching below the table, Jonness lifted a shallow wood box containing three objects—a writing pen, a signet ring, and a copper ink dish. "Are these yours?"

Suddenly faint, Batush swallowed hard. As his gaze rushed forward and his peripheral vision blurred, he saw the tools at the end of a long tunnel. "I–I ..."

"Do not fear. I am with you."

He turned to his right, expecting Zophar's cupped hand at his ear, but Zophar was on his left. "Raphael?"

"What did you say? I will ask again—are these yours?" Jonness pointed with the cross, his face narrowing like a poised viper.

"Without inspecting them, I do not know. But..."

Except for the rapid scrabbling of quill on parchment, the room waited in silence.

"These were found in the burial chamber of Celsus, below the library dedicated to his name. They were scattered on the floor as were the governor's desecrated bones." Jonness extended the signet ring toward Batush, holding it between thumb and forefinger. "This ring bears the name of the church as well as your mark, faithful servant. Tell us why you desecrated and robbed the tomb of a high official—the governor and a senator. Why did you do this—tell us." Reaching forward, his hand on the table, Jonness stood.

Batush felt Raphael's open hand on his back as heat radiated through his body like a tingling fire. He closed his eyes. Warmth melting fear, replaced with peace and power, filled his frame.

"An angel came to me and showed me the tomb. He told me I would find a book there at the feet of Celsus."

"An angel?" Jonness again spread his wings to the others. "And you saw this angel?"

"Yes, he appeared to me in the library."

"And did this angel have a name?" He tapped the cross against his open palm.

"Yes. He is the Archangel Raphael. He said he was sent by God and I had been chosen to find the book." Batush held the bishop's stare of disbelief as the young scribe's pen scratching continued.

"You sit before us and profess to have seen an archangel? Who told you to open the tomb of a Roman official and to desecrate his body?

And do you expect us to believe you moved the stone lid yourself?"

Jonness's eyes stabbed at Zophar. "Did you help him do this thing?"

"I did not." Zophar stood rigid like stone.

"You did not do this alone. Who helped you?" Jonness slammed his cross to the table with a flat hand, his jaw clenched, the veins of his neck inflamed.

"Raphael helped me."

Jonness drew his hand back as if to strike, his face matching the color of his robe. "No. You fill this holy chamber with lies. And what proof do you have?"

"I have the book."

"Book—what book?"

"The book that was at the feet of Celsus. It was in the sarcophagus."

"You took this book.... You *admit* to stealing it? And you also dragged the bones of a dead man from his sleeping place and threw them on the floor? And then you crushed Celsus's skull? Tell us why— why did you do this?" Jonness strode back and forth behind the table. The wood soles of his unseen shoes slapping the floor echoed through the chamber. As he gestured wildly, his robe of crimson flapped and darted like a horseman's flag in battle.

"I did not."

"Tell us then—who did?"

"Death himself rose up from the tomb and tried to take the book from me. Raphael protected me. He crushed Celsus's head."

"Do you know Rome is looking for you? The crime of desecration is worthy of death. Do you understand this?"

Batush sat in silence.

"Tell me why this angel would appear to *you*, a scribe? If there was an angel, would he not appear to *me*? I am bishop. Why you?"

"I do not know, Your Holiness."

"Show us this book."

Batush opened the oiled flap of his writing case and withdrew the wooden tube. He then removed the scroll and cradled it in both hands.

"Read it to us." Jonness sat down, his flushed face shiny. The frenzied clawing of quill on parchment continued.

Fumbling with the book, Batush fitted it with scroll pins. He then extended it to half arm's length and cleared his throat. "The Revelation of..."

Feeling a hand cover his mouth, Batush stopped.

"Be quiet."

He mouthed the next few words, but no sound emerged.

"Why have you stopped? Read it."

Batush lifted his head, his mouth hanging open.

Jonness's gaze swept to Zophar. "What is wrong with him?"

"Perhaps an angel has closed his lips." Zophar took the book from Batush. Locking eyes with Jonness, he rolled it closed and began to speak:

"'The Revelation of Jesus Christ, which God gave Him to show to His bond-servants, the things which must soon take place, and He sent and communicated it by His angel to His bond-servant John, who testified to the word of God and to the testimony of Jesus Christ, even to all that he saw.'"

Zophar's eyes roamed from elder to elder as he spoke. He paused when he came to the passage written to the church of Ephesus. Leveling his gaze on Jonness, he continued:

"'To the angel of the church in Ephesus write: The One who holds the seven stars in His right hand, the One who walks among the seven golden lampstands, says this: I know your deeds and your toil and perseverance, and that you cannot tolerate evil men, and you put to the test those who call themselves apostles, and they are not, and you found them to be false; and you have perseverance and have endured for My name's sake, and have not grown weary. But I have this against you, that you have left your first love. Therefore remember from where you have fallen, and repent and do the deeds you did at first; or else I am coming to you and will remove your lampstand out of its place, unless you repent.

"'Yet this you do have, that you hate the deeds of the Nicolaitans, which I also hate. He who has an ear, let him hear what the Spirit says to the churches. To him who overcomes, I will grant to eat of the tree of life which is in the Paradise of God.'"

Still holding the bishop's frozen stare, Zophar paused again. Then proceeding, he quickened his pace, his gaze again grazing from elder to elder until he concluded.

Rising to a half-standing position, Jonness leaned forward, spread hands on the table. "How is it you have read and memorized this book before today, Coffee Trader?"

"I do not read, Your Holiness."

"How is that possible? You have just spoken the book."

"I have never heard these words before. Clearly, the Lord has opened my mouth."

Jonness glared, his face contorted in indignant disbelief. The men in white remained seated, their ashen faces seared with disdain and rebuke.

"Guardians!"

The guards descended in a flurry of motion as the intensity of the scribe's etching escalated.

"Jail them under my authority. Fo—for crimes against the church, they are to be held until further notice. Give me the book and get them out of here."

One of the men extended the book toward Jonness, who did not respond. Bowing, he then placed it on the table. Breathing heavily, Jonness whirled from left to right and then jerked upright, his carved chair banging into the wall. Eyes glaring, they darted from Zophar to Batush and then out to Naaman, who was writing madly.

"Let it be documented. Batush has admitted to the crime of theft. The scribe has lied to his elders and has also desecrated the body of the Roman governor. This record shall be sealed and placed in my hand."

Lifting his pen, Naaman stared at Jonness. After bobbing his head, he then dipped his quill. Returning to the parchment, the scratching continued.

<<>>

Daniel opened the door slowly and peered around its face. Entering, he nodded to the ladies, eight of them, seated around an oval table below a glass chandelier. A series of stained-glass windows behind them depicted the story of the flood, washing the room in hues of yellow, purple, green, and red.

Bubbling water greeted him with hushed reverence from the wall of stacked limestone, inspired by the Wailing Wall in Jerusalem. The variegated wall was fitted with a scupper dribbling water into a stone basin. Folded slips of paper protruded from the joints between the stones, left by those who had visited with requests for the Intercessors.

"Daniel, how nice of you to brighten our morning. We have been praying for a long time, asking the Lord to send an elder to visit with us. Is that you?" Petite Nancy Dawson, impeccably dressed in a gray suit with jade earrings and necklace matching her twinkling eyes, sat at the head of the table, a folded paper in her hand.

"I would love to." He pulled out a chair at the circle's perimeter.

"Come here, Daniel. Sit next to me."

The lady next to Nancy stood. "Take my seat—we can trade."

About to object, he yielded. "I'm honored."

"We've been reading prayers from your beautiful wall. Can you imagine? This room was once used for storage, but now, it's been transformed by you into a work of art to bless so many." Nancy's wrinkled face radiated warmth.

"You're too nice. I didn't design it. I just built it."

Like a bird, she tilted her head, her eyes big above powdered pink cheeks. "Well, we heard the prayer wall and the fountain were your ideas. Is it true?"

"I don't want to step on the architect's toes. But let's just say sometimes even contractors have some good ideas." He winked.

She patted his hand. "We were just about to read this last message. Would you like to pray over it for us? Just pray whatever you hear the Spirit speaking."

He eased the folded note from her cool fingers and closed his eyes. "Lord Almighty, You are our God, and we are Your people. We praise and bless You remembering the great and awesome things You have done." Soft mms and chatter murmured from the table's other side. "You spoke, Lord, creating all that we see—the mountains and oceans, the trees and animals, the fish and the birds. And You created us in Your image. The tongues increased. You led Your people out of Egypt and parted the sea to save them. You gave them water from a rock and fed them bread from the sky. You led them, Lord, through the desert with a pillar of smoke by day and fire by night. We praise and bless Your holy name."

He squeezed the note in his hand. "We lift this request to You, Lord, interceding now for the person who wrote it. I thank You for the heart of this person. I see—I see a young woman calling out to You. Fill her with Your Spirit to serve You for Your glory."

The mms intensified now, with two angelic whispers caressing his ears.

A hand touched his shoulder as waves of heat and emotion washed through him, tears filling his eyes. Another hand, open, rested atop his head. With eyes closed, he was looking into the sun, the sensation of tingling energy coursing through his frame. He sputtered, "We cry out to You, Lord of Lords, King of Kings."

One of the chattering voices morphed into a musical rhythm.

"Look up, Daniel. With your eyes closed, look into the face of Jesus."

Unsure if it was one of the ladies or the voice of God, he gazed heavenward and prayed, "Open our eyes and ears to hear Your voice and see Your path. Pour us out like a drink offering, that we might know You and walk with You...." Lips quivering, he wept, collapsed in the chair, limp and weak yet filled with glory. "We love You, Lord, and need You. We surrender all to You."

The chattering softened as two hands took his. He opened his eyes to Nancy's tearful smile.

"Daniel. The Lord has anointed you with the gift of prophecy and given you the hot right hand of the healer. Use these gifts to bless others for His glory. The Lord loves you, and He is so proud of you. You are to be His voice. It is your calling."

Speechless, he wavered, feeling like he was floating.

"Is this how you always pray in here?" He wiped his face and laughed.

A hand on his knee, Nancy leaned in. "Oh yes, always. See what you have been missing?" The ladies burst into laughter, all of them with tears in their eyes. "I'm teasing, of course—that was different. I'm not sure this has ever happened in here before. Now give me the note before it melts. I should have told you to read it before you prayed. But you prayed first, and now, I'm curious."

A ripple of doubt taunted his mind. *What if it's not a woman? What if it's a child or a man or the message has nothing to do with what I prayed?*

Nancy unfolded it. "I need my glasses. The ink is smeared, and it's wringing wet. Let me see... Okay—yes, it is a woman."

A gasp swept through the group.

"Now listen, ladies—'I have been attending this church for a short time with my two children. I had a dream and it was very windy and the sky was filled with ominous storm clouds. I was standing in an open field of dry wheat, stretching out as far as I could see. And then I saw a white church with a steeple in the middle of the field, and I was trying to get inside ahead of the storm. I was pulling on the door. But it was locked, and then it flew open. There were wolves inside. They were skinny and gnashing their teeth and growling. The Lord loves this church, but wolves have come in and are prowling about. The Lord says: 'Worship Him in Spirit and truth. Surrender your ways and follow Him. Pray for the healing of Faith Bible Church.'"

Nancy laid the sheet of paper on the table. She then swept it flat with her open hand as the group murmured to one another.

Daniel tightened his clasped hands as their eyes drifted to rest on him.

<<>>

The eldest Church Father, Agabus, sat at the far end of the crescent table, scratching his gaunt face. He and the others waited in silence as Naaman collected his tools and packed them into his writing case. Slinging the satchel over his shoulder, the young scribe stepped to the aisle between the benches. He stood rigidly staring at Jonness for a few moments. Scratching at short black curls, he then bobbed his head and departed.

Agabus had lived in Ephesus his entire life. When he was a boy, his grandfather had told stories about the Apostle John whom he had once met. Each night, Agabus lit candles of remembrance for the Apostle, the first Bishop of Ephesus. The candles were a reminder of his grandfather and the stories he told of wonders and miracles.

His gaze drifted down the long row of men, falling lastly on his bishop. He had supported Jonness's ascendency when the former bishop had passed to glory. It took a unanimous vote of the elders to elect a new bishop, and there had been holdouts. But Agabus had worked behind the scene, patiently building consensus for Jonness. The majority had wanted Agabus to take the seat at the table's center, but he had declined the responsibility. Perhaps it was a mistake.

"How is it the scribe found the book?" he mumbled. "Have not we each sworn our eternal souls to hold the church secrets in silence? And how also can it be the coffee trader spoke the book but does not read? He is a faithful bondservant, but not educated—of this, I can bear witness."

Jonness squeezed the jeweled cross between folded hands. "The scribe admitted to being a thief. An angel of light would not appear to a thief. Nor would an angel desecrate the body of a resting soul."

A hollow knock echoed through the chamber as he tapped his cross on the table.

"The scribe is an educated man, but he does not hear from God. I was chosen to lead this church—would not God send His messenger to me?"

The men responded with silent nods.

"Any true angel would have left the book at rest, as placed there by our Fathers. Surely, this scribe was helped by one of Satan's angels. He and the coffee trader are deceived. A demon helped the scribe and spoke for the coffee trader as well."

Thadius, the youngest within the group, spoke next, "The book will do great harm to the church. It falsely accuses and condemns us to repent. We have not fallen, and we have nothing to repent of. This book is filled with lies, and that is why the Holy Fathers sealed it in the tomb. It must be hidden again or perhaps destroyed."

Claudius asked, "What of the coffee trader? How can these words be sealed if he speaks them again? And why also did the demon close the scribe's lips?"

The rapping of wood on stone ricocheted through the chamber as Jonness began to pace again. "The scribe is crafty. He is possessed by a demon of deception, who seeks to harm us. The demon led him to the book, and together they opened the sarcophagus and desecrated the body."

"If he—"

Jonness raised his hand, silencing Agabus. "Satan wants us to turn these men over to Rome. He wants a public trial to display the blasphemy of this book against the holy church." Jonness stopped. Hand still uplifted, he closed his eyes. "But we will not be deceived nor allow these men to harm the flock. The book was sealed and shall again be put to rest. We will pray over this matter, and I will decide what is to be done."

Fingers quavering—how he hated what age had stolen from him—Agabus picked at raw scabs on his jaw. "Your Holiness, I agree with the wisdom God has revealed to you, but I am troubled."

The men turned.

"The scribe has been missing now four days, and we do not know if he made a copy of the book. Perhaps that is why the demon closed his lips—so he could not be questioned? Batush says he was with the coffee trader, who may have answers, but we do not know if either man is to be trusted. This demon is playing tricks with us. We must be gentle as doves, but also shrewd like serpents." As he spoke, he stared at the empty chair below them.

CHAPTER 26

National Security Agency, United States of America
Case Number: PDCA-6477
Investigations Division, via email

Attention: Detective Ryan Green
The subject case has been transferred to the
Federal Bureau of Investigation. You are hereby
directed to destroy all related case files both
written and electronic, including: Reports,
images, interviews, notes, and recordings.
Agency Controller

"IT ARRIVED last night at 11:33. That's when I checked the project folder and discovered it's gone. The video, the still shots, our notes, and the site report. All of it—they deleted it. Who do they think they are, entering our network and stealing our data? I want to file a complaint, but who do I even send it to?"

Propped against the doorjamb, Howard gave his coffee a swirl. "You can't fight these guys. They have the authority to do whatever they want, and they do." He gazed at the ceiling. "It happened to me back in the eighties. A judge was murdered, and it was a big deal because he had political ties. I was working the case, collecting evidence, and doing interviews. Then one day, these two dicks show up at the station—it was like *Men in Black*. They had the shiny black shoes, black pants, and skinny ties with the white shirts. Same thing, they came in and took our files. I was pissed and demanded to see a warrant. They didn't even crack a smile, but one of them flashed a badge—FBI."

"What did you do?"

"Same thing you're gonna do—nothing. I did some follow up for a while on my own time. And there was no one to give it to. My boss wouldn't touch it, and the Feds didn't even want to see it. Get this... I had talked to a guy who knew the shooter, and he told me, well, never mind—it doesn't matter. No one cared... They had their game plan, and that was it. You gotta let it go."

"This is garbage. I can't believe it." Ryan shoved away from his desk.

"Sorry, kid—it stinks. You gotta roll with it. It's part of the job."

As the old man walked out of the room, Ryan clenched his fists. *Burnout. Like someone who's been staring at the calendar waiting for the exit.*

Ryan opened his desk drawer and glanced into the corridor. Picking up a flash drive, he dropped it in his shirt pocket. He then checked his file cabinet. A quick rifling through the hanging files confirmed his dread. *The case folder—missing.*

He turned again to the empty corridor.

<<>>

Dressed in the simple cloak of a commoner, Jonness checked behind him as he lifted the latch and leaned into the heavy door. Almost falling, he caught himself as it flew open.

"Your Holiness? I—I was checking to see if there might be a delivery. I did not expect... Can I help you find something?" Face to face, Naaman's mouth hung open. His gaze quickly falling, he moved aside.

"I came to check as well." Jonness moved past him and then stopped. "Is your recording complete?" Jonness drew his hood over his head with both hands.

"No, Your Holiness. I must check it for accuracy and then make the final."

"Bring it to my chamber when it is ready."

"Yes, Your Holiness."

Jonness exited beneath the awning into the drizzle. Descending the stone ramp, he stepped into the quagmire shrouded in waist-deep fog. He then made his way along the perimeter wall to the service gates. He turned back, squinting as he pulled the cloak tight to his chin. The short young scribe's ghosted shape stood motionless on the loading dock. Using the man-gate, Jonness left the yard. From there, he followed the descending service trail to Marble Road.

Watching his step, he paced the slick road. The violent cough of a man close enough to touch startled him. He smelled him before he saw him, bent over a vegetable cart. Crossing the road, Jonness slipped and threw an arm out to catch his balance. *Careful—the last thing we need is to be rescued. I'm fasting and only wanted to walk among the flock.*

The sun's disk was barely visible when he arrived at Curetes Street. A bit farther, he spotted the stone phallus and a woman standing in the corbeled opening just beyond the fountain. When he recognized the supple shape, warmth lit his face. Rachael, older than the other women, owned the brothel.

Jonness withdrew his hood. "Greetings, my beauty."

"It's been too long—where have you been, my love?" She drew him forward, reaching between the folds of his cloak.

He moaned. "I am captive in your grasp."

"Business is slow, and some of the girls are not well. Come, my Holiness. Perhaps if you pray and lay your hands on me this fog will leave us?" She purred seduction, parting her robe to bare her heavy breasts.

"Hush!" he hissed. "Don't call me that—your girls might hear." Touching her soft flesh, his fingers lingered. "I will need a bath and a carriage. Will you wait for my return?"

She laughed. "Jonness, when you return, you will have no strength for me." She let go, clapping twice sharply. "Girls!"

Two young women quickly appeared, both dressed in laced linen.

"Bathe him and have Marius prepare the cart." Closing her robe, Rachael walked away, then stopped in the doorway. "You and I, Jonness, we are much alike, are we not?"

<<>>

Heading for the kitchen, Amber walked through the library, her phone propped against her ear with her shoulder. In her hands, she carried a mug of coffee, a plate of fruit, and five sheets of paper. Balancing on one leg, she closed the sliding glass patio door with her foot. The cool morning was quickly turning hot.

"I called while it was printing—here, I've got it in my hand. It's not the private sector, but it's very generous." She placed the mug and plate on the granite counter and then told him about the job offer and position specifics.

Richard did not respond.

Amber bit her lip. "It comes with a five-thousand-dollar signing bonus, and the church would cover our moving costs. It includes medical and dental insurance for both of us and..." She squeezed the back of the barstool. "It also comes with a two-week paid vacation and a performance bonus."

"Performance bonus—how does that work?" His voice was steady but soft.

Can't he at least pretend to be excited...?

She pulled the stool out and eased onto it. "It's based on attendance and giving numbers. The church is in serious financial trouble, but I can fix it. Honey, it would be so easy. I mean, well, it'll take some work, but I'm thinking with just a few changes, we could easily double the congregation. They have about nine hundred attending on Sundays, and the annual budget is a little over two million. Palm Desert is filled with retirement communities, and I'm thinking we could bus people in. They've got to be bored silly, and I understand it'll take some logistics. But..."

Her toes on the footrail, she rotated back and forth to silence. "The campus is older but has some great facilities, and they're debt free. I'm thinking... There are just so many ideas I have and—well, what do you think?"

"If anyone could make a difference, it's you, Amby. I've been praying about it, quite a lot. I've also been praying for you. So how are you doing?"

"I'm great. I'm also surprised by how excited I am about this. But you know me—always drawn to a challenge."

"So, what's the salary?"

"It's more than I expected—but there'll be a lot of responsibility. And, well—it's based on regional data, and—not including the signing bonus it's ninety thousand."

"Wow, that's amazing. I'm not sure what our pastor makes, but I know it's not that much. But we're a lot smaller, and we don't have a school or the staff. Wow." Again, Richard was quiet. "So, what have you been hearing from the Lord?"

Asmodeus whispered, *"The Lord will do great and mighty things for those who trust Him. I will lead my people to the promised land...."*

"I haven't given it a lot of thought. But right now, I'm hearing step out in faith and trust the Lord for great and mighty things. And also that we've been wandering in the wilderness and the people are hungry and thirsty. And the Lord is saying: I will lead you into the Promised Land."

"That sounds significant. You know I want you to be happy, but the move, it'll be hard. I guess I hadn't considered we might actually do this. Leaving our friends and church family... But, if it's the Lord, we need to be listening."

Richard spoke distantly, as if from a dream.

"There's one more thing.... They want me to start right away."

"How soon is right away?"

"Monday at eight. To meet the staff. Nick Hamilton, he's one of the elders, would be introducing me. I think that's why they're offering the signing bonus, so I can buy some things. They said I can stay in the loft. The owner's never in town and would let me—or both of us even—stay as long as we want."

Amber's rotation on the stool and her breathing glided to a stop.

"I would need to at least stay through the midterm. You know that, right?"

"I do. But you could join me later. I could fly up, and we would drive back together. It would only be for six weeks. The church needs us, and they need me right away. Some big decisions need to be made before the holidays. And, well—what do you think? It's your call. I'll do whatever you say." She bit her lip again.

"I want to pray and fast for a couple days. When do they need to know?"

"Tomorrow by five. But I'm sure they can wait a little longer if I ask."

It was quiet again.

"Let's pray about it and talk tomorrow. How does that sound?"

"That sounds great." She stared at the document in her hand. She'd already signed it.

<<>>

The fog had thinned. Hanging in the still air like a blanket of smoke, it muffled the clopping hoofs. Brush-clad hills surrounded them, visibility to no more than a stone's throw. The drizzle had transitioned to a fine-beaded mist that swirled within the fog, permeating every surface. Asmodeus licked at the air. He could almost drink it.

The cart was fitted with plank benches and a weather canopy fashioned from sackcloth and tied to vertical posts. At least the crude vehicle was horse-drawn. Horses were stronger and far more predictable than donkeys. Besides, he hated donkeys. Jostling to and fro, he lamented vehicles of the modern era, although he'd seen far worse, and the road, constructed by Rome with interlocking pavers, was quite good. This northern route linked with other towns and cities, but its primary destination was the Temple of Artemis.

He sat next to the driver. Facing backward, he stared at the bishop. A large man, his thick wavy white mantle framed a high forehead. His neatly trimmed short beard accentuated his puffy red cheeks and bulbous nose. It was the eyebrows that stood out, unwieldy with protruding whisker-like hairs. The combination was a bit striking, the brows leaping out of his face in contradiction to the impeccably manicured curls.

Arms folded over his chest, Jonness belched from indigestion every few minutes. With his smooth pallor and soft hands, he clearly spent little time in the sun and didn't bother with physical work. A man of power and position, typically surrounded by an entourage, but today, he traveled alone.

Taking the man would not be difficult, and Asmodeus would do it by force if necessary. But an invitation was typically cleaner, and he was in no hurry. Indwelling the body of an obese older man would not be his first choice. The body noises alone would be considerable for someone who ate and drank like this man.

He preferred humans who were wholly functional and physically fit. Athletes and warriors were typically quite good, but his robe of choice was a beautiful woman. Although physique was important, power was key, and this man wielded authority as well as a title.

And Asmodeus relished power. It was the elixir of the physical realm, an aphrodisiac of sorts that highlighted his existence.

Pounding hoofs announced the arrival of a chariot closing rapidly. Jonness withdrew a mask from his cloak and slipped it over his face.

Asmodeus huffed. Costume masks were quite common among Romans for parties and festivals and helpful also when one didn't want to be recognized. The unspoken protocol was not to acknowledge the mask wearer, even when their identity was obvious. After all, without seeing the face, it was impossible to know for sure, allowing for the freedom of expression without accusation or condemnation.

Jonness nodded as the chariot rushed past with two Roman soldiers.

Asmodeus leaned in to study the mask crafted from perforated copper and colorful feathers. The plumage swept back from exposed metal to form the face, a hawk-like effect with protruding beak and shiny round eyes concealing horizontal view slits. Quite beautiful but surely uncomfortable, considering the quills exposed on the interior.

Jonness pulled the mask to his forehead. Leaning over the side of the cart, he sneezed. He then blew his nose into his hands and slung the mucus to the road.

Asmodeus made a face, disgusted yet resigned to his assignment. He would bide his time.

<<>>

Sunrise was overtaking darkness as Nick executed the trade. Drawing a sip of dark roast, he whispered, "Zen Master—Yes." Behind the L-shaped array of monitors, he watched the stochastic graph turning down with volume rising. He confirmed the trade and did the calculations. *Twenty-six eight, in nineteen minutes. Like stealing candy from a baby—too easy. Just think if we had placed all of it?*

He scanned his list of discretionary accounts, which included four of his fellow elders. He'd traded with their money, as well as six others, using none of his own. They had each risked 5 percent of their portfolios but would receive just 10 percent of the profit generated from their contributions, the balance going to him.

It had become routine. Check the news and foreign markets, along with the price of the dollar and precious metals. Lights out, alarm goes off, climb out of bed. Brew the coffee while the machine boots, then bring up the platform and check for breaking news. Strap in and sip coffee while scoring some cash, all before heading to the office.

He was ahead over twenty thousand in his first month of real trading with just a handful of down days. He'd broken even a couple of times but typically was up and gaining confidence.

Mammon encouraged, "*What a way to start the day! This is fun. We should have been doing this all along? But don't get cocky and remember— tithe to the clients and the church.*"

Nick was moving the monies back to the client accounts when the phone rang. Fear twinged his mind as he read the caller display: Palm Desert Police. He glanced at his list of accounts. *There's no way...*

"Hello, Nick Hamilton speaking."

"Good morning, this is Detective Ryan Green with Palm Desert PD. I hope it's not too early to call?"

"Not at all... I'm just sipping my coffee and about to leave for work."

"Relax."

"I was assigned to the Karen Peterson case, and I'm following up on the investigation into her death."

"Investigation? I didn't know there was an investigation."

"Yes. The circumstances of Karen's death were quite unusual, and we're trying to close some loose ends. I understand you knew Karen, and she was meeting you at the loft on the day she was killed. Is that right?"

"Yes. Karen worked for the church. She was our receptionist, a wonderful woman. Everyone loved her. I was doing an interview, and Karen was on her way to join us. She was going to take notes."

"Can you tell me who it was you were interviewing?"

"Amber Lash—we're in the process of hiring her, and I'm one of the elders. That's why I was meeting her—she was in town, and I was interviewing her at the loft. One of our congregants owns it, and Amber is staying there. That's why Karen was coming over... Because it would not be appropriate, well, to be there alone with a woman."

"Just answer his questions. You sound ridiculous."

"I understand the maintenance guy did it. Is that, right? The guy who jumped and killed himself?"

"It looks that way. But someone else was there, and that's what we're looking at."

"Are you saying someone else was involved?"

"You're doing it again."

"No. But the security cameras showed an individual was there shortly after it happened. So we're talking to people who were in the building, to see if we can locate the potential witness. Would it be possible to meet with you and Ms. Lash?"

"Ah, sure, that would be fine. Both of us would be happy to help. If you like, we can meet at the church. Amber will be there on Monday— does that sound good?" He threw his open hand into the air, stopping short of his forehead.

"You mentioned Ms. Lash is staying at the loft. Sometimes being at the scene is helpful in remembering something you might otherwise overlook. Could we meet there?"

"I can try to set it up. When would you want to do it?"

"How's today? Could we do it at, say, four?"

"Thursday, let me think. It's short notice, but it's good for me. I'll call Ms. Lash and get back to you." He thought of Brooke then.

"No reason to tell her. It might be disturbing. Besides, she might not like you at the loft again with Amber—Don't tell her."

Nick hung up. Looking to his monitor, he saw his pick slogging uphill. *Damn, missed the second score, but no need to be greedy. Besides, it's a good sign.*

Mammon whispered, *"Thirsty Thursdays... Tell Brooke not to worry—it's an emergency elder meeting, and it could run late...."*

CHAPTER 27

THEY SANG the song of Moses, struggling to remember many of the words but not the chorus:

"...I will sing to the Lord, for He is exalted. The horse and its rider He has hurled into the sea. The Lord is my strength and song. And He is my salvation. This is my God, and I will extol Him. The Lord is a warrior. The Lord is His name..."

Their voices echoed through the stone labyrinth. A man they could not see sang with them from a distant location. In the adjacent cell, an old man slept on a bed with straw matting, his head hanging over the edge, a string of drool clinging to his dirty beard.

"That song brings remembrance to me of a time long past."

"Tell me of this memory, good friend." Zophar's eyes glinted with roguish mirth.

Batush rubbed his hands together for warmth. "My father took me to the mountains of Masis when I was just becoming a man. It was late in the year and very windy. We climbed the southern peak and were within reach of the summit, and we were both weary. My father put his hand on my shoulder and said, 'Batush, can you make it? If not, we must return now.' But I could not answer. All around us, ice hung in the air and clung to the rocks. It was cold, and my legs were crying out. We could not see the top because it was hidden in the clouds. And so, I prayed—it was very short."

Zophar grinned in wonder.

"I prayed, 'Lord God, You brought me here, and I am afraid. If You want me to climb on, I will, but I need a sign—give me a sign, Lord.' And then..."

"What happened? What did the Lord say?"

Tears filled Batush's eyes. Unable to speak, he fanned his arms while shaking his head. The torchlight outside the iron bars danced on Zophar's face as he waited. Batush blinked back the stench of burning oil and stale refuse. He then scratched his stubbled chin. His head bobbing, he continued.

"He did not say anything. I lifted my gaze, somehow knowing—I will never forget. The sky parted—like a giant fish suspended in a moving stream. The clouds opened—like an eye. And a golden beam of light came down and lit the mountaintop. And then it closed, and...” Batush's voice trembled.

“What happened? Did you climb on?”

“I heard the voice of God then. It was the very first time. Perhaps it was the voice of an angel, but I believe it was the Spirit of God. He said, ‘Come closer, Batush. I am here. Come to me.’ I could only look at my father. I nodded yes and pointed. And so we climbed on. He led, with me in his footsteps.”

“Did you make it to the top?”

“Yes, and we hid from the wind behind a boulder. I was shivering, and sand was grinding into my eyes. My teeth were banging together—oy, I was so cold! Father asked if I was well. But I could not form words to speak. He suggested we wait for me to warm, but I only grew colder. And so we headed back down. I knew then—I was in the hand of God. He could take me if He chose, or He could save me.”

Zophar nudged him with a meaty elbow. “And He saved you because you are here with me today in jail.”

They laughed.

Facing each other on separate cots, Batush gripped the damp mat and tugged on a clump of straw. Across from them, the old man began to cough and then growl. Magnified by the hard surfaces, the sound boomed through the cavernous space like a roaring lion.

They continued to laugh until the ruckus subsided.

“When we got down from the highest point, it was not so windy. My father asked if I could feel my feet, but I could not. He told me then to take off my boots, and he rubbed my feet. Very fast—like this. And then...” He stopped again.

“What did you learn?”

“It opened again—the sky. Again, it was the eye, but this time on its side. It opened and then closed.” He extended his arms, waving them apart and then together. “We saw the whole world—stretching out for a great distance. It seemed the Lord was showing it to me, and He said, ‘I am calling you, Batush. You will speak My words to the nations.’ And I knew then I would become a scribe. Preserving the words of God—it is a noble thing, I think. Yes?” Batush opened his hands, a tilted smile on his face.

"But what did I learn on the mountain, and what did God say? He said, 'Give me your every breath—all of you. I want your very life, and I will use it for My glory.' That is what I heard, and that is what I learned." Batush leaned against the smooth stone wall, the chill drawing the warmth from his frame. From the small opening in the deep wall, no bigger than his open hand, he heard the steady patter of rain again.

Zophar leaned forward, elbows on his knees. "What are you thinking?"

"What of the book? What will the Church Fathers do with the words of God, written by the beloved friend of Jesus?"

"You have done that which was asked, Batush. That is all you can do. The book is in His hands, and that is a good place. You know this from the mountain, do you not?"

"Again, you minister to me, Zophar. I am humbled but also sorry you are in prison because of me."

"I am blessed to be here. And I am not afraid—what can they do? This world is not our home. They cannot take heaven from us, can they? And you minister to me also. These things you are telling me—I cannot imagine or even understand."

Batush clamped his hand on Zophar's shoulder. "Being here is like the mountain. We are giving up our bodies to serve the Lord, even if our lives are taken from us—it is much like fasting." He stared at the stale chunk of bread and the metal water cup that had been on the floor since their arrival. "Are you going to eat that?"

"No. We should wait until our families hear of this and bring food and water. We should fast for three days, praying for the Lord's deliverance."

They sat for a while, and then Zophar asked, "Does your body hurt from the beating?"

"Not too much. Remember to be persecuted for the Lord is joy, yes?"

"It is, my friend. It is, indeed."

Through the corridor drifted a soft whimpering. An unseen deep voice responded with a shouting demand for silence.

"Why did they not beat you, I wonder? It seemed the guard enjoyed beating me. Perhaps he likes your coffee too much?"

"You could be right. The guards are at my shop every day. Maybe his arm was tired, and he will come back to beat me later?"

Again, they laughed, the comforting sound warming the cold stone.

"Do you have another song, Batush?"

"The one we sang last week in church—you know the one." He started, and Zophar joined, the man in the far cell now silent.

"*...I will extol You, my God, O King, and I will bless Your name forever and ever. Men shall speak of the power of Your awesome acts, and I will tell of Your greatness. They shall utter the memory of Your goodness and shout joyfully of Your righteousness. The LORD is good to all, and His mercies are over all His works...*"

"Now it is your turn, Zophar. Sing to me in your native tongue—I would like that."

Zophar hesitated and then closed his eyes. Opening his mouth, he sang with closed eyes, his head tilted back.

Waves of adoration radiated through Batush's core as the song echoed through the stone walls. The rhythm slowed in pace and then softened to a whisper as Zophar's chin met his chest.

"You sing with the voice of an angel. I did not know you had the gift of tongues. Tell me the words of this song—I must know them."

Zophar rubbed his face, the familiar twinkle in his eye. "You know this song. It is the one we were just singing."

"Be quiet, or I will beat you again." The guard stood glaring at the bars. He then unlocked the old man's cell. "Get up, Jethro. It is time to go home." He kicked the bed platform, and the old man jerked from his stupor. "Your wife is here for you. And if I ever see you again, I will beat you to death. I am tired of your drinking."

"I will pray to Caesar for strength." Stuttering, Jethro suddenly vomited.

Jumping backward, the guard lifted his hand to strike. "This is what I am talking about. I will get your wife, and when I return—if I even smell it—I will be back with the whip, and you will have no skin when I am finished. Perhaps you like it here because your wife abuses you—I see she is quite strong. Maybe I will ravage her as you watch, and she will like it." The guard walked away laughing.

Dropping to his knees, Jethro began to wipe up the mess using the straw.

<<>>

The treadmill accelerated with a whir as Amber tapped the green arrow. In front of her, the digital screen displayed a London streetscape approaching her, complete with other runners and a black taxicab. Breathing heavily, she swiped the white gym towel from her shoulders and wiped her forehead. Across the room, a heavyset shirtless bald man in blue swim trunks smiled at her while sitting on a bicycle. Pretending not to notice, she drew her phone from the hip pocket of her black spandex one-piece. She was about to open her email when the display lit with a call from Nick. When she punched the red arrow, the treadmill rapidly decelerated, allowing her to safely step down to the floor.

"Hello, Amber Lash."

"Hi, Amber—it's Nick. Have a minute?"

"I do, but I'm out of breath. Sorry." Amber panted. "I just discovered the building has a gym. Whew, I was on the treadmill when you called." Amber leaned against the window-wall chair-rail. Propping the phone at her ear, she drew deep breaths. "That's better, whew. What's up?"

The man in blue dismounted from the bike and girded his belly with a towel.

"I'm sorry to interrupt, but something just came up. It sounds fairly important, but first—I wanted to ask how you're doing?"

"That's fine. I was about to take a break." Amber sat on a weight bench. "I'm doing great and enjoying the loft. It's wonderful."

"It's hard not to like. I was thinking how great it would be to serve with you, and I'm wondering if you've made a decision?"

Asmodeus whispered, *"Play hard to get."*

"The opportunity is exciting, and the offer is quite generous. To be honest, I wasn't expecting all of this so fast, and, well, Richard and I are going to need some time to pray about it. It's a big step, and with the move—it's not an easy decision."

"Don't mention Richard again."

"How does Richard feel about it? Is he ready for Palm Desert?"

She bit her tongue. "He's a little overwhelmed. I think it's going to take some time for him to process."

Standing in front of an ice-filled water dispenser, the hairy-chested man was now sipping from a small white cup. Again, he smiled as she turned away.

"I'll be praying for you both, and I completely understand. Lots of guys are like Richard. I'm sorry it seems like I'm pressing. I guess I'm more like you."

"Change the subject before he embarrasses himself."

Amber wiped her forehead. "You mentioned something important came up?"

"Yes. I got a call from a Detective Green. He's investigating Karen's death and wants to meet with us because Karen was on her way to join us when it happened."

"That's interesting." She imagined him shrugging.

"He also mentioned someone may have seen Karen fall, and they're trying to locate that person. I'm not sure we can help, but I told him we would certainly cooperate."

"Well, of course—that goes without saying. When would he like to meet?"

"Today at four, at the loft. I can tell him next week if it's too short of notice, but I told him I'd ask."

"I'd planned to do some shopping, but I'd rather get this out of the way. Next week could be busy. Yes, today is fine."

"Okay then. I'll confirm. Thanks. I know you must be thinking about a thousand things right now. But I agree—we should get it over with."

"I'm not looking forward to it. Talking about it again and remembering... I'm just glad you'll be with me." She stood and then walked back to the glass. Looking down, she stared at the sidewalk and streetlight below.

<<>>

Muggy and increasingly uncomfortable, his palms and temples slick, Jonness adjusted his position on the bench seat as the prickly mask scratched at his skin. Tempted to remove it, Jonness waited while they passed a procession of pilgrims.

Dressed in white robes, they were crowned with ornate headdresses crafted from green leaves, twigs, and flowers. About half of the group sported masks, mostly depicting forest animals. Several stags, complete with antlers and fur, convened with bears, lions, panthers, and birds. The majority also bore idols, wearing them like necklaces, some tied with twine and others in small cages and boxes.

The pagan procession of Artemis occurred four times a year. Today's celebration had opened at the Temple of Hadrian, with the pilgrims enjoying a light feast of grilled meats and new wine. The ceremony included four stops, one at each of the city's prominent monuments where fees were collected from the partakers. Today's pilgrimage would culminate at the Temple of Artemis, one of the world's seven wonders. People had traveled from all corners of the earth to see it over the centuries. Today's group was small, about two hundred.

The cart had nearly passed when he saw it—a waving flag embroidered with Caesar's olive-leaf wreath encircling the purple cross of his faith. How he loathed the Nicolaitans who proclaimed to follow Christ but, upon conversion, refused to surrender their pagan rites! Instead, they merely added a convoluted version of Christianity to their heathen lifestyle. He smoldered inside his mask, a piercing pressure behind his ears. He wanted to rebuke them, especially those bearing caged crosses swinging to and fro about their necks.

A cheer erupted when a young boy was first to call out the temple sighting, considered to be good luck. Jonness shifted his position to admire its enormity, emerging from the fog. The fact that a building could draw so much attention filled him with awe and jealousy. They came to see it and worship Artemis the Huntress, nocturnal goddess of the moon. The Greeks had built the original structure, later destroyed by fire and then replaced by Rome. Upon completion, the Romans changed its name in dedication to Diana. But the people continued to call it by the former name, worshiping both fertility gods with a single sacrifice.

As they drew closer, the temple's balanced proportions were unveiled. Classic Greek, it presented with a rectangular footprint, elevated at the perimeter with steps. A double row of fluted Corinthian columns bound the platform's four sides with pediments rising on the roof's gabled ends. Ornately carved relief panels above the entry depicted Rome's prominent gods—four on each side facing the epiphany window. Sometimes Artemis herself mysteriously appeared in the oval window, blessing those who came to worship her.

Jonness clenched his fists. Someday, the church would possess a building of worship rivaling this. Awe-inspiring, the structure would have soaring spaces and artwork lit with colored glass. Pilgrims of the true faith would travel great distances, entering with penitent hearts ready to confess their darkest sins and make offerings to the church, to which they owed their very salvation. *Yes, one day it will come to pass, God willing.*

The cart eased to a stop a short distance from a crowd now gathering before the stone altar on the temple square. He handed two small coins to the driver. Avoiding his reaction, Jonness turned away as a cheer swept over the crowd. Emerging from behind a wall, a robed priest waved a fist-sized bloody object above his head. Placing it on top of the stone altar, he bowed with face to the ground as the cheering intensified. It started with a poof of flame about the size of a bush, then subsided, leaving the wood smoldering.

A man cried out, "Fire from heaven—look."

A hush fell over the crowd as a woman shrieked and pointed to a figure in the epiphany window. Wearing only a white veil and crown of leaves, Artemis danced to the beat of unseen drums. The crowd responded with wild cheers as she undulated, stroking her long red hair and full breasts. Disappearing with a wave, she then reappeared to a roaring ovation. A silver phallus in her hoisted fist, she waved it above her head.

The Nicolaitan with the flag shouted and laughed, exclaiming to anyone who might be listening, "She blesses me! She blesses me."

Disgust twisting his gut and lips, Jonness shook his head. *Clearly, the fire was lit from below by an unseen workman, and the goddess is a mere prostitute. Surely, they see the facade of deception but do not care. How is the church to compete with this—and the Nicolaitans...? They join in and embrace it. We must have a building. It is the only way.*

CHAPTER 28

"CAN YOU tell me why the three of you were meeting here?"

While the detective spoke from the couch across the coffee table, a glass of ice water on a coaster in front of him, along with his accordion file, Nick sat up straight. With Amber settled next to him on the matching couch, they held glasses of ice water. A silk pillow between them, Amber swept sandy curls from her shoulders and then smoothed her gray skirt into place. Nick breathed in deeply. Savoring her soft clean scent, he tried to remember the last time Brooke had worn perfume.

"I—" Amber edged forward as he lifted his hand to stop her.

"I believe it's appropriate for me to address that question. As I mentioned, I'm one of the elders at Faith Church—or Faith Bible Community Church, that is. We've been working our way through a search process for a new executive pastor and interviewed Amber Lash. We were quite impressed and hope Amber will be joining us." He rested a hand on the smooth leather couch and smiled at her. His eyes lingered on her slender ivory neck. "Anyway, I felt we needed to bring her up to speed—before meeting with the larger group." He flexed his Rolex band while rotating his wrist. "The first meeting was with just two of us, elders that is—and also two staff members—the senior pastor and our pastor of worship and arts." He tugged at his collar.

"He doesn't need to know all that. You sound like an idiot."

"Go on."

"Anyway, we set the meeting here because Amber was traveling and this loft, belonging to one of our parishioners, was available, and I wanted Karen—the deceased..."

With a deep breath, he drew a circle in the air with his finger. "I wanted Karen to take notes and to be available to help with questions. And also to be sure, well, as I said on the phone, because she's a woman. It wouldn't be appropriate without another person present. Karen is—or was—our executive assistant."

"Did the three of you drive together?"

"No. I had a meeting later in the day and wasn't sure if I might need to leave early. Karen was at the church, and so we had set the meeting. And no—we drove separately." He shifted in his seat.

"Did either of you know the maintenance technician, Thomas Chapman?"

"The guy who did it?"

"Officially, he's still a suspect. But the evidence certainly points to him. He went by Tank, but his given name was Thomas."

"No. Neither of us ever saw him before. Well, I saw him in the lobby on my way up—on the day Karen was killed. But not before."

"Had you ever seen him before, Ms. Lash?"

Nick interrupted, "I'm sorry, Detective. I shouldn't have spoken for Amber. I just assumed..."

"Shut up."

"No, the first time I ever saw him was on my way up." Her finger floated along the lip of her glass.

"Did either of you see anyone else in the building before the incident or anyone leaving afterward? Anyone at all?"

"I didn't, or... No one—besides the people we saw from above, gathered around him after he jumped. That was all I saw." He rotated toward Amber, his knee bumping her thigh as his attention jolted back to the detective.

Detective Green remained motionless.

"That would be the same for me as well." Her red-painted nail glided to a stop on the rim of the glass. "I didn't see anyone in the building or leaving the building."

"Did you hear anything?"

"We both heard the scream—through the elevator shaft."

"Did you hear her, Amber?"

A shiver rippling over her, she bit her lip and glanced away. "I did, yes—I heard her."

"I'm sorry. I understand it's hard, but I have just two more questions. You mentioned seeing the body below. And because your windows are directly below the spot where he left the roof, I need to ask—did either of you see him or hear anything when he went off the roof? And tell me where you were exactly when that happened?"

"No, we didn't see anything. We heard the scream—or a scream from below. It sounded like a woman, but we didn't hear or see him jump." Nick felt warm. "We were standing right over there when we heard Karen. We could tell she was going down the shaft—or the scream was. About a minute or so later, we were in the corridor, checking to see if anyone was there. Then we heard the second scream and ran out to the balcony. And that was when we saw him on the pavement."

"What about you, Ms. Lash?"

"Quit answering for her!" Mammon shouted.

"I didn't see him leave the roof or hear him. We both heard the woman scream from below. Like Nick said, we were in the corridor and then ran to the balcony."

"Okay, just one last question." Detective Green folded his hands. "I mentioned to you, Nick, the building has a camera system. In fact, it was very helpful in gathering evidence. We know someone witnessed the incident because we have his picture. I should mention, he's not a suspect, but he is a person of interest."

He opened his accordion file. "We got a face shot, but it's blurry. Anyway, the camera equipment has different settings, and I was able to enhance it using some filters. Technology is amazing, and I'm not very good at using it. But I'd like you to look. This was taken in infrared, so I had to guess on skin color. This first one is what he looks like if he's Caucasian. And this would be African. This last one is between the two if he's Hispanic or Arabic, Native American or possibly Asian. I had to guess on the eye color also, so all of them are brown." He laid the photos on the coffee table. "Have either of you ever seen this guy? Take your time."

Nick leaned forward. "Wow, he's strong. That's a striking face—I would remember if I had ever seen him. No, I've never seen him."

Amber's elbow brushed him as she moved the couch pillow, sliding closer.

~~

Asmodeus lied, *"I've never seen him before. I would remember."*

"No—I've never seen him before. I'm sure I would remember." Amber squeezed her water glass as a wave of fear swept over her.

"Which one would you say matches best with his facial features? There's no right or wrong answer. I'm just curious. What do you think?"

Amber pointed. "That one—the one in bronze."

<<>>

Asmodeus enjoyed clothing himself in flesh because it opened a realm of opportunities. The range of emotions and physical sensations were magnified until almost palatable. Pain and death especially intrigued him, even though he'd experienced both on countless occasions within a mortal. And their blindness to the spiritual dimension—astonishing. If humans had eyes to see, how differently they would behave! He sighed. While he'd never fully understand humans, he longed to.

Jonness headed directly toward the cleansing pools with Asmodeus following. Being an observer for so long, he was almost never surprised. *So predictable. The second bath in a single day—clearly, he is not here on official business only.*

Wading into the heated pool, Asmodeus was tempted to take Jonness by force. Those watching would attribute the commotion to a spiritual experience. After all, it was the sacred pool of Artemis. He snorted at a heavyset woman bathing herself just ahead. *Imagine if I took him now and then engaged her while throwing off his mask? A display like that would rock the foundations of many. However, it would likely displease the master. Besides, mischief making of that sort is better suited for the tormentors and havoc makers.*

Asmodeus whispered as they passed. *"I want you."*

Emerging from the pool, he studied the bishop, who seemed quite comfortable in his nakedness. The others around them were drying off and putting their robes back on, but Jonness did neither. Instead, he walked with cloak in hand, through the grand hall wearing only his mask.

The humans, overcome by the magnitude and grandeur of the space, gazed upward, wavering with arms outstretched as they received the experience into their conscience. The reaction he observed had value in reinforcing the vision. True, the Temple of Artemis did not include human sacrifices, but the worship of one's flesh and decadence was nothing to disregard. In many ways, lust and self-focus could be even greater for distraction and confusion, which, of course, was the point.

An idea began to emerge. *Perhaps fighting the adversary's efforts to build is a mistake? After all, they will soon have their churches where they will proudly display their wretched cross, a symbol of the lost great battle.*

But maybe—maybe, it could be more profitable to focus on shaping those who will ultimately construct the buildings? What is the difference? After all, an idol is an idol, whether a golden calf or cross of stone? I must share this revelation with the comrades.

<<>>

The chunk of dried bread was nearly twice his size, but he was persistent. The mouse had first tried to push it, with little success, and was now dragging it. Stopping, he took his fill and then scurried to the metal cup to perch atop its rim. Leaning forward, he extended his tail for balance. When he dropped his head, it disappeared inside. Popping up, he vigorously scrubbed his face, then paused to stare at his audience.

Batush looked to Zophar, who leaned against the wall. "He can have the bread, but I wish he would tip over the cup so I can stop dreaming of it." He could hardly form the words with his parched mouth. "If we were not fasting, would we be so thirsty, or is it because we can only think of water? How long do you think before they find us?"

"They will be here tomorrow. Right now, they are wondering why we are late and beginning to worry. In the morning, Gibeon will go first to the church."

"Will the Church Fathers tell him, do you think?" He knew the answer before asking.

"Perhaps someone will. If not, he will next come here to see if the authorities know where we are. They will come tomorrow."

"Are you as thirsty as I, dear brother?"

"I am thirsty with you, but not thirsty for water."

CHAPTER 29

AS NICK ushered the detective from the room, Amber stroked her lower lip. *A fully functioning man and quite handsome, but what am I thinking? What am I even doing here?* After closing the door, he turned around. Meeting her gaze, he shook out his arms.

"I don't know why I was so nervous, maybe it was the badge, I'm just glad he finally left. I think I need a drink. How 'bout you?" Nick paused in front of the couch and then headed for the kitchen. Outside, the sun was approaching the mountain ridge.

"That sounds nice, yes. Someone restocked the wine cooler and refrigerator when I was out. Mr. Bernhardt knows how to shop and seems to know my taste." Amber kicked her sandals off and curled into the corner of the couch.

"Wow, there's a killer platter of hors d'oeuvres in here waiting for us. This will be perfect with a glass of white. Let's see we've got Chalk Hill and..."

Nick was turning the next bottle when Amber said, "Chalk Hill sounds good. Let's have that."

Asmodeus blurted, *"Tell him to bring the second bottle. And the cooler, it's too cold. Have him turn it up three degrees."*

"I love cold wine, but it gets me in trouble. I'll need to be careful—you might take advantage."

"You can have as much as you like—remember, you're not driving? It's me you might need to worry about."

Eyes widening with a stifled twinkle, he settled next to her and presented the platter while negotiating the bottle and glasses. He worked the blade opener with the skill of a server in a fine restaurant. "There was a corkscrew in the drawer, but I like doing it the old-fashioned way. The trick is—you need a real cork for this to work, and they're becoming more and more rare. Bernhardt's stock doesn't have a lot of fake corks."

"What about screw tops?"

"Ha. If there's one of those here, you'll find it under the sink, next to the drain cleaner." They laughed as he poured into the crystal chard glasses, stopping at the one-third point. Lifting their glasses, they paused as their eyes met.

"Here's to you. I'm hoping my new pastor—or minister, I mean—and partner?" He tilted his head. "Well...? You could at least tease me."

"It's yes for me. But I need to let Richard make the decision." Cradling the glass in her palm, she drew a sip. "Mm, that's really crisp and clean. I usually like it sweeter, but this is nice, almost like champagne without the bubbles."

"What if he says no?"

"He won't. We've been talking about making a change. Richard's very thoughtful and needs time to pray. He's not one for snap decisions. That would be me. I'm so impulsive." She watched his hands as he opened a package of smoked salmon. Working with two small forks, he broke it into chunks and then transferred it to the platter. "What about you—would you say you're impulsive or thoughtful?"

"Both. I look at decisions and weigh the opportunities, and then make my move. Sometimes, it takes a while—if I need to do some research or measure the pros and cons. And, of course, when others are involved..." He picked up a small paring knife. About to slice into a poblano pepper, he placed the knife down and met her eyes. "I also ask Brooke for input, but typically, she lets me decide—but that's because I make good decisions. Yeah, she pretty much trusts me." He spread some goat cheese on a butterfly-shaped cracker and capped it with two green olive slices.

"Should she?" Amber smiled, leaning forward with bowed head. Her hair fell over her bare shoulders. She held the glass in both hands, inches from her mouth.

"*Careful...*"

"I think so. I'm a trustworthy guy, and I take good care of her."

"So how did you meet? Was it love at first sight?" She set the glass down and turned her focus to a rye cracker and the pine-nut hummus.

"We met in school—Princeton, where I got my Bachelor's in Economics. Then later, I was at Yale for my PhD. Brooke was a couple years behind me and studying music. Piano and voice, you'll hear her play in church. She's really good. But she never finished her degree." He picked up a pepper cracker, spread it with cream cheese, and then crowned it with a mound of salmon. "I was in a fraternity, Phi Delta

Theta." He waved the cracker toward her and seemed to be expecting a reaction. His expression fading, he focused on the cracker. "Anyway, it was rush week. Brooke was pledging with Tri Delta, and we met at a party. We spent the entire evening sitting in a corner talking. She told me about her love for music and animals, about living in her hometown and playing tennis and being a cheerleader in high school. And about her dad who was a lawyer and their house in Texas. She was so innocent and pure. And shy—about who she was and her family."

Amber brushed crumbs from her hands and then tilted her head, flipping her hair back. "What do you mean?"

"Well, the next day, I was telling my buddies about Brooke, and one of the guys told me her dad is a senator and the house is a mansion. But Brooke never mentioned it. Funny—I haven't thought about that in a long time." Nick's voice trailed off.

"Sounds like you found a nice girl. I look forward to meeting her." She extended her glass as Nick poured.

"One night with the guys we were talking about our dreams and who we were going to become, and it came to me. I said—Brooke is the perfect woman. She's beautiful and smart. She has a family name, and her father has power and wealth. And I spoke it straight out."

"What?" Amber settled back against the cushions and pulled a pillow into her lap, one brow arching. "What did you say?"

"We'd just met, and I hadn't even asked her out yet. But I said it straight up—I am going to marry Brooke Stevens. And I did. We dated for two years and married right after I graduated. It was a really big wedding—amazing in fact. The vice president came and the governor too. And, well—that's how we met."

Asmodeus whispered, *"Did you love her?"*

Amber paused, the glass almost touching her lips. "Did you love her?"

"I was in love with everything about her. She was beautiful, and we were young and attracted to each other. And I admit—I wanted her family and the doors that would open. But yes—I loved her."

"Ask him."

She tipped the glass to her lips. Drawing a sip into her mouth, she held it and then swallowed. "Do you still love her?"

He glanced at the window and the mountains beyond.

"I'm sorry—it's none of my business. I shouldn't have asked."

"No, it's okay. You have a way of being direct, Amber, and I like that. I'm a lot like that myself." He swirled the glass, dropping his gaze.

"Touch him."

She nudged his knee with three fingers. "I understand."

"I do, but the passion's gone. It's been gone for a long time. I guess, when you get older, it fades and that's normal. But..." His eyes met hers, the briefest caress before sweeping back to the window. "The other day I was looking at her... It was early, and she was sleeping—and I was standing there. And it sort of washed over me." He waved the glass slowly. "When you know something, but you're suddenly seeing it—in the flesh I guess you could say." As he set the glass down, a slight shrug rolled his shoulders. "Knowing that something, that was so much part of who you were, is gone.... It's behind you, and you can't go back. Do you know what I'm saying?" He cleared his throat and started to stand. "I think we need the other bottle."

"Stop him."

Amber put her hand on his wrist. "You can tell me if you want, but I don't need to know. I'm sorry and I understand, more than you know—really, I do. It seems we have a lot in common."

"So, tell me about you and Richard. Is it hard, I mean because...?" He eased into the cushion.

"It was so fast, like a light going out. We were young and full of passion. We were traveling, and life was exciting, everything moving at a hundred miles an hour. And then he had the accident, and everything changed." Amber took another sip, the wine numbing her inhibitions. "I felt guilty for a long time, like somehow... And I was angry. I was mad at God, and it was hard taking care of him—especially at first. But it was even harder for him. Everything was ripped away in a blink—his manhood and profession, the excitement and pace, not to mention the money. His dream and all that he was and all that we were together—gone like that. Baseball... I guess that one word says it all."

She gave the glass a swirl. "Eventually, the money ran out, and I had to become the provider." She opened her hand with a small wave. "That part was easy for me, but hard for Richard, and that was rough on both of us. And having your physical relationship taken away was frustrating for Richard. But it was for me too—and I felt guilty. He was the one who was disabled, and I didn't feel like I deserved to have physical desires. But I did, and the guilt of it and..."

"Let him comfort you."

She set the glass down and swiped away tears. "I haven't talked about this in a long time. I didn't mean to." She leaned against his chest.

"It's okay—it's okay." His hand warmed her shoulder. Letting go, she pressed in sobbing. Crying and convulsing in his arms as he held her tight felt good.

"Let it go, Amber. It's okay."

"Beautiful. Now compose yourself."

She pulled away. Wiping tears from her face, she exhaled a laugh. "I'm sorry, I must look a wreck. This is so unprofessional I cannot believe it." Discarding the pillow, she drew her knees to her chin, tucking her gray skirt around her legs. "I think you were right—we better open that next bottle."

"Don't feel bad. I started it. I was the one whining and feeling sorry for myself. But you've been through so much more. I should be saying sorry, not you. And I am." He tilted forward with bowed head before looking up. "Forgive me?"

"Yes, of course, but only if you forgive me too. And only if you pour me another glass while you're at it."

They laughed and then sat in silence as Nick opened the second bottle.

"Do you have any regrets?"

"What do you mean?"

"Your youth..." He poured. "If you had it to do over, would you have done it differently?"

"I think I would have, yes. I would've valued it more and taken advantage of the time we had. So often, I pushed Richard away when he wanted to be intimate and I was tired or upset. To be honest, I pushed him away because he wasn't giving me the attention I wanted, and I felt he didn't deserve me—and that was wrong. And then, after the accident, that part of our life ended, and we didn't have any more chances. If I could go back, I wouldn't push him away... Then again, maybe I would have been just the same." She stared into her glass, feeling empty.

"What's his fantasy? Ask him."

"We lived in a condo with a balcony. And Richard used to ask me over and over if I would... Never mind, I shouldn't say..."

"What did he ask? You can tell me."

"Well, he wanted to do it on the balcony, and I always said no. Someone would see us up there, and even if they didn't, well, it would feel like someone was watching. I think that's why he wanted to—it was a fantasy he had. But now—if I could go back—I would do it on the balcony, even if someone was watching." She laughed and drew a sip. "All guys are like that. You're no different, are you? Tell me about your fantasy—did you ever have one with Brooke?"

"No, I don't think I did." He tilted his head to the side. "Well, yes, actually... But it's been a long time since I've thought about it."

"Tell me. I want to know."

Nick shook his head, a mischievous grin twinging his face.

"Tease him."

Amber extended her toe, poking his knee. *"I told you...."*

The grin spread across his face as his brows lifted. "Well, before we were married, we were good. I mean, we were both raised in Christian homes, and well, we tried—and most of the time, we were. Of course, when you're young, it's hard, and once we were engaged, it was even harder. But Brooke had this robe." He paused, shaking his head, the grin persisting.

"Come on. You can trust me."

"A robe...? What robe—come on, you can trust me."

"It was pink and soft. And we had made out a few times when she was wearing the robe in her parents' house. Brooke was living at home, and I'd come over late, and... Well, she would be wearing just the robe, if you know what I mean. And we would be close, and it was exciting— but she would never open the robe. She was the strong one, and I was trying to get inside the robe. Anyway, I had this fantasy, and I told her. Or suggested—now this was after we were married—I would tell her or ask..."

Amber dropped her chin, offering a smile of devilish expectation. *"Yes...?"*

"It would be nighttime, and I would go outside to the front door and knock. She would open the door wearing the pink robe, and she would open it up to me. And we would embrace and kiss and then make love. But we would never say a word—it would be like we were outside of ourselves, as if we were both someone else. And then I would leave and sneak in later. And it would be like it never happened—like a secret memory to cherish, but never speak of." He glanced away, taking a large swallow. "I'm sorry I shouldn't have told you."

"Did she ever do that for you?"

"Did she ever do that for you? You don't have to tell me."

"No... She never did. I kept mentioning it—for probably the first five years we were married, and then I finally dropped it. It was silly, I guess, like the balcony thing with you and Richard. Guys and girls are just different."

"I would have done that for you."

"It's not silly. I've had that fantasy. Dream sex, that's what I call it—as if it never happened. I would have done that for y—" She stopped short. "I'm sorry. I didn't mean to say that. I don't know where that came from. I must be tipsy."

"It's okay. You and me, Amber, we're a lot alike, aren't we?"

"We are, and I like that. I hope you won't change your mind about hiring me after all this?" She smiled warmly.

"Are you kidding? You were honest and vulnerable with me. Both of us—we were ministering to each other just now. That's what the church should be doing. That's what it's all about. We need each other, Amber, trust me—I'm right about this. We are going to be great together, or... working together, I mean. I'm sure of it."

CHAPTER 30

THE GRAND ATRIUM was a conditioned space. Having a raised floor, it could be heated or cooled with tempered water channeled through a crawlspace beneath it. Today, steam rose from the open joints between its stone pavers. Jonness spotted him reclining at a low table on a floor mat. Governor Maximillianus Lucius Proculus Quintilianus held a silver bowl filled with pomegranate seeds and rice wine. The libation was called Nectar of the Gods, a popular temple drink believed to enhance vigor.

The emperor had selected Lucius for the open governorship following the death of his father. The appointment was one of several, which were moving the empire away from its rigid past, toward a new liberality of tolerance. Persecution persisted however and was not uncommon. The authorities did little to interfere when mobs rose up to execute justice, especially when Christians were involved. But times were changing, and even a few government officials were stepping forward to be counted among the faithful.

With an array of colorful cushions and tapestries spread over a purple floor mattress, Lucius propped his torso up with a body pillow, his hand resting on a raised knee. An intimidating man, large in stature with a walrus face, his tanned body was fully shaved. Except for a body drape tented over his raised knee, Lucius was naked. Seldom alone, he shared the mat with five worship attendants. Two of the bare-chested women rubbed his back, while the others, heavily adorned in various renditions of jewelry and body paint, lounged on the cushions. All of them were less than half the governor's age.

Jonness approached. His eyes, darting from girl to girl, fondled their taut shapes and soft curves. Raising her head, one of them offered a half smile of drugged seduction while grazing the governor's neck. Her emerald robe, knit from open-loop silk, gave her body an efflorescent shimmer in the torchlight. Transfixed by the erect nipple protruding through her netted skin, he stared.

As she dropped her head, she took the nipple between thumb and forefinger. Releasing it with a twisting pull, her hand then floated up and over her hip to disappear beneath the governor's drape. Her distant gaze returned to Jonness. Liquid eyes painting his face, she opened her mouth and languidly licked her lower lip.

"Jonness, I thought that was you. How are you, my Holiness?"

Inside the mask, Jonness's face flushed with heat as he clenched his jaw. Twisting about, he scanned the room.

"Don't worry, Jonness. It is only the two of us—trust me, they do not understand. The twins are Hittite, purchased only last week. It seems I have forgotten their names. These two are Moabite—or perhaps Girgashite. Who can say? But this one, she is special—Artemis in the flesh, fallen from the heavens to earth. Did you see her in the window?" Lucius laughed, then drew a sip from the silver bowl. Placing it on the table, he tapped Artemis on the arm with his open hand. "The seat of power has its privileges, my friend. Not everyone can be serviced by a god who is paid for by the people. But you, my Holiness, would pay dearly for a temple blessing from this one—I can tell you. Perhaps you should join me on the council? You could then remove that foolish mask and enjoy yourself."

He fanned his arm out to the atrium. "Come sit. Join us and tell me what is on your mind." He waved Jonness forward while lifting his body drape. Artemis stared at Jonness as she shifted position, crouching like a cat. Thick red curls covering her arms, her head then disappeared beneath the tent. Dropping slowly, it then rose.

Jonness fumbled with a pillow as Lucius nodded to the Hittites, who crawled toward Jonness.

"Governor Quintilianus, I—"

"Lucius. Please, my friend, call me Lucius."

"I have come seeking your wisdom and counsel." Jonness cleared his throat, glancing to the sisters, now fawning at him on each side. "You understand, Excellency—it is the Lord and the holy church I serve."

Lucius burst into laughter. "Who could help but notice who it is you serve? I see you have reversed your circumcision. Tell me, friend, who was your physician? I must recommend him to my Jewish friends. He is quite skilled. I hardly noticed the scaring."

Lucius drew another sip. "You know I am only jesting. Now tell me, how can we help each other today? If you have come to talk about your temple again, you are not the first. Your friend, Bishop Gallus

Publios, the Nicolaitan, was just here. Did you know he shares your ambition? And Bishop Gallus embraces our gods, which you do not."

Hidden within his shell, Jonness fumed, his entire being rearing with hatred and disdain. "He is not worthy of the title Bishop. The Nicolaitan is a wolf, who will do you no benefit. His followers have no need for a temple—they have plenty to choose from. And what do you think they would do if they had one? They would only steal pilgrims from visiting the temples of Rome, collecting the sacrifices and tithes that belong to you. The Nicolaitans worship only themselves. Gallus is..." Jonness stopped, trimming the speed of his tongue. "Your Excellency—Lucius. You are a man of honor and wisdom. Forgive me, but... Clearly, you are not deceived by that imposter's trickery?"

Lucius laughed again nearly choking. "Jonness, we are all the same. You worship one god, and we worship many. And Bishop Gallus— forgive me, Gallus the Wolf—does both. Now tell me—why is this not good for Rome?"

"Do these Nicolaitans bring you tithe, Your Excellency? And do they pay rent for the use of your public buildings? They do not. They have no need to do so because they worship here with all of Rome. The Nicolaitans burn incense and make sacrifices to Artemis and also to Caesar—and the Christ. You may think this is not a bad thing for Rome, but what of my flock?"

Jonness composed himself. "We are growing in numbers and will continue to do so. We are peaceful, and we help the widows and orphans. After all, who will feed and care for Rome's poor if not the church? The Nicolaitans do nothing for you. The Senate and Caesar will notice your wisdom if you embrace us. And as you said, how different are we from you?" He mirrored the governor's previous gesture, fanning an arm to the plaza.

Lucius shrugged. "You have good arguments, and we have discussed this, many times. I will think about your request. But the council will rule on this and only if I bring it to them." Lucius suddenly dropped the bowl, grasping the tented drape in his fist. Head tilted back, his body went rigid. No one moved or spoke. After several moments, he relaxed. "But that is not why you are here today, now is it?" Still holding the drape in his clenched fist, Lucius raised his brows.

"You are perceptive, Your Excellency. Another matter concerns us both, a matter that will benefit you."

He released his grip, and the rhythmic motion recommenced. "Tell me of this matter."

"You are looking for those who desecrated the tomb of Celsus, are you not? I know who these men are."

"Tell me, are these men the ones you put in my jail this morning? The two arrested without formal charges?"

Jonness swallowed. "Yes. They are criminals."

"The coffee trader and your scribe—surely, there is a mistake? Who would believe they have done this? Tell me now what you want and how it helps me?"

"The scribe—his name is Batush. He has admitted to the crimes in front of witnesses—it is documented. The scribe desecrated the body and also robbed the tomb."

"I was not aware anything was missing. What was taken?"

"A book belonging to the church. It was placed there, with Rome's permission, by our Fathers."

"And what does the coffee trader have to do with this?"

"He read the book to us. He is a witness of the scribe's testimony and spoke words that dishonor the church. It is blasphemy."

Lucius laughed again. "You fear the book. The coffee trader has only read to you. This is not a crime. The scribe desecrated and robbed the tomb. Now this, this, is a crime." He shook his head. "You want to hide this book that makes you look foolish. That is what you want. And you want me to kill them for you? Your scribe and the coffee trader— tell me how this helps me?"

"Your Excellency, you are wise and discerning. True, we wish to have the book returned to rest where our Holy Fathers placed it. The council and people will look upon justice, delivered for crimes against Rome, with favor. They will respect you and fear you, yielding to your leadership."

"Jonness, this does not help me. I have executed justice upon my enemies many times. Trust me—the council and the people fear me. But Celsus was hated. He overtaxed the people and killed many in the arena. The people remember. You ask me to kill a scribe for desecrating the tomb of a hated oppressor—and the coffee trader too? The people love his coffee and I do also—it is better even than my cook brews. It would be better for me to kill the cook."

Lucius's body rocked as he roared to tears. "A dead man's bones scattered about in a dark cellar and a missing book? No one knows of this or even cares." He poured nectar into the silver bowl. "Unless you press formal charges against these men in three days, you will need to let them go. You know the law. And make sure you do not charge them with desecration because I have no time for it. Perhaps you can charge them with late fees for the missing library book." He chuckled as he slurped from the bowl. "If you want the scribe killed, you will need to do it yourself. But leave the coffee trader alone."

Jonness flinched as one of the Hittites kissed his ear.

"You may go—business awaits me." Lucius nodded in the direction of two men beyond earshot. "Next time you want to meet—can we please discuss something which interests me?" He laughed again, looking down to his lap.

Jonness stood. "My Excellency, but how can—or...? You know that I... the church cannot..." He glanced again to the waiting men. "We are Christians. We cannot kill a man. How would...?"

"It has been done before, has it not?" Lucius waved the men forward.

"But..."

"Jonness, my friend, have you not noticed so many are coughing? Only yesterday, twelve were killed by this plague. And today, my soldiers removed another twenty from the village—mostly children and the elderly." Lucius lifted his brows. "Who could be causing this? How difficult would it be for someone to end this pestilence?" He winked as he placed his hand atop the tent.

With a backward step and another glance at the girls, Jonness bowed. "Thank you, Your Excellency. You have been most... helpful." He looked away as he passed the approaching men. Crossing the plaza, he headed for the room without light, known as the Den of Darkness.

CHAPTER 31

A STEADY STREAM of vehicles crawled in both directions along the boulevard, just beyond the retail center's parking lot. It was early evening, but rush-hour traffic was showing no signs of relenting. Richard adjusted the position of his wheelchair beneath the iron mesh patio table. His stomach growled in response to the savory aroma of barbeque coming from the restaurant next door.

He looked to his friend and mentor as Clive Staples poured a packet of raw sugar into his black coffee. "Are you hearing anything?"

They had been meeting for several years, typically on the first Friday of each month at six thirty a.m. When conflicts arose, they would reschedule. Other times they met off schedule, calling those encounters emergency sessions, typically when Richard needed counsel on church-related business.

Today's meeting was the first time they had met in the evening. Having a different vibe, the coffee shop was gloomy and depressing. *That's it—the timing's off.*

"You're the one who gets the feelings about things. I'm the engineer who gravitates toward logic and knowledge. However, I do have a sense, or it could be I'm hearing something. But I'm conflicted, so I'm reluctant."

"It might be important for me to hear." Richard stirred the ice in his coffee with a black straw, his eyes trying to read Clive's face. "I'm not sure you've ever shared anything you thought the Lord might be speaking to you. Tell me."

"You mentioned Amber wants to take the job. The two of you have also been talking about making a move. And Scripture says the Lord gives us the desires of our heart, so if you both have that same desire, logically it would be in God's will. But I can't make that decision for you, and I'll certainly miss our times together. But if the Lord is calling you both, you should go. That's simple—it's called obedience."

"I agree. But tell me about the conflicting part."

"Well, like I said, I'm not sure about this because it's not like me. But each time I pray, I'm hearing the word *betrayal.*" His friend spoke softly almost mouthing the word.

Richard tried to decipher what he was seeing and hearing. Clive was the last person he would expect to utter a prophetic word of knowledge. *This must be significant, Lord. Give me ears to hear and eyes to see.*

"I don't know what it means, or if it means something to you? And it seems to conflict with being obedient to the desire you both have."

The soft clink of metal on ceramic lifted from Clive's cup as he stirred his coffee. "I'm not sure why you would go if betrayal is involved? I also don't know who it might apply to. It could be for you or Amber or the church leadership or the congregation. I certainly could be off base on this too. You're the one who hears from the Lord. You tell me?"

Richard poked at the ice in his drink. Meeting Clive's eyes, he slowly shook his head. "I think I'm getting the same thing, but it could be because I'm too close to it. I do sense we're being called, and that's the decision part. But I'm uneasy. Something's not right—a sense of foreboding."

Clive brought his spread fingertips together and then apart, repeating the motion in a slow and silent clap. "It reminds me of Paul in the Book of Acts, when he's saying goodbye to the elders in Ephesus and he's going back to Jerusalem. He tells them he doesn't know what's going to happen, but the Spirit testifies that bonds and chains are waiting for him—which they are. But he goes anyway out of obedience. Maybe that's what it is? It could be painful, but somehow, the Lord will use it for His ultimate glory."

"Let's ask for Amber's protection and for surrender to the Lord's will."

They prayed as the sun dipped below the metro skyline in a beautiful sunset of reds and orange.

<<>>

"The balcony... Ask him."

"I haven't been back out there... since..." Amber looked to the balcony and the sky beyond. The sun was about to disappear behind the mountain ridgeline. A canopy of wispy clouds lit the sky in a palette of pinks shifting to orange.

Nick stood. Lifting his brows, he fanned an arm toward the glass door. "I subscribe to facing one's fears. Besides, there's nothing like a desert sunset. Come on—I'm here for you."

"Will you hold it?" She extended her hand, feeling a bit silly. Taking it, he led her toward the sky of fire. Dry air flooded over her as he slid the door open.

"Wow, you were right. Mm..." Amber hesitated. "You first."

He stepped through and then extended his hand with a bow as one might ask for a dance. Hand clasping his fingertips, she met the warm breeze, purring as it washed away all residual apprehension. Floating to his side, she drew a deep breath and closed her eyes. Slightly dizzy, she placed her hand on his chest. "Mm, this is so nice. I hope you don't mind. I'm a little tipsy."

"I got you. It's okay."

"I don't want to look over. Can we stay here? I'm afraid." Her eyes still closed, she smiled, savoring the floating sensation. She thought of the lace curtains then, and the day from her past when everything was about to change. "You lead, and I'll close my eyes and hang on."

"It's fine. Now open your eyes before you miss it. It's gorgeous."

"Ask him to kiss you."

She opened her eyes, centering herself. A spectrum of color, ranging from yellow orange to a series of luxuriant reds, lit the sky. As she rolled her head back, the canvas transitioned to violet and purple. "It's nice to share this with you—thanks."

"Ask him. He wants you to... Ask him."

"This is... I'm sorry... We shouldn't..."

"He wants to but needs you to ask—ask him. Do it."

She withdrew her hand from his chest. "It feels right, sharing this with you—it's a precious moment I'll always cherish." As she met his eyes, the sunset warmed her face. She put her hand back on his chest. Her breast pressing against his side, she lifted her head to meet him.

It interrupted then, the pulsating buzz.

"I'm sorry."

"Let it ring."

"Kiss him. Kiss him now—Now!"

"I'm sorry—bad timing." Nick pulled the phone from his pocket.

Watching him, she knew, as if reading the display herself.

"Hi, babe. I'm still in the meeting. I'm stepping out." He turned his back, taking three steps. "We're with Amber right now, and then we'll be discussing it... The job decision... It could be a while and then who knows what else might come up."

He took another two steps before looking back. Their eyes touched. "I think she's going to take it, but it's not final. ... Okay, sure. That sounds fun. What are you going to see? ... I heard it was good. Okay... Try to park near the entry and be careful on your way out. I love you too."

He hung up, and they stood there, eyes comingling. He set his phone on the railing and turned to the horizon, now fading to ruby.

"Thanks again for helping me face my fears. I'll never forget this."

A quiet smile grazed his lips, his eyes heavy with something she could not read. "Me too—and..." He glanced again to the sunset and then back. "I'll be looking forward to your decision. Do you think you'll be letting us know soon?" He put his hands in his pockets. "It's late. I should go."

She nodded.

<<>>

Two paces behind, Asmodeus followed Jonness into the great hall bustling with bodies of flesh in pursuit of shelter from the rain. Asmodeus rallied his comrades who were more plentiful than the humans. Several responded with teasing jeers and encouraging shouts.

Rufus, a tormentor, chided, "Take him down master—he's yours."

Withdrawing his goo-covered head from a young woman's abdomen, Lasher, known as the Negotiator, sneered, "We welcome your arrival on the inside."

A pair of body-hopping mischief-makers, called out, "Kill him slowly, mighty leader. Yes, with insanity and great despair."

As they passed a line of pilgrims waiting to make offerings to the Fire Stone, Asmodeus sneered. *Like moths to the flame...*

Humans believed Zeus himself had hurled the mighty stone to earth as a sign the gods had chosen this location for the great temple. They worshiped it for good luck and fertility. Bowing and laying offerings at its base, they would rub it and even copulate against it for a blessing. Over the years, the perpetual polishing from millions of hands and body parts had turned the stone shiny dark silver.

Asmodeus gave a thumbs-up to Gusher, the lust specialist.

"Just taking a breather, good sir." Gusher cocked his head toward a young couple ravaging one another on the stone. "I only just introduced them. They didn't even exchange names—glorious." Wiping his brow, he grinned.

The flames of a torch lampstand licked at the walls before the Den of Darkness. At its side, an alms box was chained to the floor next to an empty attendant chair.

Asmodeus huffed as Jonness pretended to drop something in the box.

The narrow entrance corridor reversed direction four times, the light reducing with each successive turn. The switchback then opened into a stone chamber furnished with a variety of couches and beds placed randomly to accommodate a practice known as Sacred Encounters. When filled to capacity, the Den of Darkness could serve more than two hundred worshipers and prostitutes.

Water gurgling and breath panting filled his ears. It was still early with just twenty or so humans present. Several were washing in the central fountain with others engaged in various acts of worship. A few staggered about with outstretched arms, seeking a suitable partner or group to join. An older prostitute, covered with the white blotches of early leprosy, kissed a young man. *I would love to see your face if you could only see her.*

As Jonness listed to the side with a tilted head, his arms reaching forward, Asmodeus leaned in to his ear and whispered, "What's it going to be? A woman or young girl—a man perhaps? Or maybe—yes, that sounds nice—a boy."

<<>>

Sitting in his white Escalade, Nick stared through the windshield into the courtyard, lit in string lights. He then turned to the elevator lobby as Karen and Tank flashed through his mind. *Strange how it unfolded, throwing us together.*

Mammon whispered, *"It felt so good—holding her—so soft and vulnerable..."*

Nick shook his head. *She's married—I'm married. I must be misreading it. This is crazy.*

"She wanted you to kiss her—you blew it. She's beautiful and exciting—what the hell is wrong with you?!" Mammon shouted.

Nick bit his upper lip. *What if I had kissed her and she didn't want me too? That would have been awful. What would I have even done?*

"Are you kidding? How blind can you be? She was looking into your eyes with her hand on your chest. She couldn't have been any clearer. You're going to regret it for the rest of your life."

Should I call—but what would I say?

"You forgot something, and can you come up."

That might scare her. And if she didn't want me to, she'd feel pressured, and I'm about to be her boss. I can't do that, and besides...

"Come on, man. What do you got to lose? Just call and see what happens. You can always walk away."

Nick pinched his brows between his thumb and forefinger. *What do I say—what to say... What's my excuse?*

"Anything—it doesn't matter."

He inserted his key into the ignition and held it there. *I could say I'm sorry if I gave her the wrong idea—or...?*

"What do you mean—the wrong idea? No, that's all wrong."

I can say... I left my notes. Are they on the counter? And then, if she wants me to come up, but then...

"Now you're thinking—give her the option. She wants you to come back up."

He reached to his pocket. *My phone—the balcony—the railing. Damn... How do I even...?* His unseeing eyes came into focus on the lobby desk phone.

He locked the Escalade and walked to the lobby. Holding the receiver, he stared at the large push buttons. Not remembering Amber's number, he dialed his own. *Maybe she'll hear it or see it light up? It's not likely, but if it's meant to be...?*

CHAPTER 32

JONNESS STOOD in the cool blackness. The hairs on his body standing erect, his hands swept over his torso. Lifting his mask to his forehead, he listened. The cave-like room magnified the fountain's gurgle, but the background sounds held his attention. Chanting tongues of breath, whispering and panting, rising and falling behind the bubbling water's clip-clopping echo. He inhaled the sensations of naked freedom and fearful expectation. His heart quickened.

He faced a woman's rhythmic moan, close at hand, two of them. Stepping forward, he wavered with an arm extended. His forearm met flesh. His hand, quickly following, cupped a swinging breast.

From behind, coiling arms entwined her body as a flat hand met his thigh, sweeping to his belly. He yielded as she pulled him forward, her face pressing into his side. Every muscle tense, he received her shaved and oiled head. The presence of her partner met him with bursts of slapping breath. A hot hand pressed his chest. Another wrapped his neck.

His palm found a second pair of breasts, firm and moist. He leaned forward, exploring with his mouth. Slender fingers then took his face, cheek grazing jaw. He inhaled perfumed breath. Muzzling the musty aroma of thick locks, an open mouth grazed his lips. Pulling away, four hands pushed him back.

His face flushed with heat as they burst into laughter.

Moving on, he took short sidesteps, again groping with outstretched arms. A man exhaled ecstasy on the room's far side as a woman to his right huffed in strained endurance. A small hand then found him, chosen almost, as if by one who could see in the dark. Wrapping two of his fingers, the unseen companion gently squeezed them.

Jonness felt a soft kiss on the back of his wrist. He reached down and palmed the small head. His heart surged as a tingling wave of excitement swept through his frame. He followed with the boy leading.

<<>>

Amber stepped out of the shower, wiping away what remained of the day's stress. She faced the mirror. *It's for the best. Besides, we're going to be working together.* Entering the bedroom, she glanced at the armoire. *Neither outfit will work for the staff meeting or the service.... What to buy and how many outfits?* She bit her lip. *How long before I'm home again, and what if Richard says no?*

"He'll say yes." He had to.

As she opened the large doors, her mouth fell open. The cabinet was filled with women's clothing swaying before her.

She selected a high-necked stretchy dress that appeared to be a fit. *Red will complement my eyes while conveying authority. Hmm, no label...* Not bothering with underwear, she pulled it over her head. *Perfect.*

Turning, she checked her profile. *It could be tailored. Dignified authority with a quiet seduction.* Fanning through the wardrobe, she counted another seven outfits, similar in size and taste, along with several impeccable blouses and pants that would mix and match at will. Two horizontal shelves of shoes offered nine pairs to cover any occasion. After trying a pair of open-toed pumps, she slipped into another perfect fit. Kicking them off, she again checked for labels. "I've never... How?"

Drawn next to the ebony dresser, she found a treasure trove of carefully folded wares—assorted socks and nylons, shorts and casual tops, laced underwear and lingerie.

A tinge of fear rippled through her as she lifted a shimmering negligee. She looked around the room, feeling like the angel in the painting was watching. It was then she noticed it—centered on top of the dresser wrapped in brown paper. About the size of a pillow, tied with twine. A small envelope tucked under the bow. Unsealed without writing.

After lifting the flap, she removed an embossed card with raised lettering.

~~

Enjoy your stay with us
Love, Karl

~~

"Karl—Bernhardt."

The refrigerator, stocked with food and wine, and now the clothes.

"But... How on earth?" She touched the bow. Taking the loose end, she gave it a pull and then unfolded the paper. She knew immediately what it was, soft and fluffy. It was the color that froze her. Pink.

"Put it on."

Amber snuggled it to her cheek. "Mm..."

After tugging the red dress over her head, she held the robe against her body. *So soft—I haven't worn pink since high school.*

"Put. It. On."

She slipped it on, snugging the collar to her chin. "Perfect for a movie and popcorn. I wonder...?" She headed for the kitchen and scoured the cabinets. "No popcorn—seriously? Maybe Karl doesn't know everything after all."

In the refrigerator, she spotted a bowl of strawberries. *Healthier I guess.*

Dimming the lights, she absorbed the twinkling city. It caught her eye then, the pulsing light at the railing.

"Get it—before it falls."

She dashed to the ringing phone. "Hello, this is Amber."

"Hi, it's me. I wasn't expecting you to pick up. But you did, and... I'm downstairs in the lobby. I... Well, I took a walk and then realized I left my phone. I'll be at church on Sunday. Would you be able to leave it for me in the reception center?"

"Nonsense."

"Nonsense. That's silly. I'll call you up." Back inside, she headed for the elevator and then froze. *I better...*

"Leave it on."

She stood in front of the keypad. "Are you there?" Nick's voice came through.

"Yes, can you wait a minute? I need to change."

"Leave it on. Call him up."

Her heart pounding, she watched her hand rise to the keypad as if belonging to someone else. Entering the code, she heard the elevator spring to life. *Still time—hurry!*

"Wait."

Reaching for the dimmer, she switched the lights off and untied the belt. The robe parted between her breasts. The doors opened then, flooding her in white.

Nick froze, glancing down and then back to her eyes. His face reflected the feelings pumping through her veins—fear and wonder, anticipation and decision.

"Wait."

She was about to turn away when the doors chimed, beginning to close.

As he blocked with his arm, the doors lurched back. They stared. He then stepped through the opening, standing in front of her, almost touching.

"Open it."

She opened it, the soft fluffy pink framing her body lit in brilliant light. Chiming again, the doors closed, and they stood in the city's glow. Taking the robe in his hands, he tugged her forward. Their bodies touched. His hands finding her, skin on skin, he caressed her hips.

Her heart pounded as she tilted her head, offering her neck. As he kissed her shoulder, his cheek grazed her jaw, and she felt his heart thundering against her.

He started to whisper, "I..."

"Stop him."

Pulling back, she put her hand on his lips. He drew her fingertips into his mouth. *Like it never happened... A secret gift shared...*

"Kiss him."

And they did. The two of them kissed Nick Hamilton.

<<>>

Watching Moaz lead the buffoon was quite amusing. *Humans are all alike—blind, stupid, and naked.* Rising from the chair, Asmodeus met them.

Moaz grinned, hardly able to contain himself. Holding Jonness's hand, he maneuvered him in a circle to sit.

They spoke, mind to mind. *"Keep it under control, Moaz. I want this to be clean."*

"Master, I will."

Moaz stroked the man's face, kissing him on the lips. He stepped back as Jonness leaned forward. Moaz clenched his hand into a fist. Then drawing his arm back in a winding-up motion, he followed through with a thrust that stopped just short of the bishop's crotch. Still grinning, he looked up.

Asmodeus bit his tongue as Jonness flailed with his arms. When he started to stand, Asmodeus pushed him back. Fear contorted Jonness's bloated face as he began to tremble. Asmodeus let the man find his torso. Jonness gasped and jerked his hand back as if touching a hot stove, nearly toppling. Striking like a snake, Asmodeus seized the man's throat.

Jonness began to thrash about.

"That's right, *Jonnesssss*," Asmodeus hissed. "How does it feel to be in the presence of a god? Are you afraid? If I were you, I would be very afraid."

He squeezed a bit tighter, sneering hatred as Jonness gulped, his hands tearing and slapping at Asmodeus's iron wrists.

"That's it... No need to resist, my *Holiness*. I'm all that you've been longing for—the reason you crave the darkness." Asmodeus ripped Jonness's mask off and tossed it to the floor. He then yanked him up and out of the chair and studied the squirming human's puffy red face. "Blind and naked in the grip of fear, this is what I see. And you and I are about to be one. However, I find myself repulsed."

Shaking his head, Asmodeus turned to Moaz, who was hopping from one foot to the other, singing one of his ridiculous made-up songs: "...*Pain and darkness, death and shame—here we come, oh yes, we come... We come in the darkness. Yes, we do—we're here to kill and live in you....*"

Asmodeus drew Jonness to his mouth, sucking the remaining breath from his lungs. Standing on his toes, Jonness squirmed and then relented, going rigid. Asmodeus then breathed himself into the man's body. Seizing territory, he swept through every crevice of the human's being as Jonness fell to his knees.

Gasping, Jonness began to crawl.

With a cackle, Moaz kicked the mask across the room. "I'm right here, Holiness. Do you still want your little boy?" He punched Jonness in the face. "Yes, I think you still want me, don't you?"

Singing again, Moaz spun on one hand and swept the bishop's arms out from under him. Falling forward, Jonness landed face-first on the floor of cold stone.

"...*Pain and darkness, death and shame—here we come, oh yes, we come. We come in the darkness, yes, we do—yes, it's true, we're inside you...*"

<<>>

"Wake up. You have visitors."

Batush rubbed his eyes and then turned to Zophar, who seemed to be sleeping while standing.

When the guard kicked the plate and water cup, a cockroach scurried away. "I see you do not like our cooking. Perhaps you would rather have a plate of excrement and piss to drink? If you want to live, you will learn to eat what I bring. Do you hear me?"

The guard snorted, then cocked his chin down the corridor. "Come."

Rushing forward, Gibeon slowed as he passed the guard. "Father, we have been searching for both of you. What happened?"

Zophar met his son at the bars, their fingers locking. "We are safe. You must tell Meraiah and Sarah."

"But why are you here. I do not understand?"

"I will explain everything later." Zophar lowered his voice. "The fear of men binds us, my son. They will free us—you will see."

Gibeon glanced at the plate and cup.

"We are fasting. In two days, the Lord will free us. Tell Meraiah and Sarah not to worry—the Lord will provide. Our strength is in Him... Go."

CHAPTER 33

KICKING OPEN the door, Asmodeus swept into the chamber. Known for its intense heat, the undulating kidney-shaped Well of Souls randomly quaked and groaned. Like gnarled roots of a rainforest, oozing with liver-colored goo, the chamber cradled a cauldron growing up and out of the ever-shifting floor. Today, it smoldered with a steaming concoction, carefully prepared over many years.

Head held high, Asmodeus approached his second in command. "Mammon, you ugly old maggot, what's the report?"

"All is well. We are making excellent progress." Mammon let go of the large stirring spoon, which continued to spin in the bubbling sludge, rising slowly to the surface.

Asmodeus bent over the pot, inhaling deeply. "You have done a fine job with this one. He is nearly ready to be poured."

"We are ready, on your command."

Asmodeus scanned the perimeter doors. Five were fully open, another two cracked. Others were closed, and one barricaded with a beam and chains.

"The report, Mammon—we don't have a lot of time."

"Mayhem and Madness are working his mind as we speak. And Gusher himself is below working the organs. I am keeping watch over the cook." A smile revealed decaying sharp black teeth as Mammon gestured to the pot. "We are ready for reinforcements and will put them to work immediately—at your discretion, of course."

"You are doing well and will be rewarded." Asmodeus thrust his chin toward the barricaded door. "The enemy looks to be secure, and we must keep it so. Today's victory will be helpful." He clamped a hand on Mammon's shoulder. "Be sure this is the grandest of times he ever experienced. It must exceed all prior encounters, including that of his mate. Do you understand?"

"Of course, master. He will cherish this, returning again and again to feed. We will make sure of it." Mammon picked up the spoon and gave the sludge another turn. "Tell me. Which of the doors are to be opened?"

Asmodeus flexed his clawed fingers and spoke softly, "Several, but two will be especially useful. I will be sending another twelve, including Ziglag and Dagon. Both have territory rights yet to be exploited."

"Tell me, master, that I may prepare for their placement." The hunchbacked demon twisted his neck, peering up to him.

"Betrayal and Suicide..." Asmodeus released the words as one might serve a forbidden delicacy on a silver platter.

Mammon's translucent bat-like ears twitched. "How many generations?"

"Seven for Suicide, sealed my friend—with a human blood curse." Lifting a long finger, Asmodeus rotated his hand, palm raised, his fingers unfurled as if holding a bowl. "And one for Betrayal—her father."

"Thank you, master. We will not let you down—you can count on us. Again, I am blessed to be in your service."

"Keep him engaged, Mammon. I am not worried about her, but he must not fall short. No less than two of their hours, and we will be helping with the woman. And keep the Tormentors under control—we must work together."

"I give you my word—he is under close control, and we are stronger together. No less than two."

Cocking his head, Asmodeus whirled around and then departed.

~~

They rolled over, her palms grinding into his chest. Amber breathed deeply, raking her fingers through her hair, her heart pounding.

"That's it. Take your time..."

She gazed at the painting over the bed. Pressing in, she moaned. *How would it feel to be her, Raven Wing, soaring into the night's sky?*

<<>>

Hanging from the citrus tree in the corner of the yard, the bug zapper illuminated with a violet flash and buzz. Overhead, a canopy of Italian string lights lit the patio with a twinkling glow. In front of them, the pool light washed the desert-scape in a dancing aqua shimmer. The smell of creosote was as heavy in the air as the mosquitos. Daniel slapped at his ankle as he rocked in the stretched fabric chair, four of them, circling the square tabletop clad in raja slate.

"So, what do you think? What's going to happen?" Rhema swept her copper curls into a knot and secured them with a scrunchy as he stared into the soft blue glow.

"She'll accept. And who knows? Maybe, Amber will be just what we need. I guess I'm wondering if what I know about her might be clouding my perspective. It just feels like it's not going to be good." Twisting from side to side, he inspected his exposed legs and then kicked off his flip-flops. "And I keep thinking about the woman's vision with the storm and wolves. It feels like it's happening, and I don't know what to do. Can you imagine if I was to tell the elders?"

"Maybe you should. It wasn't your vision. You'd just be telling them about what happened at the prayer meeting." She uncrossed her legs. Positioning another chair closer, she used it as a footrest.

"They'd think I'm wacked. I'm sure they would listen and ask some questions, but I can see it. They'd be nodding their heads and saying—hmm, that's interesting and who again was it that had the vision? They would be more concerned with making sure the woman was shut up, and then later, they would be laughing and talking behind my back. 'Oh man, Daniel's losing it. We need to be praying for him. Maybe he's got a demon.'"

Rhema reached across the table and touched his arm. "You don't know what they'd be thinking. I think they would respect you for being honest. You should ask the Lord what to do."

"I have, but I'm not hearing anything."

"I love you, and I'm proud of you." She took his hand and squeezed it.

"They're good guys, and they love the Lord. But... I guess we have different experiences and perspectives, and that's what we bring into the room. We start and close with prayer—but in between, it's just business. I guess I'm being judgmental."

His phone chimed. "It's from Nick." He swiped the screen and read the message silently.

```
Brothers,
Amber received the blessing from her husband and
has accepted the position. I have advised Pastor
Jason to make the announcement on Sunday, and all
elders should plan to be on deck. Amber and I will
be meeting with staff on Monday. Be strong and
```

courageous as we turn the page on a new future.
May the Lord lead and guide us. In His Service,
Nick

He passed it to her. "What do you think?"

A frown twisting her copper eyebrows, she set the phone aside. "The message should be coming from Paul Chambers." A flicker of purple lit her face as the zapper again seared the night.

"Nick acts like he's chairman—actually, he really is. Can you imagine if I tried that? If I just told everyone what to do and that I would be meeting with the staff, they would freak. But Nick—he just takes over—and we let him."

"Someone should stand up to him."

Feeling a prick, Daniel slapped his calf and then clapped his hands together in front of his face. "It's possible he talked to Paul, but I doubt it."

Except for the chirp of crickets, they sat in silence.

"I was reading my Bible this morning, and I think the Lord gave me a Word for you." She picked up the phone, swiping and then tapping its face several times. "Here it is." She waited for his eyes to meet her. "'How lovely on the mountains are the feet of him who brings good news. Who announces peace and brings good news of happiness. Who announces salvation, and says to Zion, Your God reigns! Listen! Your watchmen lift up their voices, and shout joyfully together, for they will see with their own eyes when the Lord restores Zion.'"

His chest constricting, tears welled in his eyes. "Yeah. That was for me—thanks."

"I think you're a watchman, Danny. The Lord is saying, I put you in that room for a purpose, and your job is to watch and listen. In Isaiah's time, the watchman would stand on the walls of Jerusalem and call out when he saw something dangerous or important." She took his hand again. Her warm fingers threaded through his and then squeezed with a strength that always surprised him. "Maybe that's you? We need to be praying and listening so we can hear and see what's coming."

<<>>

Swallowing was extremely painful. His mouth and throat were so swollen completing the maneuver was nearly impossible. Weak and dizzy, Batush needed water. His eyes were seeing with a heightened clarity, with colors almost vibrating. In spite of the parched mouth, he was holding up.

Zophar continued to stand, hardly moving. *How does he do it? Fasting three days while standing? And how does he balance when sleeping? Or is he also fasting sleep? I will ask him later.*

Again, Batush tried to swallow.

"Stand." The guard held a ring of keys. "You should be glad I feel sorry for you, old man, or I would beat you for sport. Your wife is here to carry you home. Both of you will leave me. And take your refuse with you."

Surfacing from his hibernation, Zophar strode to the corner and picked up the bucket. He then offered an arm to Batush. "Fasting was good, was it not?"

Batush wavered in a bent-over position with hands on his knees. Everything went white. His ears ringing, he held the position as his vision regained focus. He took the arm then, amazed by Zophar's strength.

"Yes, it was good. I am weak but strong in the Lord." Batush offered a half smile as he straightened up, struggling to form the words.

"You do not look very strong, little man." The guard guffawed. "Why, I think with one small punch you would be dead before hitting the floor." The guard's roaring laugh boomed through the labyrinth of stone.

As they hobbled down the corridor, Batush felt like he was floating, watching from outside his body. He saw her then in the arched opening, surrounded by a glowing luminance. There were others. Five of them—guards. Batush commanded strength to fill his frame. Stepping into the overcast light, he squinted and took her hands. Warmth coursing through him, he struggled to swallow. How he loved her! Had he ever seen her so clearly before? Loved her so deeply?

Meraiah helped with a jug. "I have water. Drink—slowly, Batush."

His lips stung, splitting open as he drew a mouthful. He felt it nourishing his swollen tongue and tissues. After spitting it out, he then swallowed and extended the jug to Zophar.

The men began to circle. One of them grabbed Batush's arm. "The bishop has sent for you. The coffee trader may go, but you will come with us."

PART III

But I have this against you, that you have left your first love. Therefore remember from where you have fallen, and repent and do the deeds you did at first; or else I am coming to you and will remove your lampstand out of its place, unless you repent. Yet this you do have, that you hate the deeds of the Nicolaitans, which I also hate.

Revelation 2:4-6

CHAPTER 34

STANDING ON the sea of glass was somewhat like walking on water. It was a humbling experience, even for an angel. A layered fluid, thinner at the surface, transitioned to a thicker consistency below. It felt like wet clay, supported by the cool substance, yet unrestricted when walking.

To an observer, it would look like he was standing on a perfectly flat mirror that cut through his flesh at the ankle. Raphael lifted his foot and watched it vanish as he placed it back down.

The motionless surface reflected the kaleidoscope above, constantly moving in waves that swelled and yielded in response to the ever-singing cherubim. Sky song reminded him of the ocean, rising and falling, crashing and then gathering again. Today it was cool, smelling sweet and crisp, like honeysuckle. He stood in wonder, basking in the song of joy. Yes, that was it—soft joy radiating from the sky and reflecting up from the sea in which he stood.

Myriads upon myriads of cherubim rose in radial layers from the distant horizon, corbeling inward toward the open center. As though he were inside a beehive, the singing creatures stacked in oscillating layers rotated in opposite directions. *Does the song come from their mouths or their wings—perhaps from both?* They sang with a single purpose, verse upon verse, overlapping with the next:

"...*Holy, Holy, Holy is the Lord God Almighty... Worthy is the Lamb who was slain... Worthy is the Lamb who was slain... Who stands in the presence of the most high God... Who was, who is, and is to come... Who was, who is, and is to come... Who stands in the presence of the Most High God...*"

One could not stand for long in the throne room, as the sensations of motion, color, song, and emotion were overpowering. As he dropped to one knee, his hand disappeared into the mirrored surface. Lifting it out, he flexed his fingers as liquid power tingled through the extremity and dissipated into his body. He inhaled the presence and essence of all, consuming him in waves of truth, love, glory, and power.

And he waited. In front of him, three sweeping steps rose from the sea, each knee-height and sharp-cornered, appeared to be formed from the thicker material supporting him. Having never ascended them, he was unsure. The steps, extending in both directions, formed the circular platform centered beneath the hive dome. Covered in churning cloud and lit from within by flashes of lightning, the Almighty walked among peals of rolling thunder. *Can the cherubim see Him from above? The question remained a mystery.*

The elders stood in a wide circle, equally spaced around the platform base. He could see three in each direction, the others disappearing behind the cloud. They stood like sentries, apparently having assigned positions. Sometimes one would walk along the perimeter to speak with the next. Other times, one or more would leave the room. But all were in attendance when the clouds lifted for the convening of the courts. Twenty-three were present now.

He knelt in the missing elder's position, the billowing cloud towering above. *Will there be enough?*

He dipped cupped hands into the sea and was about to splash his face when the missing man emerged out of the cloud. Dressed in a flowing white robe, he strode toward Raphael with a poise and grace matching his youthful physique. He cradled a bowl in both hands, careful not to let it tip.

Raphael studied his face for a clue as he descended the steps. "What do we have, John?"

"Not a lot—but possibly enough." John extended the bowl, about the size of one's open palm cut in white pearl with a flat lip, toward Raphael. John swirled it.

Thick fluid rolled up its side, thinning into a film and then coalescing as it rolled down. About two drops worth, it moved like golden mercury.

"Do you need them now, or do you want to wait?" John lifted his brows to Raphael.

"I better take them now." Raphael pulled the cork from a small bottle strung around his neck. As he held it steady, John poured, then smiled and nodded. Yes, Raphael had requested assistance from the right man. Each elder was special, but none possessed the measure of love John had. And love was what Raphael needed for the battle—he was sure of it.

"God's glory, Raphael. I'm interceding for you."

Capping the flask, Raphael inspected the empty bowl engraved with script along the flat rim. The letters on one side were a language Raphael could not read. A mirrored inscription on the opposing side bore the name Daniel Jeremiah Fairmont.

CHAPTER 35

ARRIVING as planned, Amber was five minutes late. Nick had mentioned she would likely be introduced at the end of the service. It would be informal, but she should be prepared to share a few remarks, in the event Pastor Jason asked her to speak. The elders would also likely be called forward to pray over her. Amber imagined they would gather around and lay hands on her as they had in the boardroom. With head bowed, she would be standing there in submission. *Surely, they wouldn't ask me to kneel. That would be too much. Nick would have mentioned it.*

Asmodeus whispered, *"You'll look weak in front of the staff and congregation. They're trying to dominate you—don't let them."*

She pushed the remote, and the BMW replied with a chirping wink. Walking briskly, she headed for the worship center, relieved the dry morning was holding the heat at bay. She smiled at a greeter on the plaza. Welcoming late arrivers, the frumpy woman wore a bright-orange vest.

Who would put someone like that out front to greet visitors—in orange plastic? She looks like a traffic cop or, worse, a Home Depot clerk. Amber waved as she made an abrupt turn toward a side entry.

The organ greeted her ahead of a carved oak door. The hymn was familiar, but the title escaped her.

"Crown Him with many crowns,
The Lamb upon His throne.
La—la, la—la, la, la—la—la...
La, la—la—la—la—la...
Awake my soul and sing,
Of Him who died for thee,
And hail Him as, la, la—la—la...
La, la—la—la—la—la..."

The song is nice enough, and the organ's beautiful. But neither will attract youth. It's a tradeoff—younger families are the future, but old folks have the money. The hymns need to go, but maybe the organ could work for senior singalong services.

Asmodeus suggested, *"Cover it up."*

She pulled the door open. *Maybe a veil? And, if it was backlit, you would still be able to see it. We could gradually dim the lights. Later, when they're used to it being covered and can hardly see it, we could remove it, and no one would notice.*

Looking up, she was startled by the dark figure. The door half open, she froze. Tom Evans stood before colored glass, morning light silhouetting his body. Fear gripped her throat, the same fear she experienced when shaking his hand.

Dropping his head, Tom nodded while holding her gaze. She forced a tight smile. Realizing she had opened the prayer-room door, she backed out and headed for the foyer's double doors.

"Tom needs to go. He's dangerous."

A red-faced usher handed Amber a bulletin. *Perfect timing.* The crowd was milling about, shaking hands, and chatting while Pastor Jason stood at the podium. Walking down the sloping side aisle, she spotted an open seat near the front.

"It's a blessing to be with you on this glorious day in the house of the Lord."

Amber sat.

"On my drive in this morning, the sun was rising, and I thought about God's creation and how good He is. Now, some of you know I like to get here early to spend some time with the Lord before I speak. But I know all of you get up early to pray on Sundays—and you saw that beautiful sunrise too. How many of you saw it? Raise your hands."

The congregation laughed and clapped with several turning to tease each other. *They have a connection with him.*

"Stover needs to go. It's the only way."

Pastor Jason paused. "Father God, we thank You for this beautiful day and for this family—Your church. Open my mouth to speak now and protect me from error. We pray in Jesus's name. Amen."

He looked directly at her and then scanned the crowd. "Last week we started a new series in the Book of Revelation, and I was intending to continue with it today. However, during the week, the Spirit impressed on me that He had something else to say. And so, the message you were expecting will need to wait another week.

"Turn with me to First John, chapter 4, in the back of your Bible, just before Revelation. This was written by the Apostle John near the end of his life. Now, John was known as the beloved disciple. Remember, he was the one who laid his head on Jesus's chest at the last supper. He was also the only disciple present when Jesus was crucified. And when Jesus was hanging on the cross, it was John He asked to take care of his mother Mary.

"You may know John was also the only apostle not martyred for his faith. And John is believed to have been the first bishop at the church in Ephesus. It's also believed that John took care of Mary, there in Ephesus, where he spent the last days of his life and likely when he wrote this book.

"Historians record that, when he was very old, John needed to be carried on a stretcher. And he got to the point where he could hardly speak. But he would repeat a single phrase over and over." Jason let the statement float in the hushed auditorium. "Love one another. Just love one another—over and over. That was the most important thing he wanted the church to remember. Or, maybe, he wasn't seeing a lot of love. Maybe the church John had known—and the church his Savior Jesus had given to the world—had lost something? Maybe they had forgotten their love for the Lord or their love for one another—maybe both?

"Read with me, beginning at verse 7."

Amber scanned the pew in front of her, seeing no Bibles as pages rustled all around her. She exhaled relief when the passage appeared on a large screen.

Beloved, let us love one another, for love is from God, and everyone who loves is born of God and knows God. The one who does not love does not know God, for God is love. By this the love of God was manifested in us, that God sent His only begotten Son into the world so that we might live through Him. In this is love, not that we loved God, but that He loved us and sent His Son to be the payment for our sins. Beloved, if God so loved us, we also ought to love one another.

Pastor Jason swept a hand to his flock. "Are we doing that? I'm struggling with this because a lot of the time it doesn't seem like it. I'll ask again—do we, as a body of believers, a family... Do we actually love one another, and does it show? And if it doesn't, what would it look like? Have we lost something here?"

"This is preemptive. He's trying to protect his job."

Amber bit down on her tongue, her mind treading in fast water. *Could it be a coincidence, or did someone tell him? It seems strategic.*

"He knows. We'll need to move quickly."

Jason concluded his message with a prayer, following with an announcement. "As you know, we've been functioning without an executive pastor for several months. The elders and staff have been praying and seeking wisdom for the right person to fill that position. Trust me, I've been praying more than anyone because the executive pastor helps me run the church. But today..."

"He's maneuvering. We need to nip this now."

"...I'm pleased to announce the search is over, and we've filled the position with a very capable woman. I would like to ask Amber Lash and the elders to come join me now. Let's give Amber a friendly welcome." Pastor Jason extended a hand toward Amber as the congregation clapped.

"Relax. You got this."

Her heart accelerated as six hundred people watched. Jason met her when she ascended the platform. *Prepare to be schooled, Jason. You've never met a woman like me before.*

"Take his hand."

Amber did, letting go as she faced the audience. The lights blinded her while a fearful excitement filled her.

"Wait... Gracious and beautiful..."

She stood at the podium beside Jason with the elders forming a crescent behind them. Taking a step back, he fanned her forward. "It is my pleasure to introduce our new executive minister, Amber Lash."

"Now," Asmodeus barked.

She stepped forward, her open hand on her chest. "Wow. I was not expecting this. I am so pleased to be here—thank you. I cannot say how welcome I have been made to feel this past week. Everyone has been so friendly and kind, and I'm looking forward to meeting each and every one of you. I want to thank you and the elders, and also my staff, including Pastor Stover."

"Careful... Don't overstep."

"I want you to know how blessed you are to have these godly men serving you. I also want to thank Pastor Stover for asking me to share a few words."

Pastor Jason took a half step forward and then eased back, a flash of concern darkening his eyes.

"Hold your ground."

"This morning when I got up to pray, *before* that beautiful sunrise." She rotated toward Jason as the crowd erupted. "Actually, I need to confess—I missed the sunrise. But I was reading my Bible, and I want to share something the Lord showed me. From the book of Isaiah." She unfolded a piece of paper. "'Do not call to mind the former things, Or ponder things of the past. Behold, I will do something new, Now it will spring forth; Will you not be aware of it? I will make a roadway in the wilderness, Rivers in the desert. The people whom I formed for Myself Will declare My praise.'"

She looked up. "Did you catch that? This is for us. And when I read this, well—I just can't tell you how excited I was. I heard that soft still voice, saying: This is what I am going to do." She beamed, her hands in front of her like open flowers. "This is saying we need to let go of the past and get ready for something new here in the desert. That's us— Faith Bible Church. Our new path is going to be a roadway out of the wilderness. It's going to be like a fresh stream, bringing new growth to a parched desert. And when it's complete, we will be singing praises."

The crowd was quiet except for a couple mms.

"I don't know about you, but I'm thrilled."

"Submission..."

"As your executive pastor—or minister, I mean—I want you to know it's humbling to know these men, your elders and pastors are entrusting me with the responsibility to lead this organization."

"Church—Submission!"

"I said organization, but it's more than that. We're the church, but we're also family. And in a family, every member is important and plays a role. There's also a design for headship to shepherd the family. In our case, that leadership role is carried by the elders and staff. As your executive pastor, it's my job to lead the staff and pastors and to glean wisdom from my elders, and I will do that to the best of my ability." She swallowed, her mouth suddenly dry as the audience sat in silence.

"Submission—you're a slave."

"The Lord showed me another passage I'd like to share. It's from the gospel of John when Jesus was washing the disciple's feet. Think about that, God's only Son on His knees—washing the dirt and grime from His friend's feet. And Jesus said, 'If you want to be the greatest leader, you need to be the greatest slave first.'

"To summarize, I want to leave you with this. I believe we are facing an exciting future. We're being asked to let go of the past and prepare for something new. It's going to spring forth, and it's going to bring us out of the wilderness to new life. And I've been called to lead in that adventure. It's a huge responsibility, but as your executive pastor, I promise to remember I've also been called to be the greatest slave of all. And that means, when I meet with my pastors and elders, I will be submitting to their authority, washing their feet, if you will. I want you to remember that, family."

She turned to Jason as the audience began to clap. "Pastor, I have a question for the church, if it's okay?"

Jason smiled weakly, the concern lingering.

Amber leaned forward. "I'm not sure if this is okay, being a woman and being new, but I was wondering...?"

A female voice called out, "You go, girl."

"Well okay, then. When I was a little girl, my father would take me to church—we were Lutheran. And at the end of the service, the pastor would give the Benediction. It was always the same. I know it by heart. Would it be okay with all of you, if I blessed our pastors and elders in closing?"

The congregation began to clap.

"Don't yield."

Pastor Jason stepped forward. "That would be nice. Yes, Pastor Lash, please."

Amber raised her right hand. "'May the Lord bless you and keep you. May His face shine upon you and be gracious to you. May He lift up his countenance upon you and give you peace. Go in peace, Church. You are loved.'"

CHAPTER 36

JONNESS LEANED against the thick wall in the comforting darkness of the radial corridor. The glow of torchlight danced across his feet in front of the opening behind his seat at the crescent table. A numb ringing in his ears, he squeezed the wooden scroll tube that he clutched to his chest. Cold and clammy, heart racing, he felt like he was standing on the edge of a high cliff. His stomach churned.

A voice inside whispered, *"Breathe in, breathe out. This will pass."*

Jonness listened to the voices of his men, sounding like they were speaking from the depths of a deep well.

"He went into the city wearing the cloak of a shepherd. His Holiness has done this before. He was compelled to be close to the people, to talk with them freely about the Lord. But he was attacked by robbers and beaten." The mumbling words came from Agabus.

The young elder spoke next. "This was an attack of Satan. But the gates of hell will not prevail against the church and the Lord's anointed."

Asmodeus spoke gently. *"It is time now. You must be strong."*

The men fell silent as he emerged from the opening. Wavering a bit, he grasped the back of the heavy chair. It groaned as he dragged it. Head down, he took his seat.

Alone in the dimly lit chamber, they watched his every move. Unrolling a scroll, he braced trembling hands on the table as he pretended to read. His left eye was swollen shut, and his nose bandaged. Half his face was blackened as if covered in soot.

While staring at the scroll, he began with a blurting stammer. "The Lord has testified the scribe shall be shown mercy. I requested his release from Rome earlier today. Batush shall serve as my personal attendant and scribe." Drawing a breath, he focused his eyes on the soft disk of light inching its way across the mosaic floor.

"Slowly, take your time."

As he breathed deeply, his bearings began to settle. "I have letters for the bishops and will be calling a council of the churches. The scribe can help in this and will live here. He will quarter with the clergy until the Lord releases him from my service."

Agabus nodded approval as he scratched at an open sore on his chin. "My Holiness, you show the love and mercy of Christ Himself and will be rewarded in heaven. You also show great wisdom in holding the scribe close. He can be questioned further to determine if he has made copies of the book." The senior elder folded his hands, his eyes locking on Jonness. "And what of the coffee trader?"

"I ordered his release also. He is not a learned man, and if he speaks the book again, he will do so as a blasphemer. The flock will not listen to him." Jonness continued to stare at the disk of light.

"Again, you show great mercy and—"

Jonness cocked his head and shouted, "Bring in the scribe."

Two guards appeared, escorting Batush to the central chair.

Jonness rolled the scroll tight and then slowly inserted it into the tube. "Batush. I have decided to show you mercy. It was I who ordered your release from jail and your companion also. Additionally, I have decided your crimes of desecration and theft shall remain unreported to Rome. If I had reported this, Batush, you would no longer be walking among us. Rome would likely have crucified you by now or fed you to wild beasts in the arena. But I have decided you may live for now."

Batush sat in silence.

Asmodeus whispered, *"Did he make a copy?"*

"I have a question for you, Batush. And I will remind you, when answering the bishop of Ephesus, you are speaking to your Christ—and you will speak truth. Have you made a copy of the book?"

"Yes."

"How many...?"

"Have you made more than one—are there more?"

"Only one."

"Where is it?"

"Tell us, where it is?"

"I cannot."

Jonness pointed with the scroll tube. Drawing it to his ear, he thrust it forward and blurted, "And why not?"

"It was taken, and I do not know where it is."

"This is an outrage—he shows dishonor."

Hands flat on the hammered stone table, Jonness rose, leaning forward. "Who took it from you?"

"As I said, I was working late at the library. When leaving, I was attacked on the road and rendered unconscious. Zophar found me and my writing case. The book, which you now have, was in the case, but some of my things were missing. Zophar did not find the copy of the book in my writing case. The angel told me..."

"Rebuke him."

"Silence!" Jonness slammed his fist on the table.

"What did the angel tell you?"

"The angel, yes... What did he tell you?"

"He told me to bring the book to you, which I have done."

"And did the angel tell you to make the copy also?"

"Yes."

"And what did the angel tell you to do with the copy?" Jonness strode behind the row of chairs, spreading his arms. The wings of his crimson robe opened.

"He told me to hide it. It is now gone, so that has been accomplished." Head down, Batush spoke softly with no emotion.

"He lies. Bind him until he surrenders it."

"I do not believe..." Jonness pivoted to Batush. "I believe the location of this copy will be revealed to you. You shall reside here, serving the church as my assistant, until the location of the copy is revealed to you and brought to us."

"Your Holiness... my family, they... Please, I beg you."

"Leave us."

The guards ushered Batush from the chamber.

Jonness whirled from one side to the other. "I said leave us. All of you, leave us."

<<>>

"Did you notice she avoided letting us pray over her?" Hands resting on the wheel, Daniel drove slowly.

"I did." Rhema shifted in her seat, the shoulder strap cutting across her cotton blouse as she faced him. "I also noticed how she took the Isaiah passage out of context. I really get tired of that."

He glanced at her before navigating a left turn. "What do you mean?"

"Using that passage to justify this or that new thing the church wants to do. I remember when Pastor Turner used the same passage. Remember? Right before they told us they were going to tear down the old buildings and build a new campus? It was God's plan, and then they changed their minds after four hundred people left because they had donated the money for the original buildings." She shook her head, her curls bouncing in a blur of copper. "It makes me angry. But who am I to say? No one ever asks the congregation before they do anything."

Daniel's foot floated over the brake pedal. Reacting then, he hit the gas to clear the intersection on yellow. "You're right, Coach. I know it doesn't help, but the thinking is we can't say what we're going to do ahead of time because it upsets people. And if we do ask, and then decide against whatever it is, the people don't understand and get mad."

"So? They should still ask, but they don't—because they don't care or want to know what we think. We're just the dumb sheep."

Daniel pursed a smile as he pulled into the driveway. His phone chimed.

"Who is it?"

"Bruce Peterson. Pastor Jason mentioned he left a voicemail for Bruce, offering to have the elders come pray with him. He wants to know if we can do it on Thursday evening so I'll need to message the guys."

"That's great. You should spend some time praying between now and then. He's grieving, and you might hear something for him." She stared out the window. "It's interesting he reached out to you and not Pastor Jason or one of the other elders."

<<>>

Engine idling and AC blasting, Amber sat alone in the parking lot. Biting her lower lip, she opted for a text instead of calling: The service was great. Pastor Jason introduced me up front, and elders prayed for me. Tomorrow I will meet my staff and get started. Be home soon and...

Hmm.

She retyped. Can't wait to see you but need to stay for now. May need you to send me some things. Will call.

Again, she adjusted the message. May need you to send some things. Will let you know. I love you and miss you soooo much.

Hmm. No, not that either.

Fumbling with the phone, she retyped. I miss you!
She then pushed Send.

<<>>

Nick Hamilton drew a sip, glancing at the corner of his monitor. The staff meeting was at nine, but he wanted to arrive early. *Three hours...* Day by day, he'd grown in confidence—sometimes, he could almost believe he controlled the graphs with his mind. He knew when to get in, when to double down, and most importantly, when to exit. He'd never been a touchy-feely sort of guy, but this was different. *Relax— embrace the stream. The only difference is the amount. Trust your instincts and listen.*

The trading symbol was NXG, a pharmaceutical recommended by Troy, a friend who worked for the company. Its beta was extremely high with the price fluctuating daily between one and two dollars. Up nearly 30 percent in the past week, it had closed at fifteen and change. The volatility revolved around the anticipated FDA approval of a new cancer drug, undergoing final testing with results to be announced at any time. Nick had traded the stock several times over the past month with solid gains. Today's pool included monies from his three largest client portfolios, along with a handful of other significant accounts. *One hundred and fifty thousand is no different from fifteen hundred. If it goes bad, these guys can afford it—but it won't. We've prepared, and besides, if it doesn't open down, we sit tight. But if it does, we score. The Zen Trader is invincible. Enter the stream. The fly is tied, and the hook is sharp.*

~~

The atmosphere was wet and rich in the Well of Souls, the temperature exceptionally hot. Rumbling and churning, the undulating goo-coated surfaces were stable for now. Heavy with acid and a tinge of ammonia, the scent smelled of fear and lust or was it greed? The variations were subtle and difficult to identify. However, the foundation ingredient was known with certainty—pride.

Mammon looked up from the smoldering pot. "Are the messengers ready?"

Gusher leaped to the cauldron edge, landing in a squatting position. After dipping a cupped hand into the sludge, he brought it to his nose. "Yes, General. The legions are ready—on your command."

"Whoa there. Easy on the brew." Mammon frowned.

Gusher smeared the goo on his face. "The smell of greed in the morning. There is nothing better. It smells like—victory..." Gusher laughed. Hopping to the floor, he stepped into the opening rift to huddle with the messengers who then darted away, delivering the word to a host of demons, each having the ear of several hundred day traders throughout the United States and a few foreign countries.

"At the ready... Keep it clean. The money is going to come off the table fast. Cover the premarket orders and be sure to bail when the fools start to make their moves. Mammon has the call..."

Traveling at light speed, the entire process took less than a millisecond on the human clock. Gusher leaped back to the edge of the pot. "All set. This will be glorious."

~~

Nick prayed, "Father, bless me. Expand my territory that I may testify of Your glory." As he drew a sip, the graph lurched vertically. "Damn." He lifted his index finger from the mouse. He then raked his fingers through his hair, stretching his face back. "Damn."

"*Watch*," Mammon whispered. "*Here it comes. These guys are all suckers. It's about to turn. Do you feel it? Will it to turn, and it will. Wait... Wait...*" The price continued to pulse higher, but volume was fading with cresting stochastics.

He glanced at his buy order in the queue and returned his finger to the mouse. *We've never shorted.... But what difference does it make? We can score either way.* With a click, he changed his order from buy to short-sell.

"*No risk, no glory—time to get some balls on.*" Mammon encouraged, "*It's about to turn. You are the Zen Master. It's turning.... All in—do it.*"

Typing quickly, Nick doubled his short-sell to ten thousand shares.

"Now... Now..." His finger dropped. Executing the order, he then checked for confirmation.

~~

"Sell... Sell... Now! Sell!" Gusher screamed to the messengers who vanished, bursting into human souls, each echoing the command to the legions who shouted into the minds of the traders.

~~

Nick tensed as the price pulsed higher with one last push. Turning then, it fell like a rock. He whispered, "Yeah baby. Yeah... Freefall...

Yes." He shook clenched fists as the graph plummeted like a cliff face. "Fifteen sixty... Fifteen thirty, twenty-six... Wow—truly glorious. Thank You, Lord."

"Ready now. This is going to be huge—don't miss it."

Nick brought up the trading tab, staging his next moves. First, a buy to cover the short-sell, followed with a long buy, and lastly the final sell. Fingers flying, he set his trades, each for ten thousand shares. The numbers raced through his mind, up nearly fifteen thousand in a minute and a half. Every muscle in his body rigid, he placed the second order.

~~

Mammon nodded to Gusher. "It's done."

Gusher relayed the command to the messengers, who immediately passed it on.

~~

The leveling price began to climb again. Nick rode it for several minutes, bailing at fifteen seventy-nine. The graphs indicated there was more to come, but he was out. *Safe and strong—it's done.* Referring to a piece of scratch paper, he returned the pooled funds to his client accounts. He then moved the profits to his account.

We earned it—every penny. That was insane. His mind still sprinting, he wiped sweat from his forehead. *Thirty-eight thousand and change in less than an hour. Zen Master rules—yeah baby.*

~~

Mammon bowed to Gusher, who thanked the comrades. "Is it not a glorious day, brothers? Oh yes, quite glorious."

CHAPTER 37

BATUSH SAT alone, in the cold darkness. Heavy air enveloped him, like a damp blanket smelling of limestone and decaying plaster. Centered just below the ceiling, a small opening, no more than the size of his head, provided a connection to the outdoors. A cot and a tired chair with a desk to match furnished the room, accessible by two plank doors, which locked from the outside.

Bowing his head, he prayed softly, "Holy God, I do not understand, but I worship and praise Your glorious name. You allowed me to deliver the book to the elders and to write the copy also. You sent Raphael to help and protect me from evil in the darkness. And You provided Zophar to minister to me, to revive me, and to fellowship with me in prison. I ask only that You watch over my family. Keep them safe and hold them close." He continued in silence, his lips moving. *Protect the book, Father. Watch over Your Holy Word and deliver it from evil... Amen.*

<<>>

Alone in her new office, Amber put the finishing touches on her agenda for the staff meeting. Saving the file, she closed her laptop and leaned back. With a few changes, the corner office with spacious windows and an oversized oak desk would soon feel like hers. Everything would need to go, but for now, she would make do with the faded green couch, small round table, and metal file cabinet. Her only fingerprint on the space so far was a digital Big Ben desk clock she had borrowed from the loft. After adjusting the time, she tried to figure out how to turn off the simulated ticktock feature. She then rubbed the bridge of her nose, the smell of mothballs bringing to mind her grandmother's dusty den.

Nick pushed the half-open door with his foot. "I've got coffee. The stuff around here is horrible unless you like burning your tongue on scalding water." He held a tall green and white paper cup in each hand.

Clock in hand, she tilted her head up to him and settled back, the lumpy chair's cracked leather scrapping her thighs. "Thanks. That was sweet of you."

He took a seat in front of her and inched closer. "How are you doing?"

"He's asking about Thursday," Asmodeus whispered.

"I'm eager to meet my staff, but the first encounter can be tricky. I guess I'm a little nervous. Thanks for being here."

He slid the coffee toward her. "I meant after the other night?"

She touched the tip of his finger as she took the cup. "What other night are you talking about? I don't remember a thing, except having an incredible dream." Tipping her head, she let a coy smile part her lips. "And I'm sure nothing happened, but I hope it won't be the last time—nothing happens."

His head jerked, wonderment glazing his face. With a quick glance at the door, he lifted his cup. "I was thinking I might escort you in and make the introduction, if that sounds good? It would convey the message that I'm, or we're, passing the torch if you will—entrusting leadership and authority into your very capable hands."

His tailored black suit with blended green silk tie and shirt were impeccable. Perhaps for a wedding, it could work, but for a staff meeting, it was a bit over the top. Then again, his brutal good looks contrasting with his boyish grin were quite charming. She thought about asking him to remove the vest but decided against. *He's dressed for me—what have I gotten myself into? He's my boss and I'm married, and I haven't even started the job yet? Then again...?*

"I like that. And then, when the timing's right, you sit, and I'll take the reins. Pastor Jason will be the wild card. After yesterday, I'm not sure what to expect."

"If need be, I'll jump in. I don't mind rebuking him if necessary. He works for the elders, and sometimes the staff doesn't seem to understand." He squared his shoulders.

She stifled a giggle, but truthfully, the image was ridiculously cute. "I appreciate that, but I think it's important I handle whatever happens. It could be the moment that makes or breaks me as their leader."

"Careful... Diffuse it."

"But if he starts shouting or comes across the table at me, that would be different. You might need to rescue me."

They laughed.

After taking the stairs, they exited through the reception area, crossed the plaza, and headed for the classroom building. Five after nine.

"Have you thought about filling the receptionist position?"

"I have a temp coming in at eleven, and I'm interviewing two candidates this afternoon."

Nick opened the door to a rush of clapping from the staff on their feet, about thirty, nearly filling the classroom. "Good morning, and what a beautiful morning it is. Some of you met Amber yesterday, but I wanted to take this opportunity to introduce her. I think all of you are going to be very impressed."

She scanned the room. *No Pastor Jason.*

"That's good. Use it."

Nick spoke for nearly an hour with great oration and detail, conveying her credentials and leadership skills as he read from notes. "There's a lot I could add, but for now, I'll turn it over to Amber." He took a seat in the front row of white plastic chairs with Amber standing behind the table that served as a podium.

Amber smiled, taking a moment to meet each person's eyes before spreading her arms in a wide embrace. "I know many have been blessed because of your service, and I'm thanking and praising the Lord for that."

"Enough with the fawning. They need to fear you."

"I appreciate how many of you reached out to say hello and make me feel welcome. It truly means a lot." Amber smiled as they stared.

"That's enough."

"I've been working on your names, so I'll also appreciate your patience. But I noticed Pastor Jason is missing. Does anyone know if he's ill or maybe having car trouble? I'm a little surprised he's not here." She raised her brows to the music pastor. "John, did you hear from Pastor Jason?"

"He doesn't typically work on Mondays. He spends all week preparing his message. It's a lot of work. This is his day off."

"That's garbage."

"Well, I don't want to waste any more time on this, but I'll need to talk to the pastor later. For now, I'd like to share some observations." She stepped closer to the table and woke her laptop. "I've spent time with the elders and prepared some data emphasizing our challenges. I'm not one to hide things from my staff so I requested everyone be here. What I'm about to present is confidential and needs to remain in this room."

"Perfect. It'll spread like wildfire."

"This first slide graphs the growth and decline of Faith Bible Church. You can see the initial spurt—it was a moon shot, from zero to six thousand in just five years. It then levels off, and the big slide follows to where we are now, with just two thousand members." Amber tilted her head. A lawnmower droned outdoors. "That's not a good sign, is it? I've been hired to bring us back—and I plan to do that. And if I don't, well, let's just say I won't be here for long."

The room responded with blank stares. In the back row, a younger woman appeared to be scrolling on her phone.

"Here we go, solid and confident."

"This next slide adds some data to the graph. Green indicates yearly giving dollars, and yellow shows population within a five-mile radius. I understand demographics have changed, and other churches have come in to compete. But our congregation and giving have declined as the city grows. This shows we're missing something. I see this, and the elders see this also. Something's wrong."

"No mercy."

"This last slide adds our staffing in red. It starts with one individual, the founding pastor, and then grows. Now, look. When the church had six-thousand members, we were operating with twenty-two full-time staff. And now, at just a third the size, our staff has actually increased. The good news is we have no debt. However, operating costs are sucking us dry with our largest expenses being salaries and health care."

She closed her laptop and folded her hands. "So, this is where we are. I understand staff has increased in response to ministry expansion, but we're in trouble. The simple truth is—if we can't fix this by year's end, we're going to be broke, and we'll need to close the doors. And none of us want that."

They continued to stare, even the woman on her phone looked up.

"I want three documents from each of you by two o'clock on Friday. The first should list your name and title along with a description of your job responsibilities with data, including how many people you're working with, growth figures, or anything else measurable. The second document will be your résumé so include the typical information—your education and prior experience, how long you've been here, etcetera. The final document will be your ministry overview, describing your vision and goals. Tell me why you're here and what your dreams are for this church."

A handful took notes.

"Mission accomplished. Wrap it up."

"You likely discern we have some tough decisions ahead. The elders and I will be working together on that, and we ask for your prayers. If we are going to survive as a church, we will need to right size our expenses. Beginning today, I want all of you to be looking for ways to cut costs. Send any ideas you have, because we need to cut expenses by fifty percent. Any questions?"

A part-time intern raised his hand. "Does this mean you're planning to cut half the job positions?"

Nick pushed back his chair, stood, and smoothed a crease in his pants. "A good question. I'd like to address it if I can?" Amber smiled as he stepped to her side. "It's exactly as Amber said—we need to cut expenses. That could mean half the job positions, but that's not realistic. However, we do need to reduce the cash burn significantly. The elders will be setting up a committee to look at options and leaning heavily on Amber's expertise. Does that help?"

The intern bobbed his head slowly. A half smile molded on his open mouth.

"Thanks, Nick. That's exactly what I would have said."

"It's best if they hear it now."

"As you know, I accepted my position last Thursday—making two staffing decisions already. First, I'll be interviewing candidates to fill the receptionist position. The receptionist is the face of every organization, so finding the right person is crucial.

"The second decision I made was to release someone, which I did on Friday." Several within the group exchanged glances. "Looking over the various departments, I found we're top-heavy in maintenance. I understand this is a large campus, but six full-time employees are too many. I decided, and Nick—Elder Hamilton agrees—we don't need a manager. Simple work assignments issued by email will be more efficient." Ignoring the gasp from the audience, she continued, "I understand Tom Evans has been here a long time and everyone likes him. But considering the decisions ahead, we—or I—let him go."

The intern jumped to his feet. "He's still here. Look, there he is!"

His face lit with a wide grin as he pointed. Her audience spun to the window. On the far side of the plaza, the strong dark man was riding a lawnmower.

<<>>

The clank of the slide bolt was followed with a command, "Come."

Pushing on the heavy plank door, Batush entered the bishop's private study. A zebra-skin couch lounged before a stone fireplace, while a carved desk and cushioned chair rested on a Persian rug. Shelves, overburdened with scrolls and books, sagged along the return wall beside his desk. Opposite them, a glazed window opened to the building's atrium where a birdbath stood below a canopy of cypress.

Jonness read a letter for several minutes as Batush stood. Jonness then picked up an empty crate from beside his feet and crossed the room to the shelves, never acknowledging Batush. Scratching his chin, he paced while scanning up and down, the box under his arm. He then randomly grabbed several scrolls and shoved them into the box, filling it.

"I will need three copies of these." Sitting again, he shoved the box across the desk. "You will also transcribe your scheduled training sessions and draft letters when I call. Your regular wages will continue and will be delivered to your wife by messenger."

"Thank you—"

Jonness lifted his hand. "You will speak to no one except me, answering only when I ask you a direct question. This is now your life, Batush, and it will remain so until the day you remember where the copy of the book is and tell me. Do you understand?"

Batush swallowed, responding with a nod.

"Do you understand, Batush?"

"Yes, Your Holiness."

<<>>

Nick opened his mouth as he kissed her neck, teasing with his tongue. Cocking her head, Amber recoiled and drew her shoulder to her ear. "That tickles."

Rolling above her, Nick pressed in with his face.

"Stop. I can't take it." She pushed against his chest as he let go. "You better be careful, or you'll give me a hickey. That would be quite the sight at my first elder meeting."

Cupping her breast, he drew her flesh into his mouth.

"We better not start again. You're too much for me.... Mmm."

Moving to her mouth, he slipped his hand under the small of her back.

"No... Stop. It's almost nine. You need to get home to your wife."

He relented with his boyish grin. "I'm not sure I could please you again, but I could give it my best shot."

"I'm sure you could, but I doubt I could keep up."

"Now you're lying to me, girl."

She drew a purple pillow to her chest and flipped her curls back. "So what's up with Tom Evans? That was unbelievable—I was so angry. I think he did it on purpose. Why else would he be mowing the lawn when he knew we were meeting in the classroom building? My first staff meeting, and he makes a fool out of me. Do you think anyone noticed I was upset?"

"No, it was fine. You were in control, and they got the message—I certainly did. They're on notice, and you're running the show."

"Except for the big black guy. He was just out mowing the lawn— after I fired him. Maybe he didn't understand the memo, but seriously, could I have been any clearer? Dear Mr. Evans, We would like to thank you for your service, but your position has been eliminated. Please pick up your final check from Elder Hamilton, who will transition your benefits." She threw her hands open as the pillow fell away. Nick's eyes darted to her chest, and she grabbed it up again. "And stop staring at my breasts."

"They are impressive, incredible in fact." He grinned while lifting his brows.

"Men, you're all the same." She wagged her finger, a cross look pinching her face.

"I understand you wanted to draw blood, but you should have asked me first."

"Why?"

"Firing Tom isn't going to save a lot. The entire time I've been handling payroll, he's never taken a penny."

Certain she misunderstood, she cocked her head. "What do you mean?"

"We pay him every two weeks, and he has full benefits—or did, I mean. Anyway, I cut his check, and he picks it up and then cashes it like everyone else. And then every Sunday, his offering is exactly half his check amount."

"You're saying he tithes a hundred percent?" Amber dropped her mouth open.

"Yep. And as far as I know, he's never used his benefits either. Never made an insurance claim or taken a single vacation day."

"So he just works and never takes anything. He's working for *free*?"

"You got it."

"Does anyone else know?"

"Just me—the giving information is confidential."

"What about Daniel—how much does he give?"

"Daniel?" Nick stiffened and arched a brow. "Why do you ask?"

"I don't know.... I get a bad vibe from him. I'm just curious."

Nick shrugged. "He gives about a third of where I'd guess his tithe is. But he could be giving to other organizations. There's no way to know."

"As an elder, shouldn't he be giving at least ten percent to his own church?"

Nick straightened up, rolling his shoulders back. "I think he should. But each of the guys has a different opinion. The New Testament isn't clear, but the Old Testament says everyone should bring ten percent to the temple storehouse."

"Perhaps we should address that as a policy. It would help with the numbers if all the elders were tithing. And we could use it as a wedge if someone's causing friction."

"What do you mean?"

"You know. If we wanted to get rid of someone and they were breaking a policy. All of the elders should be following the policies, right?"

"That's good, Amber. We can work on that."

"So, what do I do about Tom? I can't let him defy me and keep working."

Crossing his legs, Nick drew the tips of his fingers together. "What about liability? He's no longer insured. And what if the lawnmower threw a blade and cut off his foot? The church would be at risk if he sued us."

"Right. Or what if he sexually assaulted one of the schoolkids? A suit from the parents could wipe us out."

His fingers slipped apart as Nick laughed. "That's a stretch. Tom's the last guy I could imagine doing something like that. He's a saint and everyone loves him. That's another reason he wasn't your best choice."

She bowed her head. "Do you think there's going to be pushback?"

"Oh yeah—count on it. But don't worry. Besides, I'll back you up, and we can work together on the cleanup." He offered a warm smile.

"You're the best." Amber lowered the pillow.

CHAPTER 38

FAITH BIBLE Church's boardroom was a battlefield. The campaign had spanned more than forty human years and mostly been slow going, especially early on. But investments were paying off. A firing here and a sex scandal there, a couple church splits, not to mention the music wars—all were counted as battles won in the long war. Of course, each conflict had taken great effort and cunning strategy. But steadily, they were gaining territory, and ultimate victory was deliciously close—so close, in fact, they tasted the blood in their mouths.

Moaz leaped to the conference table, landing like a surfer riding a wave. Standing upright, he yawned and then clapped his hands. "Wake up. Stay frosty... The enemy could be prowling in the shadows." Rotating slowly, his head bobbing up and down, he gauged the scene. The frozen humans sat around the slab of mahogany with heads bowed. "Focus, guys. They might call in a strike." Moaz circled, stopping to chat with comrades. Two leaching demons clung to their hosts while others peered out from interior positions. Moaz bowed like a Shakespearian actor and then crossed his arms. "Ramoth, you ugly sack of vomit. What say you?"

Ramoth withdrew a small clawed hand from an elder's eye. Licking at the goo, he slid it back in. "Slow and steady. Blindness is closer today and quite tasty." Clad with grayish-white oily skin, the leaching demon's appearance was much like that of a hairless sloth with the shrunken head of an old man.

"Very good, sir, carry on." Moaz stopped in front of Paul Chambers. "Sluggo, my man, how's it hanging?"

The nickname stuck to Lachish from a time long past. Sluggo hung from his tail wrapped around the chairman's neck. His appearance being almost identical to the other leaching demons, subtle skin coloration and facial features offered his only distinguishing characteristics. He typically worked in tandem with various addiction tormentors. His exterior position afforded excellent access to the ear when whispering encouragements, while the tormentors' job was inside drudgery, mostly working the organs, clawing and picking. Sluggo carried his trademarked spiked war club, being an expert in its use.

"Can you give him a shot? I've been working on your windup move but can't seem to quite master it." Sluggo's delivery of the migraine blow was legendary. "Show me, Sluggo—sock it to him." Moaz hopped from one foot to the next.

Withdrawing his head from the elder's side, Sluggo rubbed his face with both hands like a rodent moving in slow motion. "Moaz, you're interrupting progress. We're working a sector and nearly complete. Can it wait?"

"No, it can't—and besides, we need this one alive. The sector can wait. It's not going anywhere. I want to see your move—come on, man?"

Sluggo released a long exhaling breath, his head swinging back and forth. "Okay, okay—but just one pop. And that's it. Okay?" His tail unwound as he climbed slowly, up and over Paul's back. "Here we go—watch and learn." Standing on Paul's shoulder, he hoisted his weapon and leaned outward. Stroking the club in and out, he stopped just short of contact, like a batter at the plate.

"Sock it to him, sock it to him. Yeah, Sluggo—hit him good." Moaz leaped up and down, clapping and hooting.

Sluggo drew a sucking breath. Reaching back, he held the position for dramatic effect and then loosed the swing. It made a sharp shooting noise, like an arrow released from a taut bow. The impact followed with a crunch, the club head buried below the surface of the elder's temple. Sluggo then heaved, levering the club up and down. Bracing a foot against Paul's head, he yanked it free.

"That's what I'm talking about—you are the man." Moaz strutted bowlegged with elbows extended, bobbing from side to side. He missed seeing the warping shimmer as the rift opened and closed behind the powerful being. Caught off guard, he spun to face the towering archangel. He straightened up, composed himself, and puffed his chest out.

"Raphael, we were just talking about how we hoped you might join us for the meeting. Look, they're praying for you."

~~

He felt it then, a tingling shimmer of energy in the room. Daniel almost looked up but instead twisted in his seat to look behind. No one was there. He rubbed chills from his arms. The room was hot. He then scanned the faces of each man at the table—nothing. *Surely, they felt it?*

Paul Chambers squeezed his temples between thumb and forefinger. "That's enough. It doesn't matter who spilled the beans. Anytime you share something with that group, it's gonna leak within an hour." He waved his plastic hammer. "I called the meeting without Amber's presence because we need to hash this out. Look—we hired Amber to lead. Any leader, who takes over a corporation, starts by drawing blood. It's like the new guy in prison. The first thing he does is beat the heck out of the biggest badass he sees."

Laying the hammer down, he rubbed his face. "Maybe that's a bad analogy, but the principle is there. Amber was establishing herself. In our case, the guy she punched happened to be Tom Evans."

"I agree, and—"

"Wait." Paul lifted an open hand. "Daniel first. Then Henry and then Nick."

Daniel waited for their attention. "First of all, this isn't a prison or a corporation. And yes, we're called to lead, all of us—and especially Amber, because of the role we've placed her in. But I'm talking about servant leadership and shepherding. We're supposed to humble ourselves, washing the feet of the staff and congregation. But to walk in and fire the guy who's loved more than anyone else in the entire church—on her very first day? And then to say, 'Oh, and by the way, we're getting ready to fire half of you too.' Talk about first impressions—seriously?"

He spread his hands. "In our first meeting, Amber said she'd come in and listen to the music, get to know the staff and the people before making any changes. You were there, Nick. She said it would be like a conductor, coming in during the middle of a song and taking the wand without anyone noticing. What happened to that? And another thing, why would she... My point is..." His words trailed off.

"Okay. Henry next, then Nick."

Henry straightened up. "We hired Amber to lead, and she's doing that—you know, based on her experience. I mean, let's face it—this woman really knows her stuff. You know, running her real estate company and making the changes she did. She's a smart cookie all right, and the Holy Spirit is working. I think we need to sort of sit back and see what the Lord has in mind—this is what I'm saying here."

~~

Moaz sat cross-legged at the center of the table, staring at the men. Jumping to his feet, he shouted, "Do you think this is fun? Sitting here day after stinking day waiting for you to move. Say something, you fools!"

Rolling his eyes, he looked at Raphael. With a headshake, he then snorted. "Hey, I got it—how 'bout a dance?" Moaz bowed gracefully, one arm raised above his head. "Thank you—thank you. Such a wild ovation. Okay—settle down, be patient." He began to hum. Then gyrating, he spun like an ice-skater. Planting his right foot, he morphed into a strut, elbows extended while thrusting his head from side to side leading with his chin. "See that, Raphael? The Rooster Walk—that's my move, I invented it." Moaz crooned a high-pitched out-of-tune rendition of "Sympathy for the Devil".

"Here we go again—you're such a little liar."

His lower jaw protruding enough to jab his teeth out, Moaz pivoted, stopping midsong. "Who said that?"

Leaping into the air, he planted his feet into Vince's laptop keys. He then took a squatting stance and began to pull on his cheeks, composing a ghoulish face. Leaning forward, he sneered, nose to nose with Vince, whose fingers hovered above the keys. "You there. That's right, fly-bait—I'm calling you out." Standing upright, Moaz thrust his hips forward. "I think you'd like some of this—wouldn't you?" He grinned at Raphael.

"That's enough, Moaz." Raphael stood behind Daniel's shoulder.

Moaz cocked his head. "'That's enough, Moaz. Quit messing around, Moaz. How come you're always teasing the humans, Moaz? What's wrong with you, Moaz?'" Vaulting to the table surface, he moonwalked past the bowl of stale popcorn.

Pouncing then, he landed on Daniel's notepad. "I'm coming for you next. That's right, joker. My friends and I are messing with you now, but we're coming for you later." He pointed a crooked finger. "You better watch yourself because I'm gonna be inside your head. That's right, a-face, inside your ugly-ass head." He glanced at Raphael then back again. "You think he can protect you? Ha—Raphael, the *crying* angel? He can't stop me because he knows I'll kick his ass—that's right. And that one over there, Nick Hamilton? We got major territory inside him—six of us right now. And did I mention Asmodeus? You ever heard of him? You better—because Asmo comes and goes as he pleases inside that fool."

Raphael reached behind his right shoulder and drew his weapon.

Moaz folded his arms, pretending to yawn. He then flicked his wrist in and out and glanced down as if checking a wristwatch.

The sword glinted as Raphael brought it forward in a fluid arc. The shimmering weapon was nearly twice as long as the demon was tall.

Moaz drummed his fingertips against his wrist. He then swung with a batting hand that passed through the blade as four knuckles fell in front of his face. Bouncing, they rolled across the table.

"Get that out of my face." Moaz stooped, sweeping up the fingertips with his good hand. When he took a step back and then two sidesteps, the sword tip followed. "Get it away—I said I don't like that." He placed the severed fingers back on the stubs of his wounded hand. Flexing them in and out, he made a fist. "What are you going to do now? You think you're such a big shot with your sword? I could whip you with my little—"

Raphael flipped his wrist with the precision of a surgeon. Moaz's head lifted from his torso. Flipping through the air, it landed facedown in the popcorn.

Moaz screamed, but the words were garbled. Dropping to a knee, he picked up his head, tossed it into the air as one might check a melon all while his head continued to laugh. As he planted it on his neck, the laugh transformed into a throaty cackle.

Moonwalking again, Moaz floated toward Paul Chambers, his head on backward. "It's so much easier when you can see where you're going. Do you get it, Raphael—do you get it? It's a joke."

~~

Feeling nauseous, Daniel stared at the large plastic bowl of stale popcorn. A paper bowl in his hand, Henry used it as a scoop, dipping it into the large bowl. Stuffing his mouth, he picked up another paper bowl and arched his brows to Daniel. His stomach churning, Daniel shook his head.

"Okay, Nick's next." Paul pointed with his yellow hammer.

Standing behind his chair, Nick used it as a podium. "I agree with

Daniel—we're each called to lead. But I see it differently in how that looks. The sheep are hungry for leadership. They need a shepherd with a staff for protection, yes, but they also need a shepherd who carries a rod. And they fear that rod because, when they stray, they know they'll get a whack. It's no different from raising children. Every child needs to be loved, but true love is going to be tough—there will be boundaries. Children need that. And the flock, including the staff, are no different."

Leaving the chair, he paced while gesturing with his hands. "Gentlemen, we are watching a masterful leader in the woman Amber Lash. I'm with Paul—I like what I see. And I disagree with Daniel on servant leadership. Let's face it—this organization is a business. We're a corporation with paid staff, and that's a key difference compared to Bible times. The staff work for us. They're employees, and they deserve real leadership. They need boundaries and discipline. In fact, without it, they don't know what to do."

He tilted his head as if listening. "It's like a cauldron of steaming excrement. Excuse my description, but that's what it is. The pot is filled with thick goo, and it reeks. It smells like fear, rumors, and deception—and that's good. Because we can sit back and watch it spinning around. We pull up our sleeves and reach in and stir it a bit. Our arms come up, and some of the poo sticks—its dirty work." Wrinkling his nose, he lifted his arms and let them dangle from the elbows.

"Amber's no dummy. She knew everything she said was going to leak—it was brilliant." He tugged on his chin. "Let's see what comes out of the smoldering pot—what stinks and what sticks. All of it will help with the tough decisions—but our job is to sit back and watch. Enjoy the show because it's going to get interesting." He paused. "I have a proposal to place on the table."

A glance exchanged between Paul and Nick.

"I recommend we establish a leadership selection committee to work with the executive pastor in review of the forthcoming employee feedback, in order to make sound recommendations to us. I'd also like to volunteer myself for consideration to chair the committee."

Paul shielded his eyes, squinting. "That makes sense. What do you think, guys—should we set up a committee to help Amber?"

The men responded in nodding agreement.

"Okay. I don't think we need a vote, but we should record the decision in the minutes."

Vince nodded as he typed.

"Does anyone else want to serve on the committee, and do we agree Nick should chair it? Come on, guys, I need at least one more to balance it out. I won't look so good if it's just Nick and Amber."

Daniel was tempted. A voice inside seemed to be saying no, but his mind was saying yes. He was about to lift his hand when Henry volunteered.

"Okay. Henry and Nick will work with Amber. Let's be praying for the committee, because we've got some rough water ahead, but that's why they pay us the big bucks."

A couple of the men chuckled.

Back at his podium, Nick said, "Men, we've made a strategic hire, and it's time to forge ahead with boldness. But I'd like to draw attention to that thing on the wall." He pointed to the schoolroom clock. "The holidays will be here before we can blink, and our new structure needs to be set before we get there."

Paul rubbed his temples. "Nick's right. The last thing we need is to be firing people just before Christmas. The sooner we work through this the better it's going to be for everyone. And with that, I'd like to wrap it up. It's late, and I've got a tee time in about"—Paul lifted his head, squinting at the clock—"six hours."

~~

Quiet assurance filled Raphael as the demon's face washed from glee to ashen concern. "What's that, Raphael—what do you got? Is that power? What are you going to do?" Moaz gawked at the flask hanging from Raphael's neck.

"I think you know." Raphael lifted the necklace over his head and eased out the cork. Extending his hand, he held it above Daniel's head.

"That's not very much." Moaz stood up straight, his eyes darting from the flask to the sword still fixed in front of his face. Whimpering, his words escalated into a cry, "Noooo... No, no, no! Don't."

Raphael tilted the clear vial just below level. The golden liquid flattened, rolling forward. It paused at the lip. Reconstituting into a reflective droplet, it hung for a moment. It then fell like the weight of an enormous boulder, floating yet cutting through time and space.

Watching the power enter was a fascinating thing. The droplet was there and then gone, disappearing into the being's shell. Raphael wasn't exactly sure how it worked, but it did, falling directly to the Spirit within. It made sense that pure power, true power, is the only essence that can be added to the Spirit of God. His power essentially poured into Himself.

The shimmer effect followed. He'd never tired of seeing it. It presented at the entry point, slightly delayed from the moment the droplet entered. The delay was equal to the time the vanishing droplet expended in falling to the human's core, his heart, the well of souls. The shimmer then followed, washing over the being's surface, in this case from head to toe.

What must it feel like as the crackling wave of golden glory electrified Daniel's body? He'd seen humans stagger or fall when the power entered. However, Moaz was correct today—there wasn't a lot to pour.

Though small, it took effect on Daniel, who was now radiating light. The glow extending from his body to about the distance of an open hand. It would also emanate from his mouth. As he spoke, the words would be seen and felt by the angels. How long the effect would last varied from being to being. Again, the amount was small, but it usually lasted a day or two before dissipating.

Raphael lowered the sword, redirecting his attention to Moaz, now crouching in front of Paul Chambers. Lifting his arms, Moaz spun around while holding his head in place, his eyes riveted on the chairman. Standing upright, he turned to Raphael. "Okay, okay, I'll stop. Lighten up, Raphael—you're so serious."

~~

Everything was clouded—his vision, the men's voices, the feel of his clothing, even the smell of the popcorn. As if submerged in icy water, Daniel clung to the edge of the mahogany slab.

"Nick, can you please close us? My head is pounding." Paul was hunched over, his head almost laying on the table.

"I have a question." Daniel spoke not knowing what he'd say. It hit him then, a tingling sensation of heat washing through his frame. It started at his head and moved down and through his extremities. He stared at his hands, flexing his fingers, suddenly lightheaded.

"Sure—why not. What is it, Daniel—we're dying to know?" Paul pushed himself back, glancing to the clock. "It's something simple, I hope—right?"

Daniel opened his mouth, the words flowing out as if speaking on their own. "Tom Evans. What about Tom?" The strength in his voice startled him, his question sounding more like a declaration.

The men turned to him as if he'd just walked into the room.

"Yeah, thanks for the reminder." Paul straightened up. "I was going to bring that up. What do we think, guys? Does someone need to talk to Tom?"

"And tell him what—he can't volunteer anymore?" Daniel turned from side to side. "Isn't that what we're always asking for? More volunteers serving and using their gifts to build up the body?"

Two of the men offered stilted nods.

Nick exhaled. "It's more complicated than that. You're smart enough to understand, Daniel. Tom Evans is taking a stand against Amber. It's a challenge to her authority and ours as well because we hired her. The staff were smiling and laughing when they saw Mr. Evans riding the lawnmower—after he was fired. He's defying our new pastor and shaking his fist at us. Pure and simple, that's rebellion."

Protruding lower lips bolstered the men's responding nods.

Daniel stood. "This is the point I made earlier. We're called to be servants, and that's who Tom is—it's his gift. When was the last time you were at any church function and you didn't see him? His job has nothing to do with it. He's always serving because he loves the people and he loves the Lord."

The men dropped their heads.

Paul rubbed his face. "Okay... Do we let him keep working or does someone go talk to him?"

Nick folded his arms. "I'll handle it. This is leadership, men. But I won't be talking to Tom—that would be inappropriate. I'll talk to Amber and let her know we're backing her up. She fired him, so she'll need to straighten it out."

Vince Fogel asked, "What do we do if he keeps working?"

"That'll be up to Amber, but I'll be advising her to call the police if necessary."

Daniel's throat tightened as he blurted. "The police—you can't be serious? And what are we going to say, 'Hey... can you come over to the church and arrest one of our members? He's volunteering to help too much?'" Daniel huffed.

"I would and it's not funny. We need to consider the liability if he's working without insurance coverage. We can't have him operating machinery without supervision. He could get hurt and sue the church. And what would happen if he sexually assaulted one of the schoolkids? We could be sued out of existence."

Nick had to be kidding. Daniel threw his arms out, his chin thrust forward. "That's ridiculous. He's not going to assault one of the kids. And besides, we let people work in the nursery and help with campus cleanup all the time without being employees or having insurance." He made eye contact with Henry, who offered a head tilt.

"Okay. It looks like we're mostly in agreement. Should Nick talk to Amber about this? And let me add, Nick... You will speak gently to Amber, and you will be sure she understands she will be gentle with Tom. Yes?"

"Absolutely." Nick avoided Daniel's stare.

"Nick, can you please now end this meeting with a prayer?"

CHAPTER 39

BATUSH RUBBED his eyes, struggling to focus. He stood and stretched and then began to pace, a procedure he'd repeated several times during the day. The bishop had been clear—he was to remain in his small room unless called upon. He was allowed to open the door, but only to place his refuse bucket in the corridor where it was picked up twice daily. He was also allowed use of the bishop's personal study, located between Batush's room and the bishop's private quarters, provided the heavy door between the two rooms was unlocked. When the bishop was present, Batush was to withdraw to his room immediately unless called upon to remain.

Batush approached the entrance door. Hearing nothing, he tried the latch to find it unlocked. Woozy and hungry, he grimaced when his stomach growled. Dusk's glow faded from the small window. *Will there be food tonight, and will there be more than a single meal per day?*

He touched the overflowing box of scrolls. *All day and only one of twelve scrolls copied for the book of Enoch—with five books to follow. Twenty-six scrolls in all and three copies each? Working all day, it will take at least six months. And will there be transcriptions also?*

Batush refilled the oil lamps in both rooms. Hearing the patter of rain again, he moved to the study to light a fire. *The warmth will be comforting, and the dancing flames will provide company. For now, at least, we have plenty of logs and kindling.* He was building the fuel structure when footsteps approached in the corridor.

As Batush entered his room, the door between him and the corridor swung open. "Naaman—greetings. I see you have brought nourishment for an old man."

Naaman stared at the tray in his hands.

"What news do you have for one who is hungry for words?"

Naaman hesitated, nodding toward the small desk as Batush stepped aside to let him pass. When he placed a plate of vegetable stew on the table, Naaman hesitated again and then hurried to leave. Pausing in the doorway, he lifted his eyes to meet Batush's. "I'm sorry..."

The door closed, followed by a heavy clank as the iron bolt slid into the jamb socket. Batush tilted his head to the small window as the thought of fire entered his mind. *I have done what You ask, Lord, but I do not understand? What am I to do?*

<<>>

Two women sat in the villa courtyard next to a statue of Zeus. They spoke in rapid hushed tones. "The bishop knows who desecrated the tomb."

"Who...?"

"One of the church Christians, but I do not have a name. The tomb was robbed also."

"One of the Christians? Why, and for what reason? This... it is hard to believe."

"But it is true. I heard it from Lidia. She heard her husband speaking of it with another member of the Senate. It must certainly be true."

"Did she hear of what was stolen?" The older women lifted her neck scarf to cover her mouth.

"A book sacred to the Christians. It was sealed in the tomb."

The younger woman's eyes darted from side to side and then to the balcony above. "And why has the bishop not been arrested?"

"One cannot know. Perhaps the governor does not care about the crime. After all, Celsus was hated by the people—and why also, would the governor care about a book sacred to the Christians?" The older woman leaned closer. "See if you can find out who did this and tell no one I am asking. This information could be valuable to certain persons. It could be dangerous also—be cautious."

<<>>

Daniel didn't see any cars he recognized. Shutting off the engine, he checked his phone—6:37. *Looks like it's just me. Probably for the best.* After picking up his Bible, he turned to the two-story home. His preparation in becoming an elder had included a required seven-week training class, which dealt primarily with the Biblical qualifications for pastors and elders. It also covered church organization and policies, as well as two sessions on the importance of humility and sexual purity.

Pastors are elders and elders are pastors. Daniel had forgotten much of what the class covered, but he did remember that statement. He also thought of Rhema telling him people usually just need someone to be there and listen. She'd told him to ask the Lord for words. *Use me, Lord, to be Your Son for Bruce in his time of need.*

He opened his eyes. Taillights glared red in the open garage bay. He locked his truck as the sleek convertible eased into the driveway.

"Wow, nice ride. Is this the 911?"

"No, it's a Cayman." Bruce Peterson, looking to be in his midforties with a medium build and short dark hair, sat in the body-hugging saddle-tan bucket with bright-orange stitching, his hand on the gearbox shifter. "It's only a car. Hey, I just sent you a text. Something came up, and I need to dash. We can reschedule if you like, or you can join me? It's a nice evening for a spirited drive."

"I can't turn down an invitation like that. I've only ridden in a Porsche once a long time ago. I think it was the 914—nothing like this." Daniel crawled into the chalk-white convertible, his face at the same height as his Ford's bumper. "Wow, this sits really low."

Bruce slid the shifter into reverse with a warm smile. Dressed in jeans and cotton, short-sleeves, he adjusted a worn 49ers baseball cap. "I bought it from a guy that did some modifications. It's got just three inches of clearance, so it's really glued to the road."

"I bet it is. So where are we going?"

"A woman from church, Amy Moore, needs prayer. She's been in the hospital for two months. She's also been to a bunch of specialists, but they can't figure it out. They finally sent her home and told her to get her affairs in order. A friend is taking care of her because she's too weak to even dress herself. They think it might be some sort of immune disorder or maybe lupus. Anyway, I got the call to go pray for her."

"Amy Moore? I don't think I know her."

"Not your church, my church. Karen and I go—or *went*—to different churches."

The three-point harness clicked as Daniel buckled in. "I didn't realize that. I would only see you..."

Bruce lifted his hand from the wheel with a dismissive wave. "No, that's fine. Most people would expect a couple to attend the same church. But we both felt called to different ministries. I don't have anything against Faith Bible. It's a great church." He eased the Cayman over the rolled curb at an angle while checking his mirror.

"So where do you attend?"

"Church of Living Water... It's really small, about sixty of us." Leaving the neighborhood, they headed north on Eldorado Drive. He watched the temperature gauge now at the one-fourth mark.

"So tell me about your church—how do you like it?"

"It's really good. I love it. Don't get me wrong—it's not perfect. We've got some issues. But that's because it's a church, and there's people there. As an elder, I'm sure you understand.... But the people are great, and they're filled with the Spirit." Pushing the clutch in, he eased on the brake pedal as they slowed before the red traffic light, his wristwatch face reflecting the dash-glow of overlapping retro gauges rimed in brushed aluminum. He turned to Daniel. "We're full gospel."

"What do you mean—full gospel?"

"We believe in the supernatural. I know Faith Bible doesn't agree— and a lot of churches don't. And that's fine because God uses His churches in different ways. Sometimes it gets a little wild—but the key is the foundation. We keep our focus on God's Word but also embrace spiritual gifts. We believe in healing and prophecy, tongues and miracles. And deliverance too—spiritual warfare is real. Demons are too." Again, he glanced at Daniel. In third gear, with no radio noise, the refined engine-note hummed with a medium high-pitched whine begging for release. "You might be seeing one tonight—that's what I'm hearing from the Lord. A lot of times when sickness manifests, demons are involved. Especially when doctors can't figure it out. Have you ever seen a demon?"

Daniel tilted his head, firmly seated in the Recaro bucket and also his heart. "No. But I know they exist—they're in Scripture. Just look at how many times Jesus cast out demons. I'm in agreement with you, but well..." They were both watching the gauge, now pegged vertical.

Bruce merged onto the I-10 on-ramp and smiled. "I got another cap if you want it?"

"No, I think I'm good." Daniel reached for the handle grip as Bruce punched it, his shifting swift and precise, his hands poised and relaxed. The German machine surged forward with a rising crescendo of screaming acceleration, feeling like a jet on takeoff, only faster. With his body pressed into the leather seat, the tachometer needle and his head snapped back and then forward with each shift. Daniel grinned as wind and road, streetscape and taillights, rushed toward them. The sensation—freedom unleashed.

<<>>

"The Anointed One said nothing of a crime or a sacred book. I am present at all church meetings, including the council, and I have heard nothing of this." The vicar eyed the young woman up and down.

She pulled her cloak tight to her neck. "Are you sure of what you speak? My source is reliable and tells me Rome is searching for these criminals. I am told also the bishop has knowledge of this wrongdoing and possesses the stolen book. Certainly, if anyone is hiding information about such a crime, they could pay with their life."

"I will ask the Anointed One upon his return."

"When are you expecting him?"

"If not tonight, he will return in the morning. He is on a pilgrimage to make sacrifices to Caesar and other gods—seeking a blessing for the church." Scanning the plaza, the vicar was tempted to touch her. He had seen the bishop do it before with much success. Although she was only a woman, she was also the slave of a senator's wife. "Will there be a reward if I can obtain this information?" He groped her with his eyes.

"We will see, once you talk to your bishop. My lady's husband seeks vengeance against those who committed this crime, and the book is evidence." As she released her grip on the garment, it parted, exposing her neck.

"I will see what I can learn, but you must understand—sacred knowledge is valuable to the Nicolaitans. It is by knowledge we escape damnation, and the way of salvation is narrow. If the Anointed One has this sacred book, he will not easily part with it."

"But you are a learned man and could read this knowledge for yourself. You could then give the evidence to me—along with the criminals' names. There could be a reward for one who might do this." The young woman tugged at the edge of her cloak, revealing the cleavage of her small firm breasts. Her finger stroked the underside of her chin, gliding down then over and up like an artist might paint with a feather. Her finger then drew back, pointing at the vicar's raised hand. Cinching her garment tight again, she glanced to see if anyone might be watching.

CHAPTER 40

THEY STOOD at the front door of the small ranch house. The porch light was out, but the buzzing streetlight provided just enough illumination for Daniel to read Bruce's face.

Bruce asked, "Have you done this before?"

"Prayed for someone?"

"No, I mean for healing as an elder?"

"I guess this will be my first time."

"Okay—here's the setup. We're representing two churches, and Scripture gives us authority as elders to pray for the sick. We pray knowing God heals. Whether or not He does is up to Him—but we ask in faith, believing." Bruce dropped his chin in a half nod. "Are you tracking with me?"

"I am."

"Let me lead. I've done this before. Be praying and listening for the Lord's voice. Pray with your eyes open and don't be afraid to jump in if you're hearing something." He reached into his shirt pocket. "Here, you do the anointing—it's frankincense and myrrh. There's nothing special about the oil. It's a symbol of God's power being poured out. Just anoint her in the name of the Trinity. Got it?"

Daniel took the vile with two fingers. Unsure of what to say, he nodded.

Bruce turned to knock when the door opened.

"Bruce." An older woman with black-framed glasses and shoulder-length blondish brittle hair covered her mouth. "You scared me. Hi—I'm Sandra. I'm sorry it's so dark out here. The bulb burned out last week, and I haven't had a chance to replace it. Please come in."

The door entered directly into a dimly lit living room, sparsely decorated with a couch, two sitting chairs, an end table, and a single framed landscape. The dry air was hard to breathe. Lifting a finger to his nose, Daniel applied pressure at the bridge and sniffed. Hearing the rustle of a sheet, he turned and saw her in the corner of the couch, propped up on one arm. The sheet draped over one shoulder slid to her lap.

"Hi, Amy. How are you?" Bruce pulled one of the chairs forward and sat before her.

"Not so good I guess." The dry whisper lingered in the air, barely audible.

Daniel motioned to the other chair. "No, no—please sit." Sandra backed away, adjusting the lamp. "She's sensitive to the light. It hurts her skin."

He drew up the other chair next to Bruce, still holding his Bible. Short dry, dusty-gray hair, which should have been black, framed a pasty gray face, matching the wall color. But Bruce had said the frail woman, looking to be in her sixties, was just thirty-two. Amy opened her eyes halfway, the whites grayish yellow. They closed again as slowly as they had opened as the faint smile faded.

"I'm sorry you had to come."

"Don't say that. Being here is an honor." Bruce began with a few questions, learning Amy was from Malaysia and worked with a nonprofit agency. She had an older brother in the Chicago area, and their parents lived in a small Malaysian village.

Suddenly lightheaded, as though outside his body, Daniel seemed to be watching a scene, which included himself. He could comprehend the discussion—distant and muffled. *What are You saying, Lord?*

"Feel what you are seeing and see what you are feeling." The soft voice, so reassuring, spoke from within, heard not with his ears, but his soul.

He sensed it then, the heavy dry dullness. Like a blanket, the dull color of the house, the walls, the burned-out bulb, and the buzzing streetlamp ... the wasteland room, ashen face, and lifeless voice. *Death...* It hung in the air, the room, and the home itself. Enveloping her, it seemed to be watching and waiting.

"My brother and I are very close—he's Christian. But my parents are not."

"When was the last time you saw them?"

"Before I got sick, about two years ago. I was afraid to go, but I had to. I love them so much, and I'm always praying for them."

"Why were you afraid to see them?"

"Because my father is so angry that my brother and I are Christians. He will not even talk to us." Amy's chin dropped, and then her head bobbed. When Bruce nudged her knee, she opened her eyes. "My mother said that, when they got a letter from my brother telling them he was Christian, our father burned it. And then he smashed all the family pictures with my brother and me in them. When I was there..." Eyes closed, her head twitched again. "I–I had to stay in a small house, separate from the temple where they live. My father is a Tau High Priest—he is like a pastor."

Bruce leaned forward. "Does he preach?"

"No. He leads the ceremonies and makes sacrifices. They worship idols in the temple, and they are there too."

Bruce touched her knee again. "What do you mean—they are there, too?"

"Demons—they are there in the temple."

"When you think about that place—tell me—what scares you the most?"

Amy lifted a hand to her shoulder and swallowed. Opening her eyes again, she drew her knees in. "A man, he is like a witch doctor. He makes curses and even kills people." Her voice grew stronger, and her jaw tightened. "When I see him—I'm so afraid—I can feel his evil. I can hardly stand to be there, but I love my parents very much. They are worshiping evil but don't understand."

Daniel gripped the seat of his chair, a shiver rolling his torso. He was swimming in the dryness of death, almost suffocating. *Lord, give me Your eyes and ears. Help me know how to pray.*

Bruce pulled a small pad from his pocket and drew a circle. "Let me show you something."

Amy straightened her back, pressing into the couch with a rigid arm. Her head tilted back, she struggled to bring her knees forward. Sandra stepped forward then. Taking Amy's hand, she lifted as Amy managed to put her legs on the floor and sit upright. The sheet slid to the floor, revealing her gaunt shape drowning in a lavender floral-pattern nightgown.

"God has three parts—Father, Son, and Holy Spirit. And He designed each of us with three parts too—body, soul, and spirit. The body is the physical part, and the soul is our intellect and personality, which makes us unique. And our spirit is the part of us that communicates with God."

Bruce divided the circle into three sections. "What happens is that life wounds most of us, including Daniel and myself. The wounds are like wedges between the parts." He colored a sliver between two of the pie slices. "The wounds are weak places where the enemy can attach and attack us from. Does that make sense?"

She lifted and dropped her head as her throat gulped to swallow. Her trembling hand then reached for a water glass on the end table. Daniel began to rise when Sandra again assisted, guiding the glass to Amy's lips.

"Usually, we get wounded when we're young. It happens when we're older too, but the deepest wounds are typically when we're little. That's because we don't understand or it happens before we know the Lord or before we're stronger in our faith. We can carry those wounds for a long time without knowing it. Would it be okay for me to ask you about wounds you might have and talk to those wounded parts of you?"

Amy nodded as her eyes again faded shut.

Catching Daniel's eye, Bruce mouthed the word *oil*.

Opening the vile, Daniel covered it with the tip of his finger and gave it a shake. "Can we anoint you with oil and lay hands on you?" When she agreed, Daniel scooted forward. "Amy, we anoint you in the name of the Father, the Son, and the Holy Spirit."

Bruce prayed, "Lord, we ask You now divide soul and spirit, in the name of Jesus. Amy, I want you to think about the worst thing that has ever happened to you. Do you remember?" He softened his voice. "How old were you?"

"I think I was about four or five."

"Can you tell us where you were?"

"In the temple, playing with my little dog and dolly."

"As you remember, tell us what you see."

"Tables around the room, curtains made out of beads. And I'm under the tables, but I can see out. The room is big—it's made of trees pulled together at the tops and covered with thatch. The sun is shining through the cracks. I smell incense burning, and smoke is rising. I see the idols—they're ugly with big teeth and scary faces. I don't like them, but I have my dog and dolly. And then he comes in..."

"Who comes in?"

"The witch doctor..."

Her body tightened.

"What does he look like?"

"His face is painted black, and he's wearing a mask covered with holes. He's wearing pants and a blue shirt, and he's barefoot. I see his feet, and I'm afraid. I want to cry, but he will hear. My dog is afraid too, and he runs. And the witch doctor—he grabs him."

"What's your dog's name?"

"Bobo—he yelps. The witch doctor squeezes, and he's struggling— but I can't help."

"Then what happens?"

"He stops kicking, but he's still moving. The witch doctor puts him on the stone table and holds him down. I see the smoke rising and his knife. He holds it up high, and he's praying and then..." She coughed out the words. "He kills Bobo. He cuts his throat and holds him by his legs, upside down, and the blood is running out. It splashes into a bowl and on the ground. I'm squeezing my eyes closed."

"I'm so sorry, Amy. Can you tell us what happened then?"

Daniel was about to say stop when he heard a soft whisper, *"Wait..."*

"I'm crying but trying to be quiet, and then... I open my eyes, and he is staring at me. He's crouching down, holding Bobo and the knife. His black eyes are looking at me through the curtain. I scream and run away. I am so afraid, and... I hate him—I hate him so much!"

"Who do you hate?"

Panting, she shook her head.

"Who do you hate, Amy?"

"My... father! I ran to my mother and told her, and I heard them shouting. My father did nothing to the witch doctor. He let him kill Bobo and babies too. He loves the idols and the temple, but he doesn't care about my mother or my brother."

"What about you? Does he love you?"

"No. He's filled with evil and hate. I hate him."

Daniel tightened his grip on the chair, his fingers numb squeezing on wood, the room spinning.

"I'm talking to big Amy now. Can you hear me?"

"Yes."

"Does little Amy, the one who saw the witch doctor kill Bobo, the one who hid under the table and hates her father. Does little Amy know Jesus like you do?"

"N–no... She doesn't."

"Can we ask Jesus to come talk to little Amy?"

Tears appeared in the corners of her closed eyes.

"Yes, He can come."

"Jesus, we ask You to come now and talk to little Amy." Bruce waited. "Is He there—is Jesus there?"

"Yes. I see Him—He's holding her hand."

"What does He say?"

Her voice began to break as tears ran down her cheeks. "He says 'I was with you under the table. I protected you, and I love you with an everlasting love....' He says 'Don't be afraid because I am always with you.'"

"Thank You, Jesus. Does He say anything else?"

"Forgive your father...like I forgive you." She covered her face with both hands and wept, her body going slack. "I forgive both of them, Jesus—my father and my mother—and myself also. Thank You, Jesus—I'm so sorry."

"Can little Amy go with Jesus? Is it okay for her to go?"

Amy's head rose and fell. Lifting a hand, she wiped her cheek.

"Do you see her, Amy? What do you see?"

"I see her leaving with Jesus, and the mountain is gone."

"What mountain?"

"I saw both of us. The little girl went with Jesus, and I was holding a rock in my hands. It was huge—like a mountain. And I threw it into the ocean."

"Amy. That feeling you have right now—of the burden coming off?—that's the presence of the Lord. I want you to hold on to it."

Bruce began to pray again, rattling off several items of business. First, he asked for a fortress of angels to be stationed around the house. He then requested the courts of heaven be convened, asking the Lord to prepare a judgment of fire for all demonic forces present, in the event they did not comply with the court's directives. Lastly, he requested the lead demon dwelling within Amy be escorted to the courts of heaven by warrior angels. He then stopped and waited.

"Demon... Are you there, and what is your name?"

Her demeanor transformed. Squaring her shoulders, she sat up straight and glared at Daniel.

"I know who he is, but who the hell are you?" The words were leveled from her mouth, but the voice was someone else. Male, it spoke with arrogant disdain.

Bruce interrupted, "Demon, I'm warning you. You're playing with fire. Answer my question. What is your name?"

"Hatred."

"Hatred... You will answer my questions. You will tell no lies, and you will tell me only what you have been allowed to say. Do we understand each other?"

Amy's head rotated to stare at Bruce.

"Are we clear?" Bruce raised his voice.

"Yessss... We are."

"Tell me when you entered Amy and do you come and go?"

"I was there before she was born. And yes—I come and go as I please."

The chill returned as Daniel swam in a concoction of skin-crawling evil and disbelief.

"Did you enter by blood sacrifice?"

"Hell, yes."

"Was it animal or human and how long ago?"

"You name it—men, women, babies, and countless animals. Fourteen generations."

Daniel clung to the chair with both hands, the hair on his neck standing upright.

"What did you trade for?"

The demon exhaled a burst of breath. "The usual... power and money..."

"How long did it last?"

Hatred puffed. "Not long—it was a lie, of course."

"Tell me what you've done to Amy's calling."

His lips curled into a smile. "She's so weak. We're crushing her spirit."

"So there are others. Tell me, how you're crushing her spirit?"

"She's been called to teach the nations." Hatred shook his head. "But we're stopping that. She will teach no one because we're filling her with lies."

"What lies are you telling her?" Somehow, Bruce spoke calmly.

The demon was silent.

"You're going to the pit today, Hatred, so you might as well tell me unless you want the lake of fire. Your choice."

The sound low and riling, Hatred sighed. "That she's worthless and feeble. Nobody loves her, she's a failure, and God doesn't care about her."

"Is that true? Tell us what the Father says to Amy."

"It makes me sick." Hatred looked away.

"Tell me, Hatred."

"He loves her so much—it's disgusting. He loved her since the beginning of time, and He's calling her... to shine His love to all the world—I can't stand it."

"Anything else...?"

"No." Smoldering contempt emanated from Hatred's eyes as he stared at Bruce.

"What have you done to her physically?"

"See for yourself. We're squeezing her to death and drying her out. We're nearly finished—you can't stop us."

"Is there anything else?"

"No, well... Cancer—he's in her brain and womb. She'll never bear a child. That's it. That's all."

Daniel's mind was reeling, struggling to comprehend. Bruce prayed, "In the name of Jesus, I command all demons who are tormenting our sister—who are in her, on her, and around her—bind yourselves to Hatred and loose without any ripping or tearing. Leave no one behind. No parts of yourselves. And take all dark spirits that are with you here in this place. Go now with Hatred—all of you. Go to the pit."

Bruce lifted his hands and voice. "Lord, I ask for warriors of light to bind Hatred and all other angels of darkness and cast them into the pit. We ask now for Amy's restoration and healing."

He nodded to Daniel, who continued with a broken voice, "God Almighty, we worship and praise You, lifting hands to You. We thank You for Amy. You created her in Your image and know every cell within her body. We thank You for setting her free and ask that You touch her with Your healing hand."

Feeling a nudge, he opened his eyes. Amy was back, quietly crying with open hands raised, her head bent forward. "Amy, can I put my hand on your back? I think I'm hearing the Lord ask me to do that."

"Yes—yes, please."

He continued with open eyes, "Father, we ask for the restoration of all that was stolen from Amy. We thank You for delivering her from the enemy's lies, and we thank You for filling her with forgiveness. We pray also for Amy's parents, throwing the burden of their salvation into the sea. We surrender them to Your care, asking that You reveal Yourself to them in Your timing and Your way. Lord, we ask You touch Amy with Your hand of mercy and healing. We pray against cancer and lupus and all other disorders and disease in Jesus's name, by the power of His blood and resurrection and by the power of Your Spirit. We ask in faith, for Your purpose and glory. Amen."

~~

The sound was like a thousand horsemen thundering toward them at full speed. Crashing, the wave of power ripped them loose and lifted them into the air. Twisting and flailing, they lashed out with splayed claws trying to open a wound, any wound. Screaming in anguish, they floated above the precious territory they'd cultivated for so very long as each word struck with the force of a giant club.

Hatred shouted, "Bastards! Noooo! She's ours. We won't gooooo...."

The deafening echo reverberated through the chamber.

"Diviiisssiiionnnn... offff... Sooouuullll... anndddd... Spirrritttttttt..."

The second wave took Hatred, grabbing him by the hair and ripping him away for a very long time. Then thrown back, he was bound with cords. He struggled like a moth trying to escape its cocoon. The others watched in hopeless disbelief as waves of power interrogated him. His eyes darted from comrade to comrade while he tried to be strong but saw in their eyes a reflection of his horror.

"...Teelllll... meeee, Haaattrrreeddddd..."

Made a fool in front of his warriors, he contorted, resisting the worst question of all, wanting desperately to lie. The image flashed through his mind of the great lake, smoldering and churning, stench and smoke forever swirling above. He considered the alternative, bondage within the great walls of despair. He had served time there before and would do so again—anything was better than the fire.

Clenching his teeth, he nearly gagged on his answer. "He loves her so much.... He loved her since the beginning of time, and He's calling her... to shine His love to all the world. It's so disgusting—I can't stand it." Unable to look at his companions, he knew the shock he'd see in their faces.

The interrogation continued for what seemed an eternity. When the final wave struck, they were exhausted, almost welcoming it. Like a tidal wave, it crashed into them.

"...Gooooeee noooowwwwww... Allll, offff, yooouuu... Gooooeee, tooooo tthhhhheeeeee... piiiiittttttt...." Churning and sloshing, the purifying effervescence of truth and love flushed them away like acid.

~~

"How do you feel?"

As Bruce smiled, Daniel noticed he was blinking back tears of joy.

"I feel so light—the weight, it's gone."

Bruce put his hand on her shoulder. "You're free, Amy, but there's one more thing we need to do. Is it okay to keep going a little longer?" At her nod, he became serious again. "I want to talk to your inner being now. The dark part of you who let the demons inside and listened to them—can I speak to that one?"

"What do you want?" Her voice changed again.

Daniel thought it was Hatred at first but then realized it was her.

"Amy. Do you renounce the demons that were lying to you? Do you realize it was wrong to listen to them, and do you want that part of you to leave and go away?"

"Yes, I do. I want to be completely free."

"Go ahead—ask her to leave, Amy."

She prayed softly, "Lord, thank You for sending Bruce and Daniel to pray for me. Forgive me for listening to the demons. I never knew they were even there. Please take my dark self away. Go with the little wounded girl and stay away. Thank You, Jesus. Amen."

When Daniel opened his eyes to a radiant smile washing Amy's face in warmth, he could feel the burden had been lifted from her. And the room as well, no longer dry and gray, seemed to be crackling now with an electric charge of joy.

Sandra reappeared, walking them to the door. "Thank you so much. You have no idea how much we appreciate this."

He wiped a tear from the corner of his eye. "Keep us posted and don't be shy about asking us to come back. It's a blessing for us, and I mean that." He pointed. "Hey, look at that. The porch light—it's working. It's lit."

CHAPTER 41

THE CRAWLING clouds parted as the crowd erupted beyond the towering wall of stone. The vicar was grateful for the brief shaft of sunlight. He watched the Nicolaitan bishop as shadow again washed over them. Middle-aged with a medium build, the bishop was not one to hide his emotions or motives and, if displeased, was known to turn on another with much wrath. The scar was his most distinguishing feature. Wide and dark maroon, it extended from his earlobe to the corner of his mouth. The vicar stared at it.

"You learned of this book from the senator's slave girl, is this true?" Gallus adjusted his position while cinching his tunic. They sat on cantilevered stone hoops in the public latrine, a channel of flowing water beneath them.

"Yes, just yesterday, and I came to you immediately." The gangly vicar swept his greasy locks back, glancing up as the clouds parted again. Two men sat on the opposing row of seats, while another three stood before the trough's open section. In addition to the linear urinal, the open-air facility boasted two rows of ten seats each.

Gallus cocked his head as a cheer rose from the arena. He then glanced at the tunnel entrance beneath the stadium bleachers. "Get on with it—I don't want to miss the tigers."

"A sacred book was stolen from the tomb of Celsus. We heard of the desecration but not of a book. The girl said the book was in your possession."

"I have no knowledge of this book."

"I told her this as well, and yet she was certain."

Gallus placed his hand on the seat between them leaning in. The vicar turned to meet him, resisting the impulse to pull away from his breath, rank with alcohol and decaying teeth. "Jonness... The slave girl overheard the senator speaking of a bishop, and she naturally thought of me. Jonness the Snake must have it." The roar erupted again. "What more did she speak?"

"She said the senator is searching for the criminals who desecrated the tomb. There must be political value in his quest because the governor is not involved."

"You were wise to bring this to me. We must secure this book before the senator apprehends the thieves and it is lost. Did she tell you anything else?"

"No, Your Holiness, that is all." The crowd clapped in unison as the Anointed One eased himself forward giving his left hand a downward sling. Standing, he moved to the upstream wash station, where entering water flowed through a channel cut into the stone counter. From there it cascaded through a scupper into the sloping waste trough, where it then disappeared into a spillway and eventually found its way to the river and sea.

~~

Gallus immersed his hands into the stream. Lifting them, he repeated the slinging shake with both hands. He glanced back and then nodded to the vicar before ducking into the tunnel, a grin tautening his face as he emerged. On the other side of the stadium, the gate rose to the sight of three tigers being prodded forward with a long pole. The rhythmic clapping erupted in a roar as the tigers emerged.

Two men stood in the circular arena, separately bound to a large post with a length of chain attached to one ankle. Government officials, they'd been convicted of stealing tax money. Rumor claimed they were enemies of the governor and falsely charged. The crowd didn't care and neither did Gallus. It was always entertaining to watch what someone might do when facing death, especially the rich and powerful.

Cupping his hands to his mouth, he shouted, "Eat them—eat them alive!"

<<>>

Asmodeus spoke mind to mind with Mammon only and then shook his head, "*These two are becoming a waste of our time and expertise. Since joining souls, there is little encouragement they even need from us. Stay vigilant, however. The mission is not complete, and the advantage can shift in a moment.*"

"I agree with you. I'm just taking the counter position for the sake of discussion. I understand we need to mix it up and Pastor Jason is the best way to do that, actually the only way." Nick leaned back in the leather chair, his folded hands on the reading table. "I hope you know it's hard to concentrate when you're wearing that thing."

"This thing, which you can't keep your eyes off, happens to be custom tailored and a gift. A special gift from Karl, and I happen to love it. It highlights my shape but doesn't reveal too much. Don't you agree?"

"Umm, yeah... It's perfect, but that's why I can't focus. Do you think we should fool around first and then finish this?"

"No, I do not. We need to finish this first, and then we'll be able to relax and enjoy ourselves."

"Talk, talk, talk, this is all they do! It would be so easy if only we were human—we would not even need them." Asmodeus set his jaw. Clenching his fist, he drew it back. About to punch her in the heart, he stopped himself. Then, placing flat hands on the walls of the pounding organ, he dropped his head and groaned.

Mammon comforted him. *"But alas, Master, it is not so. And as you said, we must be vigilant. It is our calling."*

"I have a confession." A hint of a smile teased his face. "I forgot to invite Henry Williams. He is part of the Reorg. Committee. Do you think we should call and see if he can join us?"

"Oh, don't worry. I invited Henry—he should be here any minute." She opened her mouth and eyes in gape surprise as they laughed.

"Now I see why you wanted to wait. Henry's probably a wild man in the sack, but I'm not so sure about the three of us."

"You never know—you never know."

Broiling with impatience, Asmodeus shouted, *"Focus. Get on with it, and then we play."*

"Okay, I got it—focus. Marcy Short—she doesn't understand teamwork, and she's disrespectful. And Jason, for maximum impact. Karen's gone, and I agree we need a different look up front. All of the greeters, along with the four old-guy ushers, whose names I can't remember, and Tom Evans." Nick tugged on his chin. "It would be quite bold, but I'm thinking John Warner as well."

"I'm not so..."

"Let me finish—I'm just thinking out loud. John is really good with the music, but he's old school. And like you've been saying, we need the youth—they're the future. So... yank the organ and get a band? Clean slate. All things new... New pastor, new music... Maybe a hipster who's good with videos and social media. What do you think?" Nick's eyes dropped again to the stretchy negligee.

Asmodeus arched her back and thrust her chest forward with a deep breath.

"I don't think you're thinking very clearly. Yes, the music needs an overhaul, but all at once—you can't be serious?" Amber gestured with her hands as she spoke. "Changing pastors is a huge step, but so is the music. Step one, new pastor and new vision. The music is second, and the school goes last. We might consider the music and the school at the same time, but we'll decide when we get there. And that will protect the elders because everyone who doesn't like either decision will blame me. For sure, the pastor will cost us some members, but changing the music too could cost us the church." Looking up, she caught him. "You're right. I should have worn something else. You're not even listening."

"Sorry, Your Honor, guilty as charged. I think I'm—uh, falling in love with you." He offered his sheepish grin.

Asmodeus threw his arms up. *If only I was back in Celsus's body, I wouldn't have to put up with such tripe. Help me, someone—please...!"*

"You're not falling in love with me—you're falling in love with just one thing."

"I think you're right again, umm.... But they—or I mean *you*—are so beautiful." Nick blinked. "Okay—I agree with everything you said, but we haven't talked about the intern. That little dweeb who jumped up grinning from ear to ear—he's got to go."

She lifted her notes, covering her chest. "I like Luke. I think he's cute and full of energy. I can rein him in."

"Rein him in—umm. I'm not so sure I like the sound of that?"

Amber lowered her notes, drawing a finger between the deeply cut garment.

"Okay, Luke can stay, but I'm going to be watching the both of you."

She extended the tip of her tongue from the side of her ruby lips, biting gently. "I think I want some champagne—how 'bout you?"

"Excellent idea."

"How much time do we have?"

"Can't be sure... Sometimes elder meetings can last for hours."

<<>>

Nick had forced himself to get up early, and setting his trades ahead of the open had paid off. Clicking Execute, he smiled and stretched back, hands folded behind his head as the volume bar rose in response to his sell order. It was his largest trade to date, and the monies had been in play for less than eight minutes. Twelve thousand shares bought and sold for a gain of almost eighteen thousand dollars and none of it his money, except for the profit.

"Who needs research when you're one with the markets? Zen Master... God of the markets...?"

He considered the question. Zen Master was better, the alternative scaring him a little. Confirming the transaction, he returned the principal amounts to his clients. Today he had pooled 5 percent from all of his clients, including those without discretionary authorization. The single exception was the Faith Bible Church accounts.

The graphs crested downward, a trend he sensed would continue for some time. *Zen Master, for sure—this much is true.* He flexed his fingers as he considered a short play but instead closed his trading platform and opened his email. *Henry, Henry... Reorg. Committee Next Steps, here we go, Monday morning.*

Nick clicked Reply All and went to work. First, he changed the subject line to Reorg. Committee Call to Prayer & Fasting and then edited the time for later in the day. He then erased the message and replaced it with a note suggesting they pray and fast while seeking the Lord's direction. Then, highlighting the header, he copied and pasted it above his now modified message, applying a sent time of Wednesday afternoon.

He pulled away from the keyboard. *I doubt Henry even knows he has a server, let alone how to check it. But Amber... will she think it's funny and clever or foolish and risky? Then again, she might view it as deceptive and lose trust?*

Mammon whispered, *"Don't take the risk. You can always explain it later if she finds out, but she won't."*

He edited Amber's address, replacing the *M* in her name with an *N*. *Just Henry... Better safe than sorry.* He then banged out a message from two days prior but never sent:

    Dear Brother and Sister,

       I hope you are both doing well with the fast. I had forgotten how difficult it is to

go without food and water but have allowed
myself a few ice chips. I must confess I have
missed the closeness to our Lord that comes
when denying one's self. I have been praying
for you both and thank you for your prayers as
well. I have been asking the Lord to lead and
guide you in truth and wisdom for our
leadership.

I would like to suggest we meet tomorrow for
lunch. We can break our fast together and
discuss what the Lord has been speaking. As
mentioned, please focus your prayers on whom
the Lord may be calling us to release from
service and who also He may be calling for
reassignment.

The Lord woke me this morning at three a.m.
and told me to go to my prayer closet, which I
did. In the first hour, I heard nothing, so I
worshiped and praised the Lord. When I was
about to go back to bed, I clearly heard the
Lord say He is calling three as He called
Abraham. They will not know where they are
going but will step out in faith. The Lord
said this is a time to be strong and
courageous. He also said He has chosen us to
bless His church.

I was not sure if I should share this.
However, following more prayer it seemed clear
the Lord wanted you to hear this
encouragement. Please respond to this message
if you are not able to make tomorrow's lunch
meeting. If I do not hear back, I will assume
you will be in attendance.
In His Service, Nick

Scrolling to the top, he typed a third and final new message:

Dear Brother,

I am sorry you were not able to attend
yesterday's lunch meeting (see invite below).

Amber and I prayed for you and hope you are
okay.

Laughter shook him. Composing himself, he continued:

Be aware, our meeting was quite productive,
with both of us receiving confirmations of
whom the Lord is calling as His Abrahams.
Neither of us expected the Lord to move so
quickly, and we are anxious to learn if the
Lord may have spoken the same message to you
during your fast. Be aware, we will present
recommendations to the elders on Tuesday. I
will try to meet with you between now and
then. However, I am traveling and very busy.
If we are not able to connect, I will try to
give you a head's up before the meeting
begins.

Serving with you in Grace, Nick

Nick reviewed the message string, beginning at the bottom and
moving up. Laughing again, he clicked Send.

CHAPTER 42

NICK WAITED as Earl Dempsey, last to arrive, shuffled in taking his seat. Looking from face to face, Nick drew a steady breath. The outcome of tonight's meeting was critical and would impact Faith Bible Church for years to come. The resulting growth and prosperity would also lay the foundation for his book to follow—*Reshaping the Church for Tomorrow.* He thought about the title as his gaze fell to Amber.

"This is an executive session, but I've asked Amber to join us. We've got just one item on the agenda, and with that, I'll turn it over to the Reorg. Committee, Nick and Amber. Oh, and Henry—I'm sorry, Henry's on the committee also." Paul smiled, glancing at Nick and then Amber, who looked at her notes.

Mammon whispered, *"You got this Zen Master. Time to mold the mush."*

Tapping his laptop, Nick washed the wall in white light as Paul switched off the fluorescents. "Gentlemen and lady. What you see on the wall represents where we are. A white sheet—a blank page, if you will. Our future. And it's ours to write. And yes, we face enormous challenges, but we also face enormous opportunity.

"I, for one, choose not to fight challenges but embrace them. The kung fu warrior does the same. When confronted by the enemy, he doesn't duck and cover or run away. Instead, he receives the force with poised control and uses it, deflecting the threat away from himself and back to the enemy. In a sense, he leverages the challenge and exploits it for victory. The point being, we have a choice—we can duck and cover or, like the kung fu warrior, leverage our challenges for victory?

"Think about our position for a moment. Imagine if we were talking about starting a new church, and someone came to us and said, 'Hey, guys, I want to give you a ten-acre piece of property. It's got a worship center seating eleven-hundred people, a school, and a bunch of offices. I'll throw in a thousand people to kick-start your church, and a hundred thousand dollars cash. Oh, I've also got a trained staff to run the place. You can take it over and do whatever you want—it's all yours, free and clear."

The men exchanged nods. Inwardly, he smiled, enjoying the chance to show off in front of Amber, and besides, they were finally beginning to get it.

"White sheet, guys—it's our destiny." He pointed at the wall. "All that's required is the courage to act, but the key is unity. We can debate the issues, and we will—that's good. But once decided, we need to stand together." He leveled his gaze at Daniel.

"Wear them down. Don't stop until they're all nodding like sheep."

~~

Daniel shifted again as Nick laid out the problems with a series of graphs and charts, all painting a picture of grim decline. The church was overstaffed, underfunded, and imploding financially. Again and again, he hammered away on the theme of failed leadership.

Daniel squeezed the edge of the table, feeling dizzy. *He's wearing them down. Can't they see it? We've been talking about this for weeks. There's nothing new here.*

The men seemed to be transfixed, nodding and taking notes, with Amber following on printed copies of the slides.

The body language between them...a look and smile, a nod and then another. *It's a dance. He's wooing her.*

The presentation continued for an hour and twenty minutes. The final slide, a picture of Faith Church, transformed into a swirl of color and then faded to white. "Hear me now... If it's the only thing you take away tonight, receive this word."

Nick waited.

"Vision... That's what we lack and what we'll embrace. We will not stumble or be tossed and turned by distraction. We will define who we are and chart a clear path. Like Joshua—when the Israelites crossed the Jordan River. The risks were huge, but they crossed in faith, entering the Promised Land. And we will do the same. I want all of you to know Amber, Henry, and myself have prayed and fasted and we stand in unity."

Henry glanced at Amber and then back to Nick. "That's right. We prayed and fasted, and the Lord spoke. Let's face it, when the Holy Spirit speaks, that's when you do what He's saying. You can bet your bottom dollar, and the Lord is speaking right now."

Daniel exhaled slowly, the table damp beneath his palms.

Nick spread his arms. "To summarize what Henry's saying is the committee's together on this."

Paul fanned his plastic hammer. "Guys, I don't know what Nick is about to propose, but I want to remind us of something. When we pray and then send out a group to do a bunch of work, we need to listen. There's way too much involved in running a church for us to be beating up every proposal and decision. Because when we do that, well, we end up like we always do—never getting anything done. The committee is unified, so we need to accept what they've got for us. It's called trust."

~~

Longshanks entered through a sizzling tear in space, his eyes fixed on the archangel standing behind Daniel. Disrupting his peripheral senses, Moaz bowed with his face to the table and then leaped to his feet, gesturing wildly with his arms while jabbering his usual nonsense.

"Welcome, great sir, you haven't missed a thing. The fool at the head of the table has been droning on and on—he won't shut up. I've got Mammon working the inside, but he's ready if needed. And Asmo is here as well but will remain inside the woman unless all heaven breaks loose. The others you requested are assembled, and as you see, Raphael has joined us also. I was about to engage him but..."

Longshanks fanned a flat hand toward Moaz—eyes unyielding, remained locked on his foe. He spoke a single word. "Please."

Moaz fell silent.

Raphael's raised double edge sword held the pesky tormentor at bay, his war club slung at his side. Raphael's body armor included polished forearm shields and shin guards, along with a lightweight chest plate.

Longshanks patted his battle-ax handle. "And so, we meet again. I see you have recovered since our last encounter."

Raphael stood motionless. "And you as well."

Longshanks smiled, unable to conceal respect for his hated opponent. "Power at bay—that's you, Raphael. Waiting for the nod— but that's your weakness, my friend."

Moaz began again. "You should have been there, comrade. On the road, it was glorious! We killed the pastor, and I rode the weapon. We..."

Slashing through space, Longshanks drew and delivered a slicing blow. The motion—swift and blinding—split the tormentor in two halves from crown to belly. Wavering from side to side, the head continued to speak from both sides of its mouth. The message fractured.

"...and then the boy. Yes, he... The truck—it flew... was crafty. Asmodeus, I saved him just in... But the boy, yes—he lunged...."

Eyes to eyes, neither warrior blinked.

~~

Feeling lightheaded, Daniel let go of the table and leaned forward. With elbows on the mahogany slab, he rubbed his forehead. *What's happening, Lord? What are we doing?*

Nick continued, "New vision requires significant change. We wouldn't be discussing this if we had clarity from current leadership, and that is why we're making the recommendation to replace three lead positions and redirect and/or release several targeted nonessential subordinate positions. The reimage will be rolled out in three phases over one year's time. With your approval, it will commence tonight."

Daniel leaned back and swallowed, his throat tight and dry. *What do you want me to do, Lord? Should I speak out or remain silent?*

"Phase 1 is designed for maximum impact—the shock and awe stage. As stated, it will include three key positions, the senior most being Pastor Stover."

"Pastor Stover?" Henry snapped upright, his mouth dropping open. "Who's going to preach, and what job would—"

Paul lifted his hand. "Hold on, Henry. We need to let Nick finish before we bog this down. We would be releasing Pastor Jason— demoting him would be unrealistic. The Lord will take care of him."

A knot clenched Daniel's stomach. "You can't be serious? The congregation loves Pastor Jason, and he loves the people."

"Now hold on." Paul cocked his head, pointing with his hammer. "No one's saying we don't love the guy or that he doesn't love the people. But don't you think the Lord could be leading in this? I, for one, agree—fixing the church will involve some changes at the top. So let Nick finish. The committee spent a lot of time on this."

Nick advanced the presentation to a chart with a pyramid of labeled boxes—two in red at the top, a row of blue below, and yellow at the bottom. Amber's name and title filled one of the red boxes, being connected to the row of blue boxes with solid lines. The blue boxes then linked to the subordinate yellow positions. Horizontal lines extended in both directions from Amber's box, one of which doglegged to a dashed box that read School. The second red box was titled Senior Pastor, connecting with a horizontal line to Amber only.

Daniel put his flat hands on the table. His head swimming, he tried to figure out who was being redirected or missing from the chart. *This makes Amber king of the church. This can't be right.*

"Gentlemen, this is the new Org Chart we're proposing in Phase 1. At this time, I'll turn it over to our executive pastor who will walk you through the details."

Amber stood, reaching out to steady herself.

Lewis Kolsby interrupted, "I'm sensing in my spirit we should stop and pray. We're facing significant decisions here. We need to be praying Kingdom Prayers."

Paul stared at Lewis as if peering over the rims of invisible glasses. "I have no idea what that means... but sure. Go for it, brother. Lead us in a Kingdom Prayer."

His eyes expanding and face taut, Lewis sat up straight. "Okay." He pushed back his chair and leaned forward with head bowed. "Father, we ask for wisdom and discernment to do what is best for those in ministry who will be impacted by our decisions. We ask that You send angels as a hedge of protection to surround this room. We pray also against the lies of Satan and his demons, in Jesus's name. Amen."

~~

Walls of fire erupted around them, cascading like a Niagara. Longshanks continued to stare at Raphael, ignoring the searing heat. The room pulsed in waves of radiating white light from the sphere of Protectors, above, below, and all around them. The minions were there as well just beyond the flames. Swarms of them, swirling in clusters like clouds of bats, darting in and out, over and back, seeking an opening.

Longshanks lifted his brows with a smile. "They can't help you, Raphael, you know that. If just one of them leaves, even for the blink of an eye, we'll breach the perimeter, and it'll be over." He began to circle the table, his weapon dangling like a priest's incense censer.

"Stupid, aren't they? You think they would call in some help? Nope, it's just the three of us. Oh wait, I forgot—a few others too."

Moaz taunted, "Yeah, we're gonna kick your ass."

Raphael bent down, cupping his hand to Daniel's ear.

Moaz waved his arms. "Hey. Stop that. What did you say to that bastard?"

"His name is Daniel Fairmont—do you know him? I think maybe you do, and he scares you. Did you notice he's growing in strength?" Raphael delivered the words void of any fluctuation in his voice.

The smile faded from Longshanks's face. "You know he can't hear you. None of them have ears to hear, and that fool doesn't scare us either. In fact, we're thinking about killing him because he's causing trouble. What do you think about that?"

"So he does scare you." Raphael smiled, bending again to Daniel's ear.

Longshanks reacted. Spinning in a blur, he loosed his weapon, the blade and wave of sound striking Raphael simultaneously. "Hey!"

~~

The words came softly. Ignoring the amen, Daniel continued, "Lord Almighty, we worship and magnify Your name above all names. We come in humility, asking for strength and wisdom. We ask You to send warriors of light to stand within this hedge of protection to fight for us now. Against the enemy that prowls about, who is nothing but a liar, thief, and murderer. Help us as we seek Your will—for Your church, which was paid for by the blood of Your Son. We pray in His name, the powerful name that every knee shall bow to and every tongue confess, the name that in the end will crush the head of Satan. In Jesus's name... Amen."

Daniel opened his eyes to Paul Chambers staring at him. "Okay... That was nice, but we need to move on now. Can we move on, Daniel?"

<<>>

The scene from the arena flashed through the mind of Gallus, the Nicolaitan bishop. It was difficult to forget, especially the high-pitched screams as the tigers ripped the limbs from the officials who had challenged the governor's authority. It could happen to anyone, especially someone of position who lacked discretion. *Choose your words carefully.*

It was sprinkling again, and the open market nearly empty. Near them, an old man clutched his cloak. Listing to one side, he snored. The two men sat across from one another at a small table beneath a tarp. He didn't know the Roman, except that he represented the governor. The heavyset hairless man wore the linen cloak of the Senate with no sash, indicating he was likely a legal assistant or advisor. His sharp nose gave him the appearance of an eagle.

The young server bowed and smiled. "Two hot coffees. Would you like sugar or milk?"

"Black." Gallus did not look up. "Does the governor confirm the book is in the hands of Bishop Jonness?"

"Yes, but the governor asks why this interests you."

Gallus drew a sip of thick brew. "If this book is sacred, it should not be in the hands of..." He rotated his clay mug. "The Nicolaitans hold truth and justice with great value. Like Rome, we wish to see those who committed this crime punished. We also want to inspect this book. If it is found to be sacred, it would be in our interest to safeguard it."

The Roman official placed his coffee on the table. "The governor has no interest in this crime or the book."

"Can you tell me who committed the crime?"

"His name is Batush. He is a scribe."

"And does the governor know where this Batush is?"

"The governor does not know, nor does he care about this man. Bishop Jonness had him arrested and jailed for three days. The scribe was then released without charge. Perhaps Jonness can help you."

The Roman official drained his mug and then stood. "That is all I can tell you. Do you have a gift for the governor?"

"I do. Please tell Governor Lucius I pray daily to the gods, for his blessing and victory over the Goths. May it be swift and without mercy." Gallus placed a small bronze statuette in the Roman's hands. "Mars—for luck." He turned to glare at the young merchant, who was again wiping down the clean table next to them.

CHAPTER 43

RAPHAEL HOISTED his forearm, blocking the projectile. Pulling back and ducking, he surged forward and thrust with his short sword. The battle-ax clashed into his forearm shield, exploding in a spray of spark, igniting the room in a flash of white. In the same instant, a ball of fire, loosed in the heavens, hurled toward the earth like a shooting star.

Longshanks spun as the blade clipped his side and opened a gash. Gasping, he repelled backward through a body of flesh and the slab of mahogany. On his back and elbows, he gaped at the incoming meteor as Raphael drew his war club, wielding it up and over his head.

The canopy of protecting fire winked open, closing behind the shooting star.

His cocky pride replaced with stunned disbelief, Longshanks cried out, "Breach!"

Springing forward, Moaz slammed into Raphael's torso, his drawn claws ripping and tearing.

Continuing his backward roll, Longshanks shouted the command already in motion, "*Attack!*"

The word shook the walls as demons surged from bodies of flesh, twelve of them including Asmodeus. The meteor exploded overhead, releasing seven warriors of light as the room erupted in a chaos of savage thunder.

~~

Amber clung to the back of the chair. "I'm sorry, this is not like me. I'm a little off balance.... Is it warm in here?" She waited, listening for her inner voice but hearing only silence. Hand on her chest, she closed her eyes.

Paul stood. "Do you need some water?" Three men reached toward the bottles at the center of the table. "You've been fasting, Amber, and you're right, it's hot in here. You should sit."

"No, I'm fine—just felt a little dizzy when I stood. All of you are such gentlemen." She uncapped the lid and took a sip. "This morning I was thinking about Nehemiah again. It relates to where we are as a church. Remember the Israelites had been in captivity and were returning to Jerusalem but floundering. The city walls were in ruin, and there was no leadership. And listening just now to Nick's presentation, I can't help but think that's us. Faith Church has been torn down, and it's time to rebuild. And that's what Nehemiah did. He helped them rebuild, but it took leadership."

The men nodded. *Like molding clay... They can't help it. They're only men.*

"This is what I heard the Lord say during my fast, and both Nick and Henry heard the same... Clear the rubble. Before rebuilding, there's work to be done. The rubble needs to be cleared out."

"I agree with what Amber is saying here, guys." Henry's head bobbed up and down as he turned from left then right.

Amber tilted her head. Hearing only the buzzing fluorescents, she felt strangely alone. "As we remove leadership positions, we will be moving others forward to fill the vacancies. We believe this strategy will breathe life into our staff through the introduction of new challenges. Any organization that's been around for a while stagnates. People get bored and tired, which then carries over in their day-to-day performance. The reorg. will inject them into new environments where two groups will emerge. There will be those who rise up and are reenergized and others who founder."

Nick jumped in, "That's the toilet-bowl effect I mentioned before. But the beauty in this is we need to cut positions anyway, and the reorg. will help us identify those who need to move along."

Daniel lifted his hand with Paul responding, "Let's hold the questions until they finish."

Same old Daniel, always quick with a comment. She tapped her laptop. "As mentioned, we're recommending the removal of Pastor Stover, and we're thinking the logical replacement is Victor Ortiz. He's young, and the college service has been growing under his preaching. Another plus for Victor is his ethnicity with our community becoming more diverse and favoring Hispanics.

"We're also proposing the removal of Marcy Short, the children's director, as she's been struggling with attendance. We believe Marcy is better suited as a counselor or teacher, and we would be recommending she look into those opportunities."

"The third position we're proposing for removal is Carson Harris our Pastor of Small Groups, which are floundering. Again, we're thinking a younger person will help us with Millennials. I haven't mentioned this to the committee, but I'm thinking Luke would be a good choice there." Amber exchanged a smile with Nick. "You'll notice we're shuffling most of the other positions, except for Music and Maintenance. We felt those rolls are fairly specific, and it makes sense to retain them in place for now. The exception would be head of maintenance, who, as you know was released last week."

Daniel, interrupted, "To clarify, that would be Tom Evans, the man you fired on your first day, the man loved by everyone in the church. To me, it sounds like your committee is proposing we fire all of our shepherds. And what about calling—did you even consider that? A lot of our staff—all of them, I hope—are serving in ministries they love. And they're doing it because they believe the Lord called them to those positions. Who are we to decide who stays and who goes and what jobs they will have? This feels like lording over to me." Daniel grabbed up his Bible and began to flip pages.

Here we go again. What a jerk.

Daniel leaned forward, the Bible in his trembling hand. "This is what I'm hearing in my spirit for this whole presentation: 'Who among you is wise and understanding? Let him show by his good behavior his deeds in the gentleness of wisdom. But if you have bitter jealousy and selfish ambition in your heart, do not be arrogant and so lie against the truth. This wisdom is not that which comes down from above, but is earthly, natural, demonic. But where jealousy and selfish ambition exist, there is disorder and every evil thing. But the wisdom from above is first pure, then peaceable, gentle, reasonable, full of mercy and good fruits, unwavering, without hypocrisy. And the seed whose fruit is righteousness is sown in peace by those who make peace.'"

Again, Amber listened for her inner counselor but heard nothing. *Who in the hell do you think you are and why are you even here? No one wants to hear this—not refrigerator man or farmer boy, Holy Roller or the prayer guy, nor mister politics, and certainly not myself or Nick!*

Daniel's hand hovered over his worn Bible.

You're preaching at me—seriously? You're nothing but a stupid contractor.

Daniel continued, "This proposal is all human wisdom. This isn't pure and peaceable—or gentle. This isn't merciful or loving or even reasonable. The spirit of this is all wrong."

Paul rose to a half-standing position. Flat hand on the table, he towered over Daniel. "I asked you to let the committee finish without interruption. I need you to show some respect and stop throwing monkey wrenches into the wheels of every issue we're discussing. This is not the first time you've done this, and it's becoming an issue for me—and the rest of us too."

Nick stood, moving to Amber's side. "Gentlemen, this is out of line—and I, for one, will not accept this any longer. This elder challenges us at every step, and tonight, he is disrespecting our new pastor. The committee has prayed and fasted over this. We also began tonight's meeting in prayer. And then you show up and lob a hand grenade. You sit there and talk about what you're hearing in your spirit? We're all believers and have the Spirit in us, but you act like you're special. I don't want to hear what you think you're hearing, and neither does anyone else."

Daniel swallowed. "Is that what the rest of you think?"

Henry gave a feeble nod, looking down.

Lewis elevated his thin hand as if requesting silence. Then brushing crumbs from the sleeve of his shirt, he turned his tired gaze to meet Daniel. "Nick's right.... I don't think you understand what you're doing when you speak out against what we're doing. We really want to be your friends."

Daniel looked to each of them. "I'm sorry—I thought we were friends."

Amber bit down on her tongue to suppress a smile. *How does it go— oh yeah, I remember. Miserable and poor, blind and naked. You're all alone, Daniel. Where you belong.*

~~

Emerging from his robe of flesh, Asmodeus was instantaneously engaged. Passion and zeal pumping through his veins, he was finally where he longed to be—the midst of battle. Not thinking or analyzing, he reacted to the greatest threat on the scene—Raphael, the magnificent archangel.

Surging forward, Asmodeus drew his sword as Raphael delivered a blow that passed through the conference table and crashed into the floor. Moaz thrashed beneath Raphael's foot as Longshanks curled into a ball. With a wail, Longshanks withdrew a crushed hand, spewing black goo like an oil rig blowout. Asmodeus swung his blade as Raphael crouched and spun to meet him. The room swam in a blur of battle song, a combination of unleashed rage, bloodlust, and fearful reaction to immediate threats.

An angel of light staggered beside Henry Williams. Stumbling, the angel flailed with an arm for balance and fell through the wall. With a gasp, he pulled a lance from his stomach and then crawled back and reengaged.

Mammon vaulted from Nick's flesh toward one of the angels defending Paul Chambers. The angelic creature drew a spiked mace and stepped forward. As they collided, the momentum propelled them backward. Passing through the chairman's body, they meshed with the building's exterior masonry wall. Pushing off, Mammon drove a foot into the angel's stomach as he wielded his twin-bladed battle-ax. His arm drawn back, he unleashed a swinging blow that ripped into the angel's side. Both cried out—one in release, the other in pain.

Asmodeus and Raphael collided in front of Daniel. Discarding his shattering weapon, Raphael rose to meet Asmodeus as he closed from above with his long sword like an ax to the chopping block. Raphael dropped a knee, lifting his short sword. He received the blow, clenching his teeth. The blades met in a crash of sound and spark, inches from Raphael's face. Absorbing the impact, with his knee kissing the floor, he heaved forward. Face to face, separated by glinting metal, pressing and rotating for balance, they exchanged bursts of breath.

Baring his fangs, Asmodeus smiled.

Blades rotating, Raphael glared into the soul of his foe.

Crying out, Asmodeus shouted into the battle, "No mercy!"

~~

Amber turned to Nick and then faced Daniel. Again, she listened for her inner voice, hearing only silence. "Everyone in this room wants what's best for the church. But honestly, Daniel, I'd like to ask you a question." She hesitated.

She heard it then, softly in the distance, *"No Mercy..."*

And delivered the blow. "Why are you even here?"

Daniel folded his hands on the table and held her eyes of fire. "Look at us—the hurt and damage we're about to cause. Is this what we're doing? Maybe you're right. Maybe I shouldn't be here." He then shifted to Nick, speaking as though she wasn't there. "In response to your accusation—I'm speaking what I believe I'm hearing from the Lord, in obedience to what I'm called to do as an elder."

Standing at her side, Nick set his jaw, eyes locked on Daniel. "In reply to Daniel's question about what we're doing—I would like to make a motion." Nick turned to Paul, who dropped his chin in a single nod. "I move we proceed with Phase 1 of the reorganization plan as proposed—with the release of Pastor Stover, Marcy Short, and Carson Harris. Additionally, related staff positions shall be redirected as described on the org chart presented tonight."

"Do I have a second...?"

Henry bobbed his head from side to side. "This is hard work, but we need to do something to save the church, guys. And the three of us were hearing from the Lord. You can ask Nick and Amber. The ones we're letting go are being called out like Abraham. That's what the Lord is doing here, and the Holy Spirit is speaking, if you know what I mean." Henry flexed his suspenders in and out. "I second the motion."

"Discussion...? I wasn't planning on a vote tonight, and this is a big decision." Paul leaned back, stroking his goatee.

Vince stopped typing. Covering his mouth with folded hands, he asked, "Will we be giving them notice? Does this include severance, and what about benefits?"

"Yes, to all of your questions. It's policy for one thing, but it's also about loving our brothers and sister." Nick waited until he had the group's attention. "I'm proposing each of the released employees receive double the severance pay they're entitled to, based on policy and time served. Additionally, I propose we continue their health insurance for six months or until they find new employment, whichever comes first. We're not required to do this, and I understand it's generous. But it's also the right thing to do."

Amber bit down on her tongue, suppressing a smile. *We've got the votes. Watch and weep, Daniel. You lose.*

Nick added, "The release plan calls for removal of the designated employees on the same day they're informed of the board's decision. They will also be asked to sign release agreements whereby they agree not to slander the church or the elders in any way. In the event of noncompliance, the agreement will include a provision whereby they forfeit all remaining severance and benefits."

Paul silently rapped his open palm with his yellow hammer. "Has the committee drafted a communication plan for all of this?"

Amber stared at the drumming hammer. *Did he steal it from his grandkid or has he been playing with it since childhood?* "We have, and that's a great question. Because the key to a successful outcome is communication—it can't be overstated. Strategically, we would pull the trigger on a Friday, in order to minimize disruption. Upon execution, we will follow with a late-afternoon staff meeting to inform everyone and hand out new job assignments." The tapping continued. *I wonder what he would do if I grabbed it out of his hands and threw it in the trash?* "On the following Sunday, we would make the announcement to the church. We're recommending the announcement be made by Pastor Jason, if he's cooperative."

With elbows on the back of the chair, Nick spread his hands. "On that same Sunday evening, we would call an all-church business meeting, with all of us up front to answer congregation questions. This is leadership, men. Someone's got to do it, and we've been called to. We're the elders."

Vince cleared his throat. "I move we add the following to the motion: Release of the three positions shall include twice the severance pay accrued, along with the continuation of health insurance for six months or until other employment is acquired. All severance benefits shall be contingent upon the signing of release agreements, which shall call for the forfeiture of said benefits in the event it is discovered the church or the elders have been slandered by the released employee."

"I second the motion." Again, Henry glanced from side to side.

Paul grabbed the head of the swinging hammer as one might catch a fly. "Henry. Technically, the second needs to amend the first motion unless we're going to read all of it back."

"Okay. I second the motion, like you said—amended by what Vince said."

"Do you have it, Vince?"

Vince nodded as he typed.

"Okay, guys. We have a motion on the floor. All in favor say aye and raise your hand. All opposed—same sign."

The men voted as she watched. All voted in favor of the motion except Daniel.

~~

The room pulsed with a warping shimmer as the angels vanished. The motion continued for a second, with the follow-through of blows and weapons loosed into empty space. Composing themselves, the demons huddled as the containment fire let go, dissolving with cloud-shaped openings from which swarms of demons swooped in. Within seconds, the breached sphere dissipated, pulsing with sporadic flares of heat. It then winked out like the final gasp of a star.

Picking himself up, Moaz gave his leg a shake as his knee snapped into joint. He pivoted to Asmodeus, who replied with a nod. Moaz then leaped to the tabletop, fanning his arms out to the group with raised palms. "We came, we saw—and we kicked some ass. That's what we did, and they ran from us—those fools ran."

His comrades replied with smiles and nods as they began the cleanup. Milling about, they stooped and retrieved loose weapons and limbs. After exchanging a few high fives and back slaps, they then departed to their shells of flesh.

Moaz strutted about the table's perimeter in front of the humans as the leaching demons climbed to their perches. For the most part, the dark spirits ignored him. He kicked at the popcorn bowl and then morphed into a jerky robotic dance. Lifting an imaginary microphone, he broke into song with another earsplitting rendition of "Sympathy for the Devil".

He then bowed to Sluggo, who was again dangling from his tail. "Hey, Sluggo. Did you know I wrote that? Madness claims he did, but don't believe it. That little turd's a liar because I wrote it—I surely did... Woo, woo."

Hanging upside down, Sluggo yawned and then slowly shook his head. "There he goes again. Lies, lies, and still more lies—Tormentors, you're all the same."

CHAPTER 44

"SCRIBE..."

Batush jerked. He then drifted to his home on the slope. Meraiah was smiling as she worked the loom, and Sarah was again chasing the spotted goat with a stick.

"Come here."

Again, he jerked. Nearly waking, he returned to Meraiah, who seemed upset. She was shouting, but he couldn't understand.

"Come here, Scribe."

Opening his eyes, he lurched to a sitting position.

Jonness stood in the doorway with a hand lamp. "I need you to write—follow me."

Batush stood, wavering in the darkness as the light retreated into the other room. Bumping into the chair, he located his cloak.

"Now!"

As he groped the desktop, his hand slapped an empty scroll tube. When he reached to catch it, it propelled to the floor with a hollow clatter. *There you are.* He grasped his writing case and entered the study. "Yes, Your Holiness."

At his desk, Jonness held the lamp above an open scroll. He belched. "Sit and write the words I speak." The lamp wavered in his hand. "Use this. You will make the final copy tomorrow." Smelling like alcohol, he pushed a scrap of brownish scroll toward Batush.

Burn damage blackened one end, and the edges were fraying. *Papyrus.* Turning it over, Batush saw Hebrew text.

"Did I ask you to read to me?"

"No, Your Holiness." Batush flipped it over and then assembled his tools, an ink jar and bowl, copper quill, blotter, and scraping knife. His hands trembled as he poured the ink. He then dipped the quill and waited.

Jonness stared at the scroll as Batush recognized it. *The Apostle's book!* All of it flashed through his mind like a rushing wind. Raphael and the tool shed. The sarcophagus and Death come to life. And then the attack on the road and Zophar's help, making the copy and looking into Sarah's innocent eyes, the elders and jail and now this? Sitting in front of his bishop in the middle of the night with pen in hand? *The book that changed everything. What is happening, Lord—I do not understand?*

Except for the bishop's uneven breathing, it was quiet.

"Write this." Jonness stared at the scroll, his pointer finger quavering. "To the angel of the church of Ephesus write: The One who holds the seven stars in His right hand, the One who walks among the seven golden lampstands, says this..."

Batush printed as his bishop dictated.

"I know your deeds and your perseverance, and that you cannot tolerate evil men, and you put to the test those who call themselves apostles, and they are not, and you found them to be false; and you have perseverance and have endured for My name's sake and have not grown weary. And you have remembered your first love and the deeds you did at first."

He lifted his pen.

Jonness's head jerked up, bloodshot eyes locking with his. The bishop's disheveled hair hung in his waxy-red face with drool at the corners of cracked lips. His shabby gray tunic draped open at the neck with a rip in one sleeve. "Why do you stop? I said write my words."

Batush's heart thundered in his chest as though resisting the words he was compelled to speak. He cleared his throat and swallowed. "Your Holiness, I believe the..."

"Silence. You will write the words I speak."

"The curse... My Holiness—surely, you do...you do not..."

Jonness slammed his fist to the desk. "You instruct *me*? I am your Christ, and you will obey me, Scribe."

Trembling seized his limbs, his pen, his tongue. "But... My Holiness, I–I can—I cannot..."

"You will write this as I speak it—Now." Jonness rose from his chair, leaning forward, the stench of his hot breath striking Batush's face.

"Yes, Your Holiness."

"And you have remembered your first love and the deeds you did at first. Therefore, remember these things and be blessed, or else I will come to you and remove your lampstand out of its place, remember..."

Jonness stopped as Batush continued to scribble. His mind racing,

Batush disregarded his training. Always when making a copy, accuracy and checking the work was crucial. Any copy of the Holy Scripture was checked three times when drafted, and then three times again by another scribe when complete. Batush had learned the hard lesson— any mistake, whatsoever, resulted in burning of the copy. The work was then redone under watchful scrutiny, followed with discipline.

Catching up, Batush again lifted his pen.

"Yet this you do have, that you hate the deeds..." Jonness tilted his head. "That is a mistake. Change it to read 'Yet this you do have, that you hate the abominations of the Nicolaitans and their leader who I also hate. He who has an ear, let him hear what the Spirit says to the churches. To him who overcomes, I will grant to eat of the tree of life which is in the Paradise of God.'"

Batush stared at the pen in his trembling hand as he waited. The lamp's flame light flapped against the bishop's slow bursts of panting breath.

"That is all for tonight—we will work again tomorrow." Glowering at the scroll, Jonness pointed to the door. "Leave us."

<<>>

Starkly furnished, with white plastered walls and limestone floor, the spacious upper room had an airy feel with a high barrel-vaulted white ceiling. Matching arched windows flanked a large fresco on the east-facing wall. The mural depicted the seduction of the naked goddess Diana, being fed a cluster of grapes from Mercury's hand.

"He took the cup and said drink. This is the New Covenant which is poured out to cover your sin. Drink and remember no more." Gallus poured wine from a clay pitcher into a silver chalice.

The elders reclined at the table, six of them along with the women. Two of them wives, the others prostitutes from the Temple of Artemis.

The Nicolaitan bishop continued, "...and this is my body which is shared with you. Remember and eat." He dipped his hand into a bowl of stewed figs. When he lifted it out, the dripping goo ran down his arm as he kissed a bare-chested woman draped over his shoulder. As he extended his cupped hand toward her, she took his wrist in both hands.

Mathias, the eldest Nicolaitan, sat cross-legged at the table's far end. Tall and thin, the full-bearded elder wore the sect's priestly white cloak with dark-brown sleeve tassels. The Sabbath love feasts had become more and more decadent under the Anointed One's leadership. In recent months, Mathias left after the meal, ahead of the predictable denigration. Increasingly, questions haunted him. *Are we any different from the pagans, who sacrifice their firstborn into the fire? And is the God of heaven pleased with our practice of sacred oneness?*

Losing patience, he asked, "What of the unnamed scribe and book of prophecy? If Jonness has the book, will he not use it to his benefit... or even destroy it?"

One of the younger elders poured wine into a prostitute's open mouth. With head tilted back, she received it in gulping swallows as the libation overflowed, running down her neck and chest. Transfixed by the ruby rivets, the young man leaned toward her. Then, hesitating, he retracted. "Mathias is wise and understanding. The sacred knowledge of this book will yield salvation to those who can afford to purchase it. We can sell it again and again, even to those who have knowledge but lack this new revelation. Certainly, we must find and secure this book." He smiled as the men nodded.

Mathias drew his long fingers together, tips meeting. He fanned them in and out, slowly drumming with thumbs together. "But how do we obtain it if Jonness has the scribe under house arrest?"

Gallus withdrew his hand from the woman's lips.

"Does this scribe not have a family? Perhaps if they were in danger, he would exchange the book for their safety." He immersed his hand into a bowl of water. He then wiped it off, using the woman's body as a towel. "I will answer these questions. The scribe is an old man named Batush. He lives in a small house on the slopes with his wife and grandchild. I have arranged for a delegation to visit them tomorrow night." Arching his head back, he gulped from the goblet.

Mathias stared at the bishop. *Could this... this*—he struggled to find the right word—*Gallus, truly be anointed to lead the holy church?* He collected his cloak and, with a nod to Gallus, departed.

<<>>

Daniel stood in the dim light of the parking structure admiring the machine—the car of his dreams, black on black, the color—perfect. The air-cooled Porsche 911 was older, but its condition pristine. Circling it slowly, he caressed the sleeping beauty's sleek lines with his eyes. At the bonnet, he reached down and depressed the chromed latch, which released with a pop, unveiling the twin turbo opposing six. The contrast between the cast aluminum and powder-coated red and black accents struck him with awe. Somehow, he had managed the find and purchase of this iconic classic. Yes—he owned it! *Craftsmanship and engineering merged with art and design in the purest form of purpose... How could I be so lucky?*

It caught his eye then, the reinforcing of the car's unibody where the tubular frame transitioned up and over the engine compartment. Crafted in laminated hardwood like the frame of a harp with joints fingered together, silky smooth with a glass-like finish. Pairs of dowels spliced the connections between the wood and metal. He bent down, leaning closer—maple? He marveled at the workmanship, amazed by the fluid shape achieved in wood.

His finger glided along the wood's eased edge as the realization began to emerge. A cold chill then lifted the hair on the back of his neck, and his heart began to quicken. *The car was in an accident and repaired. The seller must have done the work himself. It should be metal. No credible shop would use wood for such a repair. With a little pressure, it'll collapse. It's not safe.*

Daniel sat up, his skin clammy and heart pounding. *My car, what am I going to do? The Bill of Sale: As Is–No Warranty.* He stood, reaching for the wall. His heart began to slow as he wavered in the darkness.

I have the truck. At least, I didn't sell it. Wait—I don't own a Porsche. I have a pickup. It was just a dream....

He splashed his face with water. *What does it mean?*

The whisper came from within, *"It looks good from the outside, even the inside, unless you know what to look for. It's incredibly crafted, but the structure is all wrong. It will collapse under pressure, with even the slightest bump. It's not safe."*

<<>>

"What am I supposed to do with it?" Daniel drew a sip of espresso. Bitter-strong yet smooth and rich, the French Roast was capped with a layer of golden froth. "Ahh." He and Rhema sat side by side overlooking the kitchen. Sunlight poured through the window above the sink. Reflected from the granite, it was blinding.

"You're right. We're being led by human wisdom and not seeking after the Lord. I don't see any other interpretation." They sat in silence. "I don't think you're supposed to share it—at least not now." She cupped her hand on his knee. "Remember in the Bible when Daniel received his revelation about the end times? The Lord told him to seal it up because it wasn't the right time for it to be known. Maybe we'll need to be broken before we're ready to receive it?"

"I think I'm going to start a fast." He lifted his cup, admiring the sensual curling pattern of the rising steam washed in morning sun. He drew it to his nose, inhaling the rich aroma. "Mm. Today, right after I finish this."

Smiling, she held out her hand. "Come on, hand it over. We'll both fast, breakfast and lunch and break it at sundown—but we start right now."

Daniel rolled his eyes, stealing a last sip before handing it over.

<<>>

Batush jolted awake. A heavy thud and grunt trailed the crash. A sliver of light piercing the darkness. A groan came next, followed by the whining screech of heavy furniture being shoved. He sat up, lifting his weight gently. He then crossed the room with his arm extended, careful not to bend his ankles. With his flat hand on the plank door, he pressed his face to the crack of light, the wood rough against his forehead.

Bishop Jonness stood over his desk with a hand on the chair back. He lifted a chalice. His stance wavering, he jerked to attention as the drink splashed his neck and chest. Metal clonked against wood as he wobbled the cup down and wiped his face. Batush cringed when Jonness brushed an open scroll with the back of his hand. Belching, he then blotted the scroll with his tunic sleeve while Batush held his breath. Jonness slowly tipped forward, faltered, and then crashed into the desk. The cup clanged across the floor. Hugging the table, he slid backward, and the chair caught his fall.

"Scribe..."

Batush snapped to attention, stepping back.

"Scribe, come here."

Batush adjusted his robe, counted to five while bobbing his head, and then tried the door. It swung open. "Yes, Your Holiness."

"Make... a copy of this for me." With both hands, Jonness shoved the unfurled scroll at Batush.

The draft from three days dictation. The Apostle John's book desiccated with strikeouts and changes.

Batush swallowed. "Your Holiness, I–I do not know how—"

"Did I ask you to speak? You will be quiet, and you will obey. I am your bishop, and you are my scribe." Jonness belched again and gazed in the direction of the zebra-skin couch where a dripping wine skin rested on its side. Hands on the desk, he pushed himself upright and staggered toward the open shelves, selected a box, and pawed through it. Finding what he wanted, he withdrew a brownish papyrus with broken edges. "Use this—it is blank."

"But I do not underst—"

Jonness lifted his open hand. After making his way back to the desk, he flopped into the chair. He then groped in a drawer and produced the wood scroll tube, marked with the cross. Uncapping it, he slid out the book written by the Apostle's shaky hand.

"Your copy shall match his hand."

A pulse of heat surged through Batush. His skin clammy, he began to tremble. "I–I cannot. I cannot do this, Your Holiness."

"Listen to me. You will do as I ask—I am your Christ." Jonness raised the scroll in his clenched fist as it made a crackling sound. He slammed it to the table, crushing the end in a spray of brittle fragments.

"No. You do not..." Batush stopped himself, the blow crushing his body and spirit. "Please..."

Jonness sat for a moment in silence. As he unrolled the scroll, it cracked apart on the damaged end. He cocked his head and locked eyes with Batush as he tore off the top section of the book. "It will look exactly like this." Jonness held the scrap in front of Batush. "You will do as I say. You will write this, and you will also find your missing copy of this book. You will accomplish this, and if you do not, you will never see your family again. Take it."

Batush jerked and then watched his trembling hand reach out to take it. Stepping backward, he managed to find the opening and close the door behind him. He stood in the darkness, realizing he was drenched in sweat.

Who is this man?

He returned to the sliver of light. Jonness still at the desk, the damaged scroll in his hand. Listing forward, about to fall, he again lurched upright. He then extended the scroll toward the lamp.

Batush was about to scream, but no sound came from his lips. Touching the flames, the papyrus ignited with a puff. Jonness held it and then turned it over as the flames licked at his fingers. He dropped it on the stone floor.

Batush stood at the door until it was consumed.

CHAPTER 45

SITTIING IN his truck, Daniel surveyed the progress. *Wow, my framers are fast.* Just after sunrise, the project had consisted of a pile of lumber and a three-thousand-foot slab. Now, nine hours later, the building skeleton stood erect. In another month, customers would be exiting the drive-through with burgers and fries. The pop-pop of nail guns cut through the hot still air. Tomorrow, the balance of roof sheathing would be installed, and there would be shade inside for his sawhorse desk. Two blasts of air signaled the air hoses had been disengaged from the compressor.

"Hey, Daniel, you look tired." Joe, his seasoned framer, walked toward him, his movements stiff.

"I am tired."

"That's what you get for all that hard living. Partying again?"

"Nope. Planning your next job so you can improve your tan. Typical wood butcher... kicking back all day sunning yourself. I thought you would be done by now, but look—I gotta put up with you for another whole day."

"I planned it that way. If we finished today, who would you get to build your desk tomorrow—the plumber? He'd likely solder it up with pipe, but the drawings would be falling through the top. You need me, boss. Without me, you're nothing. It's us wood butchers—I mean, wood surgeons—that keep you out of trouble."

"I guess you're right, Joe. What would I do without you to build my desk?"

They laughed as Joe loaded his tools into the back of his tired green pickup. Joe pulled off his baseball cap, rigged with his signature red bandana, and swatted himself. Clouds of sawdust filled the air and settled on his mop of thick, gray-peppered hair. He then flexed his arm, bending it at the elbow and shaking it out. Joe had the wiry physique of a swimmer with the leathered skin of a Nomad. He stopped in front of Daniel's open cab.

"What's up, Joe?"

"You know me—I don't talk a lot." Putting the cap back on with a twist, Joe turned to the building.

"It's too hot to stand out there. Join me in my office—it's got air?" Daniel smiled and turned the key in the ignition. The F-150 fired with a roar, the AC blasting.

Joe hopped inside, leaving the passenger door ajar along with his right leg. "I know you go to church, and I heard you're an elder or deacon, whatever you call it."

Daniel nodded as Joe paused, his sunglasses hiding his eyes.

"I don't go to church or even own a Bible, but I am sort of religious, I guess... I pray. And, well, sometimes I hear the Lord speaking." Joe adjusted his white-frame Oakley's. "Just now, up on the roof, maybe it was the heat, but... I was praying and thanking God for my kids and stuff. Anyway, I was loading the gun with another stick when I heard Him speak—it was for you. I know this is weird—tell me to stop if you want."

"It's not weird at all. Tell me what you heard."

"I heard God say..." He pulled his glasses down. His voice trembled. "Tell Daniel he is highly esteemed, and the Lord took notice... when you started. And I think I heard: Seven days."

With the back of his hand, Daniel gently batted at his dangling keys.

Joe pushed his glasses back. Giving his hat another twist, he faced the windshield. "I'm not sure what that means and don't know why seven days. Hell, I don't even know what esteemed means. But that's what I heard, and He told me to tell you."

They sat for a moment, and then Joe slapped Daniel's knee and stepped out of the cab. "And then He said we should quit construction and start selling Amway." Joe smiled. Heading for his truck, he looked back. "Oh yeah, He also said you're cheap and you should be paying the wood butchers more."

"Thanks, Joe. I appreciate that a lot. And I think you're on to something about the Amway—we're getting too old for this." Daniel's face warmed with a smile. "But I'm not so sure about me being cheap because the Lord was telling me you're too expensive. You better pray about that some more."

He hit the window switch and leaned forward. Again swatting at the keys, he felt faint. *Seven days... That's when we started, Lord. Thanks for encouraging me through Joe, but I'm not sure what we're doing or how much longer I can keep this up? Fasting in this heat? This is crazy, and I don't get it—I'm struggling just to pray.*

He heard it then and turned to the empty passenger seat:

"RETURN TO ME IN SACKCLOTH AND ASHES... WORSHIP ME WITH PRAISE AND DEDICATE YOURSELVES TO MY WORD AND TO PRAYER—ALL WILL THEN FOLLOW..."

Simple and powerful. The words vivid like the title block on a roll of blueprints. Hands shaking as he fumbled with his day planner, he then scribbled out the message. *Sackcloth and ashes, sackcloth and ashes... Fasting, in sackcloth and ashes...* Something splashed on the back of his hand. He swiped his cheek. It was a tear.

The burden lifted, leaving him overcome.

I will worship You, Lord, and dedicate myself to Your Word and to prayer. And I will tell them, Lord, what You are speaking to us.

<<>>

They approached in the dark. Slipping, one of the men swore as he fell on muddy cobbles. A cough came from another, muffled by thick fog and swirling mist. Pulling his cloak to his chin, Gallus hoisted his torch.

The vicar pointed as they rounded a cresting bend. "There, just ahead."

Shrouded in fog, the small house was barely visible. Two black openings in the plastered wall stared into the night like the eyes of a bleached skull.

"Where, I do not... Yes—I see it." Bishop Gallus gave the word in a hushed voice, "Burn it." He drew a circle in front of him with his pointer finger. "Spread out. They will scurry to us like rats."

The group of eight fanned out, each with a torch. Watching from the trail, he waited until the men were positioned in a wide circle. He waved his torch above his head, and the flickering lights moved forward, constricting on the lonely building.

Two dancing flames disappeared through the dark window openings. Another dipped beside the straw heaped against the house. Flickering and fading, smoke billowed from the damp pile. Then igniting, flames climbed the wall. Two arcing streaks of light disappeared over the building's parapet wall, landing on the roof. A pulse of orange lit one of the skull's open eyes.

A child's high-pitched scream pierced the sleeping night.

<<>>

Raphael stepped through the warping tear in space. He stood over the old man, watching him sleep on the straw mat. The scribe's power wave was strong, extending nearly an arm's length from his body, his resting spirit displayed in a spectrum of purples, blues, and greens. Raphael smiled, recalling the day he stood in a furnace of fire with three righteous men. *This one is like Shadrach.*

He moved his scabbard aside and bent to speak into the man's ear. "The Lord knows your heart. Do not fear or fret—He will protect His word."

~~

Batush opened his eyes and rubbed them, sitting upright. He blinked twice, sensing a shimmer of light—unsure if he saw or felt it. Looking up, he felt the hair on his arms lifting.

"Raphael, are you there?" He cocked his head, and, rushing to his desk, he whispered the words, "The Lord knows my heart, and He will protect His word." He lifted the lampshade from his nightlight. The room glowed as he transferred the small flame to his work lamp. His face dropped into his hands.

"Lord, I do not understand. I have read the Apostle's revelation. Anyone who adds or takes away from Your Words will be cursed. He also will not see the tree of life or Your holy city. You know the bishop is asking me to add, and also take away, from Your Words. He has caged me and threatens my family, but... I cannot do this cursed thing."

Batush heard it again, spoken from within, *"Batush, I know your heart. Do not fear or fret. This is not your burden. I will protect My Word."*

"But the curse. Lord, are You...?"

"I have placed you here, under your bishop's authority. Your task, My son, is to walk in obedience. I will take care of My Word."

"Thank You, Lord, I–I will begin this very minute and not stop until it is finished." He uncapped his ink jar. His hands trembled, spilling a bit as he poured the black liquid into his dipping bowl. The blank papyrus, along with the forged draft, sat in front of him, already loaded in the scrolling tablet. He picked up the scrap, torn from the original. Holding it between flat hands, he whispered, "I surrender Your Word into Your hands, Lord, blessing and praising Your glorious name." He dipped his quill. Hands still shaking, he began. *Shaky is good, Lord— down and to the right...* Completing the first lines, he stopped to inspect the work, surprised by how it resembled the Apostle's hand.

The Revelation of Jesus Christ, which God gave Him to show to His bond-servants, the things which must soon take place; and He sent and communicated it by His angel to His bond-servant John...

"Wake up."

Batush jerked. The glow of sunrise washed the room. Lifting his head, he wiped drool from his cheek as Jonness stood over him.

"Give them to me."

Batush focused on the completed forgery, his back aching and his legs numb. Fumbling with the tablet, he removed the documents from the pins. Then rising from the chair, he extended them to Jonness.

Jonness tucked the draft under his arm and read the forgery while nodding. "It is good. You have completed one of the tasks I requested. You must now complete the second."

Batush struggled to swallow.

"I have shown you favor, Batush, but my patience grows faint. Do not test me."

<<>>

Sarah coughed, squeezing her burning eyes closed. She pulled the blanket to her face. She was chasing Noah in the yard again. The spotted goat had stolen her baby doll and had it in his mouth. Noah ran through the open door of the house, which was billowing smoke. "Stop! Noah, don't go in there—stop."

Opening her eyes, the ceiling on fire, she screamed. Smoke was pouring through the window into her room. Churning up and over, it rushed along the wall to join the flames. The room was filled quickly, already hiding the raging fire above. Gasping for breath, her throat burning, she slid to the floor and hugged the blanket. Hand pressed over her mouth, she drew a painful breath.

"Grandmother?" she called. Coughing into the blanket, she blinked back burning tears.

"Sarah!" The shrill reply cut through the roiling smoke and flames. "Get out. Get out. Sarah—run."

She looked to the window, gushing more and more smoke and now tongues of orange flame. Then she squinted to the doorway. Smoke flowed under the blanket hanging in the opening. A flaming piece of the roof fell. Hitting the bed, it flipped to the floor.

She tried to scream, but burning pain squeezed her chest. Crawling under the bed, she pressed the blanket to her face and squeezed her eyes shut. She tried to breathe, no air, only pain... a short burning gasp, eyes and fingers clenched, every muscle in her body taut and shaking. Her house was grinding and creaking, and then crashing, flaring flame and heat and boiling smoke.

She blinked burning eyes as a section of roof bowed toward her, then cascaded to the floor. Above, flame and smoke billowed into the sky.

"Sarah... Sarah..." The flames roared in her ears.

Where are you, Grandmother—Papa? Help me... Papa... Help.

No air, only darkness and sleep, only sleep...

A hand found her then, hugging her tight and then lifting her into his arms. Not the shaky arms of Papa, the strong arms of Father.

He spoke like he used to when he put her to bed. When she was almost asleep but could still hear him singing and whispering to her. "Run, Sarah. Run..."

"I don't want to. I want to stay here with you."

"You must run for me, my little flower." Only Father called her that. He was putting her down now.

The hot floor burned her bare feet. She felt his embrace, her arms around his neck.

Sarah opened her eyes. She was in the kitchen, in front of the open door, sagging from its hinges in a sheet of flame. Letting go, she turned back. Father was gone and she ran. Through the opening, feeling a burst of heat and then cool. She gasped, running into the night.

"I have you." A large man scooped her up. Another just ahead held a torch. "I have the child."

"Let me go—let me go." She squirmed. Legs kicking and arms pushing, she felt the coarse bristle of beard on her face. She twisted toward the raging blaze of flame and boiling smoke.

The men stepped back, away from it, with hands raised to shield their faces. No one else emerged.

The last scream shattered the night like the glancing blow of sword against stone. "Grandmother..."

CHAPTER 46

NICK EXECUTED the trade and calculated his gains. "A cool fourteen five sixty, not bad for an hour's work." While sipping coffee, he returned the monies to the client accounts. Retaining the profit, he moved it to his trading account named Rapid Rewards.

Mammon whispered, *"Zen Master of Money."*

Nick checked his balance. *Wow. Two hundred and eighty-six thousand. We're getting there. Maybe we should ease off and move some of it to funds?*

Mammon almost shouted, *"Are you kidding me? The risk is nearly zero when you can read the markets. And if we get serious, you'll be able to afford a divorce and have Amber. Besides, this is too easy."*

His hand jerked, sploshing coffee over the rim of his mug onto his hand. Technically, it was illegal. *But then again, I'm investing for them, and they're doing quite well in their long accounts. Divorce—wow, but how would I...?*

He pushed the last thought from his mind as he set the cup down and then mopped up the spill with a tissue.

"It's just rewards, a bonus for making them a ton of money. What's wrong with that? Besides, everyone's doing it. Banks, insurance and mortgage companies, equity traders—they're doing it all day long."

His phone vibrated in the kitchen. When he glanced to the phone on his desk, he realized it was Brooke's. *Damn phones—they look exactly the same. I'll need to get a colored sleeve.*

He dashed into the kitchen and smiled as he touched the screen.

I'm thirsty for Thursday. Are you in the clear—Call me. ☺

His heart accelerated. He glanced at the clock and then the stair. He then refilled his mug and walked to the back door. Unlatching it as quietly as he could, he stepped into the cool dry morning. Seated on a patio chair, he pushed Send.

"Hi there. I wasn't expecting you to call so soon. Guess what I'm doing?"

"Ah... taking a bath?"

"No, silly, it's morning. I'm on the balcony sipping a cappuccino in my pink robe. I woke up early and watched the sun come up. It's beautiful. Maybe it's wishful thinking, but I think I can smell fall in the air."

"I'm outside too, and you're right—I can smell it. Wish I was there."

"I wish you were too. Can you make it tomorrow?"

He closed his eyes, picturing her naked body in the pink robe. "I'm thinking yes, but I'll need to confirm. I'll text you later." He crossed one leg on top of his knee, settling into the wrought-iron chair cushions. "So what's on your plate for today?"

"Just work. I've got a couple staff meetings. I've been thinking about the reorg., and we're running out of time. What's your take?"

"I wanted to get a decision on timing, but then Daniel kicked over the table like he always does. I figured just getting the vote was pushing it." Pressing with his thumb, he switched off his phone's screen display. Beyond the patio, the pool sweep broke the surface, its tail shooting a jet of water across the yard. "We secured the decision and have authority as a committee. If the three of us agreed, I guess we could pull the trigger and notify the board later. It would be bold—but I'm not so sure. Without consensus, it would be disrespectful, and some of the guys would be pissed. I wouldn't blame them. But..."

"But what?"

Both Mammon and Asmodeus blurted, *"What are they going to do? They voted on it. This is no time to shrink back. Real leadership is bold and decisive."*

"Well, what are they going to do?" Her voice cutting out, he tilted the phone for better reception. "It needs to be done, and we voted on it. Maybe it would be good for the elders to see some real leadership in action?"

"A move like that would have significant ramifications. I was thinking we would map it out strategically and then get buy-in on the details. But you could be right, Amber. Maybe we need to be bold for the church and lead on this?"

"I want you right now...." Again, the demons spoke as one.

Amber whispered, "I want you right now."

He turned to the window. Brooke stood in the kitchen. "I need to sign off."

"Okay. We can talk later."

He hung up and stood. He then walked to the pool skimmer. Lifting the lid, he dumped the basket before entering the house.

"Who were you talking to?" Brooke brushed straggles from her face and then stooped under the sink. "My sink is clogged again." Standing, she held the drain cleaner.

"Let me do that. I'll take care of it."

"That's what you always say, and it never gets done. Nothing ever gets done around here." She handed the box to him, the question still on her face.

"The crawler was stuck so I went out to fix it. I was on the phone when I walked out—it was Paul. He asked if I could go pray for someone in the hospital tomorrow night. Do we have anything going on?"

"No, that's fine. I'm going out with the girls. Wendy Frost found a new place that has live music on Thursdays. Who's in the hospital?"

"He didn't know. He's going to check and call me back. All he knew was it's a woman and it doesn't look very good. He thought it was cancer."

<<>>

It was late afternoon, and the campus was empty. Daniel sat alone behind the reception counter, listening to the ticking wall clock. He and Rhema had been fasting breakfast and lunch for ten days, and he was lightheaded. He glanced at his watch. *Three hours till sundown, and then we eat. Give me strength, Lord.*

He picked up the bank statement. *There it is again. Twice last month and now five times this month. Exactly thirty thousand out of the account and returned on the same day.* He scratched his forehead. *No pattern, but usually early in the week, except once on Friday. I'll check with Nick. It's likely some sort of rollover.*

He turned back to the pile of checks and invoices, nearly an inch thick. *What's this?* Opening the legal-size envelope, he removed a packet of documents from the bank titled Equity Request. The application was filled out with information on the church, including the corporation name and declaration. The form referenced an attached summary of debt-free assets and property. The last page was a parcel map of the campus, with the original corner lot titled Exception.

Exception? That's right—the long-term lease with the tribe. The form included a credit request line of eight million dollars, along with a signature block listing the corporation officers: chairman, finance director, and treasurer. Paul and Nick had already signed.

Daniel flipped through the application. As a business, he had borrowed money a couple times to cover his subcontractors while waiting for late payments, but he didn't like it. He stared at the treasurer's signature line, listing his name highlighted in yellow marker with an arrow sticker pointing at the open line. Signing it, he moved to the pile of checks and confirmed they matched the invoice amounts. He then placed all of it in the black satchel and left it in the desk's pencil drawer for Nick, who would pick it up for processing. *This is not my gifting. Protect me, Lord, from ever having this job again.*

Looking out the window, he smiled at the sight of Tom Evans, across the plaza kneeling in a flower bed. *Still working—way to go, brother.*

His phone chimed. Selecting mail, he read the message:

```
Fellow Servants,
Phase 1 of the reorg. was executed today, in
accordance with Tuesday's board decision. Amber
and I met with designated staff, informing them
of their discharge. All three individuals signed
release agreements and then cleaned out their
desks. This occurred after the campus was
vacated. Pastor Stover received the news
graciously and agreed to inform the congregation
on Sunday. Please keep this to yourselves until
after the announcement. Be in prayer for our
congregation, for peace and unity during this
important season of transition. In His Service,
Nick Hamilton
```

Daniel swallowed, looking back to the window. *What have we done?*

CHAPTER 47

KNEELING ON the cold floor, Batush recited the prayer his grandfather had taught him. Eyes closed, he whispered softly. "'Mighty God, light of men who turn to You. Creator of all that grows and breathes, forgive my transgressions that I might be a temple fit for You. Watch over my family and protect them from evil and harm. I ask in the name of Christ, Your only child, the healer of souls. Through Him, may glory be given to You, in power and honor and praise, throughout the ages. Amen.'"

The sound of the iron latch came early. He opened his eyes as the door swung with the familiar creak, revealing a stocky short man with a torch. He drew back the hood of his brown cloak.

"Shebaniah...?"

"It is I, Batush. I have come to escort you for morning transcription." Shebaniah spoke in a hushed voice, then turned and glanced down the corridor.

"But I thought you were banished—did not...?"

"The bishop has shown mercy. Praise God—he has allowed me to work in penance for my transgressions. I now serve the brethren as deacon, and today, I have been sent for you. Come. We must go." Again, he glanced over his shoulder.

Batush rubbed his cold hands together. "It will be a blessing to get out of this room." Gathering his tools, he placed them in his writing case, then slung it over his shoulder and followed Shebaniah.

Stopping in the doorway, Shebaniah placed a hand on his shoulder. The flickering light magnified Shebaniah's furrowed brow and bulbous nose.

"What is it, my friend?"

"Zophar sends a message."

"You have spoken to him?"

"Yesterday—he was here for the council. He took me aside when no one was watching, and he told me..." Shebaniah spoke slowly, "Your home—it burned the night before last."

The words struck Batush in the stomach. "Is my family... My wife and grandchild? Are they safe? Tell me, are they safe?" His legs went slack, his knees buckling.

"I do not know. There were only ashes, but Zophar is searching."

"No, my Lord! How...? This cannot... I must go. Please, Lord—no."

Shebaniah glanced down and then back to Batush. "They will not let you go. They will send Rome to hunt you."

"Then let them. I must find my family."

A deacon passed them in the corridor.

"There is nothing you can do, Batush." Shebaniah cupped a beefy hand on Batush's shoulder. "Zophar has gone out in search of them."

Bending over, Batush put his hands on his knees. Then clenching his jaw, he lurched upright, and they walked briskly.

"I must go. I will ask the bishop. Surely, he will release me to seek my family—he must." His stomach constricting, he suddenly stopped, remembering the bishop's threats. "It cannot be so. How could... my bishop...?"

"I will assist you, Batush. For now, you must do nothing. I will return tonight and help you escape."

<<>>

The elders had assembled for an emergency session on short notice. All were in attendance except Henry Williams, who had not responded to the email Paul sent four hours earlier. Daniel stared at Amber, telling himself to breathe slowly as Earl Dempsey led the prayer. It was short.

"We acted at the direction of this board. We voted to proceed, and that's what we did." Nick leveled his response with concise deliberation.

Daniel spoke out, "We decided to proceed, but we had not decided when or how. You both knew that. We were going to pray about it, remember?"

"What makes you think we didn't pray about it—did you?"

Paul Chambers waved his yellow hammer. "Easy, guys. That's enough. We were all praying and have been for a long time." He slid the hammer handle between his fingers, gripping the head in a fist. "It's true we decided to proceed, but it's also true we hadn't decided when. We also gave the committee authority to act on our behalf. As I've said, we need to trust each other—we've talked about that a lot. Nick and Amber made the call, and I trust their judgment. What's done is done, but that's why I called us in. We need to discuss tomorrow." He leaned back, staring at his hammer as if it was tapping the table by itself. "Amber's got a communication plan to share."

The monitor lit the wall, and no one bothered to switch off the lights. "I have two words—*unity* and *communication*." Amber leveled her eyes on Daniel. "I know we all don't agree, but unity is critical. We need to be speaking with one voice. The second point is communication. Pastor Jason has agreed to speak to the congregation."

Lewis Kolsby interrupted, "Do you think that's wise—letting him speak? We have no idea what he might say."

"That's a good point." Amber stood, her eyes drifting from man to man around the table. "Nick and I agree the message needs to come from Jason, but how he presents it will be critical. So we talked to him about the importance of not hurting the sheep. We saw a lot of grace in Jason and believe he can be trusted."

His jaw clenching, Daniel's heart raced. "Did he sign the termination agreement?"

"Yes, Daniel, he did."

"Then I guess he knows it'll cost him a bunch if he speaks out against us. Is that right—he'll lose all of his severance and benefits?" Daniel held her searing eyes, not flinching. "I guess he didn't have much of a choice, did he?"

Nick stood, moving to Amber's side. "I don't like what you're implying."

"And what is it I'm implying, Nick—besides the obvious?"

"What do you mean—obvious?" Nick's hands curled into fists.

"Nothing more than what we've done. We've forced him to talk to the congregation and tell them what we want him to say. And if he says anything else, he loses six months' pay and benefits—when he's out of work and looking for a job to feed his family. I'm just asking for clarification, that's all. That's what we're doing, right? We got him by the balls, and he doesn't have a choice. We made sure of that—right?"

Red blotched Nick's neck. "I've had enough of listening to your crap. We did what was prudent and wise—for everyone. And all of us are on board, except you. You know it would be foolish to let him just get up there and talk. Who knows what he might say and what damage he might cause?"

"What if he said the truth? I guess we couldn't have that, could we?"

"Okay, wise guy. Tell us about the truth and what we're doing. Come on—tell us."

Paul broke in, "Guys, guys—this isn't..."

Nick struck the air with his pointer finger. "No. I want to hear him answer. This man comes in here, smearing garbage all over us and our new executive pastor. This needs to be quenched—right here, right now. Tell us about the truth, Daniel."

Daniel opened his hands, just above the tabletop, palms up. "Pastor Jason doesn't have a choice—we made sure of it. I guess he could tell them that. Or he could tell them he doesn't know why we're firing him because we never bothered to tell him. He might speculate it's because there aren't enough butts in the seats or money coming in. Or maybe, the elders want to reinvent the church, and he doesn't fit the mold they're wanting.... Maybe he's too old or not cool enough."

Silence held the room, and then Amber said, "But he won't be saying that, will he, Daniel? Like I said, Nick and I spoke to Pastor Jason, and he was quite gracious. He doesn't want to hurt the congregation. He wants to do the right thing for the church, and he understands we want that too."

"Does he?" Cocking his head, Daniel met her eyes.

"Yes, he does, Daniel. But I think—all of us are wondering if you do?" Turning her back to him, she faced the image on the wall. "I mentioned communication, and this is what we're proposing."

A slide titled "Talking Points" flashed across the wall. She read a series of bullet points, but he wasn't listening. His ears buzzing, he felt dizzy.

She clicked to the final slide. "Paul will come forward after tomorrow's sermon and stand next to Pastor Jason and make the announcement. We like the optics of that visual because it conveys unity. I will then join them on the platform to announce the special business meeting for tomorrow night." Again, she assaulted Daniel's gaze, a tinge of satisfaction flirting in her emerald eyes. "That's where the talking points come in because all of you will be on the platform. Paul will facilitate, and that will be when Pastor Jason speaks. He will then leave, and we will open it up for questions. We were planning to have the ushers hand out three-by-five cards for the congregation to write their questions. They will then be collected and given to all of you, who will take turns reading and then answering appropriately."

Nick interjected, "We want to emphasize the word *appropriately*. Because some of the questions may not be helpful, and we're going to need to use discernment in deciding which to read." He lifted his brows at Daniel, who responded with a half-open-mouth stare. "At the end, Paul will close the meeting with a prayer."

Paul cleared his throat. "Be praying about this, guys. Tomorrow morning and especially tomorrow night will be significant for us. It's going to be exciting to see what God does. Is there anything else?"

Pain pinching behind his ears, his vision blurring to white, Daniel saw Paul at the end of a long tunnel.

"Earl, could you close us?"

"Tell them about the dream...."

Daniel flexed his hands. They were sweating.

"I've been fasting. I'm fasting right now actually—I'm sorry. I'm a little woozy." He clenched his fists. "I had a dream the night before last. And I've been sitting here wondering if I should share it. I really don't want to, but I'm hearing the Spirit saying I should." He lifted his head to blank stares. "I was standing in front of a beautiful sports car. It was mine, and I had just bought it...." He closed his eyes. Seeing the dream unfold, he described it in detail to the silent room.

He opened his eyes. "The car is us—Faith Bible Church. The structure is all wrong—it's built on human wisdom. It's beautiful on the outside, but with a little pressure, it's going to collapse. It's not safe... it's a façade. That's what the Spirit was speaking to me in the dream, and that's what I believe He's speaking to us right now." His peripheral vision returned. A mixture of confusion, pity, and disgust contorted their faces. "We shouldn't do this. It's a mistake."

<<>>

The Church Fathers lifted their heads slowly as Batush entered the chamber. The morning training session was concluding with new converts shuffling out. Batush and Shebaniah took seats along with several deacons and clergy. Outside the arched opening in the back, Zophar spoke with two guards, one of them with a hand on his chest. Seeing Batush, Zophar pushed his way through. Desperation darkened his face.

"I gave instructions. Remove him." Jonness pointed as the guards took hold of Zophar and steered him back to the opening, his eyes calling out as he struggled.

Batush rose as Shebaniah grasped his arm.

Jonness blurted, "The scribe shall sit. It is time to begin—let us pray..." Jonness glanced again to the arched entry where someone else was now speaking with the guards, a younger thin man with longish hair. Stopping, they turned to face Jonness.

"What is it?"

One of the guards stepped away, emerging a few moments later in the opening behind Jonness. The guard leaned down and cupped his hand to the bishop's ear. Jonness placed his flat hand on the table, his eyes narrowing. "I will let him address the council. Clear the room—everyone." People began to rise. "Except for the scribe—he shall remain."

Batush clasped hands with Shebaniah as the gangly man with greasy locks descended the steps. He looked at Batush as he passed, glancing away before their eyes could meet. *Who is this man who seems to know me?* Making his way to the center of the room, he stopped beside the lonely chair.

"Speak."

Batush lifted his quill.

"I come in the name of Gallus, bishop of the Nicolaitans." Batush scratched out the words. "God sent an angel with a message for Bishop Gallus, who sent me to communicate it to you."

Rising to a half-standing position, Jonness leaned forward, his hands on the table. "That man is not a bishop. He is a jackal cloaked in the skin of a wolf. I am the one and only Holy Father and Bishop of Ephesus."

The vicar, his body rigid, wavered slightly. "The angel appeared to Bish... to Gallus two nights past—telling him you have a sacred book which belongs to the Nicolaitans. Gallus requests you humble yourself under God's mighty hand and give this book to the Holy Fa... to Gallus the Nicolaitan—he..."

Jonness slammed his fist to the table. "This wolf you speak of was not visited by an angel—but a demon." Slowly sitting, he leaned into his tall chair. "It is true we have sacred books—many of them. Why would I give any sacred book to a jackal like Gallus, who clearly speaks with demons?"

"The angel—or, messenger—told Gallus that the Scribe Batush found this book and you are holding both. He said..."

Batush's hand froze.

"Silence! You tell this wolf of yours he should fall on his knees before God Almighty and confess his sins. He speaks with demons and asks me to give him a book? Gallus is testing God who will judge his soul. Go now and tell Gallus to confess in sackcloth and ashes. Go."

The vicar took a step backward.

Batush clenched his hand. It was shaking. *My family and now the book? Lord, this cannot be.*

"The messenger also said—"

"Did I ask you to speak?" Jonness's face contorted. Chin extended, he glowered crimson. He then threw his arms out, his robe flapping. "What?"

"The messenger also said the scribe's home was touched by the finger of God two nights past. It was consumed with fire, and the scribe's grandchild was delivered to the bish... to the safety of Gallus."

Sarah? My Sarah is alive! His pen clattered to the floor as Batush sprang to his feet.

The vicar took another step back. "The messenger told Gallus the child may be exchanged for the sacred book." Retreating with two more steps, he stumbled.

Jonness pointed to Batush. "Sit—the scribe shall sit." After slamming his flat hand to the table, Jonness then stabbed his finger at the vicar. "And you... You come in the name of Gallus the wolf, who has kidnaped a child and orders *me*—the Holy Father and true Bishop of Ephesus? You tell this jackal, this wolf who speaks to demons and blasphemes the Holy God in heaven. You tell him to go to the fires of hell. I will not listen to his demands, and I will not trade my book for any child. Do you hear me?"

Batush remained standing, the room tilting, his mind reeling. He grabbed his hair in clenched fists, blinking back tears as his tablet crashed to the floor. "I must... Holy Father—you must..."

"Guards!" Jonness shouted. "Throw this boy out of here." He glared across the room. "And this old man... take him to the pit. Take him. Now."

CHAPTER 48

SHIELDING HIS eyes, Daniel squinted into the spotlight. Sweat tickling the back of his neck, he was second-guessing his decision to wear the jacket. The other elders were casually dressed in polo shirts and jeans. He brushed fragments of lint from his black slacks. They were everywhere. The blazer had hung unworn in his closet for years. *It's disintegrating. What a joke.* The other men, five of them, sat to his right on stools spread out in a crescent spanning the platform. *Give me peace, Lord.*

Steps echoed in the massive room as Paul crossed the stage to the podium. He fumbled with the microphone. Extending it at arm's length, he searched for the switch. "We'd like to thank each of you for coming out. It means a lot to know you care about this church enough to give up your evening. This morning we announced Pastor Stover and another two staff persons will be leaving us. I want you to know all of us are going to miss them, but we're also excited about where the Lord is calling them." Paul rotated with a stiff neck toward Nick and then Amber. "Pastor Jason is going to share a few words with us now."

Jason approached the podium.

A combination of confusion and concern washed the sea of faces before them. *Where are you, Tom? You need to be here.* There. Daniel exhaled. The stoic dark figure stood alone in the empty balcony.

Pastor Jason hesitated, his finger floating along the edge of the podium. "I'm not sure what to say.... This is strange. I guess life can be like that. Sometimes you get a surprise, and for me, this is one of those times. I want you to know I love every one of you. I'm not going to... This is hard. But Joyce and I are going to be okay. God is good, and His grace is sufficient. I don't understand, but I do know the elders have been praying about this.... And I have served you while submitting to their authority. They did ask me to stay while they look for an interim pastor, but... I think it's best if I leave right away. I've seen transitions where a departing pastor stays for a while, and I don't think it's healthy."

He held the lectern surface in both hands, rocking it gently forward and back and then lifted his head. "I'm going to receive this as coming from the Lord—like Abraham... Joyce and I are being called to leave. We don't know where we're going. But we trust the Lord, and we're putting our faith in Him. I want you to know it's been an honor to serve as your pastor. I guess that's about it. Joyce and I will... Thank you, all of you."

A lump swelled in Daniel's throat. On the silent faces, he saw tears in many eyes.

Nick moved to Jason's side. Taking the microphone, he placed his hand on Jason's shoulder. "Let's show our appreciation for Pastor Jason and his beautiful wife."

The crowd sat in stunned silence. A few claps came from three elders who rose and then awkwardly sat again.

"Go. Go to your pastor. Go."

Daniel rose, unsure of what to do next. He crossed the stage. Facing Nick, he put his hand out.

Indecision flickered in Nick's eyes.

"Don't back down."

Nick handed over the microphone and stepped back as Daniel turned to Jason. "I'll never forget the night you came to the house when Dad was dying. You ministered to my family in our time of need. You were Jesus to us that night, and I know you've done that for so many of us. You and Joyce have given yourselves up for us, and we've been blessed to call you Pastor." Daniel cleared his throat. "I can't say why this is happening, because, well, I don't really understand myself. But I would like to say I'm sorry for what we're doing, and I would ask"—his voice cracked—"can you... forgive us?"

Tears filled Daniel's eyes. Pastor Jason smiled and then hugged him.

A single clap came from the balcony, breaking the silence. Another followed, and then a third in measured rhythm. Others joined, each clap gaining in strength as the crowd swelled to their feet. Clap—Clap—Clap. Clap—Clap—Clap.

Daniel felt the concussion in his chest, the volume rising until it was deafening.

The elders reluctantly rose. Looking from side to side they joined, their hands barely touching.

Daniel handed the microphone to a white-faced Nick. They both stepped away from Pastor Jason, who raised his hands in protest. Jason then descended the steps and took Joyce's hand. Walking out, they nodded and waved to the now-cheering congregation.

Amber ascended the steps, receiving the microphone from Nick's hand. "Now that's what I call a warm farewell. Let's thank them, Church."

The ovation broke, dissipating again to silence.

"Wow. I'm not sure I've ever seen anything like that before. The elders and I are just overwhelmed with your love for the Stovers and your support for this church. We are both humbled and excited to see what the Lord is going to do at Faith Bible."

Daniel walked back to his stool. Stopping, he stared at it.

"Don't walk out. Stay."

After sitting, he brushed more lint from his pants.

Amber continued, "You all received three-by-five cards when you came in for your questions. Those have been collected and are now being passed to the elders who will take turns reading them and then answering. We thought the cards would be a good way to make sure everyone is heard."

Daniel bit down on the side of his tongue. Inside his mind, he shook his head. *Yeah, right... Give me a break.*

An usher handed Daniel a stack of cards. The top one was written in shaky blue ink: Why is Pastor Stover not qualified to be our pastor? Daniel turned to his right where the others shuffled through their cards.

He read the next four: Why didn't you ask us before you fired our pastor?

We love Pastor Stover! Do you know how much you are hurting us?

Why are you doing this? Marcy Short helped my daughter. Why did you fire her?

The last card, written in large block letters with several misspelled words: My mother cried all day and said you hurt her. Why are you so mean?

Seated next to the podium, Paul stood. "This one is more of a statement than a question, but I think it's a good place to start: We have been praying for you and appreciate your wisdom in seeking the Lord." Paul paused and bobbed his head. "This really means a lot and touches my heart. You know, these kinds of decisions are difficult. And like I said, we all love Pastor Jason—I mean that."

Paul handed the microphone to Nick. "Paul's right. This decision was bathed in prayer, and we're stepping out in faith. This next question is from a woman who's been a member here for thirty-two years. I'm not going to read her name, but she says, 'We are blessed to be led by men like you. I know these decisions are hard, but we support you.'" He leaned back, pulling the microphone away from his mouth and then drawing it forward. "This is truly humbling, trust me. Thank you for your support and especially for your prayers. We can't say how much they mean to us."

Lewis Kolsby read a similar question before passing the microphone to Henry Williams. "These are some really encouraging comments, if you know what I'm saying here." Henry studied the card in his hand. "This one is a little hard to read, let me see: We have seen this hoppen... Or, happen... We have seen this happen... in the past... Oh... and many left the church... Let me see, okay... It's hard on us, and it says... Why are you doeing this to us again? Doeing this..." Henry stopped, his eyes spreading wide. "Wait a minute here. We don't want anyone to be hurt. I mean, we've been praying and listening to the Lord. This is serious business, if you know what I mean. Let's face it, we've been working on this for a long time, and we're asking God to come down and bless this plan. That's what's going on here, guys."

Nick took the microphone. "Let me jump in. I think I can help. Henry's right. We've been praying about this and listening to the Lord, and we certainly don't want to hurt anyone. I want to be clear, and I want everyone to hear this." Nick fanned his hands out. "This is about obedience. As your elders, it's also our responsibility to make the hard decisions to protect the church."

Two whispering men gestured with their hands. One then rose to his feet. "This is not about protecting us. You're not even reading our questions. Why don't you let us ask our questions out loud?"

Paul leaned in to the microphone. "You need to sit down, Sander. This is not going to work if it gets out of hand. If you can sit, we'll have time for all of the questions."

Sander sat, shaking his head as the microphone was handed to Daniel.

Daniel stared at the cards in his hand.

"Read them, Daniel. Read them."

He fanned out the cards. "These are all similar. I'll read four that are fairly representative." Daniel scanned the row of elders, looked to Rhema next and then the balcony. "The first one says: Why is Pastor Stover not qualified to be our pastor?" Daniel nodded and then continued, ending with the child's question. He heard at least two hushed thanks yous. "I don't know how to answer any of these—I really don't. I'll need to defer to the others." He turned to the stunned faces on his right.

Paul lurched to the podium, his mouth draped open, his shiny face white. "I believe Nick answered this already. We don't want to hurt anyone. We've been working on this and praying for a long time, and this is what we're hearing the Holy Spirit say. We're asking for your trust."

Sander, on his feet again, raised his voice. "That's not good enough. What makes you think you're the only ones who can hear the Holy Spirit? Don't blame this on Him. And what about us—you didn't even ask."

"Sander, you need to sit down. Now listen..."

"No. You listen. This is wrong." Sander shook his head, sidestepping out of the pew. He walked briskly toward the exit with five or six following.

Nick stepped to Paul's side. "That's okay. We understand all are not going to agree with us. But I'd like to ask you to hear us out. And I would say to the gentleman who just shook his fist at his elders: If you don't like what we're doing, come on up—step up and serve. We've been on our knees—seeking the Lord and having meetings and more meetings, agonizing over this stuff—and it's not easy."

He spread open hands. "When you make a decision like this one, after prayer and fasting—that's right, we've been fasting. In the end, you're forced to ask a question: Are these people—that the Lord is saying need to leave—a good fit? We asked that question about Pastor Stover and the others. And I admit—we're struggling a bit to explain. It's like trying on gloves. You ask yourself is this one a good fit?" He wiggled the fingers of his open hand. "In the end, we heard the Lord saying it wasn't." He stared at his hand.

Four people stood, blurting out questions at the same time.

"What do you mean?"

"What if we liked that glove?"

"Yeah, it was fitting just fine."

"What *are* you talking about?"

"Stop," Paul interrupted. "Please, stop. This is not edifying or helpful." He waited for silence. "You need to know that we know... stuff... about these three staff persons you don't know. And we can't tell you those things—we're just not going to. You're just going to need to trust us."

One by one, the four returned to their seats.

"What stuff? What things? That's not true. Set it straight.... Stand up."

His heart racing, Daniel swiped at the lint on his pants with sweaty hands. In the crowd, shaking heads turned from side to side and gradually began to bow. He thought of Tom. Glancing to the balcony, he swallowed. It was empty.

<<>>

"Keep moving." Along with a punching push to the back, the command came from the heavyset guard.

Propelled forward, Batush watched his shadow dance forward and back, to the side and then back again. Dank blackness chilled his clammy skin like a moldy blanket. The single light source was the torch held by the smaller guard, who limped behind. The corridor ended at a low opening supported by a listing header beam.

"Move along." A shaft of light briefly illuminated a narrow landing with descending steps. "Move."

Batush touched cold walls, which crumbled in his fingers. Testing with his foot, he found the first step's slick surface as the light followed. The shaft was pitched at a steep angle with variegated steps, the air colder and thicker as they descended. Trickling water dribbled ahead, the stair base disappearing into a black tunnel.

His hand on the last step, Batush dropped into shallow icy water. They were in a cave, roughly three or four strides wide and just tall enough to stand. Slogging for several minutes, they entered a larger chamber, the water knee deep. The cavern's taller side rose with a vertical wall of stone. The ceiling then sloped downward and away to the far side where it sliced into the water.

The shorter man hoisted his lamp, swinging it with a nod toward the wall where leather straps dangled from two iron rings bolted into the stone.

"Take off your clothes."

"My family... They are missing. My wife and..." Batush removed his soaking cloak as the larger guard brandished the club that dangled from his belt.

"The tunic and shoes also."

Batush obeyed. Standing naked and shivering, he held his clothes. When the shorter man pointed to a flat stone above the water line, Batush placed his bundle on the rock, and the larger man grabbed his wrist. "Please—no."

After slipping his torch into a wall sconce, the shorter guard sloshed through the water to one of the straps. Pushing Batush against the cold rock, the guards tied his wrists. They then released the cords at the ends, still threaded through the rings, and pulled as his arms stretched upward.

"Please..."

Using their weight for leverage, they cinched the straps tighter.

"No..." Batush gasped as pain ripped through his arm sockets. They yanked again, and he cried out, his knees buckling as his arms leveled. Bent over, he cocked his head from side to side as they secured the straps. He tried to stand upright, gasping as pain shot through his shoulders and back. "No—please. You can't leave me like this—my family."

The light flashed and pulsed as the guards slogged toward the steps. It then faded to an ebbing glow, disappearing into blackness. Shivering and racked with pain, he tried again to straighten up. Crying out, he relented to the stooping position. With knees bent, he shouted out, "No! You can't leave—no." *Lord, help me. I–I cannot sustain—I will pass out. And my arms...* He exhaled bursts of breath, echoing in the shivering pain and darkness. *Shebaniah... He will be coming, but how? Meraiah, Sarah... Help me, Lord. Please.*

<<>>

Nick drew a sip from white ceramic, followed by an exhaling ah. A bit strong for his taste, the black Sumatra's temperature was perfect. Nearly full, most of the seats were occupied with students and young professionals perusing laptops and stroking phones. Grateful for the overly loud background music, he rapped his thumb and index finger against the tabletop—the beat "Feel It Still".

Scanning the coffee shop, he leaned forward. "We have to do something."

"Maybe someone should take him aside and talk to him?" Paul poked at his iced tea with a green-striped paper straw.

"We've done that. The whole group has talked to him. He knows where we stand, and he's not on board." Nick set his mug down as whirring blenders chewing ice overpowered all conversation. "We need to get rid of him. You saw what he did—he nearly blew up the church."

"Maybe he didn't understand what would happen when he read the comments?"

"No. Just because he's blue collar doesn't mean he's stupid." He rotated the mug on its napkin. "He's like you. You're both in blue-collar occupations. But you're smart, and you own your own business. That takes intelligence, not to mention guts." Watching Paul's eyes, Nick tilted his mug to his mouth.

"So what are you thinking?"

"I'm not sure, but something needs to give."

Mammon blurted, *Are you kidding me—that fool needs to go."*

"He needs to go." Still watching, Nick drew another sip.

"Daniel doesn't impress me as the kind of guy who would resign if we asked him. We could always take a vote. It only takes two-thirds to remove someone."

"That wouldn't look good. He needs to be motivated."

"I think that would be a mistake. It wouldn't look good, especially after what went down on Sunday. I'm thinking it would be better for everyone if Daniel stepped down on his own." Nick slurped another sip. The brew now slightly cooler, he noticed the chestnut accent. "I'm thinking he needs some motivation. He's no different from any of us. We all have pressures and responsibilities—they can get to us."

"What are you saying?"

"He just needs a little extra pressure." He looked over the rims of his glasses.

"Go on—I'm listening."

"If Daniel's world started to unravel... Maybe that would motivate him—to call it quits. It happens all the time."

"And you know how to do that? Make his world unravel...?" Paul braced his elbows on the table, lacing his thick fingers together. "Are you saying you can do that?"

"Don't agree to anything."

"I wouldn't do what I think you're implying. I'm just saying if Daniel's life did start to unravel, he might surprise us and do the right thing... to simplify his life." Nick's eyes widened with the slightest hint of a head fade.

"You could be right. He might surprise us."

Nick lifted his mug to Paul, who responded, tilting his cup. "Here's to the church."

<<>>

Sarah's tears had dried up, and her throat hurt. Struggling to swallow, she rubbed her swollen eyes. *Please, God, tell them to let me go.*

Tired and frightened, she knelt to the crack of light beneath the locked door. Empty besides a jug of water and a sack of grain, the moldy closet had no windows. Muffled voices came and went outside the door.

Hearing them now, she scurried across the dusty floor to crouch with the bag of wheat.

The door clanked and then swung open, and a woman with wavy black hair backed her hip against the doorway. She freed a hand from beneath her red and blue shawl to fiddle with the gold necklace wrapped tightly around her neck. As she smiled, green and gold painted around her dark eyes sparkled like peacock feathers.

"Are you hungry, little one—I have food?" Kneeling just inside the door, she extended a plate. "You're a very pretty girl, aren't you?"

Sarah pressed closer to the musty bag and pulled her knees tight against her chest.

"Are you sure? I have cheese and grapes and a piece of honey cake? I will leave it for later when you are hungry." The beautiful woman smiled and then turned. Looking into the room behind her, she set the plate down and tilted forward. "The bishop says your grandfather will be coming. It won't be long—you will see."

Sarah's eyes opened wide, but she did not move.

<<>>

"Baaa...tuuu...shhh..."

Throbbing pain and tingling numbness, a groan, and then a flash of light.

"Who...? Where?" Batush tried to lift his head. His back and shoulders wailed in resistance. "Ahhh..."

He wanted to float away with the embrace of darkness, but consciousness cried out, "Meraiah! Sarah!"

A flash and darkness again.

"Where... my..."

"Batush, wake up." Pressure's embrace. Numbing pain racked his body. Eyes opened, then closed. The echo of water rising and falling, then fading again. Stretching tension in his arms and back, then releasing, he crumpled forward. Someone cradled his head.

"Raphael? Are you... Is it you?"

"Batush, it is I."

His body floating through space with his arms at his sides. A blanket of warmth and the sloshing echo. *The chamber.* He opened his eyes to the dancing light of torches and a face above him.

"Shebaniah? How...?" Pain surged through his shoulder and back as he felt his arm being lifted. "Ahhh..."

"I am... sorry, brother. I will... quick." Then a grip on his wrist. Opening his eyes again, Batush saw men around him and Shebaniah holding his arm. Then shooting pain as his piercing scream engulfed the chamber. Darkness rushed to him as he let go, swept away in the current of comfortable numbness.

CHAPTER 49

THE WHITE Escalade crawled through the half-filled parking lot, dominated by larger makes and older models. Scratching his three-day beard, Nick checked the mirror. He wore a tee shirt, shorts, and flip-flops, along with a baseball cap he'd won at a men's retreat. He adjusted his sunglasses and locked the Escalade. Then, head down, he crossed the lot.

He squinted as he ascended blinding-white steps, a blast of cold air greeting him at the sliding glass doors. A plump woman with overly long white hair blinked at him through horned glasses, giving her the appearance of an owl. She sat behind a round reception desk directly in front of him.

"Library card?" She removed the glasses. As she dropped them, they dangled from a beaded necklace against the ruffles of her high-necked dress.

"This is my first time." Nick smiled. "Do I need a card?"

"Everyone needs a library card. You'll need to fill out this form, and then your card will be mailed to you. You should receive it within a week."

"You mean I'll need to come back?"

"Oh no, sir—I can give you a visitor pass for today, but you'll need to fill out the form." She extended a clipboard toward him with the application and pen attached. "We can't give you the pass without it, and we'll also need it for your permanent card."

He forced another smile. "That's great. I'll take the pass, but you won't need to bother with the permanent card because I'll probably never be back." He bit his tongue as her face drooped. He took the form and filled it out using the name Frank Jones, along with a made-up address and phone number.

A row of computer stations banked one side of a central reading area where several seniors sat at tables and stuffed armchairs. All of the computers were open. *What a waste of money.*

He selected the terminal on the far end and swiped his pass through its card reader. Waking the machine, he opened the browser and typed

Internal Revenue Service in the search line. The welcome page opened with a display of smiling taxpayers and the tagline Government Hard at Work for You. With a huff, he scanned the menu buttons. Opting for the search bar, he typed Reporting Tax Fraud. A new page quickly displayed a list of topics and forms. He clicked on a link to form 3949-A, Information Referral. *Here we go... Mr. Fairmont, your life is about to become uncomfortable.*

He filled most of the open fields from memory, checking his notes just once for Daniel's mailing address and social security number. The form included a list of suspected violations. Nick checked the boxes for Unreported Income and Kickbacks. Rubbing his chin, he considered the box for Wagering/Gambling. Deciding against, he scrolled to the next section, which included an open field. The heading read: Describe Suspected Illegal Activity, Including an Explanation of How This Information Has Come to Your Attention.

> I am one of Daniel Fairmont's regular clients and wish to remain anonymous. I became suspicious when Mr. Fairmont, of Sahara Constructors, offered a discount for my new restaurant project. Mr. Fairmont explained I could save 10 percent on the construction cost if I were to make electronic payments to an offshore business entity under the name of his construction company. I took advantage of the discount on five projects over the last two years, saving more than $260,000.

Mammon shouted, *"That's chump change—Daniel needs to pay. He was bragging about how he ripped them off."*

Nick highlighted the figure and changed it to $860,000. He then added:

> After completion of our last project, Mr. Fairmont conveyed he hates the IRS, doing all he can to pay as little in taxes as possible. He then bragged, telling me over the past twelve years he has paid less than one-third of what he owes the IRS.

He moved to the next section biting his lip as the cursor floated over a yes or no question: Do you consider the taxpayer dangerous?

"After what he did—hell, yes, he's dangerous!"

He selected yes and scrolled to the final section that asked for his optional contact information. Leaving it blank, he clicked Submit.

"Hi, Nick."

His head spun around to the young woman. Glancing back, he minimized the window.

"Marcy Short—from church. I brought the kids for story time. It's every Tuesday, and I'm the reader today. IRS..." She puckered her lips with a head tilt. "Are they catching up to you?"

"Oh... No. My internet... It went down, and I needed to file a tax report. It's amazing how dependent we get on the internet. You don't realize until it stops working. How are you doing?"

"We're managing. It's hard when you lose your job. But I understand you were all praying and the church is hurting."

"I'm glad you're doing well, but I need to run. I have a meeting." He closed the browser and glanced at the doors and then back to Marcy.

"What you did really hurts. Do you know that?" Tears glazed her eyes.

"We did what was best for the church. I know—it's hard, and I wish there was something I could say. But God will... He will provide—and He has a plan."

He extended his hand as she turned away. "I need to go. I'll see you around." He headed for the glass doors, welcoming the blast of heat as he exited. Spotting the telephone pedestal across the plaza, he sighed.

"Either here or the airport. Get it over with."

Nick dialed the number on his notepad. "Hello? Yes, can you connect me with a detective? I need to report a crime."

<<>>

The room began to glow soft orange. A glimpse of Meraiah with the morning sunlight on her face floated to consciousness and then faded. The luminance intensified, surging to fill the room in blinding white. Batush raised an arm and squinted in fearful wonder. Eyes adjusting, he saw a figure before him burning like the noonday sun. Large and powerful, he held a shimmering sword glinting with a flash of blue. Batush curled to his knees. He then leaned forward with a tilted head, shielding his face.

"Worship me."

"Raphael...?" Light rushed into the spiritual being like water into a thirsty sponge, his body radiating a shimmer of orange and white.

"It is you—Raphael?" Batush rose to a kneeling position.

"Scribe, it is I." The angel lifted the blade in both hands, centered to his lips.

"Have you come to...?"

"I sent Shebaniah. You must find the book—he will help you." The angel smiled, his lips curling at the corners.

"But...? Yes."

A pulse of light then flashed as the angel reared backward. Spinning to crouch, he wielded the sword upward and tight to his shoulder. A high-pitched clash of spark exploded from the blade as the angel arched back with knees bent.

Batush recoiled to the floor, his arms covering his head. For an instant, he heard muffled laughter rushing into the distant darkness.

"Batuuu—sh. Wake... It is me."

His shoulders and back racked with pain, his legs and feet numb and stiff, Batush opened his eyes.

"Shebaniah? The book—Zophar and Sarah. We must find them."

"I will help you. You must dress and collect your things."

"Where are the others?"

"Who?"

"I–I remember... The chamber—there were others with you."

"It was only I. I found you." Shebaniah placed a lamp on a box table and picked up a cup. "Perhaps the others you saw were angels? Here, I have bread and new wine. You need strength—drink."

Batush tugged at the blanket. Lifting his head, he tried to prop himself up, but instead surrendered to the pillow and listened to the patter of rain. A fire was burning on a small stove against the wall. Besides the bed and table, the cramped room was much like his with the same high window and single chair.

"We must leave before sunrise. Did you say Zophar has the book?"

"I saw... an angel. The angel said he sent you to help me."

<<>>

The room was swimming in buzzing white light, the smell of the mozzarella and mushroom making him dizzy. Daniel pushed back in his chair and leaned forward, elbows on his knees with mirrored fingertips together, his head wavered just above the mahogany slab. Ending his fast each day at sundown, he had made an exception for board meetings, when he extended it until arriving home. *Satisfy me with Your grace, Lord.* He lifted his eyes and focused on the two flat boxes with raised lids. Straightening up, he reached for another bottled water.

"Anyone want the last slice? Daniel?" Nick picked it up. Taking a large bite, he pulled the slice away from his mouth as it flopped to the plate, just below his chin. "I don't even know why I'm eating this—I'm stuffed. You would think three slices would be enough, but this is really good. And for once, it's hot."

Again, Daniel lowered his head, fighting the buzzing white light.

Paul picked up the letter. "Thankfully, this is the last one. It's from Ben and Nora." He held it at arm's length, his hand trembling.

Dear Elders,

With deep sadness and yet perfect peace, Nora and I have decided to withdraw our membership from Faith Bible Church. As we have attended and served for thirty-six years, this decision was not made in haste but rather following much prayer and heartache.

Your recent decision to fire Pastor Stover and other beloved staff was the final straw for us. Sadly, the hope we once had for our church has died within our souls, and we can no longer support the decisions you are making.

As you know, we have coordinated the eldercare ministry over the past eighteen years and will now turn it over to you. It is our prayer this ministry will continue as it has a special place in our hearts. Our love for Faith Bible will remain forever with us.

In perfect peace,

Ben and Nora Ballard

Paul placed the letter facedown and then rubbed his cheek. Except for Nick's chewing, the room was silent. Turning his back, Nick dropped the plate into the trash with a swooshing thud.

"The Lord is purging and refining us. He's removing those of little faith."

"The Ballards were—*are*—two of the most faithful people you could ever know." Daniel bit on his thumb knuckle as the others shifted toward him. "We've lost half the church in less than a month, not to mention half the income. We dipped below twenty grand last week, and the reserve account is down to eighty-six thousand." Folding his hands, Daniel glared through the blinding-white light into the darkness across the table—Nick. "What happened to your revelation?"

Nick continued to chew.

"I have a revelation to share. That's what you said. We're not going to lose a single congregant. Do you remember saying that?"

"This is what I'm talking about. One of our own is losing faith in front of our eyes." Nick pointed a greasy finger. "Maybe you should join them, Daniel? Give up and quit." He swallowed and then wiped tomato sauce from his lips with a napkin. "I, for one, am not bound in fear like this man. Where's the faith—it's time to press in with prayer, not fear. The money will be back. Wait and see—I'm right about this."

Paul stoked the air with his plastic hammer. "This isn't productive, and we've got a lot to cover. These letters were the easy stuff." He reached into his satchel and withdrew a manila folder. After pulling a sheet of paper out, he propped it up with his hands on the table. "This is from Pastor Warner. There's two of them." Paul glanced at Nick and then back to the letter. "The other one's from Pastor Ricardo. Both are resignations."

"Resignations?" Henry sat up and slapped the table. "Oh boy. Guys—this is bad. How long before they leave?"

Paul lifted a wavering hand. "They both gave us their two-week notice. The letters were emailed at the same time, which tells us they were likely coordinated. I'm not going to read these, because they're both fairly immature and pretty much say the same thing. They wish us well, but the Lord is calling them to leave. You can be sure they've been sending out résumés—you know how it goes."

"Ho boy..." Henry continued to shake his head. "What are we going to do? I mean, let's face it, guys, we're really in trouble here. Who's going to do the music and preaching? Oh boy—this is not good, not good at all."

Daniel was about to speak when he heard, *"Be still—rest and watch."*

Paul leaned forward. "We'll ask Jenny to lead the music—she's good at that. I don't know why we think we need to pay someone to lead the music anyway. And we'll handle the preaching ourselves. After all, pastors are elders and elders are pastors, right?"

"*Us?* Oh boy..." Henry blew between praying hands and then rubbed them together looking like he had just come in from the cold. He then dropped his face into his open hands, again shaking his head.

"Just those who are gifted and feeling led to do it. Nick is going to teach on Sunday, and I've talked to Amber. She's putting out some feelers and lining up guest speakers. Anyone else want to throw your name in the hat?"

Earl said no as Vince looked up. "I'm willing."

Daniel felt his heart accelerate as the room spun to white again.

"What about you, Lewis, Daniel? Either of you wanna preach?"

Covering his mouth, Lewis shook his head.

Daniel nodded. "Put me down as a maybe. I need to pray about it."

Nick puffed, the hint of a smile tilting his face. "Amber's willing. I talked to her. She's been the keynote speaker at a couple women's conferences, and she's quite good. You can check her out on YouTube. She's eager, and I think we should let her."

A snap from Henry's suspenders interrupted, "She's a smart cookie that girl. We all heard her when she was introduced up front. I mean, let's face it, guys, Amber is *very* sharp."

Paul scribbled. "We'll need to talk about that—but I agree we should let her preach."

<<>>

The cloaked men approached in the gray morning mist. One, short and stocky, was helping the other who walked with a limp.

Shebaniah pivoted to Batush. "You told Zophar to bring it here?"

"What better place to hide a book, than a library full of old books no one reads?" Batush offered a weak smile.

"You are very smart, my friend, but where did he hide it?"

"The top floor. It is dedicated for storage and nearly empty except for a few dusty shelves... and old books."

Shebaniah tipped his head toward the looming structure's high openings, which stared into the thick gray fog. A dog barked as a figure dumped a rubbish bucket in the street.

"You must go alone. I am too weak to climb the steps, and there could be questions. I will wait here. With my hood, I will be a beggar should anyone notice." As his friend shook his head in protest, Batush added, "You will find it in a small box with some other books. It is in a scroll tube marked with the cross of the church."

"Why would there be questions? You said no one would be here."

"Yes, no one, except for the caretaker. Sometimes he comes early for repairs. He lives in the tool hut." Batush pointed with a head nod.

"See? There is no light—he could be in the library."

"What should I say if he is there?"

"You come on church business—sent by the elders to fetch a book. You serve the bishop, do you not?" He nudged Shebaniah's arm.

"I will do as you say, Batush. Wait for me." Shebaniah made his way up the path and steps, then paused at the large doors with a wave before entering.

Batush waited for a full minute before retreating toward Marble Street. Moving quickly, he cinched his hood tight to his chin. The limp was gone.

CHAPTER 50

DANIEL RUBBED his eyes, trying to focus, then put his glasses on. The spreadsheet came into focus. Scrolling down, he checked his selections again reviewing to confirm he had included all applicable trades. He made two changes, opting for larger subcontractors better equipped to handle River Run Crossing. Lastly, he entered percentages to cover overhead and profit, as well as taxes and insurance.

Just over seven and a quarter million. Wow, that's big, but no different from any other job. If You want us to get this, Lord, I ask for Your wisdom and blessing. But if this is not Your will, I ask You to close the door. In either case, I will bless Your name... Amen.

He placed the cursor on his profit number and reduced it by 2 percent. Striking enter, he watched the base-bid number drop. He then rubbed his chin before clicking undo. Hands locked behind his head, he surveyed his one-man office. *You've been preparing me for twenty-six years, but I'm not sure I even want it. I ask again—protect me from this if it's more than I can handle. I trust and surrender all to You.*

He saved the bid form as a PDF and then opened his email and refreshed the page. Several messages downloaded with a chime. He scanned the list, his gaze lingering on a few quotes from subs who had missed his deadline. With a glance at the clock, he decided against any more changes. Typing a short note, he attached his proposal, along with a brochure and résumé. After clicking Send, he again checked the time. *Four weeks of effort with five minutes to spare. It's in Your hands now, Lord.*

He sighed, weak and hungry. Saving the file, he closed his spreadsheet, and then his browser. He was about to close his email when it chimed again. Reading the subject line, he froze. Internal Revenue Service - Appearance Demand.

Junk mail. It's got to be. He drew a slow breath. The heading looked official, correctly listing his company name and corporation, along with his tax EIN number. He swallowed as he opened the message.

Mr. Daniel Fairmont,

By order of the United States Internal Revenue

Service, you are hereby ordered to appear at the tax fraud investigations office, at the below listed time and location. You are further ordered to bring with you all accounting records and tax returns for the past seven years in addition to current records for this calendar year. In the event you are unable to appear at the appointed time, you may contact your investigations officer to reschedule your appointment, providing proof of hardship. In accordance with the United States Tax Code be advised, you may bring an attorney and/or accountant with you for representation. This appointment is preliminary and may be followed by subsequent meetings and notice demands.

Daniel stared at his monitor when it chimed with a second new message.

This cannot be happening. No, Lord, this cannot be. His heart raced as the room began to swirl. Reading the subject line, he was unable to breathe.

Registrar of Contractors - Notice of License Suspension

<<>>

"You have lost the book and the scribe?" Jonness slammed his fist to the table. After rising to stand, he advanced.

Shebaniah dropped to his knees and reached for the bishop's robe. "Your Holiness... Please, have mercy. It was a trick. The scribe, he–he was crafty like a snake. He hid the book in the library. He lied to me. There were too many scrolls—hundreds of them. But I will find it. I swear. Please, I—"

Jonness raised his hand. "How could you be so foolish? Of course, there were many scrolls. It is a library, is it not? I am done with you."

"No, I... Have mercy. You are my salvation—please..."

"You are right about that. But today, your salvation has been taken from you again."

"No, please... I will find it—I promise."

Jonness took a step backward. "No, Shebaniah. I showed you mercy, and you failed. On this day, you and all your family are excommunicated from the church—to the very gates of hell. In this hour, I turn your souls over to Satan himself."

Shebaniah's hand shook as he clung to the robe. Jonness took another step back, ripping his robe away as Shebaniah fell forward, his face to the floor. "Please, Father..."

<<>>

Nick watched his hand float over the soft valley of Amber's waist, rising up and over the curve of her hip. "It's time to strike."

"That sounds so serious. What do you mean?" She shifted, pulling the pillow under her arm.

"For the most part, we've cleaned house. It's time to execute the change strategy."

"I understand the change part—we've talked about that. But what do you mean when you say for the most part?"

"Daniel. He's got to go. He's not on board with anything we're doing. He's self-righteous and thinks he's a prophet or something. Telling us what he's feeling and quoting Scripture at us. And then his dream about the Porsche—the guy is clueless." Nick huffed. "If you want to fix an organization, you've got to make the tough decisions and act."

She stroked his chest with her fingertips. "You're right, of course, and I agree. But do you have a plan?"

"I'm not that devious, but I am confident the Lord will take care of it. After all, even the gates of hell will not prevail against God's church. He'll take care of it, and who knows, maybe He'll use us. The Lord works through His people, you know."

An open smile wet her lips. "What about the money? It's getting serious. The reserves are nearly depleted."

"Woman of little faith—the Lord will provide." His hand continued to float over her body's profile. "Just yesterday, we received a gift of eighteen grand from an anonymous donor."

She sat up, her mouth falling open. "What...? Who was it?"

"I can't tell you. It's confidential—you know that." His face lit with a mischievous grin. "The Lord works in mysterious ways."

Leaning forward, she kissed him softly. "It was you, wasn't it?"

He smiled again. "I'll never tell."

<<>>

Eyes burning, Rhema wiped away tears with the back of her wrist. She had learned the hard way never to touch her eyes when chopping onions, garlic, and jalapeños. Working at the sink over a bamboo cutting board, she swept the last of her veggies into the Dutch oven to the crackle of hot olive oil. It wasn't often she cooked, but when she did, her specialty was chili.

She poofed copper curls from her forehead as she scrubbed her hands. Then stirring the blooming concoction with a wooden spoon, she shook in healthy doses of her signature spices—chili powder and cumin, coriander and marjoram, chipotle powder and two dashes of Mexican oregano. The savory aroma plumed as she added ground beef, again stirring as it browned. Giving it a few minutes, she poured in the stock ingredients, pinto, kidney, and black beans, along with the tomato—sauce, paste, and crushed. Blending now, she blessed her work with pinches of sea salt and a touch of black pepper.

Lifting the spoon to her lips, she slurped it. "Mm, just right." Adjusting the burner for a slow simmer, she covered it with the heavy cast-iron lid. Outside, dusk was pushing back the afternoon sun. She smiled as she thought of Daniel and how he loved to sit at the barstool and watch her cook. The unusual phone call then replayed in her mind as the door from the garage opened and he entered.

"I just got a call from a Detective Green. He wants you to call him." Rhema stood under the can lights in front of the stove, the wooden spoon in her hand. "I wrote his number down next to the phone." When she saw his face, she dropped the spoon. Bending to pick it up, she changed her mind. "Did you finish the proposal? Is everything okay?"

"No, it's not—nothing's okay. Today was a disaster."

Pain stabbing her heart, she wound her arms around his limp body. Then easing back, she took his hands. As she tilted her head to him, he stared through her to the spoon. "And I made it worse. I should have waited to tell you about the call. What happened?"

"I finished the proposal and sent it. Just in time to find out our license was suspended, and we're being audited by the IRS. And now this—the police? I think I'm done with the fast. It's over. I don't even know why I'm doing it—I'm not hearing anything, and I can't even pray. I think I need a drink." He rubbed his temples, still staring at the spoon.

"I'm making chili. Here sit down." She drew up a barstool for him.

In his eyes, she saw something she had never seen before—fear. Taking his hands again, she pulled him close. "I'm sure the detective was just looking for a donation." She bit her lip. Rocking him in her arms, she kissed his forehead.

"This is completely crazy—all in one day?" His voice cracking, he pressed his chin into her shoulder. "I'm going to call him now. Otherwise, I won't be able to sleep."

She let go as he picked up the kitchen phone. He scrolled to recent numbers and punched in the call. Glancing up, he turned his back and walked into the living room. She scooped up the spoon and rinsed it at the sink. Then, drying it on her apron, she followed him.

"Hello. This is Daniel Fairmont returning your call? ... What? You can't be serious. ... I can't imagine. ... I understand. ..."

She froze and then swallowed.

"Tomorrow at nine thirty, yes. ... And I'll look forward to clearing this up. Thank you, Detective."

She stood in the arched opening between the dining and living room. His back still facing her, she felt the weight pressing down. Her fingers coiled around the wooden spoon. With it clenched to her chest in both hands, she hesitated. "What did he say?"

Daniel turned around with shoulders slumped. He drew a hand to his mouth, shaking his head. "Someone filed a complaint. They want me to come in to answer questions." He cocked his head, tears of glass glimmering in his steel-blue eyes. "The complaint is for theft and assault. Sexual assault—against a minor."

"What?" Her head jerked up, her hands gripping the spoon.

"It's not true. Who would...?"

She ran to him then. "Of course, it's not true. It's going to be okay, honey." Again, she held him tight. "We need to pray."

<<>>

The sun was breaking out between the crawling clouds when Batush arrived at the market. Before the coffee shop's closed awning-front, he panted as he scanned the crowded square. *Zophar, where are you?* Stepping over a puddle, he slipped then swung an arm out and gripped the canopy post to steady himself as he tucked his writing case under his other arm. Thick muck, rank with the stench of rotting food and sewage, weighted his shoes.

He wiped stinging sweat from his eyes as he stumbled about, his damp clothes clinging to his frame. *Lead me, Lord.* Then, zigzagging through the crowd, he bumped into an old woman, almost knocking her down. "Please forgive... Rehab, have you seen Zophar?"

The spice trader's leathery face lit with a smile, which transformed into concern. "Batush, you are safe. I heard about your family—everyone is talking. They are looking for you. Come with me."

"Meraiah and Sarah, I must find Zophar." Suddenly faint, he noticed the throbbing pain in his back and legs.

She removed her black shawl, gave it a shake, and then draped it over his head. Taking his arm, she hushed her voice. "I will take you to him. Look down."

Batush grabbed at the shawl, about to tear it away, but two men strode past. Dropping his head, he drew the musty fabric tight to his chin. The younger man with short black curls was scanning the crowd—*Naaman.*

Grasping Rehab's hand, he followed. The ground dimmed as the sun again retreated behind clouds. They hobbled on and then stopped in front of a heavy tarp. She pawed at a seam, which parted between overlapping layers. As they ducked inside, the aroma of dry spices enveloped them. Cinnamon and carob, with clove, sage, and garlic, as fresh and vibrant as a summer day. He pulled the wet shawl over his head.

Warmth embraced him at the sight of Zophar, his hip braced against a table covered with an array of clay jars. Behind him, a brick stove with a metal flue popped with the glow of burning wood.

"Batush." Zophar's teeth glinted in the dancing light as he capped his palms on Batush's shoulders.

"Meraiah and Sarah, have you seen them?"

"I searched the rubble but found only ashes. I sent Gibeon into the hills to search for Meraiah. If she is there, he will find her." Anguish contorted his smile. "Gallus the Nicolaitan has Sarah. I learned this from Shebaniah."

"I know this also—Gallus will exchange her for the book. I have come for the copy. Where is it—I need the book?"

"You must ask Rehab. I told her to hide it, but not to tell me where."

Rehab smiled. "It is here—safe in the rock salt. What better place to hide a scroll, than salt from the Dead Sea? It will last forever." She lifted the lid from a wooden crate filled with pinkish white crystals.

Zophar's arm disappeared through the surface as if passing through water. After withdrawing a scroll tube, he handed it to Batush, and they stood for a moment in silence.

Batush's vision blurred as a wave of despair flooded his frame. "I—I..."

Zophar touched Batush on the chest with two fingers. "You are doing the right thing. You must rescue Sarah. Do not worry about this—the Lord will protect His Word. I will help you. We will find Meraiah and get your Sarah back—I promise."

A toothless smile again parted Rehab's leathery face. "I will help you also because you are a man of God and a friend of my friend."

PART IV

He who has an ear, let him hear what the Spirit says to the churches. To him who overcomes, I will grant to eat of the tree of life which is in the Paradise of God.

Revelation 2:7

CHAPTER 51

THREE FIGURES huddled in the Well of Souls. Time was limited. The space was a chamber of sorts, every surface coated with a thick grayish slime oozing from the crimson walls and convoluted ceiling. Undulating at random intervals, it rotated in one direction or the other, the walls trading places with the ceiling and floor and then back again as the pooling goo found the shifting floor like a slow-moving mudslide.

Familiar sounds surrounded them, like the eyes of peering animals lurking in a dense forest. The ever-present wind, rushing in and then out again, overlapping with the rhythmic pounding of the drums. Boo–boom...Boo–boom...Boo–boom, interrupted by random gurgling quakes that varied in volume and intensity.

Asmodeus pondered the irony. *We dwell within the flesh of those we seek to kill and destroy, and yet we need them so desperately for shelter and the execution of operations. Truly, it is a mystery....*

Mammon and Longshanks waited with heads bowed. Asmodeus stood motionless with hands drawn to his face, his clawed fingertips just touching. "We have the advantage and hold the territory we came for."

Mammon's yellow eyes narrowed. "But what of Daniel? With each day, he grows stronger."

Longshanks elbowed closer. "And the scribe also—he has escaped and may soon have the book?"

Asmodeus lifted his pointer finger to pick at his jaw. "They both stand alone and will easily be destroyed. Who, I ask, is there to help them? The scribe we can easily kill. And Daniel is now isolated. We will soon take all that he has." Asmodeus spread his hands, splaying his talons patient to grasp all he could. "Certainly no one can stop us." Moving in unison, the three demons slogged in the same direction as a wall transitioned to floor with a rumbling gurgle.

Longshanks smiled, his hand resting on the handle on his beloved weapon. "What of Raphael? He contends with us and has defeated you—er, uh, he has defeated us—before?"

Asmodeus struck him with a sharp glance, thrusting his finger into the demon's chest. "I will destroy Raphael—mark my words." He cocked his head as the speed of the wind and drums began to wane. "It is time. Go now—back to your posts."

<<>>

Considering yesterday's events, Daniel was holding up fairly well, that is, until he saw the man in the corridor walking toward him. The floor surface hard and the two-by-four fluorescents harsh, his heartbeat accelerated. The man wore a badge attached to his belt and a shoulder-holstered pistol strapped to his chest—*the police*. The door placard read Investigations Division. Daniel drew a choppy breath and then entered.

Sitting in the small room on a metal chair before the rectangular table with folding legs, he thought of his doctor's exam room. Except for the black window and the video camera mounted on a tripod, this was similar. Two men with badges and weapons, like those of the man in the corridor, entered and sat across from him on chairs matching his. The older one clung to a black coffee mug, his eyes tired and posture slumped. The younger man offered a friendly smile. Following introductions, Detective Green placed a recorder on the table.

"Have you ever been accused of a sex crime before, Mr. Fairmont?" He lifted his finger from the recording device, nodding to the older detective.

"No... never." Daniel made eye contact with both of them. He swallowed. "This is totally out of the blue—I can't believe this."

"Try to relax. We're required to ask these questions."

"Who filed the complaint? Can you tell me?"

"There were two complaints. The first was a phone message. Left on the tip line, it was anonymous. The second was filed online from the child's mother. She said she worked for you and was afraid to come forward because she was undocumented."

"That's ridiculous. I've never employed illegals—I mean, undocumented workers. We rarely hire laborers, and when we do, we always use E-Verify. Ninety percent of our work is done through subcontractors, and we require they certify all of their labor is legal—I mean, documented."

The detectives exchanged a glance. "Did you provide construction services on a restaurant called..." Detective Green shuffled his notes.

"Tea Light Café?"

"Yes. We just completed it."

"Can you give us contact information for that project?"

"Yes—sure. It's owned by Raymond Yee. I can give you his phone number. I have it here in my phone."

"That's okay. We'll check it out. Did you steal money from Mr. Yee?"

The question struck him like a punch in the back. Daniel's jaw quivered, his mouth hanging open. "No—I certainly did not." He swallowed again.

"Did you employ undocumented workers on that project?"

"No."

"Did you fail to pay any of your subcontractors on that project, Mr. Fairmont?"

"No. Everyone's been paid in full. We have the C-of-O from the architect, and Lien Releases from all of our subs. You can ask Mr. Yee."

"We will."

"Have you ever received complaints or notices from the Registrar of Contractors or the IRS?"

He exhaled. Below the table, he clenched folded hands. "Last week. On the same day—I received notices from both agencies by email."

Again, the detectives' eyes briefly met.

"Go on..."

Relax, slow down—breathe. His heart pounding, he felt a pinching ache behind his ears that he wanted to rub. "The IRS instructed me to bring in my tax records for the last seven years. I also received a Notice of License Suspension from the Registrar. I will be meeting with them next week." *Help me, Lord.* "This looks really bad, I understand. But someone is doing this to me. None of this is true, and I'm sure you hear that from lots of people, but..."

"You're right, we do hear that a lot. We'll be checking into the allegations, and we'll also be coordinating with the IRS and the Registrar." Detective Green turned the recorder off and then opened a folder. Removing a photo, he laid it on the table.

The older detective exhaled, cocking his head. His jaw tightened, and his hand reached forward, stopped, and then withdrew as he folded his arms.

"We're just about done, but before you leave, I have one more question. This is unrelated to our discussion today, but I'd like you to look at this image and tell me if you've ever seen this individual?"

The face was striking, powerful and somewhat mysterious. *Photoshopped...?* Daniel leaned forward, his breathing and heartbeat calming. "No. I'm sure I would remember."

"Mr. Fairmont." The older detective rose to his feet. "We're done here. With regard to the accusations..." He tilted his head to Detective Green and then looked back. "If you're telling us the truth, you've got nothing to worry about. We're required to investigate because of the assault allegation.... I'm sure you understand. We'll get back to you. And thanks again for coming in."

Unsure of what to say, Daniel stood.

<<>>

Alone in her office, the phone to her ear, Amber sat up straight. "What do you mean—the Spirit told you? This is my job, Richard. I'm the executive pastor here, and you're my husband. You can't do this."

"Honey, I'm sorry." He spoke gently and then paused. It was quiet. "This is the last thing I would want to do—to any church and especially to our new church. I don't want to—I mean it." Outside the lazy drone of a propeller-driven airplane dusted the sky.

Asmodeus barked, *"This is ridiculous. He's upset because you've been gone. This is about him wanting to control you. It's always been all about him."*

Her elbow on the desk, she rubbed her forehead with two fingers between her eyes. "I think you're upset because I've been away for a while—and I don't blame you—but I don't understand. Can you tell me why?"

"I got The Wake-Up Call... at three a.m., like usual, Amby. I was in your closet, and... there were angels. I know how this sounds. The Lord spoke—it was so clear. I don't expect you to understand. It's obedience, simple obedience. I don't have a choice. I need to come."

"This is insanity. He can't do this to you."

"What are you planning to do? Just wheel yourself down the aisle on Sunday morning and rebuke the church? Make a fool out of me— your wife? And what exactly are you going to say? Hi, I'm your new pastor's husband, and the angels told me to tell you to get on your knees and repent—because you're a bunch of sinners?" Her heart racing, she couldn't still her trembling hands.

"I don't know what I'm going to say. It's better that way. I know what the message is—I got it a long time ago, you remember. I guess I'm not planning on anything really. I'm going to pray and ask the Spirit to open my mouth and speak His Words."

"This is ridiculous. You're trying to control me like you always do. You want me to quit and come home, and this is your twisted idea of how to get your way."

"He's trying to crush you, but it's not going to work."

"You're trying to crush me, but this is not going to work, Richard. If you do this, I'll–I'll leave you, and I mean that." She brushed her hair back, sweeping a tear from her cheek. Outside the window, two sparrows on a tree branch preened one another. One hopped away with the other following, then both took flight in opposite directions.

"I'm sorry. I don't have a choice.... I love you, Amby."

"He's lying. He doesn't love you. He just wants to hurt you."

She pulled the phone away from her ear. Staring at it, she hung up.

<<>>

Zophar knocked on the header beam of a mud house.

"In whose name do you come?" Long dark hair shrouded the woman's face while her silk gown coated her body like liquid metal. Bracelets bangled on her forearms, extending from wrist to elbow. Smiling with half-open eyes, she tugged her translucent veil toward her tattooed neck.

"I come in the name of Batush the Scribe. I am a friend, seeking a meeting with Gallus the Nicolaitan."

A male voice spoke from inside, "Coffee Trader, I have been waiting for you—come in."

The woman slouched against the doorjamb. Rolling her head to the side, she splayed her leg as Zophar turned sideways to pass, her knee grazing his thigh.

The thick smell of perfumed opium enveloped him in the dark room. Gallus sat cross-legged on a floor mat covered with an array of brightly colored pillows. Wearing only a loincloth, he knelt over a brass censer pot on a three-legged cradle. His face immersed in the flared opening as curling smoke rose from his head.

He drew a choppy breath and lurched upright. Then, choking back a short cough, he held his breath and opened bloodshot eyes. Waving a hand for Zophar to sit, he exhaled and then gasped breath as he swung at greasy brown tendrils. He coughed. "I am Gallus, bishop of the Nicolaitans. Do you have the book?"

"Do you have the child?" Zophar loomed over the mat.

Hovering at his side, the woman tilted her head, reached up, and touched his arm before jerking it back. "You're hot. Ar—are you a god?"

"Yes, I am." Laughing at his wit, Gallus then composed himself. "Come, Coffee Trader—sit. Yes, I have the child. Do you have the book?"

"Where is the child?"

"She is here with me. She is safe. Must I ask a third time...?"

"The book is safe. It is with Batush the Scribe."

"And where is this scribe—this Batush?"

~~

Washed in a beam of filtered sunlight, Batush stepped through the corbeled opening. "I am here." He held the wooden scroll tube in both hands.

Zophar stared at the barricaded door on the other side of the room. He then turned to Gallus. "Open the door."

Gallus lifted a hand. "No. The book first... Show it to me."

Batush drew the scroll tube to his chest. "No. My child first. Show her to us."

Gallus waved a sweeping hand, nodding to the woman, who crossed to the closet. When she raised the plank from iron post hooks, the door slowly opened. Sarah lay against a bag of seed with eyes closed, her ankle bound with a rope staked to the floor.

"Sarah." Batush lunged forward as the woman spun to crouch in front of the door, a crescent bladed knife in her hand.

Zophar reached out, grabbing Batush.

"Pa—Papa... I—I'm here. Pa..." Sarah's eyes remained closed.

Gallus laughed. "I told you she is safe. Now give me the book, and you can have the little one. Surely, you do not think I'd harm her?"

Batush spun toward Gallus. "I will kill you—if you..."

"*You* will kill me? It seems you are not as pure in spirit as I was told." A tapestry drape parted next to the closet. Two men stepped forth. Another two entered from behind. All four brandished weapons.

"Here it is. Let her go." Batush extended the tube toward Gallus.

"Show it to me." Gallus lowered his scarred face into the smoldering pot as Batush opened the tube and unrolled the parchment. Lifting his head, Gallus stared, disbelief assaulting his features. He stood and girded himself with a towel. He then staggered forward, one finger thrusting. "Do you think me a fool? I seek the ancient writing of John the Apostle. This—this book..." His face contorted. "Its ink is not even dry."

"It is an exact copy. I made it myself—please. My child...?"

"There is no power in this—this piece of rolled parchment. Where is the original?"

Jonness and the flames flashed through Batush's mind. The Apostle's scroll, falling from the bishop's fingers, and then the forged papyrus. "I–I... It is in the hands of Bishop Jonness—at the church."

"Do not call that viper bishop. I am the bishop of Ephesus and the Nicolaitans, the true church—the church of salvation and sacred knowledge." Gallus grabbed the scroll from Batush.

"Yes—yes, I can get it." Batush glanced at Sarah and then Zophar, not realizing Zophar's hand was on his shoulder.

"I will keep this for now—this, parchment." Gallus held it between two fingers. Then quickly rolling it, he stuffed it into the tube. "I will give this to you—along with the child—*when* you bring me the real book. You will do this, Batush, and do it swiftly because, as you can see, the child is not well. If you do not bring it to me, I will kill your child with my bare hands." He pointed. "I give you three days."

<<>>

Daniel felt like he was drowning in white light when the passage came to him:

Now there was a famine in the days of King David for three years, year after year... and David sought the presence of the LORD. And the LORD said, It is for Saul and his bloody house...

Opening his eyes, he tried to focus.

"So what do you think, Daniel?"

He glanced around the table, seeing them staring.

"Can you repeat the question? I'm sorry—I'm a little distracted."

"Butts in the seats... The money's holding up, but we're hemorrhaging people. We're down almost sixty percent. About a thousand—what do we do?"

"Confession..." He stared at the table.

Nick interrupted, "Confession? What are you talking about?"

"I've got something I need to share." Daniel's heart accelerated. "I had a really difficult week, and..."

Paul released an exhaling sigh. "Okay, Daniel, let's forget about the agenda. Why don't you tell us about your really difficult week?"

"I'm sorry... I'm thinking I may need to resign." A wave of peace washed over him.

"What's going on?"

The room was quiet.

Daniel scanned the table, stopping when he got to Amber. "I've been working on a proposal—I mentioned it, River Run Crossing? The retail center. Anyway, I finished it and submitted. As a matter of fact, I was short-listed."

Two of the men responded with a nod.

"But it doesn't matter because I had to withdraw my bid." His eyes moved to Nick. "Because three really bad things happened—all on the same day—right after I sent the proposal.

"First, I received a notice from the IRS, that I'm being audited because of an anonymous complaint. Then the Registrar of Contractors informed me my license was suspended because of a second complaint. I don't know what the accusations are because I haven't met with either of them yet." He held his gaze on Nick, who turned away. "And then I went home and found out I had received a call from the police."

When Paul glanced at Nick, Daniel waited for them to look back. "The next day, I met with Detective Green, the guy who met with Nick and Amber after Karen died. Anyway, there were two of them. And they told me I'm being investigated because of a third anonymous complaint—this one accusing me of hiring undocumented workers and not paying them. But that's not the worst of it." He swallowed. "They said they were required to open the investigation because there was an accusation—I had also committed a sexual assault. Against a minor."

Henry slapped the table. "That's unbelievable, guys. This must be an attack of the enemy, if you know what I'm saying here." His eyes and mouth hung open.

Paul shifted in his chair and cleared his throat. "That does sound unbelievable. All of this happened in one day?" Eyes downcast, he massaged his goatee.

"Yeah. And none of it's true—I promise you. Someone's attacking me. I don't understand it, and I don't know why."

Nick's eyes expanded as he leaned back. "Likely, it's one of your competitors. You mentioned it was a big job. I've heard contractors operate like that a lot."

Daniel puffed a half laugh, shaking his head. "I'm thinking I need to resign, regardless of where this goes. We're supposed to be above reproach—if something is said against any of us that could damage the church, we can't be here. I don't think there's any question really. I don't have a choice."

Henry patted the table with his palm. "Whew, this is big—really big. I mean, what do we do here, guys? This is serious—I mean, let's face it, a charge of sexual assault, by an elder? We need to defend our brother here, guys. This isn't right."

"...*Confession*..." Daniel heard it again, whispered into his mind.

"Confession."

The group gawked in confusion.

"To your question—about butts in the seats?"

Paul shook his head as Daniel opened his hands.

"We need to humble ourselves before the Lord and the people. I guess, what I'm facing is helping me see it. We've made a mess of things—we've hurt the church and lost more than half the congregation. A lot of peace comes with confession and getting something off your chest. I'm feeling it right now, even though none of what's been said about me is even true. We need to get on our knees and confess we've blown it."

Nick tapped his chin with his fist and then threw out his open hand. "Here we go again. Daniel's telling us to confess? When he's the one up to his eyeballs in—well... What I'm hearing is Daniel's the one who needs to confess."

Paul interrupted, "Whoa, hold on there. So far, it's just accusations. Henry's right—this sounds like a spiritual attack. But Daniel's got a point about resigning because of how it looks."

Vince had not yet opened his laptop. A folded arm across his stomach supported the weight of his other arm—bent at the elbow with hand lifted. He tugged on his chin. "We need to keep this quiet and wait to see what happens with the investigations. It could take some time, especially with the government involved, but..."

"What are you saying?" Paul squeezed his plastic hammer.

"Maybe Daniel should take a sabbatical? Step away from the board and his elder duties but retain the position. If anyone asks questions, we would tell them Daniel's taking a break. After all, who of us doesn't need a break from this?"

"What if it gets out?" Amber brushed hair away from her face as everyone turned. "This kind of stuff always gets out. We'll need a prepared response."

Folded hands against his stomach, Nick spread his fingers. "If it gets out, we tell the truth. There are accusations against Daniel, and he's taking a break until it's cleared up. We don't say what the accusations are, and if someone asks, we tell them to talk to the person who talked to them. Talking behind someone's back is gossip, and that's sin."

Paul glanced at the schoolroom clock. "What do you say, Daniel? Do you want to take a sabbatical until this clears up?"

"I'll let you guys decide. Pray about it... and then take a vote."

"Sounds good to me. What do you guys think?"

The group nodded agreement. Except for Nick, who stared into space.

Paul gave the table a tap with his hammer. "We'll meet next week. Daniel will recuse himself from the discussion, and we'll take a vote."

CHAPTER 52

OUTSIDE THE RAINS had returned in a torrent, pounding like stampeding horses on the zinc onion-dome. Beneath, the crescent table of hammered slab-quartz shimmered in the flickering torchlight, lapping at the faces of the assembled elders—cold and white.

Seeing commotion at the corbeled entry, Jonness rose. He then commanded, "Seize him."

Two guards spun to the man as he entered. Dripping wet, Batush raised his thin arms as they grabbed him.

"Bring him here." Jonness pointed at the empty chair below the dome. He then swept a hand toward his elders. "Batush, I see you are surrendering. For your sake, I hope you brought your copy of the book. If you have not, you will yearn for the days you spent in the pit." He closed his mouth—*how long was it hanging open?* He wiped drool from his chin with the sleeve of his white robe.

Asmodeus whispered. *"He shows no fear. He humiliates you."*

"Do you not fear us?"

Batush closed his eyes. "My fear is in the Lord."

"You come before your elders and blaspheme?" Jonness slammed his flat hand to the table, his cross swinging on his neck.

"I can give you what you want—the copy." Batush opened his eyes.

"Do you have it?"

"It is held by Gallus the Nicolaitan. He has my grandchild. Gallus will exchange both for the original scroll only."

"Give the grave robber what he wants. We will get the copy, and Gallus will get what he deserves."

"And if I give him this book. This book of blasphemy entombed by our Fathers and revealed to you by a demon." Jonness opened his winged arms, bowing to his left and right, and then locking eyes on Batush. "This book that tells the truth about the Nicolaitans and their leader." Jonness paced behind the crescent table.

Agabus lifted his hand. "But, Your Holiness, if we..."

"Silence!" Jonness whirled toward him, stabbing with clawed fingers.

"Give the fool what he wants, and the copy will be ours to burn."

"Gallus the Nicolaitan is a fool. He is not educated—he cannot even read. He does not know this book tells the truth about who he is. It will serve him right."

Batush opened his hands, palms raised. "Tomorrow night—at the library. Gallus will meet you there with his elders. He will bring the copy and my child." He struggled to swallow. "You will have the copy. Gallus will get the original. And my grandchild will be free."

They stared at each other for a long moment.

"The scribe must die—tell him yes."

"I will give you what you want. The child will go free in exchange for you. Your elders placed you under discipline, and you dishonored us by running away. You have not yet paid for your sins."

"The child will be set free?"

Jonness lingered.

"He will soon be in hell. Tell him what he wants to hear."

"Yes, Batush. The child will be free." Jonness glanced at Agabus, who nodded. "We will take the scribe with us. Do not let him out of your sight."

One of the guardians placed a rope around Batush's neck, jerking him forward. Stumbling, Batush looked to the back of the room as the other guard shoved him from behind. Jonness then saw him, framed in the arched opening, the ever-present burly man—Zophar the Coffee Trader.

Jonness was about to shout when Asmodeus stopped him. *"He is a harmless Watcher. He cannot stop us now."*

<<>>

The green Up button chimed when he pushed it. The doors lurched. Trying to open, they began to jitterbug. Turning sideways, Richard tugged at the half-open door. The effort merely rotated his wheelchair in a semicircle. A door swooshed at the top of the stair and then banged into the wall.

"Hello? Is someone there?" A light came on, followed by footsteps. "Daniel, is that you? Wow, it's been a long time."

"I was wondering when you'd be out to see us. Amber didn't mention you were coming. Does she know you're here?"

"It's sort of a surprise. I talked to Paul Chambers—he knows."

Daniel eyed the trembling door and then laughed. "I'm surprised it even moved. I don't think anyone's tried to use this thing in years." He punched the green button with his flat hand. The button flickered as the door continued to splutter. When he struck it again, the door began to crawl. "Is your phone charged? I'm just asking because mine's low on juice and we could be stuck for a while."

They laughed as Daniel again tried the Up button. The cab light blinked, and the doors glided shut like a runner in slow motion sliding for home.

"Now we're talking. Looks like you've got the touch." The hydraulic motor whirred from below as the cab rose, bouncing to stop at the second floor. The door again quivering, Daniel helped it with a lunging push.

"Amber and the guys are in the conference room. I was out here when I heard you downstairs." He motioned to the tired blue couch outside the closed double doors.

"They give you a 'time-out'?"

"Funny. Executive session—they're voting on my fate. Whether or not I stay on the board."

Richard leaned forward, dropping his voice. "Amber said you were struggling a bit. So how's it going, if you don't mind me asking, with the guys?"

"This is crazy, Richard. You and me—we haven't talked in years, and it's like we're picking up where we left off. You playing baseball, and the two of us hanging out and talking about almost everything. And then you, well, you remember—you stole Amber from me. But nothing ever came between us."

"That's because we're friends." Richard shrugged. "It's supposed to be that way. So tell me, how's it going with you being an elder?"

Daniel flexed his hands. "It's been hard, I guess, but also, really good. I hadn't really thought about it, but I guess I would say it's probably the hardest thing I've ever done, but also the best thing."

He eased into the cushions. "The Lord has been growing me in ways I wasn't expecting. I've tried to be honest about what I believe I'm hearing from the Lord and what I believe is right."

As Daniel looked up, tears shone in his eyes. "I've been the lone voice against some things we're doing. That's the hard part because it doesn't go over so good. But I say what's on my heart, and I'm sleeping like a baby."

"That's good, Daniel. That's what you should be doing—all of you." Richard slapped Daniel's knee. "I'm wondering if we might be on the same page with what we're hearing and maybe that's why I'm here tonight."

Daniel sat up, lifting his brows. "What do you mean?"

Richard studied his friend's accepting eyes. Daniel would understand and not judge him. But the others beyond the double doors—including Amber—he sensed they wouldn't be as receptive. Drawing a deep breath, he blew it out. "The Lord woke me up three years ago and gave me a word. It was a message for the church—only I thought it was for my church, not yours." Bobbing his head, he smiled. "I'm not sure how it's going to go over, but I'm here to speak it because the Lord told me to."

"Have you told Amber about this?"

"She knows and didn't want me to come. In fact... well, it doesn't really matter. I've got to speak it."

The door opened, and Paul stepped out. "I see you found a friend, Daniel. Come on in. We're ready for the both of you."

<<>>

Asmodeus whispered to Jonness. *"Place your hand on his shoulder."*

They sat alone in the council chamber, speaking in hushed tones. "It must not be known by the others—do you understand?"

Agabus nodded. "Yes, my Holiness. I know a man who can do this."

"How soon can it be arranged?"

"I cannot know until I speak with him."

Asmodeus blurted, *"Tomorrow night, at the library."*

Jonness slid his hand across the elder's shoulder, touching his neck. "Tomorrow night. At the library—he must do it then."

Asmodeus moved quickly from Jonness to Agabus.

Agabus leaned away, his eyes and mouth opening wide. "Tomorrow, yes. Tomorrow night at—at the library."

<<>>

Amber stood with the others, forcing a smile as Daniel and Richard entered. *He came. He actually came.*

"They're watching—go to him."

"Wow. I wasn't expecting this—what a surprise. I'm sorry, but I haven't seen my husband in a month." She bent to hug Richard, kissing his cheek. "We'll catch up later." Still smiling, she avoided looking at Nick.

Paul slid his chair away from the table and gestured Richard into his spot. "We have two more items of business. Richard asked if he could speak with us. He's come straight from the airport and hasn't even seen Amber until just now. So, I want to let him share, and then let him take his wife home. I'm sure they would love to spend their evening discussing business with all of us, but I'm not going to allow it."

The group laughed as they settled into their chairs.

Her mind racing, Amber struggled not to set her jaw or clench her fists. *Richard—here, after what I told him? Stay cool, relax—breathe.*

"I want to start by thanking you for allowing me to address you tonight. Especially on such short notice, not even knowing what I have to say. It's humbling."

Her face flushed. *Easy now...*

"This is difficult, sharing what I have for you. In fact, I'm not even sure of the message's full meaning."

Looks of awkward discomfort dulled the expressions around the table.

"I'm not sure of your position on prophecy, but I'm not a prophet. I'm just a messenger, and the meaning of what I'm about to share is between you and God. I've come in obedience to speak a message I received three years ago. The Lord woke me up and spoke it to me—it was crystal clear. In fact, I could actually see the words, like text printed on a page. Anyway, I wrote it down and put it in my Bible. And I've been carrying it with me. The Lord told me to wait, saying He would tell me when to speak it. All along, I thought it was for my church, but then two nights ago, the Lord told me to speak it to you."

Paul cleared his throat. "Well, Richard, we could sure use some words of encouragement. I'm sure you know we've been struggling, so I'm anxious to hear what you have for us."

She forced a smile, lowering her head as a couple of the men chuckled.

Richard opened his Bible and removed a folded sheet of yellow paper. *All this time, he's been saving that wretched scrap to use against me? If I'd only known, I never would have let it come to this—I would've stopped him.*

Silence fell over the room as he unfolded the worn note and a pair of reading glasses, glancing to her as he put them on.

She didn't need to hear it—she'd heard him describe it over and over, the words he'd claimed were spoken from God. Leaning back, she closed her eyes, as he read the message:

"'I WILL WITHDRAW MY SPIRIT FROM YOU. YOU REAP WHAT YOU SOW. THEREFORE, SOW TO THE SPIRIT AND NOT TO WORLDLY WISDOM.'"

"This is outrageous. He has the nerve to undercut your authority?"

Face hot, eyes tearing up, a scream building in her chest, she spoke slowly. "I am very sorry, gentlemen. My husband should have spoken to me about this ahead of time. I–I'm sorry, but I will need to leave."

Nick stood, taking a step toward her. "I should walk you down."

Paul placed his hand on the arm of Richard's wheelchair, speaking gently. "Thank you, Richard. We appreciate you sharing with us, but you should join your wife. Nick will walk you both down."

<<>>

Agabus sipped the hot drink with cupped hands, the strong brew offering a comforting contrast to the heavy morning fog. All around him, the incessant coughing and cries of children were thankfully muffled, as also the ghastly sights were shrouded. However, the lingering stench of death—inescapable. He held the clay cup close to his nose.

A lanky figure, hooded with a wispy white beard, approached. Hunched over, he clutched a tall walking staff and struggled against a slight limp.

"Agabus...?"

"Polonosis, please join me."

Gibeon appeared with a tray. "May I serve you?"

"Another boiled coffee for my friend." Agabus waited until the server left. "Again, we find ourselves in need of your expertise."

Raising his unruly white brows, Polonosis pulled his hood back. "And how can I be of help to the Church Fathers?"

"A certain scribe has blasphemed the holy church, committing crimes of desecration and grave robbery. Because he is a church scribe, it is, well, we find it difficult to execute the appropriate discipline this man requires."

Gibeon placed a steaming cup on the table.

Picking it up with a nod, Polonosis drew a sip. "The simple

pleasures of this short life are the finest—do you not agree?" When Agabus did not respond, Polonosis tipped his cup. "And what appropriate discipline is needed for this certain scribe?"

Hands wrapped around his cup, Agabus bent close and hissed a single word: "Death."

Polonosis smiled. "How is it I knew you were going to say that?"

Again, Agabus did not reply.

"And how soon will this service be needed?"

"Can you arrange to seize him tonight—at the library?"

"Tonight? This is too much—even for me. Do you think it an easy thing to organize a mob on such short notice? More time is needed." Polonosis drew another sip, the smile gone from his gaunt face.

"His Holiness demands this tonight."

It was quiet except for the muffled coughing of a man in the distance who began to choke. A woman's desperate scream followed.

Asmodeus whispered, *"The scribe has a plasmos demon. Touch him. Touch him now."*

Agabus leaned forward, his hand floating to the man's shoulder. "Did you not hear the cry? Another has passed as we sit here now. Will this plague never leave us? Some are wondering if this fog of death is the fault of a man or a demon—or possibly both."

Asmodeus moved quickly, surging from one body to the next.

<<>>

When Nick opened the door, Paul Chambers was tapping the table with his annoying hammer. Easing into his seat, Nick gave his head a shake and exhaled. "Wow... That was strange. I'm not going to challenge the guy's doctrine—and I'm sure he's sincere. But calling himself a prophet and coming in here and schooling us? He doesn't know anything about us. Or this church. I'm sorry, but that was out of line."

Leaning forward with elbows on the table, Daniel pointed. "He didn't say he was a prophet. In fact, he was very clear in saying he's not a prophet. Richard Lash is married to our executive minister, and he's also an old friend, so he does know a few things about us. He said he didn't want to speak the message, but he did it in obedience. I accept that."

Right, he accepts anything against us. Nick puffed a laugh. "There you go again, throwing a wrench into the gears. I'm going to tell you something you don't know, Daniel. Just now, in the parking lot, Richard said he has no idea who the prophecy is for. I say it's got no value at all if he doesn't even know if it's for us."

Vince and Lewis nodded as Earl twisted his gold bracelet. Then leaning back, Earl folded his arms across his belly and dropped his chin. "As I was listening to that man speak, his message wasn't resonating in my spirit. That's all I'm going to say."

Daniel shook his head in disbelief. "Why would the Lord tell him to speak it to us if it's not for us? That makes absolutely no sense."

Paul laid his hammer on the table. "Good question, Daniel, but Nick is making sense. And I agree it was a little weird and also uncomfortable. So we're going to drop it for now. Let's be praying about it, asking the Lord for clarity."

Flapping his agenda like a newspaper, Paul then placed it on the table facedown. "Okay, Daniel, we need to talk about you now. We discussed your situation and then voted. It wasn't unanimous, and we had more than one vote, on both sides." He rotated the agenda with one hand like a ticking clock.

"So—can you tell me what the motion was?"

"Sure, I'll read it. It was moved—Daniel will remain on the elder board. However, he will attend no meetings nor execute any elder duties unless reinstated by a future vote of the board. Said duties shall include serving communion, interim preaching as scheduled, and execution of his duties as treasurer... Nick would take over as treasurer."

"So which direction did it go? Am I in or out—on sabbatical or whatever?"

"It was a tie."

"Did everyone vote?"

"Yes—all of us—including Amber, we called her. I decided to let her vote, considering her position and relationship with the board."

"Which way would it have gone without her vote?" Daniel smiled.

"Um, well, actually..."

Nick clenched his jaw. *What a sanctimonious jerk.*

"Without Amber, the vote was for you to stay on. Anyway, we decided, since it ended up as a tie—"

Henry blurted, "What about the second vote?"

Paul glared at Henry. "There was a second motion... Which was to let you decide."

"And how did that one go?" Daniel lifted his brows.

Nick fired a glance at Paul, his stomach churning.

Paul squeezed his hammer. Tilting his head, he pursed a smile. "It passed."

CHAPTER 53

TROY HORSEMAN stepped out of the elevator into the sweeping space. Besides the built-out core, it was an open shell with a concrete floor, grid ceiling, and glass curtain walls. He walked toward the knee-height stack of gypsum board. Serving as a bench, the room's single furnishing stood in the far corner next to the stair tower. On the lake below, four longboats, each with a crew of eight, plus the coxswain, trained for competition.

Glancing back toward the elevators, he dialed the first of four calls. "It's me. I'm between meetings and only have a minute.... Yes, it's going to be huge. No one's talking, but it's going down on Thursday.... I'm trying but can't promise anything.... But it's ninety-nine percent.... Absolutely, I'll try..."

He watched the boats. "Yes, I'm all in, and I mean *all*. I went to cash last week, and I'm maxing out my margin. I also pulled every penny from my house and cabin equity lines.... I'm not going to tell you what to do, but that's what I'm saying—everything...."

Again, he turned to the elevators. "Just my brother and you—that's it. The FDA will be calling at nine a.m. We'll all be there—the entire team, in the conference room. The announcement follows. It's simultaneous.... I'm trying to confirm, but I'm absolutely sure on this—it's happening.... Okay—you too, thanks."

Troy hung up, turning again to watch the longboats. Exhaling, he scrolled through his contact list, located the number, and tapped Send. "Nick, it's me. I need to be quick."

<<>>

Fog enveloped the roundabout at the intersection of Marble Road and Curetes Street. Elevated with three steps, it was a common gathering place for the public display of criminal punishment, most typically by flogging or time served in stocks. Government officials also used it for the reading of legal decrees and public announcements. Additionally, the podium, as it had come to be known, was used by slave traders for the auction of their human cargo on the first day of each month.

Polonosis stood under a cypress canopy. Steady and slow, the

Ephesians slogged homeward after a long day's work. A woman dressed in black stood at his side, cradling a small bundle. Turning to her, he lifted his oil lamp, reached in, and pulled the blanket back to expose the lifeless child's ashen face, eyes closed, tiny mouth open.

"It is time."

Taking the woman's hand, he guided her forward and crossed the road to climb the steps. Five torch stands guarded the podium's perimeter. He lit the torches and swept his hood back. Cold mist stung his face. He elbowed the woman who began to wail.

"*Nooooo!* Please, God—no. Why, God—why?" She clutched the bundle to her chest.

"Citizens—look." Polonosis proclaimed, "I have something to show you."

The crowd grew as the wailing subsided to waves of sobbing, rising and falling.

When he took the bundle in his arms, the woman fell to her knees and clung to his leg moaning. "Look at this. All of you—look." He thrust the limp body above his head as the blanket fell away. "My grandchild—my *only* grandchild—taken from me."

The woman began to wail again as the crowd groaned.

"How many more will be lost before we act...?"

Silence fell over the assembly while the woman whimpered.

Polonosis fanned an arm. "This fog of death we face is a plasmos demon. It creeps along the ground, day after day and night after night. With each breath, this demon sucks the life from us. My grandchild just hours ago... And how many more will die tonight?"

A man shouted, "My father died two days ago, and my wife is failing!"

A murmur rose, followed by a woman's cry somewhere in the crowd, "My baby is sick also. She cannot stop coughing."

A man in at the podium's base spoke next. "Many have died, but what can be done? Is one to strike at the fog with a stick?"

The rumbling continued as men turned to one another, nodding.

Asmodeus barked, *"The grave robber. He has caused all of this."*

Polonosis handed the dead child back to the woman. "This man speaks truth. We cannot strike the fog, but the demon can be stopped."

Several shouted, "How? Tell us. Yes, tell us. How can it be

stopped?"

"The plasmos is in a man—a grave robber who angers the gods. This man desecrated the tomb of Celsus, the hated governor. The demon rose up from the crypt, entering the thief. The desecrator breathes his demon from his mouth to all of us—look, it is everywhere. This man has killed my child and others, and he will kill many more."

"Who has this demon? Tell us, who is this man—who?" A large man rushed up the steps, grabbing a torch. "This man with the demon must be stopped. He must be killed."

And the crowd shouted agreement.

Polonosis raised his hands. Savoring chaos so easily created, he waited for them to quiet. "He is a scribe. The Scribe Batush has the plasmos demon."

"Find him... The scribe must die—kill him."

Night was falling as the podium filled with angry men, seizing the torches. The flames lashed out at the misty fog.

Asmodeus whispered, *"Send them before they turn on us."*

His hands upheld again, Polonosis shouted, "Listen to me. The scribe is in the library."

"To the library... Kill him—the scribe, kill Batush."

<<>>

Amber stood in the kitchen, a brandy snifter in her hand. The elevator chimed. Raking her hair back, she drew a sip. *Richard or Nick?*

She exhaled. Taking another sip, she tapped the intercom, which lit with an overhead view of the lobby. The screen displayed her thin husband in his wheelchair, looking up.

Damn... She bit her lip.

"Get it over with—end it. You've been patient for so long. Meeting his every need—all while watching him disintegrate. He's dying—but you're alive. You deserve to be happy and free. You need a strong man who can take care of you. A man who can please you..."

She took another sip of the burning liquid, her vision blurring as she blinked back tears. Extending her hand, she touched the speaker button, leaned her back against the wall, and gazed upward.

"Twenty-two years is a long time, and you're not getting any younger. You don't want to end up old and alone. It's best—for the both of you."

"Richard?" She lowered the glass, cradling it in both hands.

"I'm sorry, Amber.... I love you."

She slid down the wall to sit and stared into the kitchen, her mouth a foot or so from the keypad behind her. "It's over, Richard. We need to end it."

They sat in silence.

"I don't know what to say—I love you too, but..."

"Then it's not over. We can work it out."

"No. No—no—no. It's now or never. End it!" Asmodeus shouted.

"I'm sorry. I want a divorce." She spoke softly, struggling to control her voice. A falling tear glinted before splashing in the brandy glass. Leaving a circular ripple, it was then gone.

Asmodeus whispered, *"Nick—you need him. Call him."*

"No. Leave me alone. Please just leave me be." She wept softly.

<<>>

"Almighty God, I worship and praise Your glorious name. Grant me grace, O Lord, that I might honor Thee now. Father... If Meraiah is in Your arms—I thank You. But if she is somehow still alive, I ask... Keep her safe and hold her close. I ask also for Sarah. Protect her from evil, strengthen and watch over her. I ask because You are a merciful God and Meraiah and Sarah belong to You."

Alone in the cold dark room, Batush shifted his weight in a struggle to find comfort. He had been sitting on the wooden block stool for hours, his buttocks and legs numb. He rubbed his lower back, arching and then rolling his shoulders. Lifting, he elevated to a crouching stance, about a hand's spread above the stool. The iron ring, chained to the wall, pulled against his neck from behind. It was a form of torture often employed at the podium where Curetes Street connects with the Marble Road.

The patch of light cast from the tiny window marched slowly toward the wall, fading in and out, sometimes barely visible in the jaillike room. It had turned and was now climbing the wall. *They will soon be coming.*

"Father, I beg Thee for strength and faith to finish well and to hold fast. Surround me, Lord, with peace and hope...."

The light pulsed brighter with a shimmer. The wall then warped like a hanging sheet in the breeze.

He shielded his eyes as brilliance filled the room, a wave of warmth washing over him. "Raphael...?"

The light dissipated. "Yes, I was sent to minister to you. You are my friend, Batush. I will not leave you."

The heavy door crashed open with two guardians bursting in. "We heard voices. Two voices—who were you talking to, Scribe?"

The warmth and peace he felt seemed to be radiating from the angel. The memory of Meraiah washed over him then. Sunlight pouring through the window, and he at her side, brushing a lock of hair from her forehead.

He smiled. "I am talking to my friend, the Archangel Raphael. Do you not see him? He is there, standing beside you."

<<>>

Amber poured herself another brandy. Not bothering to swirl the glass, she gulped it and choked back a cough. Batting hair away from her face, she steadied herself, then capped the bottle. She stared at the two choices—fluffy white or cushy pink? With a huff, she yanked the white robe from the hanger.

"I'd go with pink."

Spinning around, she drew the garment to her neck as brandy sloshed from the glass and washed her hand with a cold splash. "Who...?"

A silhouetted woman, taller than Amber, stood in the closet doorway. Straight jet-black hair flowed over bare shoulders and brushed her waist, while ivory skin cloaked chiseled features and piercing blue eyes. A short silver dress glossed perfect proportions.

"I'm sorry—I didn't realize you were still here. My name's Karl." She smiled. "I came from the opera—it was beautiful."

"I–I didn't..." *Karl Bernhardt?* Suddenly dizzy, Amber inhaled a soft gasp as her legs went slack. Dropping the glass, her hand splayed for the jewelry shelf.

Striking like a cobra, Karl stepped forward and caught the glass before it hit the carpet. She touched Amber's waist, their faces just a breath apart. Looking into Amber's soul, she spoke without words, *"Wear the pink. It's a gift from me to you."*

Amber's legs buckled as Karl's hand moved to the small of her back. Breast to breast, breath to breath. "Who? This can't... no..." The godlike stranger on the balcony flashed through her mind. She pushed against Karl's torso with her open hand, closing her eyes to the wave of surging power. "I..."

"Let go, Amber—let go to me." The words came softly as ruby lips parted to meet Amber's yielding mouth. Rushing forward then gulping, the angelic creature surged down Amber's throat with the imploding suction of a tornado.

Falling backward with flailing arms, Amber found herself propped against a wall of compressed fabric. Opening her eyes to the swirling room, she felt like she was still reeling backward. Blinking, she struggled for composure.

Karl was gone. *What just...?*

"Nick—you need him. Forget about Richard—it's over. The pink robe. It's for Nick. Call him...."

"I tried to tell you, Amber. Listen to us..."

Amber looked at the glass on the floor. *Pull yourself together—forget about Richard. It's going to be okay. I deserve Nick—call him.*

<<>>

Paul Chambers took another bite of the chocolate-covered chocolate donut with rainbow sprinkles. "How long has this been going on?" Outside, the sun was rising in a splash of orange and pink, matching the overly lit garish interior.

"Since the murder, it's an ongoing investigation."

He swallowed, thinking about cops and donuts. "I thought the elevator guy did it. That's what they said on the news."

Detective Green did not reply.

"Surely, you don't think the church had anything to do with it?"

"It's like I said, I'm meeting with you as a favor, to give you a heads-up."

Paul licked his fingers, rubbing them with a lime and pink polka-dot napkin. "Okay, I'm ready for the heads-up. What do you got?"

"Your treasurer, Daniel Fairmont? He gave us viewing access to your church accounts."

"Now why—why would he do that without informing us? We've been having some trouble with Daniel and..." He stopped.

"I understand you know he's under investigation for another matter."

"Yes. Daniel informed the board and offered to resign. Apparently, there's an accusation of child abuse and issues with the IRS and his contractor's license."

"We had him in for questioning. He gave us viewing rights on all his accounts. He's been very cooperative. Because he's an administrator for your church accounts, we've been watching those as well, and that's why I'm here."

Paul rubbed his temples, staring at the last bite, his head suddenly aching. *Sugar-rush, no doubt.*

"And...?"

"We've been watching some unusual activity in your checking and savings accounts."

"What kind of activity?" He spread sticky hands.

"Monies are moving out of the accounts and then coming back in—sometimes for just a few minutes, and then other times for two or three hours."

"But the money comes back in, right?" He rubbed his temples again. Smearing something sticky into his hairline, he withdrew his hands.

"That's right."

"Is the amount the same—when it comes back in?"

"Not always. Sometimes, it's exactly the same, and other times, it's greater."

"But never lower?"

"Correct."

He shifted in the bright-orange plastic seat, leaning toward the window. "I think I know what it is. We have a holding account where we get a higher interest rate. Nick Hamilton, our elder of finance, parks our savings over there quite often. Did you look at that?"

"We did."

He shielded his eyes with both hands. "I'm sorry. I've got a migraine, and the bright light is killing me. I've got to go, but I'm not sure what your concern is. Money in, money out, we're like any business. I'm sure Nick is just being diligent to earn us a few extra dollars at the higher rate."

"It's not just a few dollars. The amounts are significant."

"Nick mentioned receiving a few anonymous donations. Maybe that's what you're seeing?" Nauseous, Paul needed to lie down in a dark room.

Detective Green shifted forward, resting his elbows on the glaring white plastic table. "I attend church too, Paul. Normally I wouldn't be meeting with you, except I've seen churches get burned. Trust me—it happens more often than you think. I'm suggesting you consider changing administrators on your accounts."

"The elders would need to meet and vote on a change like that. And besides, we're in the process of taking Daniel off anyway. Nick will be taking over." Covering his eyes, Paul peered at the detective through a slit between his fingers. "I'm sorry, I've got to go."

"I recommend you pull administrator status on both of them."

"On Nick...?" Pulling his hands down, Paul squinted.

Detective Green edged closer. "There's another thing I want to tell you.... Typically, we don't get involved with people's personal lives unless they're breaking the law. But like I said, I'm a Christian brother, and I don't like seeing churches get hurt."

"What is it...?" Paul placed both hands on the table about to push off and stand. The throbbing pain felt like someone was pounding on his temples with a sledgehammer.

"I thought you might want to know your finance elder—Nick Hamilton—is sleeping with your executive pastor."

CHAPTER 54

DANIEL STARED out into the big room. The red exit signs and the single emergency light above the platform glowed in the darkness. His eyes rested on the cross, a symbol of cruel brutality yet also the beauty of grace.

He closed his eyes, praying softly. "I don't know what to do, Lord. Maybe it's too much, the IRS and the Registrar—and now... The guys don't want me, and no one understands—not even Rhema. I'm ready to resign. You know that. I know it's wrong to ask for a sign, but I need one." His head bobbed. "I'm tired and confused. I don't know why I'm fasting.... I'm weak, and I can't even hear You. I need a sign, Lord. I need...something."

"The service was canceled. Didn't you get the memo?"

His head snapped up as he spun around to the dark figure seated behind him.

"Tom? You scared me. Wow, it's good to see you." Daniel laughed the words out.

A warm grin spread over Tom's face, his eyes glinting in the dim light. "It's good to see you too. I'm not sure I've ever seen one of the elders in here praying before."

"There's something about this room when it's empty. It's magical—no, that's the wrong word. Spiritual—like worship. I can't quite put my finger on it." Daniel sighed. "I come here by myself sometimes, more and more lately. I feel close to the Lord in here."

"How are you doing?" Tom clapped a large hand on Daniel's shoulder.

"Not very good actually. The family's good, and Rhema's great. But everything else is a mess." Daniel told him about the notices from the IRS and Registrar and the false accusations and then shook his head. "But I don't really care—that's the funny thing. If this had happened a year ago, I would have been a basket case. But now..."

"Now what? What's different?"

"The board—being an elder—has changed everything. I'm scheduled to preach on Sunday, and that's a challenge. But mostly it's having the burden of the church on my shoulders... It can be really heavy." A lump swelled in his throat as he blinked back tears. They sat in silence. "I think I'm going to resign. They don't want me, and I'm always voting no when everyone else is voting yes. They asked me to quit but gave the decision to me. I'm thinking they don't have the guts to vote me out."

"Are you fasting?"

He huffed a laugh. "Did Rhema tell you that?"

"No one told me, Daniel." Tom's deep voice reverberated even in a low whisper. "It's my job to know these things, didn't you know?"

This time, they both laughed.

"Thanks, Tom. You're a good friend."

"Did you see the Intercessors?"

"I did."

"And...?"

"It was interesting." He shared the woman's vision of the storm and the small church filled with wolves. "Then at the bottom, she had written: 'The Lord loves this church, but He is not pleased.' It was a warning—that we should return to Him and turn away from our human wisdom."

"Did you share that with the elders?"

Daniel exhaled slowly. "Yeah, I did. It didn't go over so good."

"It sounds to me like you're the conscience of the board."

"I don't know about that. Maybe..."

Tom locked eyes of intensity with Daniel. "God didn't call you to be an elder just to quit. He called you to be in that room for a purpose—to speak for Him. And it makes sense that's not always going to be a popular message for others to hear. But some things are worth fighting for—no matter the cost."

"I guess I'm tired, and they're going to do what they're going to do." Daniel lowered his head, shaking it back and forth. "It's just not worth it. I'm fighting a losing battle and don't even know why I'm fighting."

His head cocked to the side, Tom placed his hand on the back of Daniel's neck. "Wanna get some coffee?"

Daniel checked his watch. "It's almost ten. I'm pretty sure Starbucks is closed."

"I know a place." Tom's face lit up, his teeth glinting white.

"Okay. But how 'bout you pray for us before we go?"

Tom tugged on a lock of Daniel's hair. "You pray."

Feeling a bit woozy, Daniel closed his eyes. His head seemed to be spinning, and he saw what looked like churning stars.

He opened his mouth. "Lord..." Daniel's head snapped back. The twinkling lights surged toward him, the sound of rushing wind in his face. His hair blowing back, his body flooded ice cold, the hairs on his skin standing upright. When he struggled to open his eyes, the wind and stars vanished in a flash of emerald light, replaced with a rhythmic hollow sound. Clop, clop, clop...

He heard people talking and laughing. A breeze in the air, damp and heavy. A distant voice called out, another was coughing. Then came a bark—*the bark of a dog?* Pulling back, Daniel felt Tom let go as his eyes released, flying open, squinting, and blinking. "Wha—?"

Blood coursed through Daniel's veins. Lightheaded, he tried to stand. Tom's hand on his shoulder restrained him. His eyes blinked, his mind swimming in the impossible. He was—he *couldn't* be!—seated at a wooden table, in a fair of sorts. People, dressed in robes, moved about awnings and tents. The clopping sound... a man dressed in armor passing them. *On... on a* horse... *a Roman soldier?*

An old woman with a mop of dirty gray hair and wrinkled face approached. A drape like a gunnysack with cutouts covered her. Sitting down, she ignored him. Facing Tom, she spoke in a rapid-fire foreign language, her hands gesturing as swiftly as her tongue.

"Who...?" Daniel again tried to pull away from the man he knew, transformed with lighter skin and a burly dark beard. His face and glinting smile the same, he wore a heavy sage robe with leather sandals.

They nodded to each other. She then stood and departed into the crowd. The woman had said... something about their friend... *What?*

"Tom?" Daniel's eyes fixed on a stone structure some distance left of Tom's shoulder. Ornately carved, it had fluted columns supporting a pediment, its roof clad with glossy red tile. With mouth hanging open, Daniel tried again. "Where—who? How...?"

"Welcome to Ephesus." Tom stood and clapped his hands. A lanky young man briskly approached with a towel and tray. "Gibeon. Two boiled coffees."

The youngster pulled up short. Dipping his knees, he tilted the tray for balance. Then, as he cocked his head, his face brightened with curiosity. "Do you have a guest, Father?"

"Yes—quickly. Bring your robe and spare shoes. Quickly, my son, go."

Daniel pressed flat palms against the rough-hewn table in stunned disbelief. They spoke in the woman's language—a language he somehow now understood.

"Tom...? Who–who are you?"

The sun faded behind the clouds. The air musty and filled with fog, everything wet.

"In this place, I am Zophar, the Coffee Trader. In another place, I am Tom Evans, Custodian. I have other names in other places. But in all places, I am watchman—angel of the church. I was told to bring you here. There is something you must see and something you must do."

<<>>

Nick sipped coffee. "It's just another trade." Except for his monitor's glow, it was dark.

Mammon whispered, "*Last trade, Zen Master. Score big, and then we're done. Forget about writing the book, you'll never need to work another day in your life, and you can leave Brooke. You'll have Amber, and the two of you can live anywhere in the world. Too good to be true... Opportunities like this come once in a lifetime. We've got the skills, and the knowledge is sacred....*"

His message was relayed to hundreds of greed demons, who whispered similar renditions into the minds of their hosts. Some were directors and CEOs of investment firms and hedge funds. Others were average investors, but the majority were day traders.

Nick had set his moves two days earlier, tracking the latest news releases, which were giving nothing away, except that the announcement was forthcoming. FDA approval was still a secret with speculations running in both directions. He skimmed the latest market news, now reporting FDA release of final Noxigen testing results at nine a.m. *Excellent. No clues with massive action...* He drew another sip, double-checking his trading graphs. *Five minutes... Bless me, Lord, with favor and fearless boldness.*

Over the past weeks, he'd made significant gains, playing the anticipation move with NexGen's price, swinging wildly almost daily.

With approval, shares would jump by at least 30 percent and could easily double or triple. He'd been careful, sharing the information with a trusted few who had the position and means to move price. They would benefit from one another. He'd also moved his Rapid Rewards holding account to a small offshore bank in the Cayman Islands.

"Watch the markets move with the stroke of your finger."

Nick checked his cell phone's dark screen, his hands trembling. *Come on, Troy. Where are you?*

"It's likely too risky for him, but it's a done deal.... Troy's all in."

Come on, Troy—I want confirmation. Talk to me, Goose.... Nick was queued up with four buys and one potential short. The buys were graduated, ranging between eighty- and five-hundred-thousand shares. *This is insane. Last time, and we're done with this forever....* The fourth block contained his entire net worth, his margin limit and every penny of available credit, including the equity line on his home. Additionally, it included the checking and savings accounts as well as the full credit line of Faith Bible Church. The balance of funds were mostly client monies, about half of which he'd pulled from discretionary accounts.

"No guts, no glory—this is our time."

The graphs jerked to life, moving forward with price and volume spiking vertically from yesterday's close at twenty-six and change. *Twenty-eight... thirty-one, thirty-two... Wow—unbelievable... Beautiful! Wait for the dip... Steady...*

"Enter the stream and let the fish come to us.... This day will be truly glorious." The message was whispered into the minds of hundreds, who sat as Nick did, ready to pull the trigger.

The price leveled and then dipped. *Thirty-two... thirty-one... Steady, hold... wait for the suckers—wait...* The volume bar began to rise, pulsing like a blood-pressure gauge. *Thirty-two, thirty-three...*

His finger twitched.

"Wait. Hold the line—hold..."

The price turned down again, hard with volume spiking.

His heart pounded. *Thirty, twenty-nine, twenty-seven, twenty-six and a half...* His fast stochastics were ready to bounce with trajectory lifting.

"Now... Now—Buy."

His finger dropped, executing his first trade, totaling 2.1 million. He ignored the impulse to check for confirmation. *Ready, read...* The price rose another half point and then plunged again. *Damn... Twenty-six, twenty-five...*

"Buy. Buy... Now."

He executed his second and third trades and covered his mouth as the graphs leveled like a held breath. "Holy shit... Eighteen point six..."

"This is what we've been training for.... Relax—breathe."

In New York, it was 8:57 a.m. Sweating, every muscle rigid, his right arm aching, he fumbled to refresh his second monitor and check market news. His hand jerked, index finger floating a quarter inch above the mouse. It hurt.

"No guts, no glory. Last chance... Do it for the church. Do it for Amber. You know you want to—do it. Do it!" Mammon screamed with every fiber of his spirit. Falling to his knees with clenched fists, he reared his head, enraged with a broiling concoction of lust and searing hatred.

Nick watched his finger jerk, clicking the button.

It's done.... All in... thirty-seven million dollars... The graphs hovered as he checked confirmations. Wiping his face, he swept his fingers through his hair and swallowed. *No guts, no glory. No guts, no glory...*

He considered his fifth trade. The short-sell queued up in Daniel Fairmont's SEP account.

"It's not worth it. With everything else, he might figure it out. Besides, it's chump change."

He stared at the figure. *Forty-five hundred shares, half of your account, what a joke.* He executed the sale with a huff. *You get what you deserve, and besides, I can afford to lose you as a client.*

His body lurched as the cell phone vibrated, lighting up with a text message. His vision then rushed into a tunnel. **Wendy Frost—Thirsty Thursday, where are we meeting?** "Wendy? My phone... Where's...?" He stood, lurching a step back, his eyes fixed on the time—8:59. "It's not too late.... Where the hell? My phone—holy shit... holy shit." Bent over the keyboard, his body rigid, he met the edge of the chair. Vision blurring, hands shaking, he managed to open the trade window.

The clock clicked to nine as he calculated the cost of bailing.

"No. Wait—it's okay... wait. Glory is within your hand. This is your moment. We've been training for this. You're the Zen Master—wait." Mammon was on his knees, whispering, face down, his fingers clawing into Nick's soul. *"It's okay. It's okay—steady, steady. It's okay.... Wait..."*

CHAPTER 55

DANIEL CLUNG to the edge of the heavy table. Zophar's hand on his shoulder, he rotated in his seat, gawking as a man passed with a chicken in his arms. Just beyond, someone dumped a bucket of rubbish in the muck with a splash. Nearly falling from the stump-block chair, he reengaged the burly dark man. "What did you say? You're an angel—but how can you be... I don't understand?" Nearby, a black raven flapped its wings on a wood post.

Zophar held up his hand. "As I told you, Daniel, I am mostly a watchman. I cannot answer all of your questions because I do not have all of the answers. I can tell you angels of light are strictly obedient. We obey no matter what, and many times the purpose in our efforts is not known."

"Tom, or—did you say? Zophar...?"

"Yes, Zophar is best."

A woman fanned her arms behind a bleating goat covered in mud. Daniel's hand rubbed the table's rough surface. "How is it no one sees me?"

"In this place, you are a half step beyond the physical into the spiritual." Zophar waved to a large man pushing an overloaded straw cart. "I am in both places—the physical and the spiritual."

"You said a half step? Is there a full step?" Daniel rubbed his nose and then swung at a pesky fly. The odor was powerfully raw—like a dairy farm laced with sewage.

"Yes, I am there also." Zophar's familiar smile crinkled his cheeks and lit his eyes with mischief. Comforting in its exuberance, it was the one thing that grounded Daniel in this bewildering place.

As he continued to clutch the table, Daniel's mind swarmed with questions and confusion, yet somehow, Zophar's hand on his shoulder fed him assurance and strength. *I'm safe. It's going to be okay.* "Can I go there?"

"You can. However, you must be certain you want to. There, you will see spiritual beings. Some of them frightful and ugly—sights you will never forget."

"If I ask you to take me... are you required to do it?"

This time his smile held mystery. "Not yet exactly, but someday—yes."

"What do you mean 'not exactly'?"

"If you ask, I can take you there, but only if it is included in my engagement rules." A booming laugh burst from behind his daunting beard. "I know your next question, and the answer is yes. I will take you there if you ask, but consider my warning. I can also take you to the physical side."

Gibeon appeared, balancing a tray of drinks. He held a robe in his other hand, a pair of dirty sandals under his arm.

"Stand up, Daniel. I will show you." Zophar glanced around and then tossed the robe over Daniel's shoulders.

Gibeon spun to Daniel, almost dropping the tray. His face brightened. "Are you one of my father's travelers?"

"Hello, yes—I'm guessing that is correct."

People were staring.

"Sit, Daniel. You are drawing attention. Gibeon will soon take you inside where you can properly change. He will then burn your clothes. It will be safer."

Daniel pulled his glasses off. Reaching inside the heavy robe, he dropped them into his shirt pocket.

Zophar nodded. "Daniel, this is Gibeon, my son."

Gibeon smiled, bowing as he placed the tray on the table. "I am happy to meet you, Master Daniel. Please enjoy the coffee. The beans are Ethiopian."

Daniel raised the clay cup, smelling the thick brew. Toasting them with a nod, he drew a sip and then exhaled a purring ah. "This is excellent."

Zophar leaned back and folded his arms across his chest, then arched his thick brows at Gibeon and fanned an arm to the other tables. When Gibeon jerked to attention and departed with another bow, Zophar placed his hands on the table as his smile faded. "I am glad you like the coffee, Daniel. Enjoy it, and then after you change, we must take a walk. It will soon be dark."

Daniel held the cup just below his nostrils, savoring the rich aroma. "Where are we going?"

His guide tugged on his curly beard. "Do you like books?"

<<>>

Tensions in the sweeping conference room were as taut as steel cable. Some of the men were talking and joking in hushed tones, feigning calm. All were keenly aware of the price, with several watching on tablets and smartphones. Those without electronics were close to those who had them. All were dressed in shirt and tie, except for the thin CFO, who wore navy pinstripes. He stood at the window-wall watching the longboats below.

Troy Horseman glanced at the clock and then back to his phone. His mind was soaking in a cocktail of adrenaline, greed, and fear. Virtually certain of the outcome, he needed confirmation from his FDA contact. *Josh, Josh.... Where are you?*

Volume was rising with price floating at twenty-five. Troy set his phone down and forced a smile. He then raised his brows to Gill. Seated on the other side of the table and three chairs over, he was sweating like a sumo wrestler in a sauna. The room's temperature— cold. *Get a grip, man. You're five minutes from being filthy rich. Relax— you're drawing attention.*

Troy again glanced toward the clock as the door opened—8:56 a.m. Benjamin Cruise turned from the glass and sat as the others squared their shoulders. John Grantham, president and CEO, slid into his seat at the head of the table. Always impeccably dressed, the imposing man with a shaved head was clad in a three-piece charcoal Armani with a diamond-patterned gold tie.

Troy searched his face for a sign. *The old man could be a poker player.... Maybe it's the tie? Yeah, it's a clue.*

John took his glasses off. Scanning the team, he made eye contact with each of them, lingering a bit on Gill. "Electronics... In the basket, gentlemen—let's go. Everything. I don't need to remind you, no one leaves the room until after the announcement."

Troy tilted his head, lower lip protruding, heart pounding.

"I want to start by thanking all of you for your efforts on Noxigen. Three years and seventeen million invested, including three trials. We've had success and a few bumps in the road, but that's the nature of this business. I don't have to tell you the stakes are high, considering the scope of this project. After all, it's quite rare that any company, let alone a startup like NexGen, gets a real shot at a serious cancer killer.

But we did, and Noxigen has shown amazing promise." John paused, looking at Benjamin, who nodded.

John brought his fingertips together. His lips slightly parted, he drew the cuff of his suitcoat back, edging the crystal of his platinum Maurice Lacroix. "As you know, we're announcing final trial results today, which are occurring as I speak. The president of the FDA, who is a personal friend, called this morning to give me a heads-up. All of us had high hopes for Noxigen."

Troy was unable to hear beyond the word *had* as the room gasped. He sat frozen for a moment, fear gripping him by the throat.

John continued as Troy and Gill reached for the basket. Troy bolted for the door, the room a blur as a chair banged into the wall.

"Benjamin. I want them ushered out. Call security and seize their computers. Neither of them leaves with anything besides their clothes and car keys." John adjusted his collar. "This is our business, men, and this is a lesson. There will be other Noxigens in our future, but there will also be successes. And I promise you, we will survive this."

<<>>

Pressing against his face, the hood reeked of dank mildew. Easy to know where they were headed, the gentle slope of the trail gave it away, followed by the three tall steps of the limestone plaza. Batush had walked across it countless times. Hearing the iron bolt slide, he was then ushered through the library's tall double doors. He twisted his hands, the rope cutting into his wrists. Someone pushed him from behind as they crossed the reading room's slate floor, greeted by the familiar echo and the smell of dusty parchment.

"Remove the hood."

Batush's head jerked back. Jonness stood rigid at his side with the elders behind them. Gallus and his men faced them across the room, the reading tables between them. Sarah huddled in front of Gallus, her eyes flooded with tears, his hands cutting into her shoulders.

When she tried to pull away, Gallus grabbed her.

Squirming and twisting in his grasp, she cried out. "Papa!"

Batush leaned forward, opening his arms as a choking tug from the noose around his neck yanked him back. A hand gripped his shoulder.

"I am here, Batush," Raphael spoke softly.

Sconce lamps lit the perimeter, Celsus's statue towering above like a sentinel cloaked in shadow from the chest line upward. Movement caught Batush's eye behind the stair. A guardian drew his blade.

"Leave him—the coffee trader is harmless. He may watch as a witness to these proceedings, if that is acceptable to you?" Jonness bowed, fanning an arm to Gallus as Zophar emerged into the light.

Gallus shrugged. "We have nothing to hide—he may stay."

Jonness stepped forward, spreading his arms in a blessing to both groups. "As you know, this man has blasphemed the church—the true church. This scribe—Batush—desecrated the tomb of Governor Celsus, located beneath the floor we stand on. This man also stole a book from the tomb, written by the Apostle John himself. How the book ended up in the tomb is a mystery. However, it is now in the hands of the church, where it belongs."

Jonness jutted his chin toward Agabus, who held Batush's writing case. Fumbling with the leather strap, Agabus handed it to Jonness, who opened it and removed a wooden scroll tube. "The scribe made a copy of this book which belongs to the holy church." Jonness waved the tube above his head. His eyes drifted to rest on Gallus. "It is known to us, Batush gave our copy of the book to you."

"It is true I have the copy, here now, in my hands." Gallus pulled a second scroll tube from his robe and lifted it above his head.

Batush stood in silence, his eyes fixed on Sarah. *Protect her, Lord—keep her safe.*

Jonness continued, "The copy belongs to the church, and we seek its return. We also desire the safe return of the kidnaped girl, who stands at your side. She is the grandchild of the scribe and a witness to his crimes. It is our right to interrogate the witness in order to carry out the scribe's discipline."

Gallus tightened his hold on Sarah, drawing her closer as a slow smile curved his thin lips. "As you know, Jonness, we are the true church—the church of power and sacred knowledge, through which one can be saved. And we are the collectors of ancient books because they possess both. We have no interest in this copy. The ink on this parchment is not even dry." Gallus tapped his flat hand with the scroll tube. "We will give you the copy you seek, but only in exchange for the original book."

"Your doctrine is false," Jonness sneered. "Parchment and ink have no power. Only the written words possess power."

Agabus placed a hand on his bishop's shoulder.

Jonness pulled away. About to strike, he stopped and spun back to Gallus. "There are two books, one for each of us. You may have the original, and we will have the copy. But you will also give us the girl."

Gallus bowed. "We accept these terms."

The bishops exchanged scroll tubes. Jonness then placed the copy in the leather writing case, handing it to Agabus.

Leaning in, Agabus whispered to Batush as he hung the writing case around his neck. "The book shall go with you to your grave."

Everyone turned then to the entry doors and the shouting. Torches flared in the distance, approaching rapidly. Batush stared at Sarah, hunger rising in his soul to hold her, to promise all would soon be well. He closed his eyes and swallowed against the hard lump in his throat. He glanced at Zophar and then back again.

"Kill the scribe—kill him. The demon must die—kill Batush...."

<<>>

"Brooke! I need my phone—it's on the dresser."

A memory flashed through Brooke's mind of the day Nick clipped his foot with the lawnmower. It was the barking cry of fear and panic. Grabbing the phone, she ran to the top of the stair. "It's here—what's wrong?"

"I need it—now."

She glanced down. "You have a message—it's from Troy."

Nick was at the keyboard typing madly.

"What does he say? Read it."

"What's your password?" The phone vibrated in her hand.

"Shit." Nick spun toward the stair and then back to his monitor. Stepping back, he shouted, "Zen39—what does he say?"

Entering the password, she tapped on mail, seeing a message from Amber Lash titled "Thirsty for You".

"It's not..." She opened the message and froze at the words—*I need you to make love to me. Richard's gone and I'm a mess. Can you get away tonight?*

"What does he say—tell me."

"Bastard... You bastard!" Brooke stumbled down the stairs. "You're sleeping with that woman—Amber Lash—your *pastor*? I hate you!"

~~

"Not now. I—you have no idea...." Nick started to turn, then spun back. Clicking the mouse, he hit Cancel instead of Execute. "Shit." Hands trembling, he reopened the trading window. "Give me the phone—I need to..."

"Look at me." Shaking and sobbing, she grabbed the back of the chair and tried to turn him around as he planted his feet. "I'm your wife—look at me."

Swinging at his shoulder, he batted her arm away. Almost falling, Brooke pulled her hand back and stumbled forward. Her eyes focused on the thick cord of the computer's power strip. She yanked it.

~~

Mammon's shouted command was passed along to hundreds of greed demons who screamed the same word, bombarding traders' minds. Some responding quicker than others, but all obeying, "Sell—Sell—Sell!"

In that same moment, havoc makers barked into the ears of market analysts and reporters scattered across the globe as they read the news flash:

Devastating news for NexGen Pharmaceuticals as FDA confirms high stroke risk associated with Noxigen withdrawing consideration of liver cancer drug in final testing.

~~

"No! What the... You have no idea what you've done." Nick spun in his chair while reaching for the cord. "Give it." Ripping it from her hands, he dropped to his knees and slammed it into the receptacle. "I'm sorry—get back." He blocked her with his forearm as he pressed the Lenovo start button. "You have no idea what's going on—no idea." He pushed back in his chair, his arm between her and the plug.

"Oh yes, I do. I know exactly what's going on." She backed away, swatting at the tears streaming down her face. Keys clattered on the counter as she found them in the kitchen.

Painstakingly slow, his machine rebooted. "Come on—come on. Please, Lord—*please*. All I ask is to be even. I'm sorry, Lord—please." A stabbing pain lanced his chest. "Slow down. It's going to be fine.... Breathe. Come on—please. Brooke!"

His home page finally appearing, he opened the browser and entered his brokerage site. Hands cramping, he logged on as a prompt displayed —Wrong Password. "Shit." After typing again, he struck enter. Then flying through the menus, he reopened his trading graph for NexGen Pharmaceuticals.

"It's a mistake—it can't."

"*Oh yes, Nick. Read it and weep—you're finished,*" Mammon gloated.

"No! Lord, please this can't... No..." The graph was flatlining at two and one-eighth, following a vertical drop. Volume and stochastics were at zero, with trajectory pointing to the grave. "No—No. This can't be—no." Nick pushed away from his keyboard, his face contorting, every muscle in his body clenched. "This can't be—no. Please—no." He jerked, reached for the keyboard, and checked again. He had the right graph. Hands trembling, he checked market news.

Trading halted today on NexGen Pharmaceuticals, pending cancellation of FDA final testing of liver cancer drug, Noxigen, on the discovery of significant stroke link. Shares of NXG tumbled from a 52-week opening high of twenty-six and five-eights. Trading interrupted and temporarily closed at two and one-eighth.

Nick's stare blurred as the garage door closed. He scarcely heard it.

~~

Mammon bowed to the tormentors. Madness spoke first with Mayhem chiming in, "*It's over, Nick—you're finished. You don't have the funds, and your clients are going to know before the day is over.*"

"*Your house, money, wife, and family...*"

"*Destroyed, Nick—you're through. Humiliated, not to mention prison...*"

"*That's right, Nick—you're going to prison.*"

"*And don't forget the church.*"

"*Yeah, Elder Nick, the church—you just lost the church.*"

Nick convulsed, "No—please, Lord. This can't be happening."

"*It is, Nick—it's done. You destroyed everything—you blew it.*"

"What do I do? Dear God, no..."

"*You know what to do.*"

"*Yeah, Nick. It's the only answer—upstairs.*"

"*It's the only option, Nick—upstairs in the closet.*"

Mammon and Madness bit their tongues grinning from ear to ear.

CHAPTER 56

ZOPHAR had just finished explaining who Batush and Sarah were and why there were two groups of elders and two bishops when Daniel saw them coming, about forty or fifty—like a scene from a Frankenstein movie. Several carried torches. Others wielded pitchforks and shovels. The wave of chaos surged into the great hall, pushing Daniel and Zophar toward the center along with the two groups of men. Jonness and Gallus raised their hands, but the pushing and shouting continued until a tall man lifted a walking staff above his head.

He looks like Merlin the magician—flowing robe and thin white beard...?

The crowd surrounded them on all sides.

Zophar lowered his voice. "They can't see you."

"But I felt them push." Daniel stepped out of the way, turning to the crowd.

Jonness spoke first, "What is the meaning of this?"

"I am the traveling Prophet Polonosis. We have come for the Scribe Batush—we will not leave without him."

A murmur rumbled through the crowd.

"I am Jonness, Holy Bishop of Ephesus. The scribe you seek is under church discipline for the crimes of desecration and theft, for which he will be punished. You have no claim on the scribe."

Gallus elbowed forward and spread his hands. "Jonness speaks truth concerning the scribe. However, he is not the bishop of the church—I am. Batush has desecrated the tomb of Governor Celsus and stolen a sacred book belonging to the Nicolaitans."

Jonness drew his hand back and then threw it toward Gallus with clawed fingers, his crimson face contorting, the veins in his neck bulging. "This wolf who stands before you is no bishop. He holds an unauthorized book of blasphemy which the scribe has illegally copied."

"Give us the scribe," a man called out, joined by others. "He must die—yes, kill him."

Polonosis again raised his staff. "I do not know which one of you is the bishop or anything of a book, and I do not care. The crimes you speak of, however, explain much." He cocked his head. "The spirits testify the scribe has a plasmos demon. Look, you can see it in his eyes. This plague we face rose from the crypt and entered the scribe. Celsus again is killing the people of Ephesus. The fog and pestilence will not stop unless the scribe is killed."

"Death to the scribe—death."

"He has a demon...."

"Stone him!"

"He killed my child. To the quarry—stone him."

The mob began to surge forward.

Daniel turned to Zophar, who gazed upward, his eyes darting back and forth. Ducking his head, he feigned from side to side and then hoisted a forearm.

Jonness walked to the center of the room, arms above his head. "Silence." Once drawing their attention, he continued, "It is true Batush has committed crimes. Rome knows this as well and seeks him also. As bishop, I speak truth. This man will be punished, but I cannot let you kill him." He glanced at Agabus, who nodded.

Gallus shrugged. "The law of Rome allows justice, for capital offenses, to be carried out by the people."

"Gallus is correct, but only when there is a witness to the crime. No one witnessed the desecration and theft of the book. However, a witness with us now saw the scribe make a copy of the stolen book. The child standing at the feet of Gallus." Jonness stabbed at her with a long pointer finger. The shadow of his drawn appendage stretched across the torch-lit room, lapping at her feet.

Polonosis responded, "Let the girl testify."

"Yes, the girl," the crowd agreed. "Make her speak—yes."

Gallus pushed Sarah toward Jonness. "Child, did you see your grandfather make a copy of this book?"

Two streams of tears ran down the girl's face while she stared at Batush. "Papa?"

When she tried to run, Jonness grabbed her as Batush opened his arms.

Kneeling at her level, his gaze embracing her as if holding her in his arms, Batush said, "It is well. Tell them."

Sarah nodded and then rubbed her eyes.

Batush started to speak, "I will—"

"Silence, Scribe." Jonness tightened his hold when Sarah squirmed in his grasp. Turning with fanning arm, he said, "We have the testimony."

Daniel shouted, "Let him speak—this is wrong." He spun to Zophar. "Do something—you're an angel. Can't you stop this?" Zophar's eyes continued to dart about as if watching flying bats.

Eyes feigning and darting, he said, "I can do nothing, but you can."

"What do you mean—they can't hear or even see me?"

"Remember what I said. You can step forward, but there is a cost. It is your choice, Daniel. You must decide."

"Yes—Yes!"

Zophar dodged to one side. Then reaching out, he touched Daniel's chest.

A blinding green flash engulfed him with a thundering boom. As he stumbled forward, everything froze, except for the flash now slowly moving away from him in all directions. Daniel stretched out his arm, watching as his hand passed through the suspended wave of emerald light. Everything stood motionless like the captured image in a photograph. *No, not completely... The shape of the torch flames, they're changing—just barely.* Turning to Zophar, Daniel realized he was frozen also.

His throat tightened. There were other beings in the room, many of them. Two groups. Several of which he instinctively knew were angels, powerful in stature, their human form dressed in gleaming white, their bodies radiating golden light. They held glinting shields and fierce weapons—swords, spears, spiked clubs, and axes.

The others were clearly demonic, monsterlike with various shapes and sizes. Some, having the appearance of gargoyles and sloths, seemed to be attached to the humans. Others were as large as the angels, outfitted with similar weapons and armor. Their bodies seemingly assembled from a parts bin of snakes and wolves, birds, reptiles, and enormous insects. Their hideous faces somehow displayed humanlike characteristics. *Frozen, all of them—or possibly moving incredibly slow.*

He swallowed. The demons and angels seemed to be staring at him. A demonic creature on the other side of the room held a battle-ax above his head. He stood frozen in a throwing position like a baseball pitcher, the ax directed at Daniel.

Maybe I should move out of the way?

An angel, standing next to the scribe was bent forward, his hands cupped at his mouth.

He's saying something—or shouting—at me. A chill of goose bumps prickled his skin. *I've seen him before. He's familiar—the photo from my interview, but...?*

Propelled forward, Daniel hit the floor, veering left and rolling to his feet. Half of the room exploded in a blur of motion and clashing sound. The shout resounded as a flashing blade grazed his shoulder, the ax exploding behind him. Like a switch being thrown, Daniel and the spiritual beings were activated, Zophar and the humans still frozen.

<<>>

The reapers waited. Seven of them dressed in flowing robes of iridescent silk with ghostlike faces of pale gray. Their job, much like that of worker ants, was the delivery of souls to victory. Highly efficient, they moved quickly but had to wait until the vessel was emptied.

The task of motivation was handled mostly by the tormentors. Moaz had point position working the exterior. Mammon was still in place on the interior, but the specialists were Madness and Mayhem. Although not present, Asmodeus was in command of the overall operation. He had been quite clear, stating several times—the man's soul was to be delivered and failure was not an option.

~~

Nick gulped another swallow of the burning liquid, alone with the bottle, darkness now approaching. He flipped on the light and slid from the footstool to the floor. Head spinning in a fog, he gave the bottle a swirl.

Moaz whispered into his ear with Madness and Mayhem chiming in, *"Two more swallows should finish it off. That's a worthy goal.... You blew it, fool—might as well do one thing right."*

"Yeah, man—finish strong."

"You can do it."

Maybe it was the tequila, the tears, or the sweat, but the shoebox was blurring out of focus. He hadn't looked inside since placing it on the shelf five years ago. Taking another swallow, he removed the lid. Then wavered there, staring at the weapon he'd never fired. It was loaded.

"*Good idea—the gun.*" Moaz licked Nick's ear.

It taunted him again, his cell phone pulsing in his pocket.

Mayhem struggled for composure, trying not to laugh. "*There he is again. It's after five, and Charlie Bushnell always checks his accounts....*"

"*Yeah, Nick,*" Madness chimed in. "*That's Charlie again—wanting to know why his account is missing seven hundred and fifty thousand dollars. Whoops, must be a rounding error....*"

He closed his eyes, rubbed his temples, the soggy box shaking in his hand, light licking the metal finish of the Ruger Magnum GP-100.

"*And the elders—when do you think they'll figure it out? Probably tomorrow morning when the bank calls. That's not good. What do you think they're gonna do...?*"

"*Can you imagine... all the money, plus eight million, they don't even have? They'll be kicking you out of the church, Nick.*"

"*Wait, what church? Hey, now that's some good news. No church—no problem.*"

"*And Brooke—she knows about Amber, and she's left you. And the kids—what do you think they're going to think when they hear about this?*"

He touched the gun, the synthetic black grip slick beneath his fingertips.

"*There you go—pick it up. Just hold it for a while until you're ready.*"

Nick picked up the .357. Cool to his touch, it lay heavy in his hand.

"*In the mouth... That's the best way—tilted up.*"

His cell phone pulsed again, and he thought of Brooke finding him. Groping in his pocket, he withdrew the phone. Then, squinting burning eyes, he blinked—*Charlie Bushnell*. He dropped the phone in the shoebox and closed the lid.

"*Don't worry about Brooke—she's not coming back. The cleaning ladies will be here tomorrow, remember? They'll find you. Don't worry. It'll be okay.*"

"*Yeah, they never clean that good anyway. It'll serve them right.*"

Nick began to sob. His head churning, he gaped at the bottle.

"*Put it in your mouth, Nick—before you pass out.*"

"*Yeah, forget the last swallow—better get it done.*"

Nick rotated the gun, placing his elbows on his knees, his thumb against the trigger. The metallic taste twinged his tongue. The barrel bounced against his teeth and the roof of his mouth. Heart racing, eyes squeezed shut, he tilted the barrel while gasping breath.

"Forgive me... Please, God, I'm sorry."

~~

Madness was about to speak when Mammon stopped him with a jabbing finger. Moaz leaned in, kissing Nick on the cheek. Hearing the familiar sound, Moaz smiled. It was the sound of rustling silk.

<<>>

The demon's grin covered the width of his face, his eyes locked on Daniel. Reaching to his belt, the monster drew another weapon, a spiked ball hanging from a chain attached to a bleached bone. Enormous with a humanlike face, he possessed the beak and eyes of an eagle, his scaled body having the proportions of an ape.

Laying on his back and elbows, Daniel was unable to move.

The demon took his time, apparently enjoying himself. With the flick of his wrist, the spiked ball lifted, suspended for a second, then vanished in a whirling overhead swing and crashed into the stone floor.

The angel across the room shouted, "Use your authority, Daniel."

Daniel heard the cry, unable to look away.

"A human, in our world? This is truly a beautiful sight." The demon advanced, yanked the ball up from the floor, and lunged forward with another swing.

Repelling backward, the impact coming, Daniel dodged as the spikes ripped through the flesh of his ear. The exploding impact stunned him, sound replaced with a high-pitched ring. Elbows digging into slate, he collapsed flat on his back and blocked with crossed arms as the demon rose above.

"Time to die, Daniel."

Raphael shouted, "Jesus's name, Daniel!"

"Jesus can't save you. Not from me—not here."

On his back, ears ringing and covered in the liquid warmth of blood, he clawed at the floor as the monster towered above. He dropped the ball on Daniel's chest, the heavy spikes punching into his rib cage.

"Remember me, Daniel? I'm Longshanks—the demon who kills

you." At a flick of his wrist, the ball rose and fell with a bounce just above Daniel's face. Longshanks smiled, winding up. The weapon disappeared in an arching blur.

A flash entered Daniel's mind. Ears ringing, heart in his throat. *Bruce Peterson—Jesus's name...* "Jesus!" His voice thundered as the walls shook. "In Jesus's name. Go—to the pit."

A blinding flash seared the room when the spiked ball passed through Daniel's head, crushing into the floor as Longshanks vanished in a blinding boom.

Daniel propped himself up and touched his ear, which seemed to be intact. *No blood...* He drew his hand back and flexed his fingers. They were warm—he was warm. A golden glow radiated from his body, his vision filtered by the haze. Head reeling and ears ringing, he managed to sit, braced against spread arms behind him. The demons gone, the angels walked toward him.

Raphael smiled warmly as he slid his sword into his shoulder scabbard. "Nice job, Daniel. You got here just in time."

Still shaking, Daniel stared in stunned wonder.

"Give me your hand, Daniel."

An electric shock rippled through him as the room surged forward in a flash of green.

<<>>

"No!" Daniel shouted as a man pushed Batush. Tumbling through the air, with hands tied behind his back, he made no sound until striking the ground with a thud. When Daniel leaned sideways to look, a cascade of pebbles rattled over the edge.

"He–he's still alive!"

Shrouded in fog, two men grabbed Batush, flipping him over like a bag of sand. Jonness lumbered toward the ledge, a large boulder in his hands.

"What are you doing? Stop. You can't—no!"

Swinging the stone back and forth, he let go. Hitting the edge, it flipped forward, then tumbled end over end, missing the man's chest by a yard or so.

Daniel turned to the crowd, now headed in the direction of a descending path. "We've got to stop this. They're going to kill him. Zophar, help me step through again."

Zophar pursed his lips. "I am sorry—I can't."

"No, you have to—I command you. Please?" Daniel chased after them, his heart and breath pumping. The mob circled around the old man, constricting like a snake. Daniel stumbled and slipped in the muck, swirling rain stinging his face. "Why are they waiting?"

Zophar pointed to the man with the staff. "Daylight... watch."

A man tossed his torch to the ground. "It is morning—let it begin."

Polonosis declared, "The witness shall throw the second stone. It shall be done in accordance with the law." He paced in front of the crowd with spread arms.

"This is insane. They're going to stone him for copying a book? And his grandchild has to start it?" Daniel whirled from Zophar to the crowd and then back again. "An–and the bishops just walked away—they're letting this happen? Jonness didn't even take the book. Batush is going to die for a book Jonness doesn't even want?"

Zophar gripped his matted wet beard with clenched fists, then swept his hands up and over his face, locking his fingers behind his head. "Perhaps he wants the book to be destroyed."

"No. This is wrong—how can... The church—I don't..."

The girl tossed a stone toward Batush. It bounced harmlessly with an echo.

"Kill him." A young man charged ahead, throwing a rock. Rifling through the air, it stuck Batush in the jaw and snapped his head back. The crowd then erupted in a frenzy of motion, shouting as stones filled the air.

"No. Stop—don't do this. No." Daniel pressed and shoved, breaking through the circle. Waving his arms and shouting, he stood in front of the old man as stones passed through his body. "Stop this—No." Falling to his knees, he began to weep. "Please... Don't do this. Please..."

Daniel tried to block a young man. A boulder propped on his shoulder, the youth lumbered forward. The sensation like a gust of wind, he passed through Daniel's body. Daniel spun around as the rock impacted with a sickening crunch, the old man's body now half buried. Sobbing, Daniel dropped to his knees at Batush's side.

Batush gazed into Daniel's eyes, then shifted to the side as if he were seeing someone else. "What of the book? I have failed you."

Batush's lips were not moving, but Daniel heard the words. He then heard a reply, recognizing the voice.

"No, my friend—you did all that was asked. The book is no longer your burden."

Daniel looked into the face of the angel he could not see. They both cried for the man now slipping from life. Batush drew a choppy breath and then two short gasps, followed by an exhaling sigh, the agony and pain flowing from him. His spirit passed through Daniel as it rose from the rubble, feeling like the caress of a soft curtain, whispering sensations of love and joy, peace and kindness, goodness, gentleness, and rest.

The touch of a powerful hand, radiating heat and strength, gripped his shoulder.

Again, the angel spoke, "Secure the book."

Blinding light engulfed him then like a firestorm sweeping him forward. Opening his eyes, Daniel was face to face with Raphael. Glory radiating from the angelic being washed over him in waves of warmth and golden light. "Nick needs your help—call him."

"I don't understand.... What...?" Kneeling beside the mound of stone, Daniel found a leather strap in his bleeding hands. As he yanked on it, the top of the writing case broke through the surface of the rubble pile. Shards of stone cutting into his knees, he reared his head to the sky as the walls of stone began to spin in a swirl of brown and gray. Zophar and the crowd were gone, and Polonosis was on the ground, curled in a quivering ball.

Reaching inside his robe, Daniel withdrew his phone from the inner pocket. The screen lit up. *Signal strength solid and power at 32 percent... But how—it couldn't possibly?*

Raphael was walking away. Stopping, he turned back. "Call Nick— he needs you." He then vanished in a ripple of light.

<<>>

"Do it, Nick. There's no other choice. Do it!" Mayhem and Madness shouted in chorus. *"It's over—end it... Now."*

Nick's phone lit, vibrating in the shoebox, his thumb on the trigger, teeth biting the barrel of steel.

"Don't answer. It doesn't matter—do it. Now. Do it now—now!"

Drenched in sweat, every nerve and muscle clenched, he quivered like a rat wrapped in a snake. Eyes blurred and burning, he screamed, "Do it—do it!" His hands pushed the gun away as he rolled to his side and drew his knees in sobbing. "Brooke—I'm sorry. I'm so sorry...."

"It's not her! Don't answer—end it."

He managed to sit, the pulsing phone not relenting. Fumbling in the box, he squinted. "Daniel...?"

"Don't talk to him. It doesn't matter—do it!"

I need to tell him—I need to...

"No—No—don't!"

"Hello, Nick—it's Daniel. Where are you?"

Nick lifted the gun.

"Do it—pull the trigger. Coward."

He choked on the words, "I–I'm in the closet...."

"Are you alone?"

"Not exactly... ha..." The gun trembled in front of his mouth. "I've got my gun.... And–and an empty bottle...."

"Where's Brooke?"

"She's gone, Daniel—she left me."

"Where's the gun right now?"

"It's...in... m–my face..."

"Don't, Nick, please. Put it down... Can you do that, please?"

"Don't listen to him. Pull the trigger... Do it."

"I've made a mess. Everything—you have no idea."

"It doesn't matter—put it down, please. Let's talk."

"You have no idea." He swallowed, dropping his head, the barrel under his chin. "I lost everything—my marriage and money. Other people's money—lots and lots of money."

"It doesn't matter, Nick. Put it down, please."

"I lost the church too. It's gone, Daniel—the paid-for church is now eight million in debt. I did that ... I did that today, to a lot of clients."

"I don't care what you've done. It doesn't matter."

"I tried to destroy you. The IRS, the Registrar, and the police—I did that to you and lost a bunch of your money too. I did it on purpose. I..."

"Nick, put the gun down. Please put it down. Can you do that for me...?"

"Actually, that's not true." Nick huffed. "Actually, Daniel, you did quite well today, by accident. I meant to lose a bunch for you. But instead, you were the only one who made anything." Quiet held him then for almost a minute—*how long has it been since I've rested in silence? I can't even remember.* "I'm going to be in prison—for a long time. Unless..."

"Please, Nick... Put it down and let me come over. Would that be okay? I know how this sounds, but it's true... God loves you. He made you and gave you the gift of life. He did that for a purpose. Can I come over? Just to talk—would that be okay?"

"No. Not okay—don't listen to him."

"In Jesus's name—please, Nick... just lay it down."

He watched his hand move, laying the gun on the carpet. He drew his knees to his chest, still weeping.

"Did you put it down? Can I come over?"

"Okay, Daniel... okay."

<<>>

Daniel stared at his phone and then out into the dark auditorium. The clock on his screen read nine thirty p.m. *Rhema... no time to call.* He sent a text:

Pray for Nick. On my way to his house—home soon.

Jumping to his feet, he bolted for the stair. *What a night—what a dream...* He was about to drop his phone in his pocket when it chimed. *Paul Chambers...?*

Emergency meeting Saturday. 8:00 a.m. Need to change your sermon. Review Matthew 18—Church Discipline Nick and Amber.

CHAPTER 57

THE TEMPLE of Artemis was bustling with activity. The entry plaza and grand atrium filled to capacity, pilgrims were hungry to worship and make sacrifice. Arriving at midmorning, Jonness circumvented the long lines by showing his special guest medallion at the members-only gate. Temple security then escorted him to the cleansing pools and from there to one of the on-call prostitute chambers reserved for government officials and high-profile entertainers. Special guests were allowed access upon invitation only. With a nod, the chamber-attendant then opened the door for Jonness, closing it behind him.

"There you are, my Holiness. We were about to give up on you—come. Sit with us." Lucius waved him forward as he gulped from a lead chalice, then wiped his chin with the back of his hand. "I heard an angry mob stoned an old man yesterday?" He arched his brows. "I also heard the man had a demon and he was one of your scribes?"

Jonness fanned his arm. "And today the sun shines in all of Ephesus."

"Thanks be to the gods."

The woman draped against the governor's arm tossed back long dark curls. Caressing her breast, she smiled.

"Why don't you take off that silly mask? Jonness, your secrets are safe in the Temple of Artemis, especially here with only us." Lucius again gulped as Jonness removed the feathered mask and rubbed his face. "There you go, my friend. Enjoy your nakedness and let us share this sweet woman."

Jonness stared at the girl and then swallowed. "Have you made a decision, Excellency?"

"You only call me by that title when you want something." Pulling a cluster of grapes away from his face, Lucius continued, "Yes, Jonness. You may have your temple—or what did you call it? Your church—yes, you earned it. The scribe has been punished, the sun shines, and the peace has been restored without a public trial."

"Thank you, Governor. Thank you." Jonness was about to kiss Lucius on the hand. Changing his mind, he bowed.

"Did you get your book, Jonness? The one you were wanting to protect? Ha."

"Yes, Your Excellency. We were able to secure it." He felt his face flushing.

"And what did you do with it? Please tell me it is in a safe place."

"Yes, Your Excellency. Thank you, but may I ask—"

A scream rang out as the three of them jolted.

"Barbarians..."

Another scream followed and then more.

Lucius stood, cinching his robe. He lifted a flat hand.

Jonness pivoted toward the room's single door. Grabbing his mask, he stood. Besides the reclining pillows, the room was empty, except for a low table and floor mat. He pulled the mat out from under the table, knocking over the wine flask and food platter.

Screams pierced the air. "Goths... Barbarians...!"

Lucius cracked the door. The chalice dangling from his finger fell to the floor with a splash. He stepped out, and the door swung closed.

Jonness locked eyes with the naked girl, his heart pounding. A puff of smoke wafted along the gap beneath the door. He strapped the mask on his face and wrapped himself in the mat. *No exit—no exit... God help us.*

Lifting the latch, he cracked the door. Ripped from his hand, it flew open and pulled him into the open forum, aflame with smoke and fire, screams and chaos. The enemy—everywhere.

A barbarian warrior dressed in animal hide shouted, "The temple is ours—Ephesus burns." He stood on top of the Stone from Heaven. Jonness fell to his knees, pulling the mask to his forehead. The barbarian held the head of Lucius, swinging it wildly by the hair.

"You!" he shouted, pointing at Jonness.

His heart in his throat, Jonness whirled. Flame and smoke blocked the exits. *The Den of Darkness—the den...*

As he spun around, a spiked club crushed his skull.

<<>>

The worship center nearly full, with more streaming in, Daniel put his arm around Rhema. A murmuring chatter, almost electric, buzzed throughout the room. He leaned in, feeling the tickle of her hair on his face.

"It always leaks out. I'm thinking Henry told Eleanor."

Daniel made eye contact with Paul Chambers. Centered in the front row, he was dressed in his black tux with a red tie. Lifting his brows to Daniel, Paul ascended the steps and crossed the stage to the lectern.

He tapped the microphone. "Is this on?" A piercing squelch drowned his booming voice, then quickly faded. "I guess that answers my question. Ah—I want to thank you all for coming out. We were scheduled for some worship and a message from Daniel Fairmont today. However, because of certain recent events, the elders convened for an emergency session early yesterday. Resulting from that meeting, we have some family business to take care of this morning." He scanned the silent crowd. "I'll turn it over to Daniel now, who will give us a report."

Daniel squeezed Rhema's hand. He walked to the podium, nodding to Paul as they passed. Then, facing the room, he drew a breath and closed his eyes.

"Let's pray. Lord God, we worship and honor You. In spite of our struggles and weaknesses, You are faithful, and You love us. We confess, Lord, that we often forget about our love for You and also for each other." He bit his lip. "I don't know what to say today.... So I ask You open my mouth to speak the words You would want to say to us. Selfishly, Lord, I also ask You fill me with Your peace. Amen."

He squinted and raised a hand to shield his eyes. "Can we turn off the spotlights?" He waited. "That's better—thanks."

As the murmur reengaged and people began turning to one another, he scanned his bullet points:
- Passage: Mathew 18:15–17
- Sins Committed: Theft / Lying / Slander / Adultery
- Participants: Nick Hamilton / Amber Lash
- Discipline: Rebuke / Removal / Legal Action

Daniel lifted his face as the audience quieted. "It occurs to me, we've gathered today for a stoning. Have you ever seen one before—a stoning? In the days of the early church—I'm talking about the first couple hundred years or so. During that time, stonings were apparently carried out by mobs incited for various reasons. Maybe a crime was committed against someone powerful... Or possibly, it was a function of ignorance—there was a drought or too much rain, and someone needed to be sacrificed to make it right. A mob might even be incited to cover up an embarrassment. I understand sometimes even the church could have been involved.

"Some of you may have heard, our debt-free church is not quite so debt free anymore. Someone stole church money and borrowed against our property and lost it. Some of you may also have heard certain persons within our leadership committed adultery." He surveyed the silent faces. "You would be right—all of those things happened. In fact, today will be the last day we meet in this building. Because it no longer belongs to us; it belongs to the bank."

The murmur rose again as Sander stood. "And who's to blame for that? Who's going to pay us back?"

Daniel placed a hand on his chest. "We are to blame—your elders. It's our fault. When we met, we found two persons guilty and decided to stone them in front of you this morning. After all, they deserve it.... That's what we're supposed to do, right?"

It was quiet.

"I'm a witness to what happened, and I'm standing up here, holding the second stone." His voice cracked. He stared at his paper and then turned it over. "I'm not going to throw it—and here's why. We're supposed to be your leaders, but we've made a mess of this church. We fired your pastor out of selfish ambition. We wanted someone young and cool. We wanted to be relevant, and we wanted to be successful. But..."

He swallowed against the lump in his throat. "We forgot about love. We forgot we're the Body of Christ. We, the church, and especially us, your leaders, are supposed to represent Him. And they, that being everyone who's watching, are supposed to know us by our love for the Lord and our love for each other."

He flattened his hands on the podium. "We failed you. We were not led by the Spirit of God—we led ourselves. Our own human wisdom led us to this moment. This ugly moment where we stand before you today—reflecting the consequences of our failure and, yes, our sin. I'm going to speak now for all of us. As a sign of our agreement in this, I'm going to ask the elders to join me up here. Because today, we are going to do one thing right. We are going to confess our failure to the Lord and to all of you. And we're going to ask..." His voice cracked as tears filled his eyes. "If you can find it in your hearts to forgive, we are going to ask you please forgive us. And we are also going to publicly ask for God's forgiveness."

It was absolutely silent.

He backed away from the microphone as the elders began to rise. All were present except Nick Hamilton.

<<>>

Zophar stood on the bluff, surveying the once-proud city of Ephesus, now smoldering in ruin. He thought of Batush when his gaze found the library, flames and smoke still rising from its hollow shell. The Goths had been swift and brutal, killing thousands. After a few days of frenzied plundering, they now ruled the harbor city.

"Father..." Gibeon approached, leading a donkey packed with supplies. He was not alone.

"Look at this—I am so very happy." The burly angel grinned with glinting teeth.

"Sarah and I found her in the hills."

"Meraiah, you are safe and alive. Why am I always the last to know these things?"

The three of them began to laugh as Meraiah smiled and Sarah entwined a small hand around two of her grandmother's fingers.

"She is healthy but confused. She does not know her name but seems to remember Sarah. Only now is she beginning to speak."

Zophar touched Meraiah's cheek. "She will heal quickly, my son. The Lord God has spoken this to me."

Sarah hugged Zophar, returning to her grandmother's side.

"I see you are packed?"

"Meraiah and Sarah will travel with me. I will see their safe delivery to the farm of Meraiah's brother." Gibeon faced the ruins of Ephesus. "I heard the bishop and most of the elders are dead—and the church, it is gone. Will you join us, Father—there is nothing here for you now?"

"Gibeon, my son, the church has not gone anywhere. It is right here, inside your heart." Zophar touched his son's chest. "The church will never be destroyed as long as believers have faith and love for their God. I would like to join you but must remain—I will help to rebuild. The church of Ephesus will live on, and besides, many need our coffee."

He grinned. "But Smyrna... Yes, Smyrna is a wise choice for our next shop, and also, not a bad place to find a wife, perhaps?" He rubbed Gibeon's hair and then checked the provisions. "Sumatra and Ethiopian—six bags each, good. And what do we have here?" He picked up the leather case hanging from its strap.

"The scroll, Father, your traveler Daniel gave it to me. He said the Spirit of God told him to give it to me. And I am to deliver it to the elders in Smyrna."

"Very good, my son—very good."

<<>>

The dry breeze greeted Amber as she exited the ladies' room at the rest stop. She was driving east but not sure where, just away with nothing except her purse. Stopping abruptly, she looked down. Taking another small step, she stopped again. Two policemen were speaking to a tow truck driver as he loaded the black BMW on a flatbed.

"Can you tell me what you're doing?" She folded her arms.

"We're impounding this car—it's evidence. Do you know a Karl Bernhardt?"

"I, well... No, I don't."

The officer glanced up, meeting her eyes. "Is this your car, ma'am?"

"No... I thought it belonged to a friend, but I was mistaken." She bit her lip and tugged on her purse strap. She took a sideways step away from the car. "Thanks, officers. I guess I'll be on my way." Walking away from them, she pulled her phone out. *Uber... Okay, let's see...?*

"Amber Lash?" an attractive sandy-haired young man asked. He stood next to the open door of a white Mercedes limousine.

"Yes. I'm Amber Lash." She folded her hands. Tilting her head, she added a smile.

"Do you need a ride?" He smiled back.

"Where are you going?" She glanced down. Lifting a heel, she twirled her toe.

"Wherever you want—Karl Bernhardt sent me."

"Well, all righty then—let's go." She stretched her legs, settling into cushy tan leather. Popping the lid of a built-in refrigerator, she checked inside.

"Which way, ma'am?" Their eyes met in the rearview mirror.

"Palm Beach..."

"How 'bout Florida... Palm Beach?"

"Yes, ma'am."

<<>>

The D9s saved the largest building for last. Besides the original chapel on the corner, the entire site was being wiped clean. Within a year, midrise apartments would fill the property.

The massive beasts took turns ramming the structure with scoop buckets. They started with the masonry columns, two of which were broken off, the entry canopy sagging in-between. As one of the tractors backed away, the other lumbered forward and struck the next support, which fractured and collapsed, dropping about three feet with a boom. The canopy seemed to defy gravity for a few seconds as if held by an invisible cable. Groaning, it yielded, buckled in the middle, and then cascaded in a roar of debris and dust.

Daniel stood on the far side of the freshly cut lawn. He smiled, thinking of Tom Evans, riding the mower one last time in spite of the scheduled destruction. *Serving the church until the very end and then walking home, just another day. I don't even know where he lives.* A laugh escaped his lips—*Would an angel live in a house?*

"What's funny?"

He turned around to see Nick behind him. About to respond, both looked back to the building as a crashing boom pounded the air. The D9s backed away while a cloud of rolling dust overtook and covered them. The diesel engines then throttled to idle, and the operators climbed out of the machines.

"Nothing, really... I guess I'm a little surprised I'm not feeling much of anything. It's okay—the church is going to be okay." The two men stood on the carpet of manicured grass in the middle of what appeared to be a war zone. Tilting his head, Daniel then placed his hand on Nick's shoulder. "I'm sorry, Nick."

"You're sorry? I'm the one who should be saying that. I caused this—all of it's my fault." Nick's gaze drifted to the carpet of green. "I've lost everything—the church, my marriage, my family. Not to mention my career and reputation—all of it. Amber too. She's gone and..." He stopped. "I don't know how to face my kids—what am I supposed to say? Your dad's a screw-up, and he's going to prison...?"

"I want you to know I'm sorry, Nick. I said things behind your back and thought things about you.... You and I are so different. We're opposites, but we're also brothers. Will you forgive me?"

Nick puffed a half laugh, his jaw tightening. "Me?" He faced the untouched building, resolute on the corner behind the chain-link fence. "That's where it all started. Forty years, and that's all that's left—fitting I guess."

"A few of us are going to meet there on Sunday. The bank wanted to buy it, but couldn't because of the ninety-nine-year lease. The tribe told them to take a hike, and then renewed the lease to an anonymous tenant—for one dollar. Now that's funny."

They laughed.

"Anyway, if you're clear, you're welcome to join us."

"What do you mean—me?" Nick placed his hand on his chest, then turned again to the auditorium. "I'm not sure I get it.... Do you have a pastor lined up or some music?"

"Not really. We're going to ask the Lord what He wants us to do. Just gather to worship and pray for an hour on Sundays until we hear something. I'm going to share a few words, and Rhema's going to read some Scripture. That's about it—it seems right."

"I can't show my face here. I couldn't do that... but thanks."

Daniel lifted his hand from Nick's shoulder. "Pray about it—it might help with some healing. We could all use a little of that."

<<>>

Rhema curled into the corner of the couch. "I'm proud of you."

They sat quietly in their place of refuge. It was late. Summer's heat finally relenting, they had opened the deck's French doors to give the AC a welcomed rest. Daniel breathed it in, savoring the pungent aroma of desert sage. Overhead, the dimmed can lights washed the fireplace before them in a glow of soft yellow. His eyes rested on the rusted iron cross, a prized garage sale find, centered on the mantel.

"How come...?" He turned to Rhema.

"You did the right thing, in spite of the pressure. And when you had the chance to get even, you didn't. Instead, you forgave and asked forgiveness." Her eyes teared up. "Most guys would have just gone along with the program or quit."

He squeezed her hand. "Thanks for standing by me. If it hadn't been for you, I would have quit."

As he stared into the unlit fireplace, she snuggled into his chest. "What are you thinking about?"

"I've been wondering about something since the vision. I've been asking the Lord to explain it, but I'm not hearing anything." He wrapped his arm around her, pulling her tight. "It was so powerful and clear when I woke up... but it's starting to fade. I'm thinking I should write it down while I can still remember." He chuckled. "That's what Batush would have done."

"That's a good idea. You should. You're a good writer, and it would certainly make an interesting story."

"I'm not sure who would want to read it."

"Well, I would." Copper curls tickled his cheek and heart as they laughed. "So, what is it you're wondering about?"

"When Tom or Zophar—you see, they were both the same angel." He stroked her shoulder, seeing confusion in her eyes. "Anyway, he read it to me from the scroll—the message for the elders in Ephesus. It was so perfect and pure. It was almost like, well, like Scripture. I wish I could remember the exact words. It was for us, Coach—that same message. We were—or are—the church of Ephesus. We were busy proclaiming God's Word and holding people to account—don't I know. But we forgot the most important thing." He sat up and spread his hands. "We lost our love for the Lord and for each other—that was our mistake."

The gentlest of breezes moved through the room to the clink of wind-bells on the deck. He rubbed his temples. "It's so close, but it's slipping away like a dream. I was thinking, if we had had that message read to us... Well, maybe we would never have done what we did in the first place." The vision receding, he stared into the fireplace, thinking about the library.

"The message to the church of Ephesus is in Scripture, honey. It's in Revelation—right here. You need to spend more time in the Word." She flipped through the pages of her Bible. Leaning forward, she laid it flat on the coffee table. "It starts where John is exiled on the island of Patmos, and he has his vision where he sees Jesus, who tells him to write it all down in a book. Here, it's in Chapter 2."

She began to read: "'To the angel of the church in Ephesus write; The One who holds the seven stars in His right hand, the One who walks among the seven golden lampstands, says thi—'"

Daniel interrupted, "That's what Zophar was saying—that's not... Remember Pastor Stover's message? About Revelation, and how it starts with the phrase: 'After these things'? And he talked about how scholars have debated that?" He took the Bible, picked up the dimmer remote, and brightened the lights, then flipped to Chapter 1.

"Honey, that's how Chapter 4 starts—look." Rhema pulled the Bible back. "Chapter 1. 'The Revelation of Jesus Christ, which God gave Him to show to His bond-servants.' That's how it starts. And this is what you were talking about, here in Chapter 4, 'After these things I looked and behold.'" Rhema pointed at the text and then looked up. A grin of knowing lit her face as she tilted her head. "I don't remember Pastor Stover preaching on that, and I've never heard anyone argue about what that means. Chapter 4 is where John goes to heaven and gets the rest of the revelation. It comes right after the messages to the seven churches."

Daniel stared at the pages, flipping them back and forth. "But this wasn't... It's different... Or—I'm confused. In the vision... It was so clear, but I guess you're right. It's right here. It's always been here. But I was—and..."

"It's good you have me to keep you on track." She pressed two fingers to his lips, stilling his stammering. "I love you."

Daniel met her twinkling eyes. "I love you too, babe."

EPILOGUE

THE STINGINIG BLOW snapped his head back, the sky and walls swirling in a blurred concoction of gray and brown. Pain shot up his neck to the top of his head as though his skull had been split apart from the blow of an ax. Sticky warmth on his neck, Batush realized his throbbing jaw was hanging open, in spite of his efforts to close it. A roaring wave of sound erupted, and a distant memory rushed in—tigers circling a wounded bull in the arena.

The second wave struck his body with punching blows from every direction, the first few seconds a crescendo of pain, followed mercifully with a stream of heavy numbness. With weight pressing down, he squeezed the angel's hand. Trying to open his eyes... Murky shades of crimson... The squeeze of Raphael's hand in his... Fighting the current compelling him to let go, Batush cried out, the message he was unable to speak.

"Will you stay with me?"

"Yes, I have your hand, Batush. I will not leave you."

"Sarah?"

"I will protect her, I promise."

Floating now, Batush surrendered to the stream of warmth. No pain, no fear, only peace perfected in love's embrace. Pictures flashed before him in soft hues—Meraiah's smiling face, and then Sarah running in the morning sun, and then himself, pen in hand, his son in front of him holding a scroll. Batush felt his body lifting and rolling over, his eye just above the stream's gentle current. *But what—what of the book? I failed—I–I...*

"No, my friend, you did all that was asked. The book is no longer your burden."

He let go, drifting again in the warm embrace of love and peace, expanding in purity as he descended. No pain, no fear, no struggle...

The sky opened then. In a brilliance of blue, it rushed toward him, swelling and accelerating. He tried for an instant to look back and then forever ahead.

Bursting through the surface into the sunlight, he opened his eyes to see what had always been. For an instant, he pondered before discarding every question. It was the staircase, extending beyond view on each side. Lifting skyward, it disappeared in a vanishing point. Calling to him—not only in sound but also with every sense magnified a thousandfold, cascading like a waterfall, reverberating through his soul. Warmth and peace, joy and sweetness of smell, the taste of love and song, color and music, laughter and tears, all colliding beyond anything he ever experienced, yet in the fullness of understanding.

Words washed through him, *"Look, Batush... Look..."*

Turning, he saw them. Powerful resolute beings, radiating grace and honor, glory and majesty—they watched him. On each side, standing on every third step, rising with the stair into the sky. The stair itself, crafted in gold having an ancient patina covered with inscriptions. The stair had always been there, waiting as it had received countless souls before him.

Still floating, he flew forward, his speed increasing, the width of the stair closing, the beings now a blur on each side—faster and faster. The blue intensified, radiating color and song like a living rainbow.

He saw it then, the light white like the sun, but so much more. He was moving toward it, or was it rushing to him? Both he decided. It didn't matter. Nothing mattered. This is where he was intended to be— perfection and purity, radiance and beauty, all around him and he in all of it.

The sensation of speed dissipated as he entered the tunnel. Was he still flying or standing still? There was no way of telling until he realized his legs were moving—he was indeed walking. Lifting a hand, he inspected it, not with his eyes really, but more so with his mind. He wasn't disoriented and instinctively seemed to know which direction to go. The shimmering color of song, the most beautiful ever to touch his soul, drew him forward.

As the white light faded, figures moved toward him. A group of fifteen or so including men and women, different sizes and shapes, some older than others, and children. His mother and father were there, along with his son, and Jacob, the elder scribe, and Claudius, son of Josephus and Phoebe too. Batush had never met several of them but knew them all more intimately than he even knew himself.

"Welcome, Batush, welcome. We have been waiting for you— come."

As he stepped forward, they vanished, and he found himself on a path, alone in a meadow of tall golden grass. He turned back—the tunnel was gone, replaced with a forest of majestic trees, the air filled with birdsong. The path led to more forest and beyond a snow-capped mountain, its summit crowned in a wisp of cloud. A crackling energy flowed through him, radiating emotions of peace and joy, laughter and kindness, goodness and love—such incredible love.

He then felt it. A rumbling sound enveloped in song much like the sea. "Wabuushhhhh... Wabuushhhhh... Wabuushhh..." Like a waterfall cascading over the edge of a cliff in waves of power.

Following the path, he entered the thick forest, the sound of the falls growing louder and louder. "Wabuushhh... Wabuushhhh..."

He began to run, feeling young again. In fact, he was. Laughing and singing praises, he danced.

The ground now shaking called to him, "Wabuushhh..."

Breaking out of the forest into the shining light, he saw him. "Zophar!"

The smiling angel stood on the path with folded arms. He dropped to one knee and bowed his head, then looked up with glinting teeth. "Welcome, master."

"Master...? What are you talking of, my friend?"

"You will understand very soon. Come. Do not keep them waiting."

Batush's mouth opened in wonder. A vertical face of polished stone rose behind Zophar, or was it glass? Perfectly smooth, it reflected the forest like a mirror. The wall extended beyond sight, disappearing into the clouds.

Batush smiled as the ground thundered, "Waaabbbuuushhhhh..."

Hand in hand, they entered a tunnel, its smooth walls radiating soft blue stretched ever onward. The rumbling sound beckoned, barely audible now. They walked on, talking and laughing for what seemed a very long time, or was it quite short?

About to ask, he realized they'd approached the tunnel's end, which terminated in a perfectly flat surface. Reaching out, Batush watched his hand pass through the reflective finish, vanish, and then reappear as he pulled it back.

"Come, Batush, it is your time." Zophar bowed, gesturing with a fanning wave.

Stepping through, they were flooded with blinding sunlight and a roaring wave of sound. Batush raised his hand to shield his eyes as he steadied himself against the thundering resound, the ground shaking as it passed.

"BBBAAATTTUUUSSSHHH..."

Eyes adjusting, he lowered his hand. He followed the roaring wave. Wavering with arms outstretched, they stood in the center of the largest arena he'd ever seen. A thousand times larger than the Coliseum in Rome. It rose on all sides like a giant bowl, filling the sky with people. Millions upon millions rising and throwing their arms into the air, then dropping to sit as the wave rolled around the arena like thick fluid in a spinning bowl, the booming ovation following.

"BBBAAATTTUUUSSSHHH... BBBAAATTTUUUSSSHHH... BBBAAATTTUUUSSSHHH..."

They shout my name. He rotated in a slow circle following them, seeing every face as if looking into their eyes yet from afar, knowing each of them, loving them and receiving them. He fell to his knees, tears streaming down his face.

Zophar knelt at his side holding his arm. The roar so loud Batush had to read his lips, "Stand, Batush. Stand up."

"Why do they call my name? I do not understand."

"All of the faithful are received like this, Batush. You will soon join them, but this is your time. Come."

As he stood, Zophar bowed, walked backward, and departed. Batush stood alone on a circular platform constructed in giant crystal blocks. The platform was dominated by an enormous purple tension structure, flanked with four large creatures, one at each corner. Powerful beings standing at attention, each with six wings and multiple faces, their legs a blur of whirling motion yet their bodies unmoving.

Batush was smiling, almost laughing, but not knowing why. A blast of trumpets, coming from a ring of angels at the arena's rim, then interrupted.

AAAWWWWWOOOOOOOOOOOOO...

The crowd erupted, every soul on their feet, hollering with arms waving as the tent opened on all sides like a theater curtain. Two figures emerged. Taking three steps, they stopped some distance from Batush, both of them twice his height. He immediately recognized Raphael holding a giant walking staff, but it was the other figure who compelled his attention. In his strong yet gentle hands, He enfolded a crown of leaves.

Raphael lifted his staff and then dropped it.

BBBOOOMMMMM... BBBOOOMMMMM... BBBOOOMMMMM...

The stadium shook with each blow, a hush of silence falling over the multitude. Transfixed with blurred vision, Batush could not look away from the One who stood next Raphael, the One who gazed into his soul—the One who knew him and had created him. Stepping forward, His size reduced as He approached to stand in front of Batush. They looked at each other, face to face, an arm's length apart.

Batush trembled as tears streamed down his cheeks. Wanting to fall to his face, he was held up by the power and Spirit standing in front of him.

Extending the crown, He smiled and then spoke in a quiet voice, the words Batush had longed to hear, peace and love, eternal joy and glory washing over and through him. "Well done, my good and faithful servant."

The assembly erupted in thundering response, the ground pounding with trumpets blasting. "BBBAAATTTUUUSSSHHH... BBBAAATTTUUUSSSHHH... BBBAAATTTUUUSSSHHH ..."

The End

AUTHOR'S NOTE

Thank you for reading my tale. I hope it touched your heart and brought a smile to your face. I would love to hear from you. Please visit our website where you can contact me and also join the conversation with other readers through our blog. Please know I would be honored and grateful if you would help other readers discover this book by leaving a brief review at Goodreads or any other media sites which post book reviews.

May God richly bless and hold you close.

JOIN US ONLINE

www.MarkAbelWriter.com

Book Tour and Events
News and Book Reviews
Works in Progress

Blog and Newsletter
Promotional Gear and More

Contact the Author

ABOUT THE AUTHOR

Mark Abel is an architect by trade but has dreamed of becoming an author for most of his life. Ephesus – A Tale of Two Kingdoms is his debut novel. Mark lives with his wife, Cheri, in Tempe, Arizona. They have three grown children and one grandchild.

Mark's writing is grounded in a passion to minister the mysteries of God through story, as an expression of worship and praise to his Lord and Savior.

STORY BEHIND THE STORY

It was my first year in college when I discovered my love of writing. I remember how proud I was when the professor announced my first paper was the best in the class. That was just before he said my grade was a D- as he threw all the papers into the trash. He then opened a magazine and read a mesmerizing short story I have never forgotten. Finishing, he said, "Forget everything you've ever learned about writing and write about something you're passionate about. And if your life is boring—lie." I'm not so sure about the lying part, but those memories remained parked in my memory. Sometimes I wonder what would have happened if I had pursued writing then. But looking back now, I see I wasn't yet ready. By the way, my second paper, in my mind was really good, scoring a B+.

In any case, life interrupted my writing as I pursued a career in architecture, got married, and, with my wife, raised and provided for a family, eventually owning our small architectural practice. But my dream of writing continued to percolate. Then in 2008, the recession hit, and we ran out of work. And the idea for a story began to emerge. Our children, like so many at that time, were swept away with story after story about teenage vampires. I shook my head in frustration while fantasizing about the idea of a story involving angels and demons. The contrast between good and evil could not be stronger I thought, and Scripture tells us spiritual warfare is real.

At that same time, my wife and I were teaching an adult Sunday school class at our church. Lessons included studies in Acts and the early church, Revelation and the Messages to the Churches, Spiritual Disciplines, The Trinity, and Spiritual Gifts, to name a few. Looking back, I can see God's hand in laying the foundation that would support the varied pieces of the story I would eventually construct.

Meanwhile, the recession pressed down as we burned through nearly every penny of our savings. One morning in October of 2011, I remember crying out to God for work. That prayer was answered in less than an hour when an old client called asking if I had the time to help him remodel two restaurants. After signing proposals, he promised to call when they were ready to begin. I then waited for two months and also began to write, and the story poured out. That phone call was the beginning of a work wave that inundated us with God's provision along with untold pressures and deadlines for seven years straight. But having started, I continued to write, typically for an hour or two each morning before switching gears to architecture, eventually completing the book as I now write this.

Jesus's messages to the churches, found in Revelation 1–3, have intrigued me ever since studying them several years ago. What makes them especially noteworthy is that Jesus returned some sixty years after His resurrection, in order to evaluate His new and struggling church and to give them a personal message. Some argue the seven messages represent the church during progressive eras of time while others make the case the messages are written for all time, with each message representing a different condition in which the church will find herself. I find myself in the second camp of thought because Jesus told John to deliver the messages to the churches, plural. Another way to look at the messages is to read them as personal. After all, as believers, each of us are parts in the Body of Christ. Therefore, the messages are important not only when evaluating one's church affiliation but also one's self. By the way, it is often the case that two or three of the church types may look familiar to each of us.

Jesus's message to Ephesus describes a church commended for persevering and working hard while holding evil persons to account, yet missing that which is most important—their love for the Lord and for one another. My story is about two Ephesus churches, one ancient and one modern, how they are different and much the same. Both churches are given the opportunity to change their ways and warned that, if they do not, they will be removed out of their place. One could argue such a message sounds harsh, and yet I believe most would also agree consequences in life result from choices and actions, whether it be a church or an individual. Therefore, there is wisdom in studying these messages.

In writing Ephesus, I have endeavored to be truthful in handling history and Scripture, while also speculating about the supernatural and how it may help explain the unexplained.

Scripture and Speculation: Because the narrative involves supernatural material and imaginative events, it was important I not violate Scriptural truths. At the same time, I allowed myself to speculate about the supernatural—provided I grounded my speculation on what is known from God's Word. As an example, winged angels and female angels are not found in Scripture. I'm not saying neither exist, but rather, that we can't know when using Scripture as our guide. As such, my angel characters, both fallen and unfallen, are unwinged male figures when appearing in the spiritual realm. I also employed deductive speculation. For example, Scripture tells us to be careful how we treat strangers as we might be entertaining angels. One can reason, because Scripture teaches demons are fallen angels, it is equally true we should be careful when entertaining strangers as they might be demons. This occurs in the scene where Amber encounters the wine-drinking Asmodeus not knowing he's a fallen angel. You might be thinking, now wait a minute, an angel drinking wine? But don't forget, Abraham entertained angels, serving them a meal with drink.

History: As half of the story takes place in the mid-third century AD, I endeavored to be accurate in terms of the era's historical record. With that in mind, I began the project in the library of Phoenix Seminary, researching such topics as Jesus's messages to the seven churches, practices and structure of the early church, Ephesus and the Nicolaitans, and similar topics. I decided on the year 262 because the Goths invaded and destroyed Ephesus in that year and I intended to purge the Ephesus church at the book's conclusion. Having established a date allowed me to focus on the third-century church in general and Ephesus in particular. Surprisingly, I, like most, mistakenly believed the early church faced constant persecution by Rome. Although Empire-wide persecution did occur during certain times, it was the exception and not the norm. Sporadic pockets of persecution were subject to flare up any time, typically by way of mob justice, with little intervention by authorities. Interestingly, the time frame of 260–303 AD is noteworthy as a period with virtually no persecution by Roman authority against Christians. Another surprising discovery was the sequence of how a new believer was received by the church. Upon conversion, new believers first underwent catechism training, followed by exorcism, and then lastly baptism into the church.

Establishment of the Catholic Church was well underway by the third century with a bishop presiding over a board of elders, who primarily functioned as his advisors. Bishops had great authority, sometimes leading to abuse. Ornately dressed, they lived as kings and government officials, moving about with an entourage of guards and treated with celebrity. The bishop was the singular authority in church proceedings—his words perceived as coming from the mouth of God, his authority absolute. He controlled salvation, which was granted through church membership and could be removed by excommunication. It should be noted the bishop of Ephesus during the time in which the story takes place is not known.

Along the way, I stumbled across a fable.... A prophet traveling through Ephesus led a mob in the stoning of an old man. The prophet proclaims the unfortunate beggar to be accursed with a plasmos demon who is plaguing the Ephesians with a crawling fog causing pestilence and death. The fable names the traveling prophet Apolonosis. I shortened the name to Polonosis as I was set on the demon name Asmodeus and the similarity would have been confusing.

I confess I may have stretched time a bit in using coffee as a drink in the ancient story. Several sources suggest coffee was discovered in 575 AD when a goatherder noticed his flock would not sleep after eating certain red berries. Finding them bitter to his taste, the herdsman threw them into his campfire from which arose a rich and pleasant aroma. Intrigued, he ground the roasted beans into a powder, which he found quite good as a drink when combined with boiling water. Another source, however, mentioned much dispute revolving around the question of which came first—coffee or tea. That source claimed tea is documented as a drink during the third century. In any case, I uncovered the coffee issue late in the book's development and liked using the beverage as an enjoyable link between both stories. Honestly, I love coffee, and who's to say an angel who travels through time didn't open the first coffee shop in Ephesus, later to be destroyed by the Goths? One can always speculate....

My compass in writing this story—and hopefully, others to follow—is summarized in my mission statement as an author:

Exploring God's Mystery Through Story.

Mark Abel - February 12, 2019

RESOURCES

Books:

Blaiklock E. M. Cities Of The New Testament. London: Pickering & Inglis 1965

Ferguson, Everett. Early Christians Speak. Abilene, Texas: Abilene Christian University Press 1999

Guy, Laurie. Introducing Early Christianity. Downers Grove, Illinois: Intervarsity Press 2004

Kerrigan, Michael. A Dark History: The Roman Emperors From Julius Caesar To The Fall Of Rome. New York, New York: Metro Books 2011

Ramsay, William M. The Letters To The Seven Churches. Whitefish Montana: Kessinger Publishing LLC 2004

Yamauchi, Edwin M. The Archaeology Of New Testament Cities In Western Asia Minor. Eugene, Oregon: Baker Book House 1980

Online Sources:
(Including articles, interviews, maps, photography, and illustrations)

City of Ephesus Ancient History / Temple of Artemis in Ephesus / History of the Church in Ephesus / Library of Celsus in Ephesus / Early Christians in Asia Minor / Church of the Virgin / Mary, Ephesus / Doctrines Held by Early Christians / Great Theatre of Ephesus / Goth Invasion of Ephesus / Public Baths of Ephesus / Bishops of the Apostolic Throne of St. John / Houses on the Slopes in Ephesus / Roman Governors of Asia / Ephesus Brothel / Joannes, Bishop of Ephesus 160 A.D. / Ephesus Public Latrines / Valerian and Christian Persecution / Market Basilica of Ephesus / Chronology of the Emperors / Temple of Hadrian in Ephesus / Doctrine and Deeds of the Nicolaitans / Temple of Domitian in Ephesus / Eidos Ephesios, Plague Demon of Ephesus / Temple of Odeion of Ephesus / Maps and photography of Ephesus / Fountains of Ancient Ephesus / Apostle Paul and John in Ephesus / City Gates of Ancient Ephesus / Secret Society at the Church of Ephesus / Prytaneion in Ephesus / Ephesus the Successful Megachurch State Agora of Ephesus / Roman Burial Practices Second Century / Governor Celsus of Ephesus

Made in the USA
Coppell, TX
03 May 2020